APRICOT'S REVENGE

APRICOT'S REVENGE

A CRIME NOVEL

SONG YING

Translated from the Chinese by
Howard Goldblatt and Sylvia Li-chun Lin

MINOTAUR BOOKS

A Thomas Dunne Book New York

A THOMAS DUNNE BOOK FOR MINOTAUR BOOKS.
An imprint of St. Martin's Publishing Group.

APRICOT'S REVENGE. Copyright © 2016 by Song Ying by agreement with Grand Agency. Translation copyright © 2016 by Howard Goldblatt and Sylvia Li-chun Lin. All rights reserved. Printed in the United States of America. For information, address St. Martin's Press, 175 Fifth Avenue, New York, N.Y. 10010.

www.thomasdunnebooks.com
www.minotaurbooks.com

The Library of Congress Cataloging-in-Publication Data is available upon request.

ISBN 978-1-250-01644-7 (hardcover)
ISBN 978-1-4668-7398-8 (e-book)

Our books may be purchased in bulk for promotional, educational, or business use. Please contact your local bookseller or the Macmillan Corporate and Premium Sales Department at 1-800-221-7945, extension 5442, or by e-mail at MacmillanSpecialMarkets@macmillan.com.

Originally published in Chinese as *Xin Shao Hong* in June 2008 by Hua Cheng Publishing House.

First U.S. Edition: February 2016

10 9 8 7 6 5 4 3 2 1

APRICOT'S REVENGE

Prologue

Hu Guohao swallowed a mouthful of brackish seawater as he felt a wave pull him under. Swimming for an hour or two was normally a breeze, why was it so hard now?

That floating white line ought to be the shark barrier. He knew he'd be all right if he could make it that far.

Hu fought to stay above water, but his head weighed him down and he choked on another mouthful.

He was starting to black out. Damn it! Where am I? Have I died and gone to Hell?

He thought he saw a great white gliding up from behind, eyeing him menacingly as it slowly opened and shut its mouth. He struggled to keep his arms moving, but everything he did was like a slow-motion movie scene, unreal and futile. The more he struggled, the faster he sank. A dozen faces—boys and girls, pale with dazzling smiles—floated up from the recesses of his memory. . . .

Now it was flames, licking in the air before his eyes. Were they real? An illusion?

A wisp of green smoke rose up lazily, spreading across the surface like bleeding ink.

Then the scene began to blur.

He tried to open his eyes, but a white mist clouding his retinas blocked out everything. Haze that would not go away turned into a gloomy, sinister abyss, sending shudders through his body.

He could sense that the Angel of Death was inching toward him. His mind was swirling as he heard a faint voice from somewhere up above say, "He's dead."

His heart erupted in a violent spasm, and he began to sink.

That was the last thing he knew.

ONE

Fog Over Lesser Meisha

— 1 —

Lesser Meisha, an enchanting beach.

A famed seaside resort in Shenzhen, it was known as the "Hawai'i of the East." Swarms of vacationing tourists came every weekend to relax on the sand, ride the waves, or just play in the water.

A line of beach tents along the water's edge created a unique scene as night fell. Shaped like yurts or pyramids, they came in a variety of colors—reds and blues and yellows—and from a distance looked like flowers blooming in the setting sun. At eighty yuan a night, they were the favorite lodging choice for young tourists and lovers on vacation, both because they were so much cheaper than the five-hundred-a-night Seaview Hotel and because they were much more romantic. The tents were thrown up as dusk descended, when a pleasant breeze blew in from the sea. Young vacationers began to sing and dance, while others slept to the relaxing accompaniment of ocean waves. Was there anything better than that?

Six o'clock, or thereabouts, on the morning of June twenty-fifth. Dawn had barely broken when a couple emerged from one of the tents. Lovers, apparently. He was wearing glasses and was dressed in jeans that failed to hide his beer belly. The woman, in a yellow T-shirt over a short white skirt, was not pretty, but her youth made up for that. He had his arm around her waist, contentment from a night of pleasure written all over his face. She smiled shyly and playfully pushed him away. They had arrived the previous afternoon. Beer Belly managed a computer company; she worked as his secretary or, to use the popular term, his Secret Sweetheart.

Obviously still savoring their night together, they looped their arms around each other and strolled along the misty early-morning beach, padding pleasurably across the spongy sand in bare feet. Gentle waves left rings of white foam on the sandy shore.

The jutting rocks of Chao Kok were visible through the thin layer of fog that lay over the ocean.

"Dapeng Bay is such a beautiful spot," the woman said.

"'All my best to you, O eternal ocean! The sound of your waves reminds me of my hometown. . . .'" Beer Belly spread his arms melodramatically as he declaimed lines of poetry.

"What's with you this morning?" She mocked him with a smile.

"That's a poem by Heine."

"Who's Heine?"

Beer Belly smirked. "You don't know Heine, the famous German poet? Then you probably haven't read his 'Ode to the Sea.'"

"No."

"I'll show it to you next time."

"I won't read it."

"I should think you'd be bored with Murakami by now."

"I like him. Especially *Dance Dance Dance*. It's beautiful."

"Right, that Sheep Man again. He's weird."

"I don't care. I like him."

"Hey, look up there." Beer Belly pointed into the sky.

She looked up in time to see white birds passing silently overhead.

"Seagulls. They're so pretty," she said with a squint.

"Wrong again. Look carefully, they're egrets."

The birds were a picture of grace and ease, long legs stretched out behind them.

"Why are there egrets at the beach?"

"Because they want to dance dance dance," Beer Belly teased.

"Stop that!"

"See those nests in the trees?" He pointed to a spot at the far end of the beach, where Qitou Ridge rose a hundred meters into the sky and cast a verdant shadow.

With a cry, the egrets flew off toward the ridge.

At the base of Qitou Ridge was another of Lesser Meisha's selling points—Lovers' Lane. Sandwiched between the hill and the beach, it meandered around a towering banyan tree and led to Guanyin Cliff at the top of the hill, where, after continuing down a dozen paces or so, it crossed a small wooden bridge that led to Chao Kok, the area's best spot for ocean viewing.

Following the direction of the flying egrets, they headed west, leaving fresh footprints in the sand.

The crags of Chao Kok, which extended into Dapeng Bay, slowly emerged from the morning fog.

They stopped just before they reached the pier at the far end of the beach, having spotted what looked like a naked man lying in the sand near the stone jetty. Not far from where he lay, craggy rocks nestled up against a breakwater that rose to about the height of an average adult. Above it was Lovers' Lane.

Curious, Beer Belly and his lover walked up to the stone jetty, suddenly sensing that something was wrong with the man.

Barefoot and wearing only a red bathing suit, he lay facedown, his legs spread out away from the water; apparently, he had washed up on the morning tide. His head was resting on his right arm, facing away from them.

Beer Belly squatted down and placed his finger under the man's nose. Nothing.

He touched the man's bare arm; it was cold.

"He . . . he's dead!" Beer Belly said in a shaky voice.

The woman's face paled; she couldn't speak.

The man looked around, no one else was in sight.

"Should we call the police?" he asked.

"What do you think?"

Their secret tryst would be exposed if they became police witnesses.

"I guess we should," Beer Belly concluded.

She nodded, reluctantly.

They rushed back, found the white cabin with a LESSER MEISHA TOURIST OFFICE plaque on the door, and woke up the night clerk.

"A drowned man washed up on the beach last night," Beer Belly said—shouted, actually.

"What did you say? Someone drowned?" The stunned clerk rubbed his sleepy eyes.

To ensure swimmers' safety, watchtowers staffed with lifeguards had been installed all up and down Lesser Meisha Beach. That, of course, was no guarantee of safety, and accidents did occur from time to time, especially when all the bathers looked like dumplings bobbing up and down in a pot. The lifeguards could not see everything, and were only on duty during the day, anyway, so people who enjoyed an evening dip took their chances. No one but an experienced swimmer or a die-hard skinny-dipper would risk going into the water alone at night.

The clerk called the local police station.

Fifteen minutes later, two uniformed cops arrived.

Since the body had been discovered near the pier, beyond the designated swimming area, the policemen reported the situation to the Public Security Bureau. Half an hour later, Cui Dajun, head of the Y District Criminal Division, drove up with a team of officers and technicians. They parked their blue-and-white Jetta police cars behind the Lovers' Lane railing above the scene and cordoned off the area with yellow tape.

By that time the sun was out, but the fog lingered.

A gentle morning light bathed the distant tents. The beach was deserted except for a few early risers down at the far end gathering seashells.

Cui Dajun, a man in his midthirties, wore his jacket unbuttoned, exposing a white-striped T-shirt. Though he was short—under five feet seven—he had eyes that could bore right through a person. He asked Beer Belly and his lover to describe how they'd discovered the body, while his young assistant, Officer Wang Xiaochuan, took their statement. Another officer, a woman by the name of Yao Li, stood next to Cui and watched intently as the eyewitnesses told their story.

The two local cops were posted at the restricted area marked by the yellow tape.

After the questioning, Wang had Beer Belly and his lover sign their statement.

"We'll contact you if we need more information."

They nodded, and Cui told them they could leave.

Meanwhile, the investigation was under way: a tall man in a vest stenciled with the word POLICE took a camera from his black case and began taking pictures from all angles.

The dead man, in his mid to late fifties and wearing only a red Lacoste bathing suit, had a medium build, though he was slightly overweight. The body lay on a smooth stretch of beach near the craggy rocks, not far from the roadbed beneath Lovers' Lane. Traces of white foam from the rising tide were visible four or five meters from his feet.

There were no footprints on the beach except for those left by the eyewitnesses, but even if there had been before that, they'd have been washed away by the incoming tide. No personal effects or clothing in the vicinity. Not far from the body, a stone jetty stretched from the pier into the water. At high tide, waves crashed against the jetty, producing a rhythmic roar from crevices among the rocks.

Tian Qing, the bespectacled medical examiner, squatted down to examine the man's back and the back of his head, gently pressing with his fingers here and there. When he turned the body over, someone remarked that the dead man's face looked familiar. Grains of sand were stuck to his broad forehead and the tip of his nose. The face was a purplish gray; so were his lips.

"He looks a little like the CEO of Landmark Properties, Hu Guohao," the chunky young officer, Wang Xiaochuan, muttered.

"You know this man?" Cui gave him a questioning look.

"I think I saw him on TV a few nights ago, on the show *Celebrity Realtors*. There was a close-up of him," Wang said.

The tall officer with the camera came to take pictures of the dead man's face.

"I think I've seen his picture, too," Yao Li, the other officer, commented.

"I guess it does look like him," Cui said after studying the man's face carefully. He continued with a surprised voice, "but how can that be?"

— 2 —

Hu Guohao was a prominent Shenzhen realty tycoon, the helmsman of Landmark Properties, South China's realty flagship. As a wealthy and influential businessman in Southern Guangdong, he was always in the limelight, was a member of the Shenzhen Political Consultative Conference, had been selected as one of the outstanding entrepreneurs of Guangdong Province, and was on the top ten list of Southern China's realty celebrities.

If it was indeed Hu Guohao, the news would rock the city.

Cui took out his cell phone and dialed 114 for information.

"I need the switchboard number for Landmark Properties . . . Got it, thanks."

He tried the number, but no one answered.

He called again, still no answer.

Someone finally picked up on the third try.

"Hello?" The operator sounded as if she had just gotten up.

"Is this Landmark Properties? I'd like to speak with your CEO."

"I'm sorry, but everyone's off today," the operator said lazily. "There's no one in the office."

Cui's face hardened as he shouted into his phone: "Are you telling me that in a big company like yours no one works on Sunday?"

"Er, hold a moment."

The call was transferred to a duty office, where a man with a deep baritone voice answered.

"May I ask what this is about?"

"I'm with the Public Security Bureau, Y District," Cui said. "I need to speak to your CEO. It's urgent."

"Oh, he's not in on Sundays."

"How can I reach him?"

"Well," the man paused. "I can give you his driver's cell number."

Two minutes later, Cui had Hu's driver, a fellow named Liu, on the phone.

"Is this Mr. Liu? Where are you at the moment?"

"Who's this? I'm home, in Beilingju."

"This is Cui Dajun, head of the criminal division of the Y District branch of Public Security. I have an urgent matter to discuss with your CEO, Mr. Hu Guohao."

"Oh, Mr. Hu went to Greater Meisha yesterday."

"Greater Meisha? What time was that?"

Cui signaled Xiaochuan with his eyes that it must be Hu Guohao; they both tensed.

"Yesterday afternoon. I drove him there."

Greater Meisha, another beach resort on Dapeng Bay, abutted Lesser Meisha. According to Liu, Hu Guohao had gone there to swim the previous day, something he did on most Saturdays, sometimes with clients, other times alone. He'd spend the night at the Seaview Hotel and return home Sunday afternoons. Liu had driven him to the beach in his black Mercedes the day before, Saturday, arriving at three fifteen. A room had been reserved under his name. Liu returned to Shenzhen after Hu told him to pick him up Sunday at four.

"Something may have happened to your boss. Come to Lesser Meisha right away."

"Did you say Lesser Meisha?" the driver asked.

"Yes. Lesser Meisha."

Cui closed his cell and told Xiaochuan and Yao Li, "Go check out the Seaview Hotel at Greater Meisha."

"We're on it." They left, following the shoreline.

The sun was up and shining brightly by then, and people were beginning to appear on the beach. Curious tourists wanting to get a closer look were stopped by the two local cops, who kept them beyond the yellow tape.

Cui looked at his watch, telling himself that news of a dead body on Lesser Meisha would soon be all over Dapeng city.

About a half hour later, Hu's driver drove up to the Seaview Hotel in the Mercedes. He seemed pale and anxious, and his red polo shirt seemed out of place at the scene.

He identified the body—as expected, it was Hu Guohao. "Mr. Hu liked to swim at night," he stammered, looking quite distressed. "He said the water was cooler."

"Was he a good swimmer?" Cui asked.

"Yes. He could swim five or six kilometers with no problem."

"So that means he could swim all the way from Greater Meisha over here to Lesser Meisha?"

"I'm pretty sure he could."

"But why did he drown?" Medical Examiner Tian asked.

"That's a good question." Liu was still in shock. He hesitated. "But Mr. Hu did have a history of heart problems."

"Heart problems?" Cui mulled that over.

Xiaochuan drove up with Yao Li from Greater Meisha in one of the Jettas. He'd barely parked the car before jumping over the railing with his report.

"We found Hu's hotel registration and some other important information at the Seaview Hotel."

"All right, tell me what you've learned." Cui led them away from the crime scene.

Xiaochuan told Cui that, according to the hotel staff, room 204 had been reserved under Hu's name on Friday and that he'd checked in Saturday afternoon at three twenty. The hotel was a stone's throw from the beach, an ideal spot to enjoy an ocean view and convenient for swimmers. The room rates were high, but Hu was a frequent guest. Xiaochuan was told that Hu was relatively free with his money and enjoyed flirting with the female staff. He was well known there. Someone had seen him enter the hotel and take the spiral staircase to the second floor the day before. Ah-yu, a waitress in the Seaview Restaurant, told them that Hu had had dinner with a tall man the night before. They'd talked for a while before Hu left alone. The tall man had sat for another ten minutes before getting up to leave.

"Did you get a name?" Cui asked.

"Yes, we did," Xiaochuan said, looking pleased with himself. "Hong Yiming, General Manager of Big East Realty."

"You're sure?" Cui persisted.

"Yes." Yao Li added, "The hostess at the restaurant, a Miss Bai, knew Hong by sight. Both men were frequent guests at the hotel."

"Very good." Cui was pleased with the report. "Did anyone see Hu go out for a swim after seven o'clock?"

"There were too many swimmers at Greater Meisha last night, and no one noticed a thing. We even went to the locker room, but didn't find Hu's clothes or anything left behind by other swimmers."

Cui liked the way things were moving.

"Hong Yiming might have been the last person to see Hu Guohao alive. Find him as soon as possible and see what he knows."

"Yes, Chief."

"I hope this is a simple drowning case," Cui said wistfully, before they gathered up their gear to head back.

If only he could convince himself of that. Greater Meisha was four or five kilometers from the tourist center of Lesser Meisha, and he was puzzled why Hu's body would wash up so far from where he'd started. Besides, they hadn't found his clothes or any personal effects either on the beach or in the locker room.

The only possible explanation was that he'd swum from Greater Meisha across the shark barrier, had suffered a heart attack and drowned. The tide had then carried his body up to the beach.

As Cui was turning to leave, his gaze fell on the stone jetty that jutted out into the bay. But why had the body washed up so close to the pier?

— 3 —

Room 707 at the White Cloud Hotel in Guangzhou.

Eight a.m., Monday morning. Nie Feng woke up to the sound of a ringing telephone.

"This is your wake-up call, sir."

"Oh, thanks." Nie yawned and leaped out of bed.

A journalist and special-feature writer for *Western Sunshine* magazine, Nie Feng was a swarthy, athletic-looking man in his early forties. Sporting a crew cut, he had a likable, smiling face. As a top student in Sichuan's C University School of Journalism, with a double major in psychology, he was highly valued by his editor-in-chief.

He'd worked until three that morning to finish a special feature for *Western Sunshine,* accomplishing the task that editor-in-chief Wu had been pushing him to wrap up. Now he could finally relax. A business trip to the Pearl River Delta area was a rare treat, so he'd made prior arrangements to visit a publisher friend in Zhuhai and see how well the magazine was doing in the south. *Western Sunshine,* a newcomer from the southwest, was a broad-ranging, full-color magazine with a cultural focus, and an influential publication with both domestic and foreign circulation. Wu was a seasoned pro who placed stringent demands on his contributors; it was he who'd come up with the *Western Sunshine* mission statement: *Unique viewpoint—New ideas—A Showcase for the cultural tastes of China's West.*

Nie quickly washed up and went downstairs to the White Cloud Terrace for morning tea.

The Cantonese love their morning tea; diners can choose from an array of dim sum in steamers on small carts pushed around by smiling waitresses. A dazzling display of steaming, bite-sized items appears when the bamboo covers are removed: green-crystal buns, shrimp dumplings, golden chestnut cakes, mara layer cakes, and so on. Naturally, each meal translates into a hefty charge. Back in Chengdu, two meaty buns, a bowl of congee, and a plate of pickled cabbage cost no more than one and a half yuan, while in Guangdong, a bowl of congee, two steamed vegetables, and a dessert easily cost thirty or forty yuan. Since breakfast was not included in the room charge, Nie rarely splurged for morning tea when he checked into a hotel to write one of his feature articles.

He walked into the crowded restaurant, where natty businessmen in groups of four or five or as few as two were smoking and talking on their cell phones or with one another. There was also a family that spanned several generations, out for morning tea and happily sending snippets of melodious but incomprehensible Cantonese his way.

Nie took a seat in a red cloth chair in a side room; a waitress in a checkered blouse came over with a tea menu.

"What kind of tea would you like, sir?"

Opening the menu, he was shocked by the prices.

Gold Brand Iron Buddha, 138 yuan per person.

Ginseng Iron Buddha, 60 yuan per person.

Royal Century, 38 yuan per person.

The list went on.

He quietly turned to the second page, where he found and

ordered the common High Mountain Iron Buddha, at ten yuan a pop. Later he learned that ordering tea was not required.

After the tea arrived, the waitress placed a yellow order form on the table, with the detailed prices for dim sum. He checked off several breakfast items: congee with lean pork and a thousand-year egg, steamed chicken feet with shredded peppers, spareribs steamed in preserved soy sauce, and a steamer of tiny meat buns.

It took hardly any time for the food to arrive, and Nie set to work. The chicken feet had a strong flavor and were quite tasty.

A newspaper rack displaying local as well as Hong Kong and Guangdong newspapers stood against the wall by the next table.

As he ate his congee, he reached out for a Guangdong morning paper.

South China newspapers are known for their more elevated approach to journalism, with serious cultural content and economic sophistication; they rarely rely on gossip and exotica to attract readers. They were Nie's favorites.

The major front-page news of the day:

CHINA "JOINING THE WORLD" ENTERS THE
SUBSTANTIVE PHASE OF MULTILATERAL TALKS

"WIND AND CLOUD" SATELLITE IS
SUCCESSFULLY LAUNCHED

There was also an item about the human genome map. According to the Associated Press, two American research groups would make a joint announcement that the map was essentially completed. Experts described the research as biology's equivalent of the Apollo Project; understanding the human genetic makeup would eventually lead to miracle drugs, and one day, the mysteries of the human aging process and illnesses would be unveiled.

When he turned to the second page, Shenzhen News, a bold headline above a half-column story jumped out at him:

HU GUOHAO, CEO OF LANDMARK REALTY, ACCIDENTALLY DROWNS WHILE SWIMMING

Nie's gaze froze, shocked to read that Landmark Realty's CEO was dead. He was incredulous, because a mere four days earlier he had interviewed Hu.

Putting down his congee bowl and the newspaper, he waved the waitress over.

"Check, please."

She handed him his check for 46 yuan, including the tea.

After paying, he left the restaurant and crossed the street to a Friendship Store newspaper kiosk, where he bought several Shenzhen and Guangdong newspapers.

He scanned them for news of Hu's drowning, and found it under bold headlines:

SHENZHEN BILLIONAIRE HU GUOHAO DIES UNEXPECTEDLY AT LESSER MEISHA BEACH

Was the cause a heart attack?

With Hu Guohao's death, who will take over Landmark?

Landmark CEO dies at Lesser Meisha, leaving many unanswered questions.

According to one of the papers:

Mr. Zhong, assistant to the CEO of Landmark Realty, confirmed that Hu Guohao, CEO and Chairman of the Board of Landmark Realty, passed away on June 24 at the age of 58. Sources say that Hu drowned while swimming beyond the shark barrier at Lesser Meisha Beach. Experts are trying to determine if it might have been the result of a heart attack. No definitive cause has yet been announced.

Another paper included Hu's portrait photo; he was dressed in a suit, with closely cropped hair and a radiant smile.

It was a smile tinged with mockery, familiar to Nie Feng. On the morning of June twenty-second, he'd interviewed Hu for three hours and had just finished the article that morning under the title "The Westward Strategy of a Real Estate Tycoon in South China." Nie could still recall Hu's ambitious buyout plans, his insightful views on real estate development in western China, as well as the tycoon's expansive manner. How could such an energetic heavyweight die so suddenly?

On the day of the interview, Hu had commented liberally on a wide range of topics, talking and laughing with confidence. He had no doubts regarding Landmark's upcoming development in the Yantian seaside district, and although Nie sensed that beneath his expansive demeanor, Hu was feeling either pressure or fatigue, he detected no omens of misfortune.

Why in the world would such an important businessman risk his life by swimming beyond the shark barrier, only to be swallowed up by the waves of Lesser Meisha?

Perhaps owing to his instincts as a journalist, Nie felt that Hu's death was too sudden.

Even though he'd eaten only half his breakfast, he raced back to his hotel room.

Endless questions flooded his mind as he dialed the number for the CEO's office.

"Landmark Realty, may I help you?"

It sounded like Ah-ying, Hu's assistant.

"Hello, this is Nie Feng."

"Oh, hello." There was a hint of reluctance in her voice.

"Is the news about Mr. Hu true?" he asked.

"Yes . . . it's true."

"How could he have just drowned?" Nie was puzzled.

"It came as a total shock to us all. It seems that the police . . ."

Ah-ying sounded evasive, obviously a sign of her own disbelief, but Nie was able to confirm Hu's death.

"Have the police reached some kind of conclusion yet?" Nie sensed something unusual.

"It seems that . . ."

She used "it seems" again. Was she puzzled or was there something she could not say?

Since there was no point in continuing, he hung up. After mulling over what to do next, he decided to leave for Shenzhen.

He rang his friend at Zhuhai Publishers.

"Sorry, pal, but something came up and I can't see you today."

"What's so urgent?"

"I'll tell you later. I can't talk about it over the phone."

"It's a scoop, isn't it?" His friend had a reporter's nose.

"Maybe, maybe not. It's got something to do with my special piece."

Then he called his editor-in-chief in Chengdu, telling him he'd finished his article late the night before and had already e-mailed it over. Nearly all of Nie Feng's stories appeared on the first page.

Wu sounded pleased on the phone, as he said brightly, "Perfect! Just in time for the next issue. I'll treat you to a meal at Lao Ma's Hot Pot when you return."

"No need for that, just up my fee for this one," Nie said half jokingly, recalling how the editorial committee underpaid him each time.

"No problem. This is a special feature, so you'll get a special fee. Say, when are you coming back?"

"I was going to take the train tomorrow, but something's come up."

"What's that?" Wu's ears pricked up.

"I'm not sure yet, I'll let you know tomorrow."

After hanging up, Nie packed his bag and checked out of the

hotel, then took a taxi to the Guangzhou Train Station, where, half an hour later, he boarded T757, a special express train for Shenzhen.

Guangzhong's gray buildings and undulating highway overpasses flew past his window, and as the train rumbled along, Nie kept thinking back to the interview at Landmark four days earlier.

He remembered every detail about his meeting with Hu. Particularly unforgettable was the luxurious office, which must have occupied at least two hundred square meters. He felt as if he'd entered a palatial hall the moment he stepped into Hu's office. In the country's interior, not even a provincial governor could boast such an impressive office.

All the furnishings were of the finest quality, including the carpet, with its auspicious design, and the linen wall hangings.

Hu had sat in his black leather chair behind a massive desk, looking quite poised as the interview began.

Dressed in a dark blue suit, he was tie-less. A bulbous nose and broad, bold face gave him a somewhat aggressive appearance, but he was personable and approachable, quite easygoing, in fact. An enormous photograph of the Landmark Building hung on the wall behind him. Glass cabinets on both sides were filled with trophies and books; a gold-plated pen set, a desk calendar, and a black record-a-phone rested on the desk, in front of which sat a gleaming lifelike black wood carving of an African crocodile, its mouth open wide.

Hu gave a brief account of Landmark's business ventures and its successes. It had started out as a small real estate company in Hainan, but with tenacity, hard work, bold vision, and an unbending will to win, he had turned it into a megacompany after years of fierce competition. Hu did not bother to conceal his pride when he talked about his rising fortunes in Hainan years before.

"Ten years ago, when I was selling real estate with a friend in Hainan, there were more than fifteen thousand real estate agencies. It was so crowded it felt like a marketplace. If a steamed bun had dropped from the sky, it could easily have killed more than one Re-altor."

Hu, who spoke with a Henan accent, swatted away the imaginary steamed bun with his hand.

"But the number of agencies dropped to a few hundred, and we were one of them. Ha-ha. Luck has been with me."

As a complacent smile creased the corners of his mouth, Hu exuded a roguish charm.

As for China's real estate development, he believed that now was the time to move westward. After ten years of large-scale development, China's real estate market was well organized and ripe for further investment, so it was simply a matter of time before outside developers came in. Whoever moved first would reap the greatest profits. Now there were two keys to success in Western China. The first was capital, the second brand name. Hu then described Landmark's ambitious acquisition plan; the first step was to acquire land in the Tiandongba area along the shore.

"The value of that land will definitely climb." A sly glint shone in his beady eyes.

The second step was to move westward. "Didn't you say there's no Landmark building in Chengdu? Well, I'll build a Landmark Building West on Renmin South Road. What do you say to that?"

Witnessing the style and behavior of a true real estate tycoon, Nie Feng realized the importance of bold vision and impressive bearing in the success of a private businessman. It was obvious that Hu was in total control of the conglomerate.

When asked about his hobbies, Hu said he liked to swim and jog, and didn't play golf.

"That's a pastime for cultured people."

As the interview neared its end, Ah-ying came in with a glass of water.

"Chairman Hu, it's time for your medicine."

Hu shook out two white tablets from a small bottle on his desk, tossed them into his mouth, took the glass from Ah-ying, and downed the pills.

"Aspirin, a cure for everything," he said in a self-mocking tone.

"Do you have a cold?" Nie asked.

"No, Mr. Hu has a heart condition," Ah-ying answered for him.

"The doctor told me I have coronary heart disease. That's utter nonsense. Do I look like I have a heart problem?"

"No." Nie said, and meant it.

TWO

Landmark Realty

— 1 —

Landmark Realty Corporation. A twenty-four-story building whose blue-tinted glass skin emitted a mysterious luster in the sunlight.

Nie Feng strode into the lobby, only to see that he'd been outpaced by more than two dozen reporters.

His only consolation was that these "crownless kings" wore unhappy looks, as they were held back by a red velvet rope.

A tall fellow who looked like a TV cameraman was muttering, "This isn't a military base. Why won't they let us in?" A female reporter with shoulder-length hair was arguing with a security guard.

Hu Guohao's sudden death had sent shock waves through the business world, and rumors about the cause had spread like wildfire overnight, which naturally drew the media's attention. Everyone was vying for firsthand, exclusive news, but Landmark Realty was being unusually guarded.

Two uniformed guards stood on the other side of the rope, their hostility plain for all to see.

The reporters came from all over, including the provincial and city papers, radio and TV stations, as well as out-of-town media.

Conglomerate employees kept the journalists at arm's length, tight-lipped and refusing all interviews.

An elevator to the left of the lobby opened, and out stepped a man of medium height in a brown suit and black tie. A middle-aged man, with the look of a driver, was right behind him. Someone recognized the man in the suit as Landmark's vice-president, Zhou Zhengxing. The reporters swarmed around him.

"Mr. Zhou, did Hu Guohao really drown?"

"Everyone says there's something odd about Hu Guohao's death. Is that true?"

"With Hu Guohao's death, who will take over as Landmark's CEO?"

"Sorry, I'm really sorry, but I'm due at City Hall for an urgent meeting."

With a heartfelt smile on his dark face, Zhou nodded apologetically and quickened his pace on his way out.

Nie Feng walked up as Zhou passed by, and his first impression was of an upright, honest man of considerable wisdom who only looked to be slightly simpleminded.

"Mr. Zhou, why was Hu Guohao swimming at Lesser Meisha in the middle of the night?"

The female reporter ran after Zhou, who waved on his way out and ducked into a black Audi. The driver slammed the door shut and drove off.

Zhou might have appeared to some to be harried, but not to Nie. If anything, the man seemed quite composed.

"Not your run-of-the-mill businessman." Nie made a mental note.

Silence returned to the lobby, at least for the moment.

The reporters remained behind the velvet rope, waiting and griping.

Suddenly, notes from what sounded like a harmonica came from the bottom floor of the building. It was a familiar tune, pleasant if a bit sad. Nie looked around, but failed to see who was playing the harmonica. Nor, surprisingly, did he spot any speakers or cassette players.

But the moment was interrupted when Zhong Tao, the Landmark CEO's assistant, came into the lobby with two staffers. He was wearing a gray suit and a red printed tie. A young man behind him was cautiously rolling up a yellow sheet of paper.

The reporters swarmed over, raising their microphones and pocket recorders.

Zhong stopped in front of the rope, where he fielded reporters' questions in a calm, poised manner. A man in his early forties, he looked both intelligent and competent, with slanting brows, a leonine nose, and bright eyes. The shadow of a beard on his cheeks left a solid and trustworthy impression.

Zhong was visibly friendly to the questioners. He explained that in the wake of an emergency meeting, the Landmark Board had agreed that the company would continue to operate normally. But this was a difficult time and everyone, from top to bottom, was busy with Mr. Hu's funeral arrangements, so he hoped that friends in the media would be understanding and forgiving of any slights.

Off to the side, the two staffers were pasting an announcement on the marble wall.

Some of the reporters rushed over.

It was the yellow sheet of paper, the black ink still dripping wet.

ANNOUNCEMENT

On the evening of June 24, Mr. Hu Guohao, CEO of Landmark Corp, suffered a heart attack and died while swimming. He was 58. All members of the Landmark family express their shock and deepest sorrow over Mr. Hu's sudden, untimely death.

The passing of Mr. Hu is a grievous loss to Landmark Realty. But the company will continue its current development strategy.

At the moment, everything is in normal operation and the Board of Trustees will soon name a qualified successor for the shareholders and the Board to make the final decision.

A memorial for Mr. Hu will be held on July 2 at the Shenzhen Funeral Home.

Office of Landmark Realty Board of Trustees

June 26

"A memorial on July second?"

"That's this Sunday."

Some of the reporters were mystified. Obviously they thought it was too soon to hold a memorial and that something else might be going on.

Nie Feng shared their reaction. Landmark Realty seemed in a hurry to put this Hu Guohao business behind them. Wanting to reduce the impact and aftermath of the CEO's death to protect the company's interests was understandable. But no one could deny that the cause of his death seemed somewhat suspicious. Based on news reports, the cause, drowning or heart attack, had yet to be determined, though the company's announcement clearly pointed to the latter.

He'd also found some unusual things in the papers he'd read that morning.

Why, for instance, if Hu had been swimming in Greater Meisha, had his body washed up at Lesser Meisha, more than three miles away?

Also, no personal effects were found near the body, neither on the beach, in suite 204 of Greater Meisha's Seaview Hotel, nor in the locker room at the beach.

"Media friends are welcome to attend the memorial," Zhong announced as the reporters began to drift away.

Nie Feng walked up to Zhong.

"Hello, Mr. Zhong."

"Oh, it's you, Mr. Nie."

They shook hands.

They'd met when Zhong arranged for Nie to interview Hu Guohao. Nie was quick to come up with his piece.

"I've already sent in my interview, but my editor wants me to verify some numbers."

"That shouldn't be a problem," Zhong said, greeting the guards as he entered the elevator with Nie. They stopped at the twenty-fourth floor, where a black stainless-steel door decorated with gold speckles opened.

Zhong led Nie into the luxuriously appointed reception room.

After they were seated in brown leather chairs and tea was poured, Zhong, in a rather laconic manner, gave Nie a brief description of the situation.

According to the ME's report, the cause of death was indeed drowning as a result of cardiac arrest while swimming. He died around midnight on the twenty-fourth. There was a three- to four-millimeter scratch on the left side of his chest, probably caused by a sharp rock. A preliminary investigation by the police showed that Hu was dead before being washed up on Lesser Meisha beach.

Nie followed that up with some questions.

"Did Hu Guohao often swim at Greater Meisha?"

"Yes."

"Was he a good swimmer?"

"Everyone in the company knew that Mr. Hu was a terrific swimmer."

"In other words, under normal circumstances, he would not likely drown."

"You could say that."

"Did he look normal to you in the days before his death?"

"Normal?" Zhong stared at Nie, "By that you mean . . ."

"Like his state of mind," Nie explained. "Or did he meet anyone out of the ordinary?"

"I don't believe so." Zhong did his best to recall.

"I see." Nie nodded.

Someone knocked at the glass door.

Zhong went over and opened the door. It was Hu's assistant, Ah-ying, wearing a dove-gray suit, and looking sad.

Casting a glance at Nie, she said to Zhong, "The police are here with more questions."

"Hello." Nie greeted her.

"Oh, you made it here fast," Ah-ying replied casually.

Zhong ushered the police into the room.

Leading the way was Cui Dajun, his keen eyes surveying the room. He was followed by two young uniformed officers, a chunky youth in his early twenties, apparently a recent academy graduate, and a petite woman with a poised manner.

Ah-ying brought everyone paper cups of tea.

"We're here on a routine check of facts," Cui said after greeting Zhong. "Who's in charge of everyday company affairs now?"

"Mr. Zhou, the deputy CEO, but he just went to report to City Hall." Zhong continued, "The Board met this morning, with Big Sister Zhu in attendance. She's still here."

"Big Sister Zhu?" Cui asked, alert to the first mention of the name.

"Mr. Hu's wife, Zhu Mei-feng. She rarely came to the office when Mr. Hu was alive, and she always stayed clear of company business," Ah-ying explained to Cui.

Noticing Nie for the first time, Cui turned to ask Zhong, "And this is?"

"He's a feature reporter for *Western Sunshine* magazine," Zhong said.

"My name is Nie Feng," Nie said with a smile as he stood up and offered his hand.

Cui gave him the cold shoulder, so Nie lowered his hand without seeming offended.

"We have no comment to make to the media," Cui said with a haughty air.

Nie gave him a funny look as he scratched his cheek.

"Mr. Nie interviewed our CEO last week and is here to double-check some facts," Zhong explained on Nie's behalf.

"I see." Cui did not relent in his indifference to the journalist.

The moon-faced male officer gave Nie a look of understanding. Nie nodded an acknowledgement.

"You're from Sichuan, aren't you?" Moon Face said to Nie.

Nie laughed when he detected the policeman's familiar Sichuanese accent.

"We're from the same province," Nie said, a common ploy to get close to someone.

"I'm Wang Xiaochuan, from Chongqing." Wang appeared to take to Nie right off.

"That's enough socializing." Cui waved his disapproval at Wang before turning back to Zhong. "We'd like to speak with Zhu Mei-feng."

— 2 —

Zhu Mei-feng, Hu Guohao's widow, ran a beauty salon. A pretty, refined woman who was always tastefully dressed, she looked to be in her thirties, though she was older than that. Everyone in the company called her Big Sister Zhu.

She met with the police in the CEO's reception room, where a beige leather sectional sofa surrounded a heavy, rectangular, glass-topped coffee table, alongside a potted "get-rich" tree, a common office sight in Guangdong.

Zhu sat on the central sofa section facing Cui and Yao Li across the table, on which an imported crystal ashtray had been placed. Xiaochuan sat on a side section, notebook in hand.

"We'd like to know more about Mr. Hu, and we're sorry to trouble you at a time like this," Cui said apologetically.

"It's all right. You can ask me anything." Zhu was intent on being cooperative.

"We've heard that Mr. Hu had a history of heart trouble. Is that right? What medicine did he normally take?" Cui asked.

"Everyone in the company knew, but he never took it seriously."

"What does that mean, never took it seriously?" Xiaochuan cut in.

"He always said he was a man of steel." Zhu cast Xiaochuan a glance, and continued in a mocking tone, "See what happened? Even a man of steel can fall."

There was a hint of irony and resignation in her words, giving the impression that she was not devastated by news of her husband's death. For all anyone knew, Hu Guohao ran a tight ship at home as well.

"What medicine was he taking," Yao Li followed up, poised but alert.

"Aspirin, four a day. And two more, something called Metoprolol and some other sort of beta blocker, I can't recall the name. But he stopped after taking them for a few days."

Xiaochuan wrote this in his notebook as Cui nodded to show he understood.

"Did he suffer from insomnia?" Yao Li asked.

"What does that have to do with his death?" Zhu turned to Yao with a questioning look.

"Well, the coroner found residue of aspirin and sleeping pills in his stomach," Cui said. "The amount of aspirin was as you said, but the dosage of sleeping pills was way over the normal amount."

"He did have trouble sleeping and frequently took sleeping pills," Zhu said calmly. "Sometimes he'd be awake all night, and it wasn't unusual for him to take more if something was bothering him."

"What sleeping aid did he normally take?" Yao asked.

"He used to take a sedative called Limbitrol. But it stopped working, so he changed to Wintermin."

Yao and Cui exchanged a look.

"I see." Cui looked relieved.

"Mrs. Hu—" Xiaochuan wanted to ask a question, but Cui stopped him with a look.

"Thank you for your cooperation, Mrs. Hu," Cui said, "Please accept our condolences for your loss. We'll be back if we need more information."

"That won't be a problem. Now, if that's all, I'd like to go home."

With a graceful nod of her head, Zhu Mei-feng stood up and left the office.

When she was gone, Xiaochuan mumbled softly, "Why did you cut me off, Chief?"

"What else was there to ask? It's clear he had a heart attack," Cui scolded the young man. "Don't complicate matters just to impress people."

"Mrs. Hu didn't seem all that sad about her husband's death," Xiaochuan argued.

"Does she need to make a show of looking sad for you? You don't know what it means to be the wife of rich man like that." Cui paused, before continuing. "Do you have any idea how many unhappy wives and mistresses there are in the paradise of Shenzhen?"

"No, I don't," Xiaochuan confessed.

"Neither do I, but Zhu Mei-feng was clearly one of them. So there you have it."

"You mean she was one of the unhappy wives?"

"What else could she be, a mistress? How could you be so dense?" Cui demanded.

"Oh." Xiaochuan scratched the back of his head, looking confused.

Yao Li covered her mouth to mask a smile.

"Based on what we've learned so far, I think we can abandon the thought that 'accidental death from drowning' was not the cause of Hu's death." Cui paused, "Unless—"

"Unless what?" Xiaochuan asked, a bit too eagerly.

"Unless we find a reason to be suspicious," Yao interjected.

Cui had nothing to add to that.

"I see, Chief." Somewhat chastened, Xiaochuan appeared to be on the same page.

— 3 —

After the police left the building, Nie Feng remained in the reception room to talk to Ah-ying, hoping he might get some behind-the-scenes information.

Ah-ying, whose full name was Feng Xueying, was an attractive white-collar worker. A graduate of the PR department at Guangzhou's J University, she was still single and had worked for Hu Guohao for four years. At the moment, her eyes were red and puffy. Her shock and sorrow at Hu's sudden death was visibly genuine. Instinct told Nie, a journalist with a master's degree in psychology, that his best bet to learn hidden details of Hu's life was to talk to his admirers. But first he had to create the right atmosphere. When suffering a loss, people need to talk to someone so as not to feel alone. But Ah-ying would not likely open up to friends, and probably not to family, either. Rather, a perfect stranger, someone likable, someone she knew only in passing, would be the one to whom she could pour out her heart.

"Mr. Hu's views on the western development of real estate were a real eye-opener," Nie Feng remarked. "He was incredibly forward looking. I was impressed. I've interviewed many renowned businessmen, but few have been as decisive as Mr. Hu."

Ah-ying looked up at him.

"Mr. Hu's picture will grace the cover of the upcoming issue of *Western Sunshine*," Nie said, and followed that up with a sigh. "What a shame he won't be able to see it. How fragile human life is."

She seemed moved by his apparent sincerity, which was enough to encourage her to reveal things about Hu Guohao, including a degree of doubt regarding the cause of death.

"There's something not quite right about his death."

"Why do you say that?"

"Just a feeling . . ."

As the conversation progressed, Ah-ying revealed something totally unexpected.

"Was he acting differently in the days before died?" Nie had asked her.

"Yes, there was something."

She told him that on the morning before his death, when she brought some files to his office, on his desk she noticed a strange piece of paper with a red sign in the shape of an ingot with a curved bottom. A series of printed numbers in bold script appeared under the sign. After Hu came in and sat down, he picked it up and examined it closely. At first he seemed puzzled; then he squinted to examine the row of numbers, and the expression on his face changed abruptly. He quickly put the paper away.

"What kind of paper?"

"An ordinary sheet, letter-size paper."

"Do you remember the numbers?"

"I just glanced at the paper and didn't pay much attention. I think the last three numbers were seven-nine-one."

"Seven-nine-one?" Nie Feng considered this new information. "Do you recall what his mood was like at that moment?"

"I can't really say, but the look on his face was strange, like he'd seen something spooky."

A hidden clue to murder?—the thought quickly flashed through his mind.

"Did you tell the police about this?"

"No."

"Why not?"

"They didn't ask," she said. "And I didn't know if I should mention it, because—"

"The paper's missing." Nie finished her thought for her.

"Yes. I searched Mr. Hu's office after his death, couldn't find it."

"What about his desk drawers?"

"I checked them all. Nothing."

"Did he have a safe?"

"No."

Nie thought she hesitated a bit, as if she weren't altogether sure.

"I searched every place I know," she added.

She seemed to be telling the truth, but he couldn't help feeling that she was referring to something specific when she said "every place I know." Since it was just a hunch, he decided not to follow it up. He also felt that there was something more to her sadness, but he couldn't put his finger on what that was.

"May I take another look at Mr. Hu's office?" he asked politely.

"Of course."

She took him back into the luxurious office, next to her own.

Walls covered in high-quality fabric, a carpet decorated with auspicious patterns, the carved wooden crocodile, and the crystal ashtray. Everything looked the same and yet, now that the occupant was gone, it was different somehow. The high-backed chair sat forlornly behind the big desk, and the giant photo of the Landmark Building hung quietly on the wall behind it.

He looked all around; there was no safe.

Through the enormous bay window, he was looking down at structures all the way to the horizon; the entire jungle of Shenzhen's buildings seemed to be within his view.

Memories of the interview from four days ago were still vivid. Five or six people had been sitting in chairs outside his office, all waiting to see Hu Guohao or to report to him. Hu Guohao had been at the helm of the entire Landmark Building, like the captain of a giant aircraft carrier. But now that he was gone, the reception area outside his office looked empty, which gave rise to a feeling that all that luxury was but a dream, and a sense of the inconstancy of the world.

. . .

That night Nie Feng placed a call to his editor-in-chief at *Western Sunshine*.

"Hello, Mr. Wu. It's Nie Feng."

"How's everything going?" Mr. Wu sounded concerned.

"Everything is a mess. I need to do some more digging and interview some people."

"That won't do. You're needed here." Wu was not happy.

"Hu Guohao's death was unusual," Nie said to convince his editor. "There's something going on here, secrets to be unearthed. Just think, a real estate tycoon dies suddenly under suspicious circumstances. I guarantee you it's a story everyone in the media will be chasing."

Wu remained unconvinced.

"I've found some clues." Nie upped the ante.

"Very well then. I'll give you a week, and you give me a followup report."

"A week may not be long enough. You can't solve a case in a week."

"All right, then, ten days."

That was clearly Wu's limit.

"Thanks, Mr. Wu. Have you read the piece I e-mailed you?"

"I did. It's good. It'll run tomorrow."

"I think you should change the title."

"Change the title? Why?"

"Add a subtitle—Hu Guohao's Final Interview."

"Genius! That'll grab the readers' attention."

No wonder Nie was Wu's favorite contributor.

THREE

Three Beneficiaries

— 1 —

The following afternoon. Y District Public Security Bureau. The criminal division leader's sixth-floor office.

Case investigation meeting. A dozen plainclothes officers were seated at three sides of a conference table, with Cui presiding at the head of the table.

Five desktop computers lined the wall to the right; a row of metal file cabinets, with a large city map on the wall behind, occupied the left. A drinking fountain and a yellow scale stood in the corner.

Cui called the meeting to order now that everyone was seated.

"Let's start with the circumstances of Hu Guohao's death. I want to hear what you all have to say, but based upon what we found yesterday at the scene, it appears to have been an accidental drowning. Still, questions remain, and we cannot discount the possibility that it was not an accident. Since Hu Guohao was such an influential figure, the Bureau has told us to step up the investigation and find out exactly what happened as soon as possible. I'll be in charge of the investigation, with Yao Li and Xiaochuan on my team. I'll increase the number if necessary." Cui lit a cigarette before continuing. "Tian, the autopsy report, please."

Tian Qing, medical examiner of the criminal investigation technical section, was seated to Cui's left. He was wearing a dark blue T-shirt and a pair of trendy glasses. Opening a gray plastic folder, he looked around before beginning in a calm, unhurried manner:

"The deceased was a hundred and eighty-six centimeters tall. His head faced the shore as he lay on the beach, bare-chested, dressed in only a Lacoste swimsuit. There were dark red liver mortis spots on his chest, his fingers were pale from heavy pressure. The corneas were blurred, the eyes dilated to about point five centimeters, bloodshot corners. There was a large quantity of seawater in his respiratory tract and lungs. His nostrils were filled with mushroom-shaped foam, which is common in drownings."

The officers listened with rapt attention to Tian, a graduate of a Shanghai medical school who had served as ME for five years and enjoyed an enviable reputation for his professional work.

He continued with his report:

"Based on my examination, we can confirm that Hu drowned between eleven o'clock on the night of the twenty-fourth and one o'clock on the morning of the twenty-fifth, the drowning most likely caused by a heart attack. His face was purplish blue, lips dark red, fingernails light blue, all signs of cardiac arrest. Cui and his team verified that Hu did have coronary disease, so it's reasonable to assume that he suffered a heart attack and drowned. Also, there was no sign of violent assault on the body, except for a three-centimeter cut on his left breast just below the nipple and a small tear on the back left of his swimsuit. I checked it under a magnifying glass and it looks new. Other than that, I found nothing unusual."

"Could the tear have been caused by the shark barrier?" Cui asked.

"No," replied Tian, "I've talked to the tourist center at Lesser Meisha. Their shark barrier was made of a special type of rope, not wire mesh."

"I see." Cui nodded.

Xiaochuan, who was next to speak, gestured liberally as he went along.

"Everything the ME has said was borne out at the scene, but Yao Li and I spoke to many people at both Greater and Lesser Meisha, and we do have a few questions."

He briefly described their visits to the hotel at Greater Meisha and to the area around Lesser Meisha, before asking an important question: "What happened to Hu Guohao's clothes?"

"The staff at the Seaview Hotel told us that Hu was wearing a green polo shirt and white slacks when he came down to eat. If he went to Greater Meisha beach to swim, then his clothes should have shown up either in his hotel suite or in one of the beach lockers, but we did not find them in either place."

Xiaochuan took a look around the table and then offered his own hypothesis. "There are only two possibilities: one, someone took his clothes; or two, he did not enter the water at Greater Meisha."

"The latter is certainly possible," offered Zheng Yong, a ladies' man attached to the criminal investigation team. "Since his body washed up on Lesser Meisha beach, he may have gone into the water there."

"That's a distinct possibility," another team member agreed.

Yao Li, who was sitting across from Xiaochuan and wearing an orange top over a pair of jeans, asked, "Then why didn't we find his clothes on the beach at Lesser Meisha?"

"Right, why is that?" Zheng Yong wondered, resting his chin in his hand.

"That's one of the mysteries confronting us," Cui said. "Hu Guohao's clothes could not have walked off by themselves."

That brought a round of laughter. Cui lit another cigarette and continued. "There was something fishy about the cause of death. Tian Qing, why don't you enlighten us?"

Tian adjusted his glasses before beginning, "After further analysis, we found two inexplicable details."

Looking at the autopsy report in its gray folder, he began. "Let me start with the aspirin. CT scans of coronary arteries, clinical studies, and autopsy reports show that blood clots usually appear in the arteries of patients experiencing cardiac arrest, meaning that clots cause the attack. Aspirin was originally used to treat the common cold and rheumatic arthritis. Later epidemiologists discovered that people taking aspirin over long periods rarely suffer coronary disease. In further tests, medical researchers have found that aspirin has a thinning effect on blood platelets.

"After requesting Hu's medical records from City Hospital, we checked his coronary artery scans. There were indeed blood clots. So there's no question that they were the cause of his heart trouble. But when I checked the contents of his stomach, I found that he had been taking aspirin. As I said, aspirin can effectively prevent blood platelets from forming clots, so how could he suffer cardiac arrest?"

No one said a word.

"There has to be a reason." Yao Li finally broke the silence. She glanced around the table and stood up. "I think there are two possibilities. First, he overexerted himself, and that led to cardiac arrest. Or, perhaps, he was given a tremendous fright."

"What?" Several people spoke at once.

"For instance," she said as she brushed the hair away from her forehead, "the sudden appearance or attack by a shark."

"Maybe the cut on his chest was a tooth mark from a shark," Zheng Yong commented.

There were snickers around the table.

"Be serious. We're talking about an unexplained death!" Cui slapped the desk with his palm.

"Of course," Yao Li continued, unruffled, "it's also possible that someone terrified him, and that someone would be our murderer. That's all I have to say."

She sat down, her eyes fixed on Cui.

"Who's next? Xiaochuan, what do you think?"

"Yao Li's analysis makes sense, fatigue or shark, or a murderer.

I'm leaning toward a murderer." Xiaochuan turned the teacup in his hand.

"Why?" Cui asked.

"I don't know; it's just a hunch."

"A hunch doesn't cut it. You need evidence, solid reasoning."

"The large quantity of sleeping pills in Hu Guohao's stomach is reason enough for me."

"Tian Qing, tell us about the sleeping pills."

Cui patted the ME on the shoulder.

With everyone's eyes on him, Tian began again.

"We found a large quantity of sleeping pill residue in his stomach fluids and his blood. The main drug ingredient was chlorpromazine, which is sold as Wintermin, a non-barbituate, commonly prescribed sleeping aid. Chlorpromazine is a powerful tranquilizer. Its primary function is to suppress the central nervous system. An overdose can cause temporary excitability, then sleepiness, and ataxia, which causes uncoordinated movements, tremors, coma, and depressed breathing, eventually leading to serious shock or suffocation from the shock. The threshold for overdose is anything over five micrograms per milliliter of liquid. In the most severe case, the patient succumbs from respiratory and circulation failures. The chlorpromazine in Hu Guohao's blood was four point two, clearly higher than the normal dosage, not enough to constitute a drug overdose, but enough to lead to a loss of consciousness."

"But according to his wife, Hu was in the habit of taking large doses of sleep aids, and that was corroborated by his assistant," Cui said. "So this doesn't tell us anything."

"Then we have to conduct an autopsy." Xiaochuan blurted out.

Everyone sat up.

"Hu Guohao was one of the superrich, a major player in Shenzhen. Do you think all you have to do is ask for an autopsy?" Cui took the wind out of his apprentice's sails.

"I think we ought to consider Xiaochuan's suggestion, Chief," Yao Li said in support of Xiaochuan.

"I brought that up, but Mrs. Hu won't OK it," Cui said, knowing that the criminal code dictated that family consent and signature would have to be obtained for autopsies in noncriminal cases.

"Why not?"

"She said she wants him buried whole. She doesn't want his body defiled, and I can understand her sentiment."

"Or maybe she's just sure it was an accidental drowning," Xiaochuan said.

"It's probably more like 'she believes' it was,'" Cui said suggestively.

"What do you mean, Chief?" Xiaochuan was confused.

"Use your head."

Cui passed cigarettes around, and columns of white smoke quickly rose in the conference room. A heavy smoker himself, Cui smoked while focusing a penetrating gaze on Xiaochuan.

Xiaochuan ventured a guess. "Do you mean she *wants* to believe that her husband's death was an accident?"

"Yes, that's what I think." That was what Cui had taken away from his interview with the widow. He could not shake the feeling that there was something hidden in Zhu Mei-feng's comment of "he thought he was invincible."

"But why?"

"Let's try to figure it out." Cui's gaze swept the table. "Who benefits most from Hu Guohao's death?"

The officers exchanged looks.

"Mrs. Hu," someone blurted out.

That woke everyone up.

"Right. Hu owned fifty-four percent of Landmark's shares. He had an ex-wife but no children, and his parents died many years ago, so legally speaking, Hu's death means that Zhu will inherit his shares."

"Oh!" was the consensus response.

"So, it makes no difference to Zhu whether Hu accidentally drowned or not. But if it wasn't an accident, or more precisely, was murder, then she would be the prime suspect, so a smart woman like her would never agree to an autopsy. And if it was an accident, then she'd naturally consider an autopsy unnecessary."

"But, there are really two more beneficiaries," Cui continued.

All eyes were trained on him.

"One is his deputy CEO, Zhou Zhengxing." Cui cleared his throat. "He's the second biggest Landmark shareholder. Employees say he's the leader of the local faction, and has had his eyes on Hu's position for quite some time. Also there was a major disagreement between the two; Zhou adamantly opposed Hu's plan of investing in Tiandongba."

Xiaochuan then reported on what he'd learned from Landmark employees.

Tiandongba was a plot of 160 acres east of the Yantian Sanatorium and a few hundred meters from the ocean. A prime location, it was a bargain financially, but carried a high degree of risk, because Yantian was hard to access. It was a long-standing problem that was brought up year after year and was a frequent topic in the media. If the area could not be made more accessible, real estate development along Shenzhen's east coast would be greatly impacted. Yantian was separated from Liantang by only a single tunnel, but the land there cost a thousand yuan a square meter less. Hu Guohao had set his heart on turning Yantian into an "oceanview luxury villa" development.

A few days before Hu's death, he and Zhou Zhengxing had engaged in a heated argument. Hu, who would allow no one to appropriate power where major decisions were concerned, was a risk-taker, while Zhou was understated and cautious. Despite their contrasting natures, they had been able to get along, at least on the surface, up till now. This time, however, irreconcilable strategic differences in approach had led to an open clash.

Someone had overheard Zhou say, "Tiandongba looks like a piece of choice pork, but in fact it's a chicken rib, tasteless though you hate to throw it away."

"Who cares if it's a chicken rib? Give me a bone, and I'll gnaw on it," Hu had replied. "How can you possibly find success if you lack the spirit and determination to gnaw on a bone?"

"I'm against betting the survival of the company on such a risky venture."

"Would Landmark be where it is today if we hadn't taken risks?"

"No matter what you say, I'm against buying Tiandongba." Zhou had dug in his heels.

"Very well then, I'll turn it over to a vote by the Board," Hu had responded coldly.

The conversation had ended, and as Zhou stormed out of Hu's office, he ran into the director of marketing operations, Huang Hongli. Huang was surprised to see the dark look on Zhou's face. The dispute was making the rounds throughout the company the next day.

"Based on what we know about Landmark, with Hu's unexpected death, Zhou is the most logical person to become the next CEO," Xiaochuan explained.

Cui then pointed out a third beneficiary.

"The last one to benefit from Hu's death is Hong Yiming, CEO of Big East Realty. We've learned that Hong was the last person to see Hu alive on the evening of the twenty-fourth. But more importantly, Big East Realty was Landmark's only competitor among bidders for Tiandongba. Everyone in the real estate business believed that Landmark and Big East were the only two real contenders for the land at Yantian. Now with Hu Guohao gone, Tiandongba could very well fall into Big East's clutches."

This news piqued everyone's interest, for if Hu Guohao's death was not an accident, then the prime suspects (those who would benefit from his death) would be:

1. His wife, Zhu Mei-feng;
2. His deputy CEO, Zhou Zhengxing;
3. Hu's business rival, Hong Yiming, CEO of Big East Realty.

Following agreement on this preliminary conclusion, Cui began planning the next step in the investigation.

"In order to get to the bottom of Hu's death, I'm going to ask for a judiciary autopsy."

Finally, closing his notebook, Cui said, "Xiaochuan and Yao Li, you two check on the three suspects' whereabouts from eleven p.m. on the twenty-fourth to one a.m. on the twenty-fifth. Make sure they all have alibis."

"We're on it, sir."

— 2 —

The Ming Tien Café in Nanyuan. A small coffee shop in green hues, with a tasteful interior design.

Nie Feng sat at a table by the window upstairs. A ponytailed waitress in a green uniform brought him a glass of ice water.

"What would you like, sir?"

"Coffee."

"Our Blue Mountain is the best," Ponytail recommended.

"OK, I'll have that."

Nie was not picky about his coffee, but he'd heard of the famous Blue Mountain and decided to give it a try.

Soon Ponytail brought him a steamy Blue Mountain in a dark brown bone-china cup. It had a wonderfully rich aroma. Nie tore open a small green paper sugar packet and began stirring the coffee with a tiny stainless-steel spoon, after pouring in some Ming Tien creamer.

Ponytail stood to the side, staring at him. She had small eyes and a garlic-bulb nose on a round face, reminding him of his nanny. He glanced at her and smiled.

"Are you here by yourself?"

"I'm waiting for a friend."

"A girl?"

"A police officer."

"Oh."

Nie picked up his cup and took a sip. It had a subtle fragrance, not all that different from the cafeteria coffee at the Sheraton in Sichuan. He'd heard that Blue Mountain was considered the aristocrat of coffee, but to him it was nothing to write home about.

"It's slightly sour."

"That's the Blue Mountain flavor, sir," she said, both to explain and praise the coffee.

At that moment Nie saw Xiaochuan rush in; he waved from his table.

"Sorry I'm late. We had a meeting about the case this afternoon," Xiaochuan apologized as he sat down across from Nie Feng.

"That's all right. I just got here."

"What would your friend like, sir?" Ponytail asked as she flashed Nie a fetching smile.

"Coffee for me, too," Xiaochuan said.

"Blue Mountain, or charcoal roast?"

Xiaochuan took a quick look at the fancy menu and ordered the cheapest one.

"Bring me a cup of Ming Tien coffee."

"Where are you staying, Mr. Nie?" Xiaochuan asked after the waitress left.

"At the Publishing Bureau guesthouse. It's cheaper than a hotel."

"This place isn't bad." Xiaochuan looked around him.

The green shop sign, the oval logo, the cheerful music, and friendly service were all part of Ming Tien's brand. The beige linen window coverings were raised, so customers could look down at the heavy traffic.

"I like the place," Nie Feng said.

"But you didn't ask me here for a cup of Ming Tien coffee, did you?"

"Coffee's the main reason, of course, but there's something else, the Hu Guohao case."

"Yesterday at Landmark, I noticed you were very curious about Hu's death, Mr. Nie."

"Please call me Nie Feng." Nie paused, before deciding to be straight with the officer. "How should I put it? Maybe it's professional sensitivity, but I don't think Hu's death was an accident. And he's on the cover of our next issue. Since I interviewed him and wrote the article, I feel I need to follow up for the sake of the magazine and our many readers."

"I share your feeling about Hu's death." Xiaochuan was somewhat animated. "But we're still looking for clues."

" 'Beauty is everywhere. And to our eyes, it's not a matter of the lack of beauty but a lack of discovery.' The same is true with clues, I think." Nie looked at Xiaochuan.

"That's from Rodin," the officer said with a hint of admiration. "And it makes sense."

"Which academy did you attend?"

"Southwest Advanced Police University. I graduated two years ago and was hired at Shenzhen."

"Southwest Advanced?" A look of familiarity appeared in Nie's eyes.

"You've been on our campus?"

"Not just been on. I know the place like the back of my hand. I spent my teenage years in the Southwest compound. The boxy buildings, the firing range, the police gym, I've been to all of them."

"Did you live in the compound?"

Ponytail walked up with a cup of steaming coffee.

"Here's your coffee, sir."

"Thank you." Xiaochuan gestured for her to put it down, without taking his eyes off Nie.

Ponytail laid down the cup and gave Nie another fetching look before walking away.

"You guessed it. But then I was admitted to the Journalism

School at C University and left the compound," Nie said. "After college, I did all sorts of work, interviewing and editing, reporting, freelancing, but nothing to make a name for myself. Now ten years have gone by."

"Now I remember." Xiaochuan's eyes lit up, as if discovering a new frontier. "No wonder I thought you looked familiar. Do you know . . . President Nie Donghai?"

"I do." Nie nodded, then continued calmly, "A stubborn old fellow. He's my father."

Xiaochuan jumped to his feet and snapped off a military salute.

"Please give President Nie my best."

That drew a curious look from people at the next table.

Nie looked around and laughed. "Please sit down. I'm not my father."

"You're right, of course." Xiaochuan sat down with an embarrassed look.

"I want to make this clear. My father and I are two different people. And you can't tell anyone."

"I won't, of course." Xiaochuan nodded. Nie Donghai, President of Southwest Advanced Police University, was a renowned administrative expert, holder of Police Commissioner First Rank, and a man who enjoyed high prestige among professionals and students.

The distance vanished between the two men, who now felt a special bond, almost as if they shared a birthplace and experiences at the Police Academy.

"That's great, good brother Nie. Just tell me what you want to know."

"I know you police have rules, and I don't expect you to share confidential information. I want to find the truth, which is a journalist's mandate. No matter how you look at it, Hu's death was too sudden."

"I think so, too," Xiaochuan agreed.

"You've just come from a meeting about the case, haven't you?"

Nie picked up his cup and signaled Xiaochuan to drink his coffee.
"If Hu was murdered," he said after taking a sip, "there must be three
suspects—Zhou Zhengxing, Zhu Mei-feng, and Hong Yiming, am
I right?"

"How did you know?" Xiaochuan was so shocked his hand
paused in midair.

"Drink your coffee." Nie nodded. "Elementary, as they say.
They're the three major beneficiaries. Zhou is deputy CEO and the
second largest shareholder at Landmark. My research shows that
Hu owned fifty-four percent of the stock and Zhou thirty-six
percent, with the remaining ten percent in the hands of Landmark
Management. When Landmark formed in Shenzhen, Hu Guohao invested thirty-six million yuan while Zhou only contrib-
uted a piece of land. The business flourished because of Hu's guts
and his willingness to take risks, but also because of Zhou's local connections. Low key by nature, Zhou wasn't entirely comfortable with Hu's bravado and domineering attitude. He particularly
disliked Hu's tendency to take risks, so problems arose between
them, to the point where they could no longer get along."

"How do you know all this?" Xiaochuan was impressed.

"It's nothing. Prior to the interview, I did some background research on Landmark." Nie winked at Xiaochuan. "A good journalist has to have a bloodhound's nose."

"So does a good police officer," Xiaochuan said to himself.

"Why did you rank Zhu Mei-feng your number two suspect?"

"Did I? I didn't say she was number two." Nie flashed an artful
smile. "With Hu's death, his shares will go to her, so she must be
considered the number one beneficiary. I learned from Landmark
employees that they were married six years ago. Before then, she'd
worked at Shenzhen's largest karaoke bar. With her voice and good
looks, she'd had a long line of rich fans, but she protected her reputation by never being involved with any of the customers. After she
married Hu, he opened a beauty salon for her. She kept her distance

from Hu's business and rarely came to the office. She probably has no idea how much her husband was worth."

"I see." Xiaochuan was mulling this all over.

"As for Big East's Hong Yiming," Nie continued, 'I'm sure the police know that his company is Landmark's strongest competitor and that he was the last person to see Hu alive. So it's natural and logical to suspect him."

"Logical?" Xiaochuan seemed puzzled.

"Right." Nie nodded to Xiaochuan as a sort of hint. "I think the last dinner at Greater Meisha and what the two men talked about may be a very important clue."

"Thanks for the tip." Xiaochuan scratched his head and reproached himself as the significance of Nie's words set in. Nie knew just about everything about the case, and he, a case officer, had missed so many details.

"Say, your coffee's getting cold." To change the subject, Nie asked with a smile, "What's your Chief Cui like?"

"He's a great police officer. He worked his way up from precinct stations and solved some major cases along the way. The only problem is, he's got a temper."

"He likes to lecture people, I suppose," Nie said. "And may be a bit overweening."

"He's actually a good guy. It's just—"

"You don't have to defend him. I'm just having a bit of fun. Will you deliver a message for me? Tell him I'd like to tag along and report on the investigation."

"Sure, I can do that."

"One more thing. Will you do me a favor?"

"Anything. Just say it."

"I'd like to take a look at Hu Guohao's body, but Cui mustn't know about it."

"That's no problem. It's at the Danzhutou Funeral Home."

"Is it far from here?"

"Quite far, actually. But I have a car and I can take you there tonight. We have to act fast, because they may be sending the body to the Public Security Hospital for an autopsy soon."

"Perfect." Nie nodded.

Xiaochuan wasn't sure whether Nie meant the trip to the funeral home or the autopsy.

They chatted about other things for a while. Nie pointed at the Ming Tien logo on the oval coaster.

"Interesting logo."

"Really?" Xiaochuan moved the coaster over to take a closer look.

"A green oval around a pair of green, slightly curved vertical lines to the left of a small green oval with little gaps at the top and bottom.

"The green lines on the left must symbolize tea leaves and the oval next to them a coffee bean."

"Excellent," Nie said, with a sparkle in his eye as he looked at the officer. "Now look again."

Xiaochuan frowned as he concentrated, like a schoolkid taking an IQ test.

"See it?"

"No." The young officer shook his head.

"It's 110," Nie Feng said, calling attention to the emergency number for the police.

"You're right, it is!" Xiaochuan clapped his hands.

"You guys in the criminal division work too hard. This is a good place to unwind. You could turn it into a police officers' club."

"Hmm." Xiaochuan looked around. "The place does have a homey feel about it."

Nie waved to the waitress, who was standing next to a post. "Check please, Miss."

Ponytail quickly went over to the cashier.

"Oh, there's one more person." Nie rapped his fingers on the tabletop as he was reminded of something. "Someone you need to look into."

"Who's that?"

Ponytail came over with a smile and the check.

Nie glanced at the check and took out his wallet. Sixty yuan for two coffees: forty for the Blue Mountain and twenty for the Ming Tien coffee. Typical for Shenzhen.

They got up and were seen out with a bow from the waitress, who said, "Please come again."

"Hu Guohao's assistant, Zhong Tao," Nie said as they walked down the stairs. "He seemed all right to me, but he was at Lesser Meisha on the day Hu died."

"Really? Why didn't we know about that?" Xiaochuan was surprised by the revelation.

"Zhong Tao told me himself. On the afternoon of the twenty-fourth he rode with Hu to the Seaview Hotel, where Hu got out. The driver then dropped Zhong off at Lesser Meisha before returning to the city. Zhong and seven college buddies who worked in Shenzhen got together for a reunion at Ocean Barbecue and partied all night."

Xiaochuan recalled how Cui had only told him to go see if the deceased was indeed Hu Guohao, and no one even thought of asking whether there might have been someone else in the car with Hu that day.

"Did he tell you the names of the other guys?"

"That's police business. It won't be hard to find them."

"I'll have to tell our Team Leader when I get back."

"Just don't tell him where you heard it."

"I won't."

Xiaochuan opened the door of his Jetta and they climbed in.

He started the car and headed off to the east.

Danzhutou was located in Buji, a town north of Shenzhen with a low mountain range behind it. It was nearly dusk when they arrived at the funeral home.

Xiaochuan drove through the gate, skirted a cement road, and stopped in front of the office, where he showed his police ID to a bespectacled, middle-aged staff member.

"This man's a journalist. We'd like to take another look at Hu Guohao's body; that's number twelve."

"But we're not open for visitations at night." The man looked at Nie from behind his glasses.

"I'm returning to Sichuan tomorrow. Won't the old gentleman kindly let us in?" Nie bowed and smiled.

"Do I look old to you?" The man laughed in spite of himself. He wasn't even in his forties.

"Come on, that's just a term of respect," Xiaochuan said in a conciliatory tone.

"All right. Follow me."

The employee led them through a shady grove of pines and cypresses to a large building with white walls and a green tiled roof.

He opened the door with a key, releasing a cold blast of air from the refrigerated holding room for bodies, a vast, empty space. Metal-handled drawers lining one wall emitted a subtle icy glint under fluorescent lights. There was no sign of life in here.

The man stopped by no. 12, put on a pair of canvas gloves, pulled out a long metal tray, and folded back the white sheet.

Hu Guohao's naked body materialized before their eyes, accompanied by cold air.

"It's him."

Though he was prepared, Nie still felt a shudder run through him.

Lying on the cold metal tray was the once-powerful real estate tycoon who, only a few days before, had been holding forth in his luxuriously appointed office on the twenty-fourth floor of the Landmark Building. He had looked arrogant, and yet undeniably impressive.

And now, he lay naked on a cold metal slab, an empty shell.

At that moment lines from a poem by Shelley flashed through Nie Feng's mind.

I met a traveler from an antique land
Who said: "Two vast and trunkless legs of stone
Stand in the desert. Near them on the sand,
Half sunk, a shattered visage lies, whose frown,
And wrinkled lip, and sneer of cold command,
Tell that its sculptor well those passions read . . .

"Mr. Nie, what's on your mind?" Xiaochuan asked, sensing something unusual in Nie's gaze.

"Oh, it's nothing." Nie recovered and looked down at Hu's body.

The skin was a grayish white, likely because of the cold storage and the length of time since his death; his broad face looked puffy, but the large leonine nose retained an aggressive appearance. His beady eyes, which had once shone with clever, ambitious light, were closed for all time.

Nie's gaze move slowly from the top of the head down to the face and paused at the left cheek, followed by a brief stop at the spot on his left chest, where below his nipple were a few noticeable cuts. Looking closely, he thought the lines formed the character for mountain, "山," but could not say for sure. There was no blood around the wounds, just a slight purple discoloration under the skin, which was probably because the body had been in the water so long.

Nie was lost in thought as he stared at the wound.

"This looks unusual," he muttered.

"Could that have been caused by jellyfish?" Xiaochuan wondered aloud.

"Is that what it would look like?" Nie had not had the fortune of being kissed by jellyfish.

"I'm not sure."

Swimmers at Dapeng Bay sometimes encountered jellyfish, those transparent, boneless creatures that came and went like ghosts, their stings like needle pricks. But the traces on Hu's body did not look like jellyfish stings, which would have produced a row of blisters; Hu's wound looked to have been made by something solid.

"You see bruises like that on bodies of drowning victims." The funeral home man had seen it all. "It could have been caused by a rock when he struggled to save himself."

"Well, that's very helpful. Thank you," Nie complimented the man. Then, before the other man knew what was happening, he took out a Pentax 928 and quickly snapped two close-ups of the wound.

"Say, you journalists have expensive cameras!"

"It's nothing special, actually." Feigning modesty, Nie flashed a foolish smile. "Just one of those idiot boxes you don't have to focus."

Xiaochuan covered a smile with his hand.

"Are we done here, Xiaochuan?" Nie turned to ask.

"Yes, we are." Xiaochuan wiped the grin off his face.

As the three men came out of the cold storage, Nie Feng asked the employee, "When will number twelve be cremated?"

"It was originally set for July second, but for some reason that's been changed."

"Was that a request from the family?"

"No. I received a notice from your people, telling me to keep the body in good shape for a possible autopsy."

Nie and Xiaochuan exchanged a glance.

"The man's already dead, and now they want to open him up. Bad karma," the man mumbled.

In the dying evening light, a few old crows were cawing loudly on one of the cypresses.

— 3 —

The Mei-feng Beauty Salon. A red BMW quietly rolled to a stop.

The door opened and out stepped Zhu Mei-feng, in a white trench coat and carrying a small purse.

Xiaochuan and Officer Yao walked up to her.

"Hello, Mrs. Hu," Xiaochuan said. "We need to check something with you."

"We can talk inside," Zhu said impassively.

"Are you sure you want to do that?" Yao Li asked.

"Yes." She smiled faintly and told them to follow her in.

"Good morning, Manager Zhu." Two young women in pink uniforms looked up and greeted Zhu Mei-feng before returning to the facials they were giving clients.

Zhu responded with a casual nod and showed the two officers into her office.

The room was roughly ten square meters in size and, furnished with a mahogany desk and a European-style sofa, was elegant in both color tone and décor.

"Please, have a seat." She gestured for them to take the sofa, while she sat behind the desk, which fronted a glass display case lined with two rows of imported cosmetic samples.

"We're here because"—Xiaochuan went straight to the point—"we want to know where you were from eleven o'clock on the night of the twenty-fourth to one o'clock the following morning."

"You're checking my alibi, is that it?" she asked calmly.

"It's just routine police procedure. I hope you understand," Yao Li said stiffly.

A pink-uniformed, moon-faced girl entered with two cups of instant black tea. She set them down on the coffee table, then turned and left, closing the door behind her.

"Lao Hu went to Greater Meisha that day alone. I didn't go with him."

"Why didn't you accompany him for a weekend stay at Greater Meisha Beach?" Yao Li asked.

"It's been a long time since I was at Greater Meisha. I'm not into swimming or surfing," Zhu explained. "My mother had a flare-up of her arthritic rheumatism on the twenty-fourth. She called from Hong Kong and asked me to come see her."

Xiaochuan and Yao Li stared at each other.

"So you went to Hong Kong?"

"Yes, I did. I took the twelve-twenty Chinalink bus from Wenjindu to Kowloon. A little after eight the next morning, I received a call from Mr. Hu's driver, who told me what had happened, so I took the first Chinalink bus back to Wenjindu."

"Which one?"

"I think it was the ten-twenty bus."

"Can you prove it?"

"Sure."

She opened her purse, took out her passport, and handed it to Xiaochuan, who removed a pair of bus tickets tucked inside the plastic cover. A quick glance told him they were for a round-trip between Wenjindu and Prince Edward Station in Kowloon. He handed them to his partner, who wrote down the dates and times on the tickets.

Xiaochuan then opened the passport for a closer look; blue triangular stamps showed her departure and entry times. The officers exchanged a knowing look before he returned the passport to Zhu.

"Thank you for the information."

"You're welcome."

Wang and Yao stood up, walked out, and climbed into their Jetta.

"Zhu Mei-feng's alibi is genuine," Yao said.

"Yes, it's iron-clad." Xiaochuan hesitated before turning on the engine. "But the timing was simply too pat."

"Did you see how calm she was?"

"She wasn't just calm. She seemed, well, more like detached," Xiaochuan said.

"Detached?"

"That's right. Where to next?"

"Let's go see Zhou Zhengxing."

"All right."

They roared off down Shennan East Road.

. . .

Back at Landmark Building. The blue glass-plated skin of the twenty-four-story high-rise was tinted from the splendid sunset.

Xiaochuan and Yao Li hurried into the lobby, where they flashed their badges at the security guard and headed for the elevator.

In the twenty-fourth-floor CEO's office, the two officers sat in the secretary's office, where Ah-ying offered them freshly brewed black tea.

"We have some questions for Mr. Zhou," Xiaochuan explained.

"Mr. Zhou is out of town."

"Oh? Out of town?" Xiaochuan was surprised.

"Where did he go?" Yao Li asked.

Ah-ying picked up the red phone on her desk and dialed an extension. "Ah-mei, do you know where Mr. Zhou went? Oh, yes, I see. Thank you. It's nothing."

"Mr. Zhou flew to Shanghai this morning."

That was unexpected.

"Mr. Zhou's secretary said it wasn't a planned trip. He left in a hurry, probably business related, but she had no idea who he was meeting there," Ah-ying added.

"Can you reach him?"

"I can try."

Ah-ying dialed Zhou's cell phone, but received a recording in a woman's voice: "Your call is being transferred to voice mail."

Xiaochuan and Yao Li exchanged glances. Yao gestured to say there was nothing they could do now.

"Think he's running away?" Xiaochuan whispered to Yao.

"I doubt it." Yao shook her head. "That would be an admission of guilt."

"All right, then," Xiaochuan said to Ah-ying, "please keep trying to reach Mr. Zhou and let us know when you hear from him."

"I will. We'll do our best to cooperate." Ah-ying looked up with lovely eyes, highlighted by dark circles, that showed a hint of sorrow.

This woman is heartbroken over Hu's death, Yao Li said to

herself. "How are things at Landmark these days?" she asked in a show of sympathy.

"Not good. Everyone is unsettled and rumors are flying." Ah-ying was noticeably upset.

When the captain of a ship, whose word is law, dies, it's only natural for tumult on deck to follow, especially if the death is suspicious. No one could tell where the ship would sail next on such stormy seas.

"Is there anything else I can do for you?" Ah-ying asked.

"Yes, thank you." Xiaochuan said, "Is Zhong Tao in?"

"He's with a client."

The door to Zhong's office, across the hallway, was open.

"Who is it?"

"Mr. Lu, the General Manager of Shenzhen Development Bank, is here, probably for a loan payment. Our Mr. Hu has only just died, and they're already here to collect."

Ah-ying was clearly unhappy.

Xiaochuan looked at his watch—5:20.

"We can wait."

"Here are some newspapers." Ah-ying handed them some local papers and left the room.

"Thank you," Yao Li said.

As they sat in the office, Yao flipped through the papers. Time slowly ticked away.

Suddenly the strains of what sounded like a harmonica floated over from somewhere nearby; the melody was familiar, but the name of the tune unknown. It had a serene yet sorrowful feel.

Xiaochuan looked around, but couldn't locate the source.

"Did you hear a harmonica?" he whispered to his partner.

She shook her head.

Now he was puzzled.

About twenty minutes later, the door to Zhong's office opened, and out stepped two middle-aged men in suits and ties. The first one, a heavyset man, had an arrogant look.

"Please rest assured, General Manager Lu," Zhong Tao said in an even tone, "that I'll pass your views to Mr. Zhou."

"Remember, no later than the middle of next month." The heavy-set man gestured.

"Absolutely," Zhong replied.

After seeing the two men to the elevator, Zhong turned and saw the two officers.

"May we have a word with you, Mr. Zhong?" Xiaochuan said.

"Of course. In here, please." Zhong showed them into his office.

It was a well-furnished office, with all the essential office equipment, including a black computer keyboard and a late-model LCD screen, but it was not particularly large.

"Those two men were—"

"Here for a loan payment." Zhong said pointedly; he poured cups of Maxwell House instant coffee for the officers while he put away the documents on his desk. "Landmark's image has suffered with the death of Mr. Hu, and the bank is afraid we'll default on a loan."

"How much is the loan?" Xiaochuan asked.

"No one knows the exact figure, nor the amount of Landmark assets. There's a rumor that Landmark's debts outstrip its assets." Zhong's response surprised the officers.

"Could that be true?" Xiaochuan asked.

"It's alarmist talk. Landmark is one of the province's model enterprises," Zhong said with a hint of mockery. "Besides, as the saying goes, a skinny dead camel is still bigger than a horse."

"Are you, Mr. Zhong, now Landmark's gatekeeper?" Yao joked.

"Oh, I'm hardly qualified for that," Zhong responded modestly. "In the wake of CEO Hu's death, Mr. Zhou is now number one, while our deputy CEO, Mr. Li, is in charge of operations. Those of us in middle management are glorified migrant workers who will likely become the proverbial monkeys who disperse after the tree falls."

Everyone in the company knew that Zhong Tao had been Hu Guohao's man, so his comments were worth parsing. People in

Landmark's inner circle were aware that Zhong was indebted to Hu for recognizing his abilities and giving him important tasks. As Hu's trusted assistant and a member of the up-and-coming generation, Zhong had a competitive edge, but stood no chance to defeat Zhou Zhengxing in a fight for control of Landmark without the backing of Hu's widow, who had inherited Hu's stock ownership.

"We want to know more about what happened on June twenty-fourth," Xiaochuan said to change the subject as he opened his notebook.

"What exactly?"

"We heard that you rode with Hu Guohao to Greater Meisha on that afternoon."

"Yes, I did. He got off at Greater Meisha and I went on to Lesser Meisha."

"What were you doing in Lesser Meisha?" Xiaochuan asked.

"A college reunion," Zhong said with a nod. "Classmates from C University who work in Shenzhen. We don't get to see each other often, so we partied all night."

"A beach party? How many were there?" Yao asked.

"Seven." Zhong sounded very much at ease.

"Where in Lesser Meisha?"

"Am I a suspect?" Zhong asked with a smile.

"No, this is just routine police work," Yao Li assured him. "We have to talk to everyone who's connected to Mr. Hu."

"We went to the barbecue pits at eight o'clock, and stayed there till about two in the morning."

Yao Li had been to the barbecue grounds with friends once in the past. There were more than a hundred individual pits, each big enough to accommodate eight to ten diners. Nicknamed the Barbecue Playground of a Thousand, it provided everything for paying guests: fatty beef, mutton, pork chops; a variety of seafood, including prawns, squid, silver cod, and so on; as well as beer, soft drinks, and other popular snacks. When night fell, the dark ocean provided a festive backdrop for merrymaking crowds around pits in which fires flared impressively.

"Did you go anywhere else that night?"

"For a while, yes."

"When?"

"Around eleven, just for a little while. I'd had too much to drink and was sick."

"Could you give us the names of your friends?" Xiaochuan asked.

"Of course."

Zhong took out a brown notebook and flipped through to find the right page, from which he copied the names and phone numbers of his friends onto a notepad.

Xiaochuan took the note; there were six names: Fu Tong, Zhang Jusheng, Qi Xiaohui, Dai Zhiqiang, Ding Lan, Luo Wei.

"Only six?" Xiaochuan questioned.

"And Zhong Tao makes seven, doesn't it?" Zhong said impishly.

Xiaochuan had to laugh at himself.

Zhong's Mandarin had a distinct Sichuan accent. Xiaochuan recalled a line he'd read somewhere that went, "No matter where you go, you'll always find a hometown friend by listening for Sichuanese Mandarin."

"You're from Sichuan, aren't you, Mr. Zhong?" he asked.

"Yes," Zhong said.

"Me too."

"My family's from Chengdu."

"Chongqing here."

"Ah, so you're a kiddo from Chongqing," Zhong quipped, using a familiar phrase.

Xiaochuan was engaged by Zhong's charm and characteristic Sichuan sense of humor.

"We were just told that Mr. Zhou is on a business trip. Urgent?" Xiaochuan probed.

"I don't know. His secretary just told me that he left in a hurry."
Zhong was obviously in the dark about Zhou's trip.

"Has something happened?"

"I hope not."

Xiaochuan looked at his watch.

Then he heard the harmonica again, this time a sad melody, like
someone pouring their heart out; to him it felt like bone-chilling
spring water flowing over his heart.

Xiaochuan's brows quavered slightly; he closed his eyes and
thought he saw a plume of flickering blue flames.

He'd heard the melody before, and though he couldn't recall its
name, the sorrowful tune tugged at his heart.

Turning to glance at Yao Li, he said, "It's getting late. We should
head back now."

"I'll treat you both to a hot pot in Jiujiulong someday." Zhong
Tao smiled.

"Thank you."

As Zhong stood up to see them out, Xiaochuan saw him stare at
something out the window. A peculiar expression came over him,
as the muscles at the corners of his mouth trembled slightly. His
hand shook so much he knocked over his coffee cup. His face was
tinted a rosy red by the fiery sunset. Tears welled up in his eyes.

Xiaochuan followed his gaze. Through the tinted windows, he
saw a Boeing jumbo jet heading southwest into the sunset, its red and
green lights pulsing on the wingtips. The plane was too low for him
to see the logo, but as it roared through the sky he felt the impact of
its power.

A confused Yao Li looked at Zhong Tao, who was oblivious to
the two of them.

But he recovered and nodded to apologize for his behavior. Still
embarrassed, he righted the coffee cup, which had been empty, thus
sparing the desk the mess of coffee stains.

The scene, which had lasted less than twenty seconds, had left a
deep impression on both officers.

"That was weird," Xiaochuan said to Yao Li in the elevator.

"It sure was. I think he saw something."

"A Boeing 747 flying toward Huangtian Airport."

"A Boeing jet?"

"That's right."

Yao Li could only shake her head in bewilderment.

FOUR

"Alibi"

— 1 —

The Y District Public Security Building. All the lights were burning in the Criminal Investigation Team's sixth-floor office.

The second case meeting was under way, and the detectives were caught up in a much more animated atmosphere. Bureau Chief Wu Jian, who was in charge of criminal investigation, was in attendance. A man of medium build, he had the look of a typical southerner, with a swarthy face and thick lips. With more than two decades in criminal work, he was an honest and forceful, no-nonsense police officer who had handled many important cases.

"This afternoon we received permission from municipal authorities to perform a judicial autopsy on Hu Guohao," Cui announced to begin the meeting. "The Public Security Hospital will work overtime to complete it as early as possible. I've told Tian Qing to observe the process."

The news energized the officers around the table.

"Hu Guohao's body will be cremated on July second, so time is of the essence." Cui drove home the tight schedule.

"Why the rush?" Zheng Yong, the squad's ladies' man, ventured softly.

"The date was chosen by Landmark's Board of Directors on the twenty-sixth, and agreed to by the widow." Cui shot him a searing look. "We can't do anything to stop them if we have no solid evidence that the death was not accidental."

"Under normal circumstances, the Board's decision makes perfect sense," Chief Wu added, in his deep, full, and infectious voice. "First, the body can't stay out too long. Also, July second is a Sunday, which lends itself to a more impressive memorial."

"Now let's hear what you all found out over the past two days."

Cui offered a cigarette to Chief Wu, who turned it down with a wave and a smile. Zheng Yong tossed the squad leader a yellow plastic lighter, which he used to light his cigarette; he took a deep drag, sending a plume of white smoke curling into the air.

Xiaochuan and Yao Li opened their notebooks and reported on their interviews with Zhu Mei-feng and Zhong Tao.

"Zhu Mei-feng told us she took the twelve-twenty Chinalink bus from Wenjindu to Hong Kong's Kowloon station on the twenty-fourth. She received a call from her husband's driver at about eight the next morning, informing her what happened to Hu, so she rushed back on the ten-twenty bus to Wenjindu Station," Yao Li reported.

"Any proof?"

"Yes, she showed us her round-trip tickets."

Xiaochuan took over. "We then went to the customs office at Wenjindu and checked their computer records. Her story checks out."

Yao Li continued her report:

"Following Team Leader Cui's instructions, we learned that Zhong Tao was also in Lesser Meisha on the night of June twenty-fourth. He and six college friends met at the barbecue pits on Lesser Meisha beach. He said there were four men and two women, all graduates of Sichuan's C University, some of whom had majored in international business, others in Chinese."

Yao flipped a page in her notebook to report on her conversation with the six friends. She was unable to speak with one of them, who was away on a business trip. What the other five said pretty much corroborated Zhong's account.

They had spent the night on the barbecue grounds, partying from dusk till about two in the morning. The five interviewed individuals told the police that Zhong was with them the whole time, except for a brief moment. He was sick from drinking too much, so Ding Lan helped him back to the vacation villa to change clothes. That happened around 11:05. Just under half an hour later, Ding and Zhong returned to the grounds, where Zhong was mocked by his friends. They remained on the beach until 2:05 before returning to their rented villas to rest.

"So Ding Lan was Zhong Tao's alibi for those twenty-five minutes," Yao Li said.

"What do we know about Ding Lan?" Chief Wu asked.

"Nothing of particular interest. She was a top student in the Chinese department at C University, a member of the college Party organization, and a scholarship winner every year. She's had many suitors but has dismissed them all. She's now the editor of a special column in a Shenzhen woman's magazine and drives a white Citroën. Her colleagues say she's a tough cookie, loves to eat and party, but is serious and professional when it comes to her work, and has had success at the magazine," Yao Li said.

"She seems to be a woman with a heart," Xiaochuan added, "and she speaks her mind."

"Then we can't really count the twenty-five minutes as an absence," Cui offered.

"That's right."

Yao continued: "Fu Tong is an international business major at C University, with average grades. A Chinese chess fanatic, he often went from dorm room to dorm room, looking for opponents.

He's known as a bit of a slacker but is well liked. He owns a trading company in Shenzhen with an annual income of six to seven hundred thousand yuan. He drives a black Honda, which he drove to Lesser Meisha that day.

"Zhang Jusheng is an English major, generally considered somewhat aloof. A top student in high school, he entered C University with the highest score in his county. A good student, he's a voracious reader, and is well versed in psychology. He succeeded in wooing the prettiest girl in his class just before graduation. Now he's involved in overseas training, running the New World Training Center, which is well known in Shenzhen.

"Qi Xiaohui, a graduate of C University's law school, is the son of a provincial deputy department head, so his family is quite well off. A heavy beer drinker in college, he also enjoys fine cigarettes. He has his own law firm in Shenzhen and handles cases of mixed importance. One involved trademark infringement, which earned him a bit of fame and a spot on a provincial TV legal program. His wife is a TV anchorwoman. That day on the beach, he and Zhong Tao had engaged in a beer-drinking contest—Zhong lost.

"Dai Zhiqiang, a bookish math major, writes software for a computer company.

"Luo Wei, a business management major, is smart and capable. Working in the loan department of a bank, and considered one of its top employees, she is a high-salaried white-collar worker. Her husband is a section head at the Municipal Finance Bureau."

"Did you check Zhong's background?" Chief Wu asked.

"We did. He was a top International Finance student at C University. With excellent grades and a cool head, he was known even then for his understated manner. In school he was generous and helpful to others; he lent out money all the time and often forgot how much someone owed him. He's an avid table tennis player who once won second prize at a college tournament. We were told that he enjoyed his classmates' support and once organized the class to overthrow a selfish class leader who flattered their teacher for his own benefit. After coming to Shenzhen, he worked for a prominent South China stockbroker, where he managed several accounts and did quite well. He then jumped to Landmark as the CEO's executive assistant. He's still single."

"Chief Cui," Xiaochuan said, "I still think we shouldn't overlook those twenty-five minutes."

"Do you mean that he and Ding Lan were up to something?" Zheng Yong asked snidely.

Someone snickered.

"That's not what I meant," Xiaochuan stammered, his face turning red.

"I think we can accept Zhong's alibi," Cui said to end the discussion.

Xiaochuan followed that up with his conversation with Hong Yiming, after revealing what Nie Feng had alluded to.

"When I met Mr. Nie two nights ago, he thought we should find out what Hong and Hu talked about at dinner that night in Greater Meisha. It could be an important clue."

"If a reporter from a mosquito press can solve a case, what do they need the police for?" Cui said, half in jest.

That got the desired result of general laughter.

"He's not from a mosquito press," Xiaochuan said in Nie Feng's defense.

"He writes for *Western Sun,* doesn't he? Well, it's easy to play detective on paper."

"It's *Western Sunshine,* not *Western Sun,*" Xiaochuan corrected his superior.

"They're the same, aren't they? Why be so stubborn? Can you have sunshine without the sun?"

Now everyone was laughing, including Chief Wu.

Xiaochuan refused to give up. "But what I learned from Hong Yiming was significant," he argued after the laughter died down.

"Tell us what you learned," Chief Wu said.

Xiaochuan told them that during the interview he learned that

Hong had an alibi. He'd played mah-jongg with some business associates all through the night of the twenty-fourth. He also told Xiaochuan about the dinner at Greater Meisha. At around six o'clock that evening, Hu invited him to dine at the Oceanview Restaurant in the Seaview Hotel. Hu ordered a tortoise pot, a spicy crab, some razor clams, and a few cold dishes. They enjoyed the meal and the conversation. A committed swimmer, Hu had no interest in golf, so the Seaview Hotel was his preferred place to meet business associates for business and for pleasure. Hong said he and Hu had known each other for years, and that he had been Hu's assistant when they had started out in Hainan. After they had acquired some capital, they came to Shenzhen to try their luck, with Hong setting out on his own. The friends then became competitors. Hu had phoned him to have dinner at Greater Meisha that evening, but their conversation was pretty much limited to talk about real estate bubbles.

"Did you ask him about the land in Tiandongba?" Cui asked.

"I did. I said, 'You're business rivals, so you must have discussed Tiandongba.' He said, 'I thought he'd want to sound me out, but he didn't say a word about the bid. That was unlike him, if you ask me.'"

"And then?"

"Then Hong added, 'Maybe he wanted to talk about it but didn't have time.' I asked him, 'What makes you say that?' Hong said, 'Hu got a phone call and said it was urgent, so we said good-bye.' I asked when the call came in, and he said it was around seven. When I asked if Hu had asked him to wait, he said no, and since Hong had arranged to meet with some banking friends at Honey Lake Resort, that was the end of it."

Yao Li took it from there.

"Hong played mah-jongg with three friends in suite number two of Honey Lake Resort all night. They were Deputy Section Head Li of the Municipal Construction Section, Bureau Chief Sun of the T District National Land Bureau, and General Manager Qian of MasterCard Worldwide. They ordered room service at around midnight."

"Check out the phone call Hu received at dinner. It's key," Cui said.

"We did check it out. It was made at 7:01 from a mobile phone to Hu's cell. It lasted less than a minute," Xiaochuan said.

"Whose mobile was it?"

"The number began with one-three-six, from Shenzhou. It was a burn phone."

"Shit!" Cui cursed angrily.

"This number is critical," Chief Wu said to Cui. "Have the phone surveillance office put a trace on it."

"Will do," Cui said as he turned to Xiaochuan. "There's something else. Tian Qing asked the city's Criminal Investigation Bureau's medical examiner to determine if a human hand had caused the scratches on Hu's chest. They appear to have been made by a sharp metal object and are in the shape of the Chinese character for mountain."

"Which means they could have been left by the perpetrator as a sign, or some kind of marker." Xiaochuan knew immediately what Cui was getting at.

"Quite likely," Cui said. "That and the mysterious phone call, plus the disappearance of Hu's clothing, all point to one thing—Hu's death was not accidental. So I've asked Chief Wu's permission to open an investigation."

"The Bureau Party Secretary has agreed," Chief Wu said. "We'll call it the June Twenty-fifth Murder, and Cui Dajun will lead the investigation. You'll need more people."

"Everyone in the team will work on this case, except for Xiao Guan and Xiao Lu, who are tied up with the Sha Tao Kok fraud case," Cui said to his suddenly animated officers.

"May I ask a question, Chief?" Xiaochuan said.

"Go ahead."

"Is it a coincidence that Hu's body was discovered near the Lesser Meisha Pier?"

Cui looked pleased.

"Good question. It's possible it was taken by motorboat to the pier and dumped on the beach. That would be an easy way to get rid of a body without leaving traces. If that's what happened, then this is a full-blown homicide."

The excitement level rose dramatically.

"You." Cui pointed to Zheng Yong. "Go with Da Wu to check out the motorboats at Greater and Lesser Meisha beaches tomorrow."

— 2 —

While the police were going over the case late into the night, Nie Feng was by Lesser Meisha Pier on his haunches, lost in thought as he stared at the rippling waves.

Under the evening sky, the stone pier stretched out into the ocean, its pylons exposed by the low tide. There were no boats tied up at the pier. Looking toward the jetty, he saw, on his left, the dark shadow of a mountain range, which the travel map marked as Back Tsai Kok Beach. To the right was the craggy Chao Kok, where sparse lights shone above the horizon, throwing distant cargo ships into silhouette.

He'd taken the 103 Bus from Luofang Road to Lesser Meisha at three that afternoon. It had taken a quarter of an hour and cost only nine yuan. He'd long wanted to visit Lesser Meisha, known as the Haiwai'i of the East, and now here he was, ready to sunbathe and take a dip in the ocean, but most importantly, to see the spot where Hu's body had been found.

Wearing a black T-shirt and a pair of beach shorts with piping, he looked carefree and smart with his beige baseball cap and a white canvas tote with the red ESPN logo.

After paying the fifteen yuan entrance fee, he walked from the main entrance to the Lesser Meisha Tourist Center, where he was immediately greeted by the smell of the ocean. Before him, coconut palms lining the path swayed gracefully in the ocean breezes while the waves lapped rhythmically.

The fine sand had a light yellow cast. Even on an overcast workday, many people were swimming, and there was a long line of beach umbrellas. Friends in Shenzhen had joked that he might find female swimming partners at the beach.

He bought a pair of black-and-red swimming trunks at the souvenir shop and changed into them right away. Then, after storing his street clothes in a locker, he went into the water, let a couple of waves wash over him, and swam out to the shark barrier buoy. It was an easy swim, so he did it twice. Nie was fond of working out, and he'd hoped to get a tan, but sunbathing was pointless on an overcast day.

After the swim, he surveyed the area. The beach was well equipped for vacationers, with villas, vacation cabins, restaurants with local cuisine, waterskiing, windsurfing, barbecue pits, and more—everything one could want to make it a vacationer's paradise. When he thought he knew his way around well enough, he went to talk to the staff at the tourist center about the morning of the twenty-fifth, when Hu's body was found.

The man on duty was a cautious, heavyset, middle-aged man, who demanded to see Nie Feng's press ID before taking him to the site.

He pointed out the spot—on the beach near the pier.

Standing on the stone jetty, Nie looked down on the spot a few feet below him, and took out his Pantex 928 to take pictures from different angles.

"So this was where Hu Guohao's body was found," he said to himself.

After looking around, he noted that the spot was thirty or forty meters from the swimming section. To his left a long row of red buoys marked the boundary for motorboats. To his right was Lovers' Lane, backed against a hill on one side and the ocean on the other.

He crouched down to measure the distance between the jetty and where the body had lain.

The tide receded in the evening and then rose again after midnight, which meant that the body had been seven or eight meters from the water at midnight. That was why there were no footprints or other marks, as Xiaochuan had said. Even if Hu's body had been dumped here, the person's footprints would have been washed away by the early morning tide. If this was indeed what had happened, then the spot and the time to drop off the body had been carefully thought out.

The barbecue ground, off to the west, was dotted with squat trees. Nie went to take a look and counted a hundred and eighteen cement pits encircled by cement benches.

Uniformed waitresses were setting out the fixings for the evening's barbecues. One of them told Nie that the squat trees were rubber trees their boss had imported to absorb the smoke from the barbecues.

He timed his walk from the barbecue ground to the pier—it took two minutes.

Nie remained crouched near the pier; he could hear loud talk and laughter over at the barbecue grounds.

Several possible scenarios occurred to him:

Under the evening sky, Hu Guohao struggled ashore and passed out on the beach;

Hu's body floated in the black ocean and washed up on the beach;

A shadowy figure carried the body and dropped it on the beach before mysteriously disappearing into the darkness.

"Could there be a fourth possibility?" he asked himself.

But there was still the puzzle of Hu's clothing.

And one more puzzle—what significance lay behind the sheet

of paper Hu received? What did the strange symbol and numbers mean?

"Seven-nine-one. Seven-nine-one," he muttered to himself.

An ocean breeze carried a chill and the smell of the sea. As Nie stood up and stretched, he decided to call the young officer, Xiaochuan. He dialed the number.

"Hey, Officer Wang. It's me, Nie Feng."

"Oh, hello, Mr. Nie."

"Is this a good time to talk?"

"I'm in a meeting at the station," Xiaochuan whispered.

"I guess you've been busy. I'm at Lesser Meisha beach."

"I see."

"Have you mentioned my request?"

"I've—"

"Who's that?" Cui cut in before Xiaochuan could finish.

"It's Mr. Nie, the reporter."

"The one from *Western Sun*?"

"It's *Western Sunshine*," Xiaochuan corrected his boss. "He wants to know what you think about his request to tag along as we investigate the case."

"Tell Mr. Reporter I'll let him come with us if he has a letter from the Provincial Public Security Office," Cui said caustically.

"Er—" Xiaochuan didn't know what to do.

"Tell him to stay out of police business," Cui said with obvious displeasure. "Now, back to the case."

"My boss said you can come, but—" Xiaochuan pressed his lips up against his phone.

"But what?"

"But you need a letter from the Provincial Public Security Office."

"A letter from the Provincial Public Security Office? Is that what he said?"

"Yes."

Xiaochuan felt awkward as he shut the phone. Nie Feng shook his head with a smile. After a moment's thought, he placed a call to his parents' home in Chengdu.

The young live-in maid picked up the phone and responded to his voice with pleasant surprise.

"Big Brother Nie! Where are you?"

"I'm in Shenzhen."

"Your mother has been wondering why you're not coming home."

"I've been delayed by some urgent business," Nie explained softly. "Say, is the old man home?"

"He is. He has guests."

"Where from?"

"I don't know, maybe an out-of-town public security bureau."

"Where's my mother?"

"Aunty is at the hospital."

"Could you call my old man to the phone?"

He wanted to see if his father knew anyone in Guangdong Public Security.

A few moments later a loud baritone voice came through the phone. "Hello."

"It's me, Dad. How are you doing? I'm still in Shenzhen on assignment, but I'll be back in a few days."

"How's it going?"

"Not bad. But the place is expensive. This is turning out to be a costly interview."

"Are you trying to get me to chip in?" the old man joked.

"Don't worry, Dad. Editor-in-chief Wu has promised extra pay for my special report. And I'll make sure he picks up any additional expenses."

"Your Mr. Wu knows how to deal with people." His father laughed.

"Say, Dad. I want to ask you something."

"What is it?"

"Do you know anyone in the Guangdong Provincial Public Security Bureau?"

"Guangdong? Sure. Deputy Chief Yao, who's in charge of criminal investigations. He and I were schoolmates."

"Perfect." It was more than Nie hoped for.

"What's so perfect about it?"

"My magazine is working on a report on the public security front. I'm heading that way and I'll pay Uncle Yao a visit." Nie paused purposefully before asking, "Would you like me to take a message along?"

"Hmm, it's been two years since I last saw Old Yao." Nie's father took the bait. "Why don't you take a couple of packets of good jasmine tea with you and tell him Old Nie from Sichuan sends his best. I've got to go. We have visitors."

"I promise to carry out my mission, Commissioner Nie." Nie Feng, the happy camper.

"No more of this Commissioner Nie stuff." His father was laughing.

— 3 —

The meeting was still under way in the crime unit conference room.

Cui passed out cigarettes, and once again columns of smoke rose.

"We have a report on Zhou Zhengxing," Xiaochuan said. "He's still on a business trip, but we got hold of him with the help of Hu's office assistant, Ah-ying."

"Where is he?"

"In Pudong, Shanghai, on finance issues, we're told."

"What did he say?"

"He didn't mince words. He said he went back to his hometown in Nan'ao for the weekend. On the afternoon of June twenty-fourth, he presided over a computer donation ceremony at a local primary school, so he couldn't have been at Lesser Meisha."

"He's from Shuitou Village in Nan'ao," Yao Li added.

Dapeng Bay, along Shenzhen's eastern coast, was over seventy kilometers long, with many blue-water, golden-sand beaches like Greater and Lesser Meisha, Xichong, Shuitousha, and Xiyong, all well-known tourist sites. Nan'ao Township, a one-time fishing village two kilometers south of Shuitousha, a stone's-throw from Hong Kong's Ping Chau Island, had been developed into a swanky coastal town.

A simple inquiry verified that Zhou had donated six computers to a primary school and had hosted a banquet at the Bayview Restaurant for the principal and the head of Shuitou Village; he'd later spent the night at his mother's house, where he'd had many visitors, including neighbors, aunts, uncles, and other relatives. They had talked till midnight. On the morning of the twenty-fifth, Zhou, a filial son, had taken his mother to a hospital in town and bought some herbal medicine for her cold. He had driven back to Shenzhen after lunch.

"Where was he on that first day after midnight?" Cui asked.

"At his mother's house."

"Did anyone see him?" Chief Wu asked.

"Only his mother."

"Close relatives like that can't provide a credible alibi," Chief Wu commented. "There's an hour gap between midnight on the twenty-fourth and one a.m. on the twenty-fifth. We need to find out what he was doing during that hour."

"Did Zhou say when he's coming back to Shenzhen?" Cui asked.

"He told us he'd be back tomorrow night for something called a 'Real Estate Elites Forum' at Guanlan Lake the following morning."

"So all four of them have an alibi." Cui summed up the situation. "But think about it, everyone, with the exception of Zhong Tao, could benefit from Hu Guohao's death, and they all have motives."

"Hong Yiming would want Hu dead for the sake of his business," Xiaochuan said, "and Zhou Zhengxing would gain control if he replaced Hu at Landmark, but Zhu Mei-feng, a graceful beauty if I've ever seen one—it's hard to see what her motive might have been."

"I heard from Landmark employees that Hu liked the ladies and that she was unhappy with him," Yao Li added.

"But enough to kill him?"

"I think something else is going on. We just have to find out what it is," Xiaochuan commented.

Team leader Cui frowned, but said nothing.

Yao Li and the others looked on, not sure what to do next. By now the office was shrouded in a pall of cigarette smoke, as they had all turned into human chimneys, except for Xiaochuan, the youngest, and Yao Li, the only woman. To all present, the case itself seemed cloaked in fog.

"The biggest mystery is how Hu Guohao's body turned up at Lesser Meisha," Chief Wu said.

"We found precious few clues at the scene." Cui was clearly unhappy.

"That's what I've been saying. Crime scene investigation is critical. It determines whether or not we can solve a case. If any single important clue is overlooked, then we might as well declare the case unsolvable," Chief Wu said emphatically. "Interviews are another routine task that can make or break an investigation. With so many tourists around Greater and Lesser Meisha coming and going, it's impossible to check on everyone, but . . . and how did Hu Guohao get from the Seaview Hotel? Did he walk, take a taxi, or did someone pick him up? Someone must have seen him, unless he knew how to make himself invisible."

"You're right, sir. We haven't been thorough enough with the tourists. We'll work on it." Cui nodded in agreement.

"The success of an investigation is usually decided by work done in the first week. Now, four days have gone by," Chief Wu stressed.

"The case will be a lost cause if we don't find more critical clues over the next few days."

"We've interviewed the doormen at the Seaview Hotel. But it was a Saturday and there were so many guests they didn't notice anything," Xiaochuan explained. "We've also shown Hu's picture to taxi drivers waiting for fares, but no one picked up Hu."

"It was after seven o'clock and getting dark, so the typical tourist or passerby wouldn't have noticed anything," Yao Li added convincingly.

Now they were truly stuck. Chief Wu knitted his bushy brows. It was getting uncomfortable in the room. Even the jokester Zheng Yong held his tongue.

In the end, it was Chief Wu who broke the silence. A seasoned investigator of criminal cases, he was able to grasp the key issues in messy cases like this. He turned toward Yao Li.

"Go ask Tian Qing if they found anything when they examined the body."

"Yes, sir." She got up and walked to the office next door.

She quickly returned with a broad smile.

"Tian called to say they have the autopsy report."

"Tell him to fax it over," Cui said.

It came in five minutes later.

It began with a general narrative, including all the usual observations, an examination of the scratch marks on the deceased's chest, and so on, followed by an important section on two anomalies, which Yao Li read aloud: "Two anomalies were discovered during the autopsy. First, a cardiac rupture led to an acute myocardial infarction. The rupture occurred in the left ventricle free wall, near the apex cordis. The cause of the rupture was an infiltration of a large quantity of neutral cells, resulting in a softening and necrosis of the diseased heart tissue. There was no clear sign of plaque buildup or blood clots in the coronary artery, which means the myocardial infarction was caused not by a blockage of blood flow, but from a case of severe fright, producing a high level of catecholamine that forced the coronary artery to contract and led to a fatal heart attack."

That got everyone's attention.

Yao cleared her throat and continued:

"Two, when the medical examiner checked the seawater in the stomach and lung tissue he found three types of odd-shaped microalgae that differed from the more common diatoms. One was a single-cell microalgae about forty millimeters long and twenty-five millimeters wide, with deep, narrow transverse surface ridges on the armor that swerve to the left above indentations. The second type was spindle-shaped, dark red in color, about fifty millimeters long and thirty-five millimeters wide. The bottom was rounded with a pair of tiny spines, the armor covered with rib-like markings. The third type had a flat back in the shape of double hammers, with short, rounded heads and hooked tails. The density of the algae cells exceeded one thousand per milliliter of water. All three structures differed from samples taken from previous drowning victims, but we have not been able to identify the species or unique characteristics, although there may be a link to a red tide. We will need to check with experts for further information in regard to marine biology and ecology."

"I see." Cui blinked, acknowledging the importance of these tiny creatures.

"This is a critical discovery," Chief Wu said. "It'll help us determine the spot where Hu drowned."

"Can you explain, Chief Wu?" Cui asked.

Wu looked around the table first. "Diatoms are common in both fresh- and seawater. In a drowning, they will be found in the victim's stomach and respiratory system. If they are not present, it's likely that drowning was not the cause of death, and that the victim was tossed into the water afterward. There are thousands of species of diatoms, unique to every water region, so we can tell where a person died by determining the type of algae found in the body. It is an effective forensic tool in drowning cases.

"The water in each section of Dapeng Bay is unique. Even in Greater and Lesser Meisha, which are only a few kilometers apart, the microbes are not all the same. So all we need to do is to take water samples from both areas and compare them to the specimens found in Hu Guohao's body, and we will know where he drowned."

This breathed new life into the room.

"And a large quantity of algae is often a sign of a red tide."

"Red tide?"

"Yes. Also known as a 'red specter.'"

Red tides were etched indelibly into Chief Wu's memory. Three years earlier, he had returned to the coastal city of Shantou, where generations of his family had been fishermen, and witnessed a red tide outbreak in a spot near Tuolin Bay. The ocean surface was dyed a russet red and did not return to normal for over a month, causing a massive death of fish and severe losses to the fishermen.

"Go to the Environmental Protection Bureau and find out if there was a red tide at either Greater or Lesser Meisha on or around June twenty-fourth."

"Zheng Yong and Xiao Jia, you two work on this," Cui said.

"Right, sir."

"And send sample slides from Hu's body to the Nanhai Environmental Monitoring Center for further tests," Chief Wu added.

"Yao Li, Xiaochuan, you'll have to make a trip to Guangzhou early tomorrow morning," Cui said.

"Right," they answered solemnly.

— 4 —

Guangzhou's Zhuhai District. A shaded area some three or four hundred meters long edging the west section of Xingang Road, a welcome sight to pedestrians. Within the metal barrier, a stand of towering trees; outside, a green belt. Rows of multistory houses were visible under the green canopy of roadside trees.

Xiaochuan and Yao Li drove up to the gate of the Nanhai Environmental Monitoring Center at the end of the shaded path. After passing through the gate, they followed a slope to the left and came to a seedling plot in front of a five-story cement structure painted a warm gray. Ten tall coconut palms fronted the structure like sentry guards. It was an ordinary-looking building, but much like a small temple with powerful magic, it housed an arm of the State Oceanic Administration, with many of the most advanced monitoring devices, as well as the most talented ocean monitoring analysts.

Xiaochuan parked the blue-and-white squad car. They got out of the car and walked to the building, where the guard told them the director's office was on the top floor. As they climbed the maroon terrazzo stairs, they were impressed by the brass spindles and curved metal railings. The middle-aged woman in charge of visitors was a bit apprehensive when she saw the uniformed officers.

"We're from Y District Public Security," Xiaochuan said, handing her a letter of introduction. "We're working on a case involving algae and need help from your experts."

"I see." She asked them to wait in the conference room while she went to report their visit.

While not big, the room was clean and orderly. Xiaochuan's gaze fell on a glass display cabinet against one wall. Inside were eighteen commemorative cups and trophies, some of which sported the national emblem.

A moment later, the receptionist returned in the company of a smart-looking middle-aged man in a blue-and-white-striped polo shirt. He looked to be in his early forties.

"This is our director," the woman said.

The director sat down at the conference table and welcomed them. "We're happy to help. Tell me what you need."

He listened intently as Xiaochuan gave him a brief description of the case and the issues with the algae.

"Our medical examiner says it might have something to do with a red tide."

"A red tide?"

The man smiled, clearly piqued by the mention of a red tide. A graduate of Ocean University in Qingdao, he had been working at the Center for nearly two decades. He'd also studied in Canada and was a renowned red tide expert, with a research focus on marine biology in Nanhai and environmental monitoring.

"We don't know a thing about red tides, so we're here to take advantage of your expertise," Xiaochuan admitted.

"So-called red tides are basically pollution caused by the overproduction of algae, which causes water to turn red or bright orange," the director began. "In fact, sometimes the contaminated water can be yellow, green, even brown. It all depends on the kind of algae overproduced."

"So different algae paint the water different colors," Yao said.

"Right. Some red tides don't actually change the color of the water. Statistics show that there are over four thousand varieties of algae in the ocean and about two hundred and sixty of them can cause a red tide. Seventy of those are toxic. You may not know it, but there's a reference to a red tide in the Bible: 'The water in the river has turned into blood, giving the river a horrible stench.' Red tides appeared in records in ancient China, but it's only been recently that the world has begun to worry about the damage they inflict, and in 1990 the United Nations included it as one of the three major ocean pollutant."

He continued to explain that some organisms in a red tide can be harmful, even fatal to humans if they consume fish or shellfish with large quantities of the toxin. Some red tides are harmless but produce a sticky secretion that clogs the gills of fish and sea creatures and chokes them to death. Moreover, the algae that form red tides reproduce at an alarmingly fast pace. The dinoflagellate, for instance, can produce a new generation every two hours. When the algae die, the decomposition consumes large quantities of oxygen in the water, unbalancing the ecosystem, which in turn causes the death of many fish and shrimp. The damage is simply astronomical."

The director moved on to describe serious incidents of red tide pollution in Nanhai in recent years.

"Three years ago, a large area of Raoping, Guandong, was infested. I witnessed the death of a substantial quantity of fish when a red tide occurred with unexpected quickness, resulting in tremendous losses to fishermen and hatcheries. One of our missions here is to detect red tides as soon as they appear and distribute information about them in the monitored areas to minimize the damage."

"Have you seen any red tides in the Shenzhen area recently?" Xiaochuan asked the question they'd come to ask.

"Yes," the director said. "About a week ago, we detected a red tide in Dapeng Bay. It started with algae drifting from Heiyanjiao, several kilometers to the south, but the polluted area was relatively small and only killed a few fish in Nan'ao. Similar red tides occur in the area every year."

Xiaochuan and Yao Li exchanged a look.

"When we received the news," the director continued, "we sent someone to Nan'ao to take water samples so we could determine the type of algae. The tests showed that the incident was caused by several kinds of algae, all in the dinoflagellate category."

"Could you tell us, sir, when exactly the red tide occurred?" Yao Li asked as she wrote in her notebook.

"Let me check. Xiao Qin, would you bring me the latest data?"

Ms. Qin nodded and left. She soon returned with a blue logbook.

The director opened the log and scanned the contents before looking up.

"An on-site inspection showed that the red tide first started on the southernmost tip of Dapeng Bay, Deer Bay, where the water turned an orange brown. Our tests showed that the algae causing this red tide consisted of *Gyrodinium instriatum*, *Gonyaulax*, and *Peridinium*, none of which are toxic. But this one was very dense, with 1,200,000 algae in one liter of water, depleting large amounts of the dissolved oxygen in the water, and we found dead fish on the surface."

He turned to a new page and continued. "Let's see. Ah, here. On June nineteenth, a small red tide was visible in the Heiyanjia area to the south of Nan'ao; the water was a yellowish brown. Two days later, the red tide slowly migrated to the area near Shuitousha Village in Nan'ao, and the pollution was at its peak from the twenty-second to the twenty-fourth. It began to disappear on the afternoon of the twenty-fifth, but it wasn't until three days ago, on June twenty-seventh, that it was completely gone and the water returned to its normal color."

"Did the red tide drift north to Lesser Meisha?" Yao Li looked up from her notebook.

"Probably not. Based on our log, the water in Lesser Meisha was not affected from the nineteenth to the twenty-seventh. The water quality was good and the swimming area was open. The same goes for Greater Meisha."

"Are you sure of that?" Yao Li persisted.

"Yes."

The director informed them that Lesser Misha had suffered red tide pollution during the swimming season the year before. It wasn't serious, but a substantial area turned red and the tourists smelled the foul odor from the beach. The Lesser Meisha Management Center kept a close watch and discussed whether or not to close the swimming area. Fortunately, the red tide disappeared and spared them from damage. This time, when the red tide was found in Nan'ao, the Shenzhen Oceanic Environmental Center and the Fishing Environment Monitoring Station paid close attention to the situation at Greater and Lesser Meisha. The staff went to both places to take water samples; the test results showed the water quality to be excellent.

"Thank you very much for the information." Yao Li thanked the director and stood up.

"I hope this helps you solve your case." The director got up to shake hands.

"Director, you have another meeting," Ms. Qin said.

"Oh." Xiaochuan wore an expectant look.

"Right. Did you bring a sample?" the director asked.

"Yes, we did," Xiaochuan replied excitedly.

"Go ask Lao Xiao to check it for them," the director said to Ms. Qin, who then took them to the third floor, which housed the lab and sample rooms.

They entered the marine biology lab. A white table along the wall in the outer room held ten different ultramodern microscopes, each covered with an acrylic glass shield.

Lao Xiao looked to be in his fifties, a kindly, gray-haired veteran algae expert. Ms. Qin called him Technician Xiao.

Seven or eight translucent plastic cases, likely used for samples, stood in the hallway outside. They were filled with closed wide-mouthed plastic containers, each marked with a combination of letters and numbers.

"What are those for?" Xiaochuan asked out of curiosity.

"They're ocean water samples," Lao Xiao said.

"The writing tells when and where the samples were taken," Ms. Qin added.

Xiaochuan took a metal case out of his pocket, opened it, and handed a slide to Xiao, who held it up to get a close look, then sat down and put it under a microscope. He focused one of the three lenses on the tiny sample specks.

The two officers stood quietly behind him.

Xiao gently turned the knob to focus as he bent down over the eyepiece.

Xiaochuan and Yao Li held their breath.

Xiao continued looking at the algae cells as he clicked a counter. That went on for some ten minutes until he turned around and signaled to Xiaochuan.

"Come take a look."

Xiaochuan bent down. What greeted him was a beautiful image of tiny translucent single-cell organisms, all about the same size but in different shapes and crowded onto a brown dot; three seemed to be dominant. The structure and pattern on each was clearly visible.

"See the one with the left swirl and hooks? Those are *Gyrodinium instriatums*."

"Yes, I see them."

"And the red ones below that look like spindles, those are called *Gonyaulax*."

"I see. There are lots of them."

"Now look at the smaller cone-shaped ones with spines. Those are *Peridiniums*."

"I see them!" Xiaochuan was beside himself with excitement.

"Let me have a look," Yao Li said, so Xiaochuan got up and gave her his seat.

She craned her neck and looked into the viewfinder.

"Wow!"

The colorful, beautiful world of algae!

Technician Xiao had verified all three types of algae.

"The same as the algae we found in the water at Nan'ao." He picked up a slide of algae they'd found in the water in Nan'ao, and repeated the process.

Xiaochuan took a second look and saw that the cell structures were identical to those they had brought; there was another kind, but in much smaller quantities.

Xiao Gong checked the counter.

"The total is 1195 per millimeter, just under 1200."

The two officers could hardly suppress their excitement, since the test showed that the algae contents in the water from Hu Guohao's lungs were the same as in the red tide that appeared between June twenty-first and twenty-fourth in Nan'ao.

Which meant that Hu had drowned in Nan'ao, Zhou Zhengxing's hometown, not in Lesser or Great Meisha.

"The crime scene was not Lesser Meisha!" Yao Li nearly shouted with joy.

"So Hu Guohao did not drown in Lesser Meisha?" Team Leader Cui was shocked when Xiaochuan called to give him the news.

"That's right," Xiaochuan said.

"I see," Cui said.

Who would have thought that Chief Wu could be so prophetic?

When Xiaochuan and Yao Li returned to the station, the other squad had also returned. Zheng Yong reported that data provided by Section Chief Xu at the District Environmental Protection Bureau, showed that there had been no pollution at either Greater or Lesser Meisha between June nineteenth and twenty-seven. The water quality was normal, and there had been no red tide.

That corroborated what they'd learned at the Nanhai Environmental Monitoring Center.

This was a major breakthrough, and Zhou Zhengxing became their prime suspect.

"So Zhou could be the man," Cui said excitedly. "Watch him carefully."

FIVE

The New Boss

— 1 —

Guanlan Lake Golf Club. The Southern Real Estate Elite Forum meeting site.

With its luxurious décor, the room was truly fit for real estate tycoons. Xiaochuan and Yao Li arrived five minutes before 9:00 A.M., when the Forum was scheduled to begin. Nearly every seat was taken, and signatures in all styles filled the red satin register at the door.

Smiling receptionists handed out gift bags and material to late arriving guests.

Xiaochuan and Yao Li went straight to the meeting room and stood in the back. Since they were in street clothes, they didn't attract any attention.

The podium was decorated with fresh flowers, formal but with a touch of style under the spotlights. Behind it a gold screen proclaimed in big bold script, "*Southern Real Estate Elite Forum*," under which were listed the sponsoring units: *N Business Post,* The Southern Housing and Real Estate Alliance, and the South City Real

Estate Association; media representatives included, STV Satellite TV, Real Estate Elite Net, and *Housing Trend Magazine*.

Those sitting behind the podium were the elite of various fields, mostly real estate figures in South China, plus the editor-in-chief of *N Business Post*, senior members of the banking industry, and economists. Most were in business attire; their faces glowed with health. The only imperfection was the absence of the real estate heavyweight of Southern Guangdong, Hu Guohao.

Reporters were frantically taking pictures of the podium, lighting up the area with flashes from their cameras.

Presiding over the forum that day was the CEO of Jiayi Real Estate Group, Wu Shi, also Chairman of the South City Real Estate Association, a dignified man with an agreeable smile. To his left and right were the editor-in-chief of *N Business Post* and the bespectacled CEO of Wanda Realty. Ceremonial flowers were pinned to their chests. Wanda Realty's CEO and Wu were engaged in a lively discussion.

Xiaochuan nudged Yao Li to check out the man in the third seat on the left. It was Landmark's deputy CEO, Zhou Zhengxing, who looked subdued and cautious. If not for the June twenty-fifth incident, it would have been Hu Guohao sitting in the seat.

One seat to Zhou's left was Big East's CEO, Hong Yiming.

The forum began on time at nine o'clock, with introductory remarks from the editor-in-chief of *N Business Post*.

"Honorable Chairman, distinguished guests, ladies and gentlemen, good morning. Today gathered here are all the leading figures in Southern Guangdong real estate, from nearly a hundred companies. We are here to talk about development trends and patterns in China's real estate. This is a rare occasion to steer real estate development in the south in a healthy direction and to continue making progress. For us in the media, this represents a way to display a sense of civic duty, which is why we organized today's forum. We wish everyone great success. Thank you."

The audience rewarded him with sustained applause.

New Century Realty's CEO was first to speak.

"Ladies and gentlemen, the title of my talk today is 'Mistakes in China's Real Estate.'"

A key player in Southern Guangdong real estate and founder of the "New Housing Movement," he had an attentive audience.

"There is a common misunderstanding in our society, which is, people believe that real estate is where you can make sudden, huge profits, while in fact the time for explosive profits is long past. That might have been true seven or eight years ago, but now we are talking about limited profits. The second misunderstanding is that people think money comes easy in this business, with very low risk. That is why so many people in other lines of work have joined the competition, without realizing that real estate is the most complex business of all. The third misunderstanding is that people think that land bids can solve all 'black box' problems, whereas the truth is, there are still issues of unfair access to capital and illegal money. The fourth misunderstanding is that people think that consumers are powerless and that developers are all-powerful, holding total control over consumers. Fifth, all problems arising from real estate development are being blamed on the developers, whereas they have rights, too. Companies with a good name that make contributions should be protected. Sixth is the phobia over unsold units . . ."

He continued to dissect the major misconceptions about the current realty situation with refreshing views that even laymen such as Xiaochuan and Yao Li found interesting.

The second speaker, the CEO of Wanda Realty, was a representative of new real estate trends in Southern Guangdong.

"Ladies and gentlemen, I would like to share my personal views of the market," he said, sounding a bit like an academic. "What is the market? Some say it is synonymous with trade, while others say the market is our lifeline. Both seem sensible, but I think that the market is the very mechanism that makes investors who believe they are right wind up slapping their own faces."

Lighthearted laughter greeted this opening comment.

He went on to analyze current conditions in the real estate market, market predictions, and the needs of consumers once the market is fully diversified. The audience reacted enthusiastically to his detailed analysis and new perspectives.

During the speech, the moderator, who was famous for his sense of humor, injected comments to liven up the forum. Earlier, when introducing guests from the finance field, he had characterized real estate developers' relationship with capital as "leaning on moneybags," which drew roars of laughter.

Next to speak was Hong Yiming, who was well known for his understated style and introspective personality; but he was decisive and firm in business decisions, an aggressive competitor, which was why his opinions often created a stir.

"I don't think anyone has a clear sense of the market yet," Hong said in a mild tone that nonetheless surprised the audience. "That's because we can look at it from many angles. It's like a prism; whatever one sees is real to the beholder, but there's no consensus as to what that is. Everyone here today is an experienced player on the stormy seas of the real estate market. Take my company, Big East, for example. We've been at it for eight years, and we continue to adjust our company's position vis-à-vis the shifting market, while we keep learning from the experts how to function in that market. That's the only reason we're still in business. I believe that a healthy market is one that is left to do what it does, without the interference of administrative directives. I'm sure you all remember the real estate bubble in Hainan some years ago. Why did that happen? And how did the bubble get so big before it burst? Because people blindly threw in their money at a time when the planned economy was transitioning to a market economy, which in turn created a real estate black hole. Luckily, my old friend, Hu Guohao, and I got out quick enough. Regrettably he can no longer join in our discussion of the market."

The room turned quiet, though there was plenty of whispering. Those in the business knew that as a soldier turned real estate tycoon, Hong talked and acted like a military man, but on that day he seemed evasive somehow. That did not escape the attention of the two officers.

"The market is the developer's god, and I hope this god of ours will bless Big East with smooth sailing." Hong Yiming ended his speech with a quasi-prayer.

Wu Shi leaned forward and spoke into the microphone: "Now please welcome Mr. Zhou Zhengxing, deputy CEO of Landmark Realty."

Zhou nodded and walked to the podium.

"Mr. Hu Guohao, the CEO of Landmark, should have been the speaker today, but you all know that he suffered a swimming accident a few days ago. I may not be the best substitute for this topic, but I'll do my best."

Hushed discussions rippled through the room, but only for a moment.

Resting his hands on the flower-festooned podium, Zhou began with confidence mellowed with modesty.

"I'll share some of my own humble views on what the previous speakers have just said." He paused. "What is the market? It is actually a changeable, unstable entity. I think we should all face the market with awe and apprehension, particularly tomorrow's market. There's a saying in England that goes, 'God will make you go crazy before he wants you dead.' Likewise, we must be careful when the market is about to go crazy. Or to put it differently, you go someplace where everyone, friends included, tells you to buy a house, and when you go home, your wife wants to jump into the buying frenzy. That's when you have to worry. That said, I must admit that I've yet to see such a frenzy in Southern Guangdong. It is, in fact, a far cry from the bubble in Hainan, when everyone was hyping the land and housing markets. But you'll notice that real estate companies elsewhere have started buying up land again. I heard that a large Realtor in Beijing is hoarding eight thousand acres of land, while the Kelly Corporation in Tianjin, trying to compete, has signed a contract to develop a parcel of fourteen thousand acres. Think about it, gentlemen, fourteen thousand acres. This is precisely why we must keep a cool head; we must never be followers. We mustn't let the market overheat or mindlessly hoard land."

Applause.

Seemingly unprepared for such a warm reception, Zhou nodded with an abashed smile as he continued:

"Over the past ten years, at Landmark, we've had our ups and our downs. We've learned from both, and that is our invisible wealth. The real estate industry has considered our development in Shenzhen, which includes the Landmark Building and New City Garden Estates, to be a success story. While developing New City Garden Estates, we borrowed the idea of "selling after furnishing" and considered the real estate production as a total cultural package, not just a housing project. Sales at the Estates set an all time high, eight hundred units in less than two months, and all twenty-five hundred units in half a year. That was a record in new housing sales in Shenzhen. Our foremost selling point was that the units came with fine furnishings. But we've also made mistakes. Two years ago, Landmark hastily bought a large parcel of land in Hexi at the cost of over a billion yuan. The land still lies vacant, a costly liability for us, which is why I'm dead set against hoarding land."

A man in an STV vest trained his video camera on Zhou.

On a velveteen desktop to the left below the podium, two young women were pecking away on their laptops. The audience was listening with rapt attention.

Zhou was known as a careful planner and strategist, not someone who made rash, risky decisions. The success of New City Garden Estates was a result of his meticulous design. His speech gave the impression that he was tough and resilient, with an unshakeable will, the exact opposite of Hu Guohao, who had swaggered with expansive gestures, and could be hot to the touch. Zhou was the personification of "great wisdom appearing to be slow-witted."

"The relationship between real estate and capital can indeed be characterized as 'leaning on moneybags,'" Zhou continued. "Our chairman's analogy was excellent. Another way to put it is, 'traveling with a giant.' But there's a potential problem with that. That is, a giant can cast you off at any time. When the giant, or an elephant, refuses to budge, it can lift its leg and crush you. Then there's the marketplace description created by pretty women. It goes, 'Eat off moneybags, drink off moneybags, lean on moneybags, then destroy moneybags to become moneybags yourself.' I agree with the conclusion drawn from the chairman's analogy—we must be alert to these two pitfalls when looking for joint ventures. Rather than mindlessly searching for a giant, we must seek out compatible traveling partners. As for the final analogy, harboring ulterior motives, with a secret desire to destroy others, is a failed strategy.

"We at Landmark pledge to work with all of you in real estate and finance, as well as the astute media, to promote and continue to develop our industry. I'd like to conclude by wishing everyone in the development and finance sectors great success. May Southern Guangdong real estate remain forever in good health."

The audience applauded enthusiastically, to which he responded with a humble smile.

The strong personal imprint of Hu Guohao on Landmark had begun to fade as Zhou stepped down off the podium. Few had imagined that a relatively nondescript individual who had always been in Hu's shadow would rise up to help Landmark shake off its rudderless image.

The two police officers were surprised to witness Zhou's performance. They had not realized that this mild-mannered man could so cleverly seize the opportunity and so easily take over from Hu Guohao on so public an occasion. Either Hu's death had given him the chance to shine, or he was a master of deception.

"That Zhou Zhengxing is quite a character," Yao Li whispered to Xiaochuan.

"He might have the talent to be an effective and inspirational leader. But then maybe he just knows how to put on a show," Xiao-chuan said as he nodded in agreement.

Zhou was surrounded by reporters as he walked out after the morning session.

"Mr. Zhou, is Landmark still going to bid for Tiandongba?"

"I'm sorry, but that is a company matter." Zhou smiled good-naturedly.

"Mr. Zhou, everyone says you'll take over as Landmark's CEO. Your comment?"

"No comment. That's just idle talk."

"I hear Landmark will soon hold a board meeting to select the next CEO. Do you think you'll win?"

"It sounds like you know more than I do about the Board," Zhou joked to skillfully skirt the sensitive issue.

"Don't you media people put a dragnet around our Mr. Zhou," Wu Shi said in jest, as he and Hong Yiming were on their way out of the hall.

A reporter thrust her pocket recorder at Hong Yiming.

"Mr. Hong, is Big East set on winning the bid for Tiandongba?"

"I'm afraid you'll have to ask Landmark's Mr. Zhou." Hong also skirted the question.

"I'm personally against mindlessly buying up land," Zhou remarked.

"So, does that mean Landmark will give up its bid for Tiandongba?" she persisted.

"We may put a hold on our plans for the land."

"Then we at Big East will reap the benefits," Hong Yiming joked.

"Tiandongba is a piece of choice meat." Wu Shi patted Hong on the shoulder.

"I guarantee you its value will double in three years," Hong said with confidence.

"Such decisiveness! Mr. Hong is a real trooper," Zhou mocked.

"A powerful dragon can't compete with the local snake lord. Ha ha."

Quietly observing the group, Xiaochuan and Yao Li could sense sparks flying.

As he turned his head, Zhou spotted the officers and greeted them with a nod.

Yao Li remained impassive, but Xiaochuan returned the greeting.

But Zhou had no intention of speaking with them; instead, he waved at the reporters and left the meeting hall alone, leaving the crownless kings to crowd around Wu Shi and the other top executives behind him.

The two officers were right behind Zhou, who climbed into a black Audi waiting at the entrance. The door slammed shut and the car quietly glided away from the club. Xiaochuan and Yao Li rushed to their blue-and-white Jetta. Xiaochuan turned the key, gunned the engine, and took off after Zhou's black Audi.

— 2 —

That same afternoon, at the Y District Public Security Bureau, the entrance to the eight-story main building was guarded by two uniformed policemen.

A visitor signed in at the reception and headed for the elevator. He was wearing casual shoes, a black T-shirt, and a beige baseball cap. With his bronze tan, he looked like a member of a walking tour, an image enhanced by the white, red-strapped ESPN tote bag. "Cool" is the best way to describe him.

Two uniformed female police officers gave him a second look in the hallway, but he ignored them and knocked on the door of room 808.

Chief Wu, who was on the phone, called out, "Just a moment." Then the door opened to reveal a smiling, honest-looking face.

"I'm Nie Feng, a reporter for *Western Sunshine*," the visitor said politely as he handed over his business card.

"Ah, come in."

Taking the card, Chief Wu offered Nie Feng the sofa with a welcoming gesture before pouring him a cup of tea.

"Propaganda Section Chief Jiang from the Provincial Bureau called. We're happy to accommodate you."

"I'm completely ignorant of police work," Nie said modestly. "I'd just like to know how the investigation is progressing."

"This is a complicated case, but we're hard at work on it."

Nie told Chief Wu that time was an issue for him, since he must return to Chengdu within the week.

"I know how tough a job you have, and we'll tell you everything we can," Chief Wu replied.

True to his word, Chief Wu personally walked Nie Feng over to the sixth-floor crime squad office, where he met Team Leader Cui outside the conference room. Nie respectfully handed Cui his letter of introduction from the Provincial Security Bureau.

Cui took a quick glance at the red official seal before fixing Nie with a meaningful gaze, as if to say, "Not bad, young man." Or maybe it was a silent grumble, "So you're here to show me up."

"I'll appreciate any help Officer Cui can give." Nie bowed and smiled, a typical Nie Feng gesture—respectful yet expansive.

With awkwardness written all over his face, Cui was obviously feeling cornered, but could say nothing, not when Nie Feng was giving him no cause for offense.

They walked into the conference room, where the squad was gathered.

Cui introduced Nie. "This is Comrade Nie Feng, a reporter from *Western Sun*. He's here to attend our discussions, with the Propaganda Section of the Provincial Security Bureau as the intermediary. Let's welcome him."

"It's *Western Sunshine*." Xiaochuan corrected Cui softly, but was ignored.

"All right," Cui said. Nie Feng nodded to each person around the table. No welcoming applause, though a few officers gazed at him curiously. Xiaochuan was the only one who wore a welcoming smile, while Yao Li cast an admiring glance.

"I'm here to benefit from the heroic spirit of the police. Much obliged." He gave them another one of his signature bows.

Cui laughed unhappily to himself, but quickly came up with a solution. He hadn't expected Nie to take him up on it when he asked for a letter from superiors. Solving a case was nothing like writing a story; it was not something to take lightly, and he would never allow a dickhead from "*Western Sun*" to muddy up his case. The crime squad enjoyed a strong sense of honor and team spirit. There was also a strict unwritten rule: while they might all be police officers, each case had its territorial boundaries, and if a case was outside one's jurisdiction, no one, not even a journalist from the boondocks, would be allowed to participate or tag along during the investigation. Police in criminal cases shunned two types of people: lawyers, who would go to any length to get information that would help their clients; and reporters, who were known to make groundless charges and, with relentless questions, stir up so much trouble it would either put the police on the defensive or make them appear incompetent.

As a responsible commanding officer, Cui was forced to abide by his superior's wishes and treat the unreasonable reporter with deference, but within limits. Best to deal with him as a spectator, or to put it more nicely, an observer. He would not be permitted to participate in any real investigative or background work. The good thing was, he wouldn't be there long.

So Cui came up with some nice words and put Nie Feng in his rightful place.

"Mr. Nie is welcome to interact with our squad. This is a complex case, and he can attend our meetings to get firsthand knowledge of how we go about solving a case. But in order to maintain security and secrecy, he may not participate in the actual investigation. Do you have anything to add, Chief Wu?"

"That sounds fine. Just cooperate with him to the best of your ability."

A detectable look of disappointment flickered on Xiaochuan's face.

But Nie Feng did not seem to mind. He'd once hoped to be a police intern, and maybe being a tag-along reporter was close enough.

"Xiaochuan, you'll be our liaison with Mr. Nie. Now, let's get down to business," Cui said.

Nie sat down as the officers gave their reports.

Yao Li reported on their surveillance of Zhou Zhengxing. After leaving the Guanlan Lake Golf Club, he'd had lunch at a roadside restaurant in town, after which he'd been driven back downtown. Xiaochuan had kept close enough to see him make a call in the car and then lean back in his seat and doze off. The Audi eventually returned to the Landmark Building, where he went straight to his office.

"We didn't see anything unusual," Xiaochuan added.

"Was there anything special about the forum?" Chief Wu asked.

"All real estate big shots," Xiaochuan replied. "Hong Yiming from Big East gave a speech. Looks like he'll finally get his hands on the Tiandongba land he's salivated over for so long."

Nie Feng listened attentively.

"Let's put that aside," Chief Wu said, "and focus on Hu Guohao's death."

The meeting shifted gears to analyze what lay behind the fact that Hu had apparently died in Nan'ao, which generated several suspicious points.

First, why had Hu gone to Nan'ao? Had he been lured there by that mysterious phone call, or had he suddenly decided to go swimming in Nan'ao? The former seemed more likely. What if it was Zhou Zhengxing who had phoned Hu, using some excuse to invite Hu to his hometown for a swim or a brief get-together? For instance, he could have asked Hu to attend the computer-donation ceremony. Hu would likely have attended.

Second, how had Hu gotten there? Had he taken the bus or a taxi, or had Zhou sent a car to Greater Meisha for him? This had to be checked.

Third, how had Hu drowned in Nan'ao? Had he suffered a heart attack while swimming? Or had Zhou been swimming with him and drowned him?

Fourth, how had Hu's body turned up at the Lesser Meisha Pier? If it had been an accidental drowning in Nan'ao, his body could not have drifted north to Lesser Meisha, some thirty kilometers away. Could it be that Hu impulsively decided to swim across Dapeng Bay, from Nan'ao back to Greater Meisha, but had made it only as far as Lesser Meisha before drowning? Could the apprehension he felt after receiving the phone call have made the idea of swimming across the bay appealing?

As they talked, Nie Feng noted everything down in his notebook. The investigation now seemed focused on Nan'ao, which appeared to be the most logical direction, based upon the algae found in Hu's body. It was a major breakthrough.

But what lay behind the fact of the algae?

Zhong Tao was obviously no longer a suspect. It would take an hour to drive from Lesser Meisha on a winding mountain road to Nan'ao, and he could not possibly have made the trip in twenty-five minutes.

Zhou Zhengxing, on the other, was a prime suspect, but they had yet to find proof.

Nie's train of thought was interrupted when Chief Wu spoke up.

"Let's think about why Hu's body showed up at Lesser Meisha beach."

"The perpetrator was obviously trying to mislead us by making Lesser Meisha the crime scene while providing himself with an alibi," Cui said.

"What have you found about boats in Greater and Lesser Meisha?"

"Greater Meisha has twenty rental boats, and Lesser Meisha

fifteen. The logbooks show no boats went out on the night of the twenty-fourth."

"They normally tie up the boats at eleven o'clock at night."

Someone pointed out that Zhou Zhengxing's hometown, Shuitou Village, was only two kilometers from Nan'ao, and that it would have been easy to transport the body from the port at Nan'ao.

"Besides, there are over a hundred motorboats fishermen use to take tourists on sightseeing tours."

"But there are patrol boats at night."

"Not over the whole area, though," Chief Wu said. "He could have driven to a spot near Lesser Meisha and then used a boat."

"Finally we've got our hands on the tail of that sly fox, Zhou Zhengxing!" Cui said harshly. "Now we must double our efforts; we have to follow his every move."

His eagerness was infectious, getting others so worked up that the room was abuzz with spirited talk.

Xiaochuan had his eye on Nie Feng, who was listening carefully, head down as he sketched something in his notebook. Xiaochuan looked over to see that Nie had drawn a diagram with three dots—Greater Meisha, Lesser Meisha, and Nan'ao—connected by bold lines to form a long narrow triangle. Nie's gaze was fixed on his drawing, a puzzled look on his face, like a student stuck on an algebra problem.

Yao Li talked about Zhou's performance at the forum in Guanlan Lake, describing him as an entrepreneur and successful leader who appeared to have a social conscience. His résumé checked out fine—born into a poor fisherman's family, he was a hard worker who welcomed challenges, and a renowned filial son, with no criminal record. The low-level employees at Landmark all thought highly of him.

"It could be a front."

"If so, then he's a superb actor."

The two sides would not budge from their assessments; Cui's cell phone rang as they argued back and forth.

"Hello? Yes? That's me. Oh, when? I'll be right there."

Cui was visibly elated.

"That was Lao Guan from the Nan'ao police station. They've found Hu's briefcase at Nan'ao Elementary School."

Cheers erupted.

Just when they thought they'd reached a dead end, a critical clue from the police station in Nan'ao could turn the case around. The squad leader left for Nan'ao with Xiaochuan and Yao Li after telling Xiao Zheng to "show Nie Feng to Lao Kun's desk so he can catch up on some reading."

Lao Kun, Cui's second in command, was on vacation. His desk was next to the air-conditioner, making the area tolerable in the middle of summer.

Zheng Yong brought over an office chair for Nie Feng, who thanked him and sat down.

— 3 —

Cui, Xiaochuan, and Yao Li raced to the Nan'ao police station, where the station head, Lao Guan, and two militiamen were waiting. After a brief greeting, Lao Guan told them what had happened.

Nan'ao Elementary, located in the western part of town, had new classroom buildings. The main brick building was six stories high and shaped like an open book, with a balcony decorated with blue stripes, giving it a fresh, lively appearance. Slogans were painted in red on each side of the third floor wall: LOVE THE COUNTRY, LOVE THE PEOPLE, AND LOVE LABOR, and LOVE SCIENCE AND LOVE SOCIALISM. The school's excellent teachers placed equal emphasis on the students' moral, intellectual, and physical development.

Over nine hundred students were enrolled in the school, a number of them children from the fishing villages. The campus was neat and clean, with lush green grass and an oval track surrounding the playground, which included a large soccer field.

That afternoon, the Section 2 fifth graders had just finished PE, and some of the children had stayed behind to play soccer. One of them, a chubby boy nicknamed Lai Zhai, had kicked the ball into the weeds outside the field. He ran over to pick it up and spotted a black object in the grass by a ditch. It was a briefcase, which he turned over to his PE teacher.

When the teacher opened the briefcase and saw what was inside, he immediately called the police.

Now the station head took the briefcase out of a drawer and placed it on his desk. Cui picked it up and held it as if he'd stumbled on hidden treasure. It was a black leather case, embossed with the Lacoste logo. There was some dirt on the outside. Cui put on his gloves before unzipping it to check the contents, which included Hu Guohao's ID, a credit card, a thick wad of hundred-yuan notes, and a notebook. He also found several colorfully wrapped condoms and two light blue, diamond-shaped pills in the side pocket.

Cui dumped everything onto the desk. The credit card was a Great Wall card, and the cash totaled nine thousand yuan. As for the two blue pills, they were each encased in clear plastic covered in tin foil. Fancy packaging.

"What are these?" Xiaochuan stared at the pills curiously, to which Cui rewarded him with a meaningful look.

"It's Viagra, what we call Towering Brother."

"Oh!" His first encounter with the pills he'd heard so much about. He made a face.

But Hu's cell phone was missing.

The notebook was a common hardcover type that served as a day planner and an address book. Cui thumbed through the pages and found a piece of paper folded four times. He unfolded it and saw a strange symbol and a string of numbers.

The symbol, in red, resembled the character for mountain, "山,"

sketched out with a thick bubble brush. Underneath the symbol were eight digits: 42602791.

"What does that 'red mountain' mean?" Yao Li wondered.

"Hm, 'red mountain'?" Cui studied the paper, but had no answer.

Xiaochuan had a sudden inspiration: it looked like the scratch marks on Hu Guohao's chest.

After checking out the contents of Hu's briefcase, the station head took them to the school to examine the spot where it was found. The playground was deserted, since school was out by then. A metal sculpture of a soaring bird stood in front of the classroom building, but all Cui could see was the fleeting image of Zhou Zhengxing's face.

How did Hu Guohao's briefcase wind up on an elementary school playground?

Nothing valuable was missing, which meant that, if he had been attacked, the perpetrator was not interested in his money.

Another major find: the "treasures" in the briefcase indicated that he had sexual encounters each time he came to Greater Meisha—but with whom? His mistress, secret sweetheart, girls provided by the hotel, or call girls? Could the mystery phone call have come from a prostitute?

On their way out of the school, Cui placed a call to Chief Wu to tell him what they'd found.

The police cast a wide net that night, interviewing all the prostitutes rounded up at Lesser Meisha a few days earlier.

A half dozen scantily dressed girls with luminous skin were being held in a room at the police station. They earned tips by accompanying men to swim in the ocean, and were generally of a higher class than those who worked out of salons. Yao Li and Xiaochuan showed them Hu Guohao's picture, but none of them recognized him.

So Yao Li and Xiaochuan returned to the Seaview Hotel, where they were surprised to see Miss Bai in an unusual state.

Staff members told them that she seemed emotionally unstable and had been acting strange since hearing the news of Hu's death. One day, one of her coworkers found her in the ladies room, alone, with a tear-streaked face. Another time she had made a mistake on a guest's bill.

So Cui and Yao met with her in the hotel's lobby bar.

A pretty woman with a round face and big eyes, she was dressed like a professional woman, in an ocean-blue dress. She sat down stiffly at a table. She did not look good.

"We want to know more about Hu Guohao," Cui began. "As a witness, we need you to tell us everything you know, to help us solve this case."

Miss Bai nodded, biting her lip.

"Don't worry," Yao said, "we're not interested in exposing any personal secrets."

Yao Li was able to coax what happened out of Miss Bai.

Hu had arranged to meet her on the night of the twenty-fourth in suite 204, but he never returned to the hotel. At first she thought he'd met another woman, but in the past he'd always called with an excuse whenever he missed one of their rendezvous. This time he didn't. So she began to worry, and didn't learn that he had died until the following morning, when Xiaochuan and Yao Li came to check out the hotel. She hadn't told the police about her and Hu because the hotel had strict rules against employees being intimate with guests. She would be fired if her relationship with Hu were exposed.

Cui agreed to keep the affair under wraps.

The twenty-two-year-old Miss Bai was an elegant young woman and a highly competent manager. Originally from Hunan, she was a graduate of the Changsha Tourism School. Hu had been attracted to her gentle and charming personality. In Shenzhen, it did not take much to seduce a girl. Girls from the countryside, in particular, who worked in hotels and restaurants, required a great deal of self-control to resist the temptations of the big city. To them, the dapper rich men who were generous with their money were idols and heroes. A seafood feast and a gold necklace were all it took to get the girls into bed within days. As for the professional women with higher educational or cultural backgrounds, "love" would be the key to their hearts, even if the so-called "love" was nothing but sweet talk piled on top of jewelry, fashionable clothes, and other objects. Rumor had it that after the owner of a fine-food restaurant in Zhongshan hired seven or eight pretty waitresses, his business took off. A rich friend, a frequent dinner guest, told him in private, "I've tried all the girls you hired over the last two months. They're very good." The owner was shocked.

It was hard to say if Hu Guohao belonged to that category, but it was clear that he was a player. The police found his fingerprints on both the condoms and the Viagra packaging.

"Did Hu Guohao use Viagra when he made love to you?" Cui asked bluntly.

Miss Bai nodded, and said shyly, "He had a bit of the—"

"The what?"

"A bit of—little brother problem of raising his head."

"I see," Cui said somewhat unnecessarily.

Feeling a bit awkward, Yao Li had to stop herself from giggling.

"So he took the pills half an hour beforehand."

"How many did he take each time?"

"Two."

No trace of Viagra had been found during Hu's autopsy, which meant that he had yet to take the two pills on the evening of the twenty-fourth. From what Miss Bai told them, Hu was not the type to be tempted by call girls walking the beach.

So the phone call must have been extremely important. But what was it about, and who had placed the call? Those remained the biggest mysteries.

On the other hand, finding Hu's long-lost briefcase was a

breakthrough. Now they could be sure that Nan'ao was where the crime had happened. Furthermore, all the evidence pointed to Zhou Zhengxing, now their number one suspect.

Team Leader Cui ordered round-the-clock surveillance of Zhou.

— 4 —

The Shenzhen Funeral Home. It was a gloomy, drizzly day. Inside, a solemn and yet extravagant memorial for Hu Guohao was about to begin.

Nie Feng was running late. When he leaped out of the taxi, the final viewing of the body was nearly under way. Xiaochuan had called to tell him that the memorial would begin at ten in the morning, with the suggestion that, since many of Shenzhen's VIPs would be in attendance, he might want to come and observe the goings-on.

The ceremony was held in a spacious memorial hall with a green glazed-tile roof. Cars were lined up on both sides of the flagstone square outside the hall. Nie walked up the green-carpeted stone stairs to the entrance, where two flower baskets stood atop a sign-in table covered with a dark velvet cloth. The signature book was surrounded by bottles of mineral water. To the left of the table, a simple announcement on a sheet of yellow paper—HU GUOHAO MEMORIAL—rested on a chrome stand.

The memorial began just as Nie Feng stepped in, as if it had been delayed for his sake.

A mistress of ceremony announced:

"Relatives of the deceased, please stand in the front row."

"Leaders of the various work units, please stand in the second row."

"All other guests, please find a place in line."

The announcement echoed and lingered in the room, an unintended effect from the microphone.

Nie walked in to see rows of wreaths and a huge crowd.

A large portrait, framed in black silk, of Hu Guohao with an aggressive smile, hung in the center of the bier. On each side of the hall lines of funeral wreaths and flower baskets stretched all the way out the door. Fresh yellow daisies were the primary components of the wreaths, but some had a red flower or a white chrysanthemum in the middle, and all were adorned with white satin ribbons with the inscription ETERNAL REPOSE and the names or titles of offices that had sent them. The enormous display of daisies created a grand scene.

Hung high in the middle of the hall, the words PROFOUND GRIEF had been inscribed on a white horizontal scroll edged with yellow.

Nie looked around, but did not see Xiaochuan or any of his colleagues.

The government was well represented by high-ranking officials. The ranks of mourners also included bank presidents, real estate tycoons, and friends of the deceased. Altogether, more than two hundred guests stood in the hall facing Hu's portrait while photojournalists and TV cameramen, armed with the tools of their trades, were crowded in the back. Camera lights flashed nonstop as video cameras turned slowly to capture the scene. Nie took out his Pentax 928, uncapped the lens, and joined in the actions of his colleagues.

The impassive voice of the MC continued:

"Please turn off your cell phones and be silent. The final viewing of Mr. Hu's body will now begin."

"Please observe a moment of silence."

A dirge was played as mourners bowed their heads. Once that was done, the white-skirted MC stood at the microphone and, facing the mourners, read telegrams of condolence in an unhurried pace, filling the auditorium with the soft timbre of her soprano voice:

"Eternal Repose to Mr. Hu Guohao."

"Unending Memories of CEO Hu Guohao."

"Unimaginable Loss to Landmark Real Estate."

Then it was time for the head of the company to give the memorial speech.

Deputy CEO Zhou Zhengxing, as the Landmark representative, spoke expansively of the late CEO. Zhu Mei-feng, dressed in black, was spotted standing in the front row, looking terribly distressed. Zhong Tao stood solemnly next to Zhou; also present were Ah-ying and several of those in the top management, all properly grave, with black satin flowers pinned to their chests.

Ah-ying lowered her head to observe another moment of silence, and when she looked up, tears sparkled in her eyes.

When the memorial speech was over, the mourners, accompanied by a soft dirge in the background, walked slowly to the bier to bid farewell to Hu; this was the climactic moment.

Hu's body lay in a glass-topped coffin, surrounded by fresh flowers. His face looked different, despite the work by funeral home cosmeticians. Ah-ying stared down at him. Zhu Mei-feng stopped and looked at her late husband's body, tears running down her face. Covering her quivering lips with a handkerchief, she sobbed quietly, presenting a sad and touching sight. When it was Zhou's turn, he stood by the coffin quietly, bowed, and observed a moment of silence. One had to wonder what was going through his mind as he looked down at the body of the company head, his boss and his partner, but also a rival who had pillaged and impeded the progress of his enterprise, as well as his emotional enemy. He was followed by various government officials, who bowed before walking slowly away, stopping briefly to shake hands with the widow and offer condolences.

Then came his real estate peers, Wu Shi of the Jiayi Group, and Wanda's CEO Lu. Standing side by side, both sadly said good-bye to a colleague who had been a formidable force in the realty business only days before. Hong Yiming was right behind them. He bowed deeply three times. Hu's sudden death should have been considered a boon to a business rival like Hong, but Nie Feng sensed that Hong displayed more grief than might be expected.

Zhong Tao was next. Dressed in a white shirt, a black satin flower pinned to his chest, he maintained a dignified yet sorrowful look. He stopped in front of the body and bowed, under Ah-ying's intense gaze. Everyone at Landmark knew that the man lying in the coffin had treated Zhong as his protégé. Once a rising star, a member of the younger generation of top management, Zhong's future had been thrown into doubt with the death of his powerful backer. When he lowered his head to show respect, Ah-ying saw the muscles near his lips twitch; either he was trying to rein in his grief or there was evidence of a strange smile.

Zhong Tao and Hong Yiming's eyes met when Zhong turned to leave. Hong nodded, but Zhong responded with a silent glance before looking off into space. The look on Zhong Tao's face was hard to read, as if he had traveled to some illusory place.

"Ah—" He seemed to hear a scream of pain that slowly faded into a dark abyss, as if sucked into the underworld. The deathly silence was terrifying.

"Qiangzi—Qiangzi—!" A heart-rending cry echoed off the cliff.

Nie Feng noticed the strange expression in Zhong Tao's eyes, but it escaped the attention of Hong Yiming, who extended his hand to Zhu Mei-feng reverently.

"Please accept my sincere condolences."

"Thank you," she said tearfully.

The memorial ended at eleven sharp.

Then something no one could have anticipated occurred. Just before the employees of the funeral home were about to send Hu's body to be cremated, a yellow minivan came to a screeching halt outside the hall.

Two workers in yellow uniforms, wearing white gloves, jumped out of the back of the van, lifted down a gigantic, mysterious blue wreath, and carried it gingerly up the stone steps into the hall.

Everyone's eyes were on them.

The shape of the wreath and the color of the flowers were unlike any of the others. Indigo petals with yellow stamens looked like tiny bells on a wind chime. The blue was so deep it was nearly purple, lending the wreath a weird beauty.

That quickly attracted the journalists, who turned their cameras on the wreath. An eerie wreath. Everyone stared wide-eyed, the name of the flowers unknown.

With a show of respect, the workers walked up and placed the wreath in front of Hu's picture. One of them took out a delivery note and handed it to the MC to sign.

Now everyone had a clear view of the elegiac couplet: bold, black inscriptions on white satin ribbons top and bottom.

The top:

> *Lofty aspirations, wild ambitions,*
> *a player's flirtations, all is illuminated*

The bottom:

> *Highly aggressive, boldly corrosive,*
> *an imposing personality soars into the air*

And across the middle the words:

> *A well-deserved death.*

It caused a considerable stir, as murmuring erupted in the hall. The mourners looked at each other and facial expressions ran the gamut, as did the views on what they were seeing. The memorial was quickly getting out of hand.

Nie Feng calmly took a picture of the wreath while observing people's reactions. It was a colossally disrespectful floral wreath meant to vent or to mock. Zhou Zhengxing stood still, refusing to react; Hong Yiming seemed out of sorts; Zhong Tao had a blank look. As Nie's eyes swept the room, the police materialized, seemingly out of nowhere. Team Leader Cui, Xiaochuan, and Yao Li, all in street clothes, hustled the workers into a lounge. Obviously they had been in attendance all along. Xiaochuan exchanged a knowing look with Nie Feng before leaving.

Inside the lounge, Cui questioned the workers about the wreath, and learned that the order had been phoned in two days before by a woman who wanted it delivered to Hu Guohao's memorial at exactly eleven o'clock that morning. She specified both the colors of the wreath and the contents of the elegies.

The yellow uniforms the men wore had HUAYI CEREMONIES logos on their back. Huayi was a major Shenzhen flower and ceremony shop that specialized in arrangements for all sorts of celebrations and memorials, including flower baskets for special occasions and wreaths for funerals, with a guarantee of speedy deliveries.

"A woman?"

Zhu Mei-feng's cold face flashed in front of Cui's eyes: the frightful terror of an avenging woman!

"Didn't it strike you people as strange?"

"Oh, no. We've had orders that were more bizarre than this. Our principle has always been to provide as many services to our customers as possible."

"Which means you'll do anything as long as there's money to be made. How much did you charge for this wreath?"

"666 yuan, since it was a special order."

"Wow!" Yao Li stuck out her tongue to show her surprise.

"How did she pay for it?"

"She sent a boy over with the money."

"What did he look like?"

"Early teens, I'd say, maybe middle school."

Apparently, the boy had not known the woman. He'd told them an "aunty" at a pay phone had given him ten yuan to deliver an envelope with the money.

"All right, you can go."

Xiaochuan took down their names and phone numbers before opening the door for them, while Cui pondered what he'd just heard. A mysterious wreath, incomprehensible sentiments, specially ordered from a flower shop, delivered by a yellow van—at the specified time of eleven o'clock in the morning. What did it all mean? And who was the mystery woman?

— 5 —

The twenty-fourth floor of the Landmark Building.

Zhu Mei-feng walked into the CEO's suite, tossed down her purse, and sat on the beige leather sofa in the waiting room.

Dressed in a purple-and-gray suit, and no necklace, she looked quite formal. She seemed calm and at peace, as if she'd recovered overnight from the sorrow and fatigue of the memorial; now her every move showed her to be a graceful, modern woman.

She looked around at Hu Guohao's elaborate suite, which she'd only visited a few times. It was as spacious as the lobby of a five-star hotel, but for some reason, it always gave her an oppressive feeling. No one had had a chance to gather up Hu's effects, so the office retained its original shape and look. The wooden crocodile in front of the desk and the trophies in the display case reflected light and instilled in her a sense of emptiness.

Ah-ying had told her that the office would stay the way it was for her to assume in the future. After Hu's body vanished from the earth the day before, she became the head of the Landmark empire. She'd heard that Hu's people were pinning their hopes on her, waiting for her to pick up where her late husband had left off and reclaim

Landmark's former glory. It was a natural course of action in their eyes, but she lacked Hu's ambition. She had no interest in real estate, and was ill equipped to run the empire.

Ah-ying walked in.

"Big Sister Zhu," she said cordially, "the Board members have all been notified. The meeting will begin at nine o'clock."

"How about Mr. Zhou?"

"He just called. He's on his way."

"And Zhong Tao?"

"Yes, him, too."

"I'd like to rest for a while. Could you get me a cup of coffee?"

"Of course."

Ah-ying left, and quickly returned with a steaming cup of Nescafé. She handed the cup to Zhu and walked out and shut the door, but not before glancing at the trophies.

In the office of the executive assistant to the CEO, shortly before the Board meeting.

Zhong Tao opened the bottom drawer of his desk, where he kept a carefully wrapped blue velvet pouch the size of a pencil box. He held it in his hand and stroked it gently, as if he were caressing a throbbing heart.

Then he gently opened the pouch and removed an old harmonica that had been twisted out of shape in a fire. Both the rubber-and-wood frame and the mouthpiece were gone, leaving only the charred, rusty metal shell.

He shut his eyes and imagined he could hear the soft harmonica sounds.

Blue flames; heartrending screams.

He opened his eyes, which were now brimming with tears. "Real men do not easily shed tears, because their hearts have not been broken." No one could know how he felt at the moment.

Someone knocked at the door; it was Ah-ying, to inform him of the meeting.

"Mr. Zhong, Big Sister Zhu would like you to be at the meeting."

"I'll be right there."

He put the pouch back and locked the drawer. Then he opened the door and walked to the conference room, where the Board would decide Landmark's fate, as well as that of everyone in top management. Prepared for the worst, Zhong Tao was ready to tender his resignation and go somewhere else.

With Hu Guohao gone, Landmark had lost its attraction, but he had one more thing he needed to do first.

A pot of red flowers sat in the center of the oval table, where the widow, Zhu Mei-feng, Deputy CEO Zhou Zhengxing, and other Board members were seated. They were looking through the documents before them. Ah-ying, in a black dress, her long hair tied in the back, sat to the side to take notes.

Zhong nodded at everyone before taking his seat.

Nine o'clock sharp, the meeting was called to order by Li Dongbao, a beefy man who was one of the VPs.

Hu Guohao had owned 54 percent of the company and Zhou Zhengxing 36 percent, while the remaining 10 percent was distributed among the senior management. The Board had seven members: Hu Guohao, Zhou Zhengxing, Li Dongbao (VP), Zhong Tao, Huang Lihong (CFO), Liu Jiali (Marketing Chief), and Xu Ming (Chief of Project Planning). Li Dongbao and Liu Jiali were considered Zhou's people; Li was his old partner, a solid and reliable person. Zhong Tao, Huang Lihong and Xu Ming were Hu's people. Ah-ying served as Board Secretary.

The first item on the agenda was to elect a new chairman of the board.

Since Hu had not left a will, the law stipulated that his shares and all his assets and personal property would go to Zhu Mei-feng. It seemed natural that she would take over as chairwoman of the board. The application to change the person legally responsible for the enterprise had been sent to the State Administration for Industry and Commerce.

The second item on the agenda: deciding on a new CEO, the seat of power.

Two views were offered: One, the "old chairman" faction, wanted Zhu Mei-feng to serve, just as Hu himself had done, making a sort of "trinity" of corporation person, chairman, and CEO.

But the "local" faction contended that the company had passed beyond the opening stage spearheaded by Hu Guohao; now that the company had entered an expansion stage, a modern style of management was required, which made it unsuitable for the chairman of the board to serve as CEO. Placing all the power in one person's hands ran the risk of bad decision-making.

Since neither side was in a mood to concede, Zhou Zhengxing employed the knockout punch of his "killer strategy" by revealing the inside story—Landmark was deeply in debt.

Zhou asked the CFO to distribute the books to everyone present. Hu had overseen Landmark's financial situation, requiring CFO Huang to report to him directly, regardless of the amount. Talk of how Landmark Realty was the trade leader, a powerful force, was simply an unfounded rumor. No one but Hu, not even senior management, had any idea how much Landmark was worth, how much it owed, or what its asset-liability ratio was. Based on Huang's data, the competing bid for Tiandongba against Big East had been a pretense, a clever maneuver to obtain capital and land sales.

Huang read from a financial report he removed from a yellow folder. As of the twenty-fourth, the day of Hu Guohao's death, Landmark owed 193,290,000 RMB on loans obtained from Guangdong banks, 7,1970,000 RMB for uncleared checks, 21,750,000 RMB for lines of credit, and 133,280,000 RMB for loan guarantee collateral. The total was 420,290,000 RMB. Deducting the 21,750,000 RMB for lines of credit that may or may not be executed, Landmark's debt to banks was a whopping 398,540,000 RMB.

"Landmark has assets of 460,000,000 and debts of nearly 400,000,000. Payment for the second half of the year is 85,650,000," Huang said dryly and closed his folder.

All those numbers meant one thing: Hu Guohao had bled the company dry. The news shocked everyone in the room.

"What about the money to buy Tiandongba?"

"Land speculation. Mr. Hu's plan was to use it to get more capital," Huang said with an awkward look while purposefully avoiding Xu Ming's and Zhong Tao's eyes.

Zhong Tao thought he could sense the man's intention to "defect."

Zhu Mei-feng was unusually calm, not appearing embarrassed or displaying a strong reaction. She did not question the numbers given by Huang or try to defend the late CEO, as if all this had nothing to do with her or that she had expected this to be the case.

"I can revive Landmark," Zhou promised solemnly before continuing to explain that he had made arrangements with friends in financial institutions in Pudong, Shanghai, to repay the 856,500,000-yuan loan using Landmark's vacant parcel of land as collateral. It was a good deal for the company, killing two birds with one stone, as it were. Hu had not been dead for ten days, and Zhou had already made plans to repair the debilitating damage to the company, impressing everyone with his ability to act swiftly and effectively in a time of crisis.

When the votes were taken, Zhou was chosen to be CEO.

The Board also decided that Zhu Mei-feng would replace Hu as chairwoman of the board and legal representative. She made it clear that owing to her lack of familiarity with Landmark's operations, she would be chairwoman in name only, while Zhou, the newly elected CEO, would be the real boss.

Applause greeted the announcements. Li Dongbao replaced Zhou as deputy CEO in charge of running the daily operations. In order to maintain a stable personnel structure, no changes were made in other positions. But to everyone's surprise, the new CEO suggested that Zhong Tao be promoted to VP as Li's replacement. The Board approved the promotion.

Ah-ying looked up from her notebook and quietly observed people's faces. She was not the only one caught off guard by Zhou's suggestion; Zhong himself had not anticipated it, and that was a perfect illustration of Zhou's cleverness, which had less to do with magnanimity than with a move to balance the power structure. No one knew if he had talked it over with Zhu beforehand or if she had at least gotten a heads-up from him. It might have been a goodwill gesture to the "CEO faction" or it could have been Zhu's condition for giving up the CEO position. But nothing seemed to matter now, since he had managed to stabilize the situation and make everyone happy.

It had all seemed so effortless on the part of Zhou, who came out as the big winner in Landmark's personnel shuffle. Throughout the negotiation process, Zhu, who was now the majority shareholder, might logically have played a pivotal role, but she'd kept a low profile, more like the Queen of England than Prime Minister Thatcher. Her behavior was intriguing, but the "CEO faction" knew that she'd never been involved in Landmark's operations, so they could not possibly have asked more of her. On the other hand, would she have been able to handle the job if she'd used her role as majority shareholder to demand the position? And would Zhou and his people have worked hard to help Hu's widow? She's a clever woman, Ah-ying said to herself.

Now that Zhou had taken control of Landmark, his first decision was to cancel the effort to buy the land at Tiandongba, which was the third item on that day's agenda.

Zhong Tao wanted to keep the plan going. Everyone in the real estate business thought it was a good idea, and they'd have had no problem finding the capital to buy it. But in Zhou's view, "our top priority is to repay the loan," and "it will take three to four years for the Tiandongba investment to generate profits." He had the support of other Board members, and so Hu Guohao's extravagant "Ocean-view Luxury Villa" project was nixed.

There was nothing Zhong Tao could do to change the situation. Zhu Mei-feng had abstained; that created an unusual Board, for Zhou would invariably have the final say on matters.

Ah-ying was upset. Zhu Mei-feng had given away the position of CEO and Zhong had been pacified by a strategic promotion, with CFO Huang defecting at the critical moment. Observing how Hu's business, aspirations, and wealth had been cavalierly abandoned by his colleagues and widow, she felt more disdain and indignation than pain.

— 6 —

The Criminal Investigation Team Office at the Y District Public Security branch.

Team Leader Cui was analyzing the case with his men. Chief Wu was present, and Nie Feng was permitted to sit in. The focus was on the mysterious wreath, which generated a variety of views and speculations.

"From the content of the scrolls and the time of delivery, we can safely say that whoever ordered the wreath has intimate knowledge of the inner workings of Landmark as well as Hu Guohao as a person. It could well be someone from Landmark," Chief Wu said.

"I concur," Cui said. "My money is on Zhu Mei-feng."

"Hu Guohao's widow?"

"She's no run-of-the-mill woman. From the beginning, I felt she was way too cool in reaction to Hu's death. It wasn't normal."

Cui's view won the others over; the focus was now on Zhu Mei-feng as the culprit.

"And why choose violets? That must mean something," Cui said as he lit a cigarette. "Did you notice that Zhu's purse was also purple?" he continued after exhaling a mouthful of smoke. "There has to be a connection. Who would be most upset over Hu's dallying? Zhu Mei-feng."

"And she knew more than anyone else about Hu," Zheng agreed.

Not everyone did, but no one had convincing arguments to the contrary.

"I can't totally agree with Team Leader Cui," Yao Li said openly. "I don't think we have sufficient reason to believe that Zhu ordered the wreath. She was, after all, the center of attention at the memorial, and the wreath meant a great loss of face to her."

"I think she's got a point," Xiaochuan said. "If she was involved in Hu's death, then why would she draw attention to herself and ruin everything?"

Nie Feng nodded, seemingly agreeing with Xiaochuan.

Xiaochuan continued, "If Zhu Mei-feng was part of a plot to kill her husband, the last thing she'd want would be to call attention to herself."

The one thing they could agree upon was that the wreath was odd. Could it have been a taunt from someone in real estate? Or a busybody's jest? An ironic twist of schadenfreude from his competitor? Or was someone making a final judgment of Hu?

None of those seemed plausible, for the wreath was really more like a curse.

It was apparent to Nie that Cui's views dominated the meeting, so he decided to keep his mouth shut. Chief Wu had different ideas. "Mr. Nie, what are your thoughts concerning the wreath?"

"Well . . ." Nie smiled lightly but was unwilling to speak his mind, not wanting to challenge the authority of the team. To be more precise, he didn't want anything he said to undermine Cui's confidence.

"Xiaochuan said you were at the scene, so tell us what you think," Chief Wu persisted.

"I'd just show my ignorance, and embarrass myself," Nie said, trying to fend it off. "I know practically nothing about solving a crime."

"Don't be so modest, Mr. Nie," Yao Li urged.

Finally Nie looked up, cleared his throat, and began. "I think the first order of business is to determine what message the wreath intended to send."

Xiaochuan and Yao Li watched him with interest.

"First of all, those weren't violets. Violets have small petals, and look more like lilacs. Those on the wreath, on the other hand, had big petals, with an unusual color, not pure blue. They had a purple tinge, and if you looked at them from the side, you would have seen that they were so purple they looked almost black."

Yao Li was surprised that Nie Feng had observed the wreath so carefully.

"So, Mr. Nie, what kind of flowers were they?" asked Zheng Yong, who was sitting to one side and had to lean forward to be seen.

"They were lisianthus, commonly known as bellflowers," Nie said, "originally from Mexico, also called prairie gentians. The ones sold in Shenzhen are imported from Holland and the flowers are mostly blue, but there are also yellow, pink, and white ones."

Yao Li could hardly hide the admiration in her eyes. "Mr. Nie knows a lot about flowers."

"Not really. I checked with the Huayi Flower and Ceremony Company, where I was told that these were a new import. And the call showed up on Huayi's caller ID, so I asked them to check the number. It came from a pay phone by a supermarket."

Chief Wu was impressed.

"They said the woman spoke Putonghua and sounded to be in her thirties."

Even Cui looked over to hear what Nie had to say next.

"At Landmark, in addition to Zhu Mei-feng," Nie continued, sounding a bit as if he were just mumbling to himself or trying to remind someone of something, "there's another woman in her thirties who also knows a lot about Hu. That would be Ah-ying, Hu's personal assistant, Feng Xueying."

Feng Xueying would indeed know about Hu, Cui thought to

himself. She'd been Hu's assistant for four years, as well as his office manager, so she would have attended just about every Board meeting. How could he have overlooked her?

The room went quiet, as the attendees began to refocus their thoughts.

Cui gave Chief Wu one of his cigarettes; Wu took it but didn't light up. Instead, he turned to ask Nie: "What's your interpretation of the scrolled memorial?" He seemed expectant, for Nie was, after all, a reporter, someone who dealt with words and their meanings.

Nie opened his notebook and glanced at his notes.

"I think there are different ways to read 'a well deserved death.' The simplest interpretation is 'a rightful death, a valuable death.' Sima Qian wrote that everyone will die, but one's death could be as important as towering Mount Tai or as insignificant as a goose feather. But I think what was meant here is the opposite. Hu was murdered, so 'a well deserved death' can only mean that he deserved to die."

A wave of murmurs rippled through the room.

"'All is illuminated,' I believe, means that the deceased knew exactly why he died. Of course this doesn't discount the possibility that it could be related to the numbers on the paper found in his briefcase. If that's the case, then the illumination refers to the strange sequence seven-nine-one."

More murmurs.

"Now let's look at 'an imposing personality soars into the air.' 'Imposing,' could mean something serious or damaging, perhaps an intolerable situation." Nie paused before continuing, "'Soars into the air' could mean an end, a closure. This is a key phrase."

That surprised them.

"And what about 'boldly corrosive'? Sounds like he was a real rotter," Yao said, drawing laugher from everyone but Nie Feng, who was struck by Yao's casual comment. He decided to let it go for the time being.

"I'm no expert, so I could very well be wrong, but thanks for listening." He stopped before the others had fully absorbed what he'd said. The room was quiet again. Cui frowned, and for a moment, the air seemed so thick you could cut it with a knife. Then the telephone by the computer rang; Cui picked it up.

"Hello? Detective Cui Dajun. Right. What did you say? That's fine. We'll be right there." He put down the phone and said to Chief Wu, "That was Big East's Hong Yiming. He has something to report and wants to see us."

"Then you should go right away."

"All right. We'll stop here. Xiaochuan, Yao Li, you come with me."

Nie Feng walked up and asked in a somewhat humorous manner: "I'm a tagalong reporter. Can I come?"

"No," Cui said firmly, but added to make him feel better, "I'll make sure Xiaochuan shares any new information with you."

"Many thanks." Nie did not mind the rejection.

— 7 —

Big East Realty, which occupied the entire eighteenth floor of East City Plaza, had a marvelous view of the bustling port.

Assuming that Hong had important information to share, the two officers and their leader hurried through the Plaza and headed straight for the elevator.

They emerged from the elevator and were greeted by Big East's logo and bright lights. Vibrant oranges, yellows, and bright reds on a gray background made the logo fresh, inviting, and ultramodern.

After Cui told the attractive receptionist who they were, she picked up the phone, and Hong's personal assistant, Ms. Lin, in a simple but elegant dress, came out to usher them into the CEO's office. Although not as luxurious as its counterpart at Landmark, the office, with its unpretentious décor, was uniquely fashionable and polished. A plasma TV and impressionistic drawings of world-famous architectural sites adorned the walls.

Hong stood, smiled, and showed them over to a white sofa.

He was dressed in a beige suit with a brown tie. A clotheshorse who cared a great deal about how he looked, he was always well-decked-out for public appearances.

Many CEOs liked to display a cigar case or a model car on their desk to show off their hobbies. Hong chose a lovely crystal case, in the shape of a lotus leaf, for candy. Those closest to him knew that he had a sweet tooth and enjoyed treating his guests to candy. Born in a poverty-stricken village in Henan, as a youngster he'd sometimes been forced to beg for food. So it was no surprise that he had yet to taste candy by the time he enrolled in middle school. Back in primary school, he once stole a small chunk of brown sugar from a classmate, and when his father found out about it, he hung the boy up and beat him so badly he was covered in bruises and laid up for two days. From that moment on, he had developed a special feeling for candy, and vowed to buy all the best candy in the world when he had enough money.

After the police took their seats, Hong pushed the dish toward them. It was filled with fine candy—mints wrapped in green paper and liqueur-filled chocolates wrapped in golden yellow paper.

"No, thanks," Cui said.

Yao Li, an unapologetic chocoholic, was tempted, but took none when she saw that neither Cui nor Xiaochuan touched the dish.

"Take some as an energy boost," Hong said, as he picked one, peeled away the golden yellow wrapping paper, and popped the chocolate into his mouth.

Xiaochuan and Yao Li exchanged a look. Yao's eyes said, "Mr. Hong is an interesting man," while Xiaochuan's said, "No wonder he's somewhat overweight."

Ms. Lin came in with three cups of coffee. She set them on the glass-topped coffee table, then walked out and closed the door behind her.

"Mr. Hong, do you have something to tell us?" Cui wasted no time.

"Yes. It's—" Appearing awkward, he rapped his finger on the edge of the crystal dish. "On the afternoon of the twenty-fourth, Hu Guohao and I didn't just talk business. We were chatting about all sorts of things when I sensed he wasn't his usual self. He seemed disturbed, apprehensive."

"What gave you that feeling?"

"He just looked different." Hong was still focused on his feeling.

"Was there anything specific?"

"I'm afraid not." Hong seemed hesitant.

"So?" Cui persisted.

"He seemed afraid, but—"

"Afraid of what?"

"He just said, 'Sooner or later this day would come—'"

"'Sooner or later this day would come,'" Cui repeated.

Yao Li and Xiaochuan exchanged another look.

"What else did he say?"

Hong looked even more hesitant. "That's it."

Midway through the conversation, Ms. Lin came in with forms for Hong's signature, which he signed with an expansive gesture before returning to his guests.

Cui wondered why Hong had waited so long to mention this to the police.

"Why didn't you tell us before?"

"Well, I didn't think much of it at the time. But later, as I thought back, it seemed odd. You see, I knew him for many years and never saw him like that. I just thought it might help you with your case."

"When did you and Mr. Hu meet?" Yao asked casually.

"Oh, we came from the same place, a dirt-poor place called Yucheng in Henan. We came out together bare-assed and determined to make names for ourselves. It's been decades." Hong appeared to be getting emotional.

"I've heard that Mr. Hong was a soldier before going into the real estate business, and he was born under a lucky star." Xiaochuan offered a bit of flattery.

"I cannot claim the lucky star, and all I've ever wanted are peace and safety. Peace and safety." Hong gave Xiaochuan the impression that he was referring to something else.

On their way out of the Plaza, Xiaochuan shared his impression with the others.

"I don't think so." Cui shook his head.

"I got the feeling that Hong didn't tell us everything," Yao said.

"He may have a reason for holding something back," Xiaochuan agreed. Cui considered what he was hearing, but couldn't make much sense of it.

After seeing off the three police officers, a dejected Hong sank into his high-back chair, as a myriad of emotions flooded his mind.

He told Miss Lin not to disturb him and to hold all calls. Then he shut himself up in the office, lost in thought. Images of his meeting with Hu Guohao on the afternoon of the twenty-fourth passed before his eyes.

They were in the Oceanview Restaurant at the Seaview Hotel. Hu had ordered an array of braised turtle, spicy crab, and razor clams, plus some cold dishes as starters. They ate and talked, mostly real estate gossip, and washed everything down with red wine.

When they were both a little tipsy, Hu fixed Hong with a searching gaze and said:

"Here's a test for you."

He wrote a string of numbers on a napkin—42602791—and asked Hong if he knew what the numbers meant.

Hong took a look and said, "No idea."

"Think again."

"Someone's phone number?"

"Horseshit." Hu cursed, a dark glint showing in his beady eyes. "Read it backward."

Hong trained his eyes on the numbers, and his face turned ashen when it finally came to him.

Hu opened his briefcase and took out a folded sheet of paper, which he spread out on the table. In the middle of the paper was a large red symbol that resembled "山," with a set of numbers underneath in a large, dark, bold font: "42062791."

"Who—who gave you this?" Hong stammered.

"I don't know."

"You should be careful."

"It's no big deal."

Though Hu tried to brush it off, his thick lips quivered, giving the impression that he was hiding fear inside.

He refolded the paper and stuck it in the notebook in his briefcase as he murmured:

"Sooner or later this day would come . . ."

The phrase presented Hong with a scary premonition. Then Hu's cell rang. He flipped it open and pressed it up to his ear.

"Oh, it's you. What do you want? I see."

A simple enough conversation.

"Something's come up. I have to go. Enjoy the turtle spawn," Hu joked as he walked off, the briefcase tucked under his arm. Hong watched his broad back disappear into the crowd at dusk. He never saw him alive again.

Hong snapped out of his reverie, his face ashen. He opened the small, middle drawer of his desk, which held a letter-size sheet of paper, which he'd found earlier that morning when he walked into his office. It was folded twice and had arrived in an envelope with the Big East address, stamped at a local post office. He glanced at the paper and quickly slammed the drawer shut. It felt like an evil omen.

His heart was gripped by a debilitating terror.

SIX

Flowers in Misty Shadows

— 1 —

At the Jianglang Chaozhou Congee Shop, Xiaochuan treated Nie Feng to a bowl of fish belly congee.

True to its reputation as a migrant city, Shenzhen boasts cuisine from all corners of China; there is enough on the small Nanyuan Road alone to satisfy even the most demanding diner—Beijing Dumpling Emporium, Old Sichuan, Chaoji Hakka Cuisine, Hunan Cuisine for Hunanese, Jiangxi Diner, Jianglang Chaozhou Congee Shop, Old Xinjiang Muslim Café, one right next to the other. The best of the bunch is the Beijing Dumpling Emporium, where authentic northern dumplings with meat and scallions are tasty and afford-able. Ten yuan gets you a big plate of plump dumplings and a dish of pickled cucumbers.

The congee the two men ordered was basically steamed rice in soup; unlike the more common slow-cooked congee, which is a sort of gruel, the kernels here had not lost their shape or texture. A few slices of crunchy fish belly floated on the surface, which convinced Nie that the people in Chaozhou had good, strong teeth. He was enjoying his meal.

The exterior and much of the diner's walls were painted red, highlighted by black and brown squares. The furniture and suspended lights were all made of wood, which, along with the substantial ceramic bowls and plates, as well as the black chopsticks, created a warm, natural atmosphere.

The two men talked as they ate.

"My editor-in-chief's deadline is fast approaching," Nie told Xiaochuan. Eight of the ten days he'd been given had passed.

"Can't you extend your stay?"

"I'm afraid not."

Xiaochuan proceeded to tell Nie about their visit with Hong Yiming.

"Mr. Hong seemed evasive. Even my boss couldn't figure out why he wanted us there and what he planned, but failed, to tell us." Xiaochuan was hoping Nie could be of some help.

"Did you say he told you 'it might help you solve the case'?" Nie asked.

"Yes."

"Then obviously he was trying to tell you that a murderer is out there somewhere."

"Could be."

"Also, it seems as if he has a feeling that the murderer is closing in on him, too."

"You mean, he thinks he's in danger?"

"Right. He even knows something about the murderer, but for some reason can't, or won't, tell the police."

"Do you think he's feeling guilty?"

"I can't say for sure. Remember, I'm just guessing. Did you bring the sheet of paper?"

"Here it is." Xiaochuan carefully removed the paper from a clear plastic folder.

"I'm sure you checked for fingerprints."

"Yes, only Hu's prints were on it."

"That means the person knew how to cover his tracks," Nie said while scrutinizing the contents and considering what the red "山" could possibly mean. He recalled how Ah-ying had told him that the curved bottom line made it look like a traditional Chinese ingot, but not the top.

"Yao Li says it looks like 'red tower mountain,'" Xiaochuan said.

"'Red tower mountain'? Sounds interesting." Nie took out the pictures of Hu's corpse to check against the symbol. It did resemble the scratch marks on Hu's chest.

Could they be the same? If so, what did it mean?

Next he turned his attention to the string of numbers: 42602791. Just as Ah-ying had said—printed in a bold, dark font, they jumped out at you.

"How did you know the last three numbers were 791?" Xiaochuan asked.

"Hu wasn't the only person who saw this before you found it."

"Really?"

"Yes. So did Hu's personal assistant, Feng Xueying."

"We're still trying to figure out what they mean."

"Eight numbers," Nie muttered.

"Most likely a telephone number."

"Right."

"But we checked; there's no such number anywhere in the country."

Nie Feng frowned. Was it really a phone number, or could it be something else? He took out his cell phone and dialed the number, only to hear, "We're sorry. The number you dialed is not in service." He tried again, this time dialing 02-42602791. "We're sorry. The number you dialed is not in service."

"We checked with the telecommunications office. No Guangdong phone numbers begin with a four, and, remember, only six cities have eight-digit phone numbers: Beijing, Guangzhou, Shenzhen, Shanghai, Chengdu, and Chongqing."

"You've been very thorough," Nie commented before calling the six cities, and sure enough, no numbers beginning with a four. Some of the recorded messages were exactly the same, with identical tones and voices. End of trace.

An eight-digit puzzle. A secret code? The beginning or ending of an ID number?

Nie was reminded of his conversation with Ah-ying. That was when he had begun to doubt that Hu's death was an accident. Why had Hu reacted so strongly to the paper only days before he died? Instinct told him it could have been "a calling card from the Angel of Death."

"What do you think?" Xiaochuan interrupted his musings.

Nie finished his fish soup and wiped his mouth.

"Criminal psychology shows that a perpetrator's MO often reflects his inner workings. So we can assume that the information transmitted through this piece of paper was meant to terrorize the victim, as a threat or some sort of intimidation. That's a common strategy by someone set on revenge, since it affords the avenger psychological gratification. The revenge will be meaningless if the victim doesn't understand the reason behind his death."

"So you think this must be premeditated murder?"

"I can't be sure yet, but it's possible." Nie's phone rang. It was the maid at home.

"Hello, Big Brother Nie, where are you?" She sounded worried.

"I'm having dinner with a friend. Is something wrong?"

"Mr. Wu, your editor-in-chief, just called; he wanted to know if you're back."

"What else did he say?"

"Not much. He just said to tell you to call him as soon as you're back."

"OK, I will." He closed his phone. "The old newshound is after me," Nie complained.

"You still have two days left, don't you?"

"I know, and I have to take advantage of those two days. I'll sniff around the crime scene once more." Nie cracked a smile, making Xiaochuan laugh. A good reporter must be a good hunting dog.

— 2 —

Greater and Lesser Meisha were like a pair of jewels inlaid on Dapeng Bay, two crescent-shaped emeralds, one big, one small. The Greater Meisha beach was longer and wider than Lesser Meisha's.

Shoes in hand, Nie Feng felt like he was in a different world as he walked the length of Greater Meisha, whose blue waters and golden sand were visited by throngs of people. A symphonic movement was created by the whistling wind through the coconut palms and the waves lapping against the shore overlaid by the frolicking laughter of the sun- and ocean-bathers.

As a public beach, free and open to all, Greater Meisha's Ocean Park drew crowds that stretched its capacity to the breaking point. The vast numbers of visitors created problems of personal safety, public security, and environmental protection, which seriously displeased local residents.

After taking a walk along the beach, Nie finally understood why it was so hard for the police to find even a single eyewitness. June twenty-fourth had fallen on a weekend, when, he'd heard, more than forty thousand people had shown up at Greater Meisha, filling the beach and the shallow water with visitors. One tourist told him, "You had to look between people to see the ocean, let alone actually step foot in it.

No wonder he felt as if he'd been swallowed up by a sea of humanity. He managed to free himself from the crowd and the heat, and rinsed his feet at an outdoor shower so he could put his shoes back on.

The gate to Greater Meisha's Ocean Park was left open, with neither a ticket booth nor a guard post. Shops selling swimming paraphernalia and snacks lined the entrance. A hundred meters beyond the entrance was the Seaview Hotel; Nie decided to take a look around.

Seaview, a resort hotel with a Southeast Asian flavor, catered to tourists, vacationers, and businessmen. It had three hundred deluxe

rooms, including several seaview suites with dark teak wood highlighted by gold-traced designs as their dominant decorating theme.
Elegant and unique, it seemed right out of a Thai resort.

At the Oceanview Restaurant, Nie ordered a fish head soup that
was quite filling. When he asked about Miss Bai, the waitress told
him she was on a leave of absence. But the other waitress, Ah-yu, a
short girl whose face was flushed, was there. Nie asked her about the
evening of the twenty-fourth, when Hu and Hong had dined at the
restaurant. He learned nothing new from Ah-yu, whose recollection squared with what he'd learned from the police. Hu had left
first, around seven o'clock, followed by Hong, some ten minutes
later. Miss Bai had charged the dinner to Hu's account.

As he was finishing his lunch, he saw Ah-yu and a few waitresses
standing off to the side, whispering and smiling at him. They must
think I'm somebody else, he thought with a laugh. The girls' gaze
followed him out the door when he left.

Taxicabs queued at the entrance. Tourists were waiting for buses
at the station across the street. Lesser Meisha was due east.

About a hundred meters down a paved path, he came upon the
Ocean Pearl Hotel, nestled among white apartment buildings. It
fronted two rows of newly completed duplexes with tiled walls and
low fences. The typical Guangdong residences were all alike, decorated with strips of yellowish-brown ceramic tiles, a favorite among
the locals. They created a rural ambience. Nie preferred the clean
Western Sichuan style of white walls and green tiles.

The owners of these small buildings were wealthy Greater Meisha residents, made rich by their proximity to the beach resort. A
soaring banyan tree towered over the buildings, its trunk so thick
it would take several people to link arms around it. A small, round
stone table surrounded by eight stone stools were arranged beneath
the tree. Nie stopped to rest on one of the stools, over which strips
of red or yellow paper hung down, some inscribed, probably good
luck prayers.

A bus and a minibus stopped to pick up passengers and then took off.

He waited for an air-conditioned bus for Lesser Meisha. According to the sign, the number 103, 360, or 364 lines all went to Lesser Meisha. The driver told him that the 360 bus ran twenty-four hours a day.

The bus followed the contours of Qitou Cliff, and as it rounded a corner, he looked out onto the rocks of Chao Kok. When the bus pulled up, he checked his watch; it had taken five minutes to get there from Greater Meisha by bus. If Hu Guohao had wanted to come here after leaving the Seaview Hotel, he could easily have walked.

Restaurants selling Sichuan and Hunan cuisine, as well as fast food, lined the street by the bus stop. Like Greater Meisha, there were also shops selling swimming paraphernalia and life preservers. The entrance to the Tourist Center faced a gentle slope that served as a parking lot, behind which vacation villas dotted the hill. There were even some trendy hair salons, with red-and-white swirling lights.

For Nie Feng, coming back to Lesser Meisha was more than just "repeatedly returning to the scene of the crime." He couldn't help feeling that they'd all missed something here. It was just a hunch, a reporter's gut instinct that there might be undiscovered clues at Lesser Meisha. Then again, he had another reason to come back— the beautiful beach had a special pull on him.

He walked along the shop-lined street until he reached the famed Lesser Meisha Hotel, a landmark structure formed by two white, stepped buildings facing each other; the unique architecture came into view as soon as you entered the tourist area. Like two white sails, the buildings invited fanciful thoughts, and the more than 150 well-appointed rooms and suites provided guests with a luxurious, comfortable home away from home.

A casual look at all the cars in the hotel's parking lot and outlying

area told him that there couldn't be many vacant rooms in the hotel. He decided to first check out the lobby, with its light green marble floor and mirrored pillars. The room rates at such an elegant
hotel had to be astronomical. Sure enough, a cursory inquiry at the
front desk told him they started at 480 yuan a night on weekdays
(660 on weekends and holidays), while rooms with an ocean view
went for 560 on weekdays (740 on weekends and holidays).

The registration desk was located to the immediate right, where
a visitor's attention was drawn to a gigantic photo behind the
desk of coconut palms against the ocean. A bar, a lobby shop, and
jewelry store were on the opposite side. Owing to the unusual
layout of the lobby, with its many pillars and winding verandas,
the services provided for guests were not immediately apparent. It
was a quiet refuge from the bustle outside, accessed through several entrances.

Nie passed a spa and sauna on his way to a tennis court in the
rear. Rows of cars were parked on the far side of the court's chain-
link fence. Another passageway took him past the jewelry store, and,
skirting the veranda by a tea shop, he came to a door with frosted
glass. He pushed the door open and was greeted by the sight of an
outdoor freshwater swimming pool. The jewelry store, like those at
hotels everywhere, had an 80% OFF SALE sign by the door, which was
flanked by two wood carvings of ferocious-looking creatures, a
hawk and a tiger.

A space toward the rear of the lobby, reached by a circuitous corridor, served Western tea. It had brown wicker chairs, black granite
tabletops, and a green carpet. Patterns of ocean fish and seaweed
were etched into the floor-to-ceiling windows.

Soon after he sat down, a waitress in a short, light green skirt
walked up.

"What can I get you, sir?"

Nie hesitated before ordering, knowing it would cost him at least
twenty yuan. He was quickly running out of funds. But he ordered
anyway. "A lemon tea." The tea came and he took a sip. Not bad.

"I hear a dead body was found on the beach a few days ago," Nie ventured.

"Uh-huh," Green Skirt said ambiguously, perhaps because she'd been told to.

"I heard it was the CEO of a major realty company." Nie switched to a blunt strategy.

"So you know."

"It's in all the papers. I interviewed the man only last week."

"Really!" Now he had Green Skirt's full attention.

"Did anyone at the hotel see him the night before it happened?"

"No. Some other people were asking the same question a couple days ago."

"Who were they?"

"Two police officers, a man and a woman."

"Was he sort of heavy and she quite slender?"

"That's right."

So Xiaochuan and Yao Li have been here asking questions, Nie said to himself.

He looked around; the lobby, with its mirrored pillars, gave the feeling that he was in a glass jungle. The tea shop's counter, blocked by a post, was not in full view. Artificial hills dotted with lush trees and flowers spread beyond the window behind him. On the other side of a white pillar, he saw a small swimming pool.

As he exited the hotel, he examined the surrounding area carefully—the lobby and the front entrance, the tennis court by the side entrance, and the small pool in the back, all under the shade of coconut palms and plenty of lush vegetation. A breakwater, proba-bly six feet high, encircled the rear of the hotel; beyond that, the golden beach and rippling blue waters of Lesser Meisha. He walked down a small path to a second entrance to the Tourist Center. He learned from the ticket taker that it was manned twenty-four hours a day, as was the main entrance.

He walked through the gate, passed a coconut-lined path, and headed east along the beach, until he was in the natural reserve, beyond the swimming area. He took a careful look at the place, and was surprised by several egrets flying overhead. Their long, thin legs were parallel to the ground, their necks stretched out ahead, pointed bills cutting through the air. There was something slightly comical about them. But he was reminded of his childhood, when his sister had taken him to a park on the outskirts of southern Chengdu, where he'd first seen egrets. Dozens of the crane-like white birds were perched on stately cypress trees. His sister even taught him a line of poetry by Du Fu: "Two yellow orioles sing among the emerald willows/A line of white egrets soars into the blue sky." Later, the egrets all but disappeared from the park, thanks to environmental pollution.

No one told him he might actually see the rare birds perched in trees at Dapeng Bay. He recalled reading a travel article that said egrets are spotted only in the Hainan mangroves these days. What a surprise to see them at a place where seagulls prevailed.

The beach ended at a backwater, where the waves surged, each higher than the one before. He turned to walk back and spotted a botanical garden beyond the embankment. A profusion of flowers peeked out from under a canopy of subtropical trees. His curiosity piqued, he hoisted himself up onto the embankment and rested his chest against the low wall of what was a seedling garden; it was like a different world. The garden abutted the lawn of the Lesser Meisha Hotel.

His thoughts turned to the events on June twenty-fourth and the paths of Hu Guohao, Hong Yiming, and Zhong Tao. All three had shown up at Greater and Lesser Meisha, but what did that mean? And then there was Zhou Zhengxing, who had been at Nan'ao Village, on the southernmost end of the same coastline.

He backtracked to the western part of the beach and walked around the barbecue ground, which was filling up quickly as dusk began to settle. Groups of seven or eight sat around barbecue pits, talking and laughing, their smiling faces brightened by the smoldering charcoal. The place was infused with the enticing aroma of roasting meat and fish. He paused, besieged by a sense that something felt different this time. A question popped into his head: why had Zhong Tao and his friends held their reunion here, instead of at Greater Meisha, where barbecue was available at a comparable cost, but which provided a much livelier ambience?

That night, Nie spent eighty yuan to rent a yellow-and-green tent, which was actually no cheaper than a guesthouse room. Lying alone in the tent, he looked through the flap at the black water and flickering lights in the distance. The sound of waves lapping against the shore was loud enough to increase the turmoil in his mind.

It began to rain around midnight, light at first and then heavier, as if the sky had opened up. Two years before, he'd traveled with a group of journalists to Thailand, ostensibly to study newspaper publication. He was working for an evening paper back then. The tour leader was the overweight, happy-go-lucky Mr. Wu, editor-in-chief of *Western Sunshine*. He recalled the night he went swimming at Pattaya, how lightning danced and thunder crackled amid the downpour. He and the other young journalist had stayed in the water, exposing only their heads for the baptism of rain; it was tantalizingly frightening and irresistibly exciting. Later he wrote a piece titled "A Frightful Night in Pattaya," which won a prize. Shortly after the trip, Mr. Wu poached him to work for his magazine. Now, on Lesser Meisha beach in the midst of a thunderstorm, history was repeating itself. His peaked-roof tent—they'd run out of the wind-resisting rounded models—was useless against the assault of the rain; even as water began to leak in, he had no choice but to stay put.

And in the midst of the raging storm, people were still out in the water.

Could Hu Guohao have died doing the same thing?

Midnight came and went, and there was no sign of the rain letting up. Having brought neither enough money to stay in a hotel nor an umbrella, he was forced to tough it out in his leaky tent. Dressed only in a pair of wet swimming trunks, he lay on his T-shirt, which he'd spread over a sheet of plastic, and his beach shorts. Both the T-shirt and the shorts were soaked, as was his base-ball cap, which hung on the tent pole outside. He was drenched in rain and sweat, and encased in a fishy, ocean smell. As he observed the roiling ocean, listening to the roar of the waves and the rain beating down on the tent, he was reminded of the military training classes during his college days.

Exhausted and cold, he dozed off around 3:00 A.M., but only briefly. He'd left sixty yuan as a deposit at the tent rental office, not nearly enough for a hotel room or even a beach towel. So he decided to return the tent, retrieve his deposit, and walk over to the Haiyi Tea Shop in slippers and swimming trunks, his waterlogged T-shirt draped over his back and a wet swimming cap on his head. He was not alone. Tourists with the same idea, some alone and some in groups of four or five, were chatting among themselves as they waited for daybreak.

The rain that night appeared heaven-sent, for when he casually asked a tea shop attendant if anything interesting had happened during the night, he was given an important clue to the case. A tour-ist from Hubei overheard him and said that he had come to the beach the previous weekend with some friends on a business trip. They'd rented a tent that night, too. Around 3:00 A.M., when he got up to pee, he heard bird sounds out by Lovers' Lane; the birds were calling to each other, as if stirred up by something. Paying little attention to the sound, he'd returned to the tent and gone back to sleep.

"There are lots of nests on the banyan tree by Lovers' Lane," the man said.

Egrets! Nie Feng's eyes lit up.

"Last weekend? Was it the night of the twenty-fourth?"

"That's right," the tourist replied. "Apparently someone drowned that night. The police were all over the place the next morning."

When day broke, Nie put on his damp T-shirt and beach shorts before going to check out Lovers' Lane, and that was how he discovered the important clue that had eluded him the first time.

— 3 —

Evening. The Milan Café.

It was an upscale coffee shop located behind a McDonald's in one of Shenzhen's busy neighborhoods, a popular hangout on a quiet lane. Zhong Tao liked the quiet atmosphere and simple décor, characterized by long tables with grainy wood and small wooden chairs with rounded backs. A fragrant cup of coffee helped you forget the clamor and concerns of the city for the moment.

Set against the old floor tiles, under orange lighting, the dark wooden doors and windows gave the café an ancient flair. The space was small enough to see all the way to the back. Black-and-white photos adorned one whole wall, most of them depicting old Hong Kong: Queen's Road, junks plying the harbor, old-fashioned tramcars, and the like. It was a study in nostalgia. A small, dark door on the opposite wall was next to a decorative Italian-style fireplace.

The waitresses wore plain green T-shirts, lending them a casual appearance.

Zhong Tao and Ding Lan were sitting in one of the three private booths against the wall. Wearing a polo shirt and jeans, Zhong Tao looked relaxed. Ding was also dressed casually. Between them on the table sat a charming little oil lamp with a brass base and mosaic glass shade in the shape of a pomegranate flower.

Their coffee came. Zhong Tao had ordered two cups of Hawaiian Kona coffee. The white ceramic cups had been warmed before the coffee was poured. A rich aroma rose with the steam.

"Their coffee is very good, so don't add too much milk," Zhong said as he handed her the small milk jar.

"I prefer Nescafé instant," Ding Lan said.

"Instant coffee is terrible." Zhong smiled and sipped his coffee. The taste, the aroma, and the richness were all first-rate. It was not something you could get just anywhere.

"Inhale the aroma and you can detect a hint of red wine," he explained.

Ding took a sip. "Very nice. It has a fruity flavor."

"Right. That's the taste of Kona coffee."

A dreamy look appeared on Ding's face.

"Do you remember . . . back when we planted coffee beans in Lanjiang?"

"Of course. 'Red, red coffee beans; green, green rubber trees.' How romantic that was," Zhong replied in a mocking tone, a blank expression on his face.

The silence was broken by music, an English song sung by a slightly hoarse baritone.

A twentysomething bartender in a black T-shirt was mixing a drink. Two of the ten bar stools were occupied by young men who were sipping Carlsbergs. A large screen in front of the fireplace was where fans congregated during soccer matches.

The song was replaced by the strains of a harmonica coming from the Shenzhen radio station. The DJ announced: "OK, everyone, here comes a harmonica solo called 'Apricot in the Rain.'" A favorite on college campuses, it opened with light, fast percussion, followed by a weepy harmonica that sounded like someone sobbing.

Zhong listened and seemed lost in thought. Ding was also entranced by the music.

The pomegranate lampshade swayed gently as the harmonica played on, sounding like music from a different realm.

"Do you remember? Back then—"

Zhong gestured to stop Ding from finishing. He was caught up in the music; a minute later he mumbled, "The past is like a dream."

"I really miss those days. They were brief, but I was so happy," Ding said fervently as she looked at him.

"We were only seventeen," he said.

"And Apricot was barely fifteen," she said sadly.

The music conjured up for Zhong the scene of apricots in the rain.

A hill in Lan'que Ridge and an apricot grove. Spring twenty-eight years earlier, when clusters of apricot flowers weighed down the branches and dyed the hill pink.

It was early evening, and Zhong Tao, along with a dozen zhiqing from Chengdu, came to the hill to sing. Part of the forced exodus of youngsters sent to the countryside during the Cultural Revolution, they belonged to the 2nd Company, 4th Battalion, XX Regiment of the Yunnan Construction Corps, all from the same Chengdu high school. Among the girls were Zhong Xing (Apricot), Xiao Yuhong, and Ding Lan. Zhong Tao and Ding Qiang were the most active boys. They sat in a circle singing a popular tune at the top of their lungs.

Xiao Yuhong, who wore long braids and had a round face and large eyes, was the prettiest girl in the corps, as well as the most talented. She sang and danced beautifully. She and Zhong Tao were childhood sweethearts.

Swarthy Zhong Tao, whose nickname was "Dark Boy," sat beside her. He had an honest face and a slightly goofy smile. He usually sang off-key.

Ding Qiang and his sister, Ding Lan, were horsing around. With a chubby face, pencil-thin brows, and slender eyes, she was not particularly pretty. Her brother, lean and solid, was a principled, stubborn youngster. Combative by nature, he was nicknamed "*Qiangzi,*" or Bossy. He and Zhong were buddies.

Zhong Tao's young sister, Apricot, accompanied the singers on her harmonica, the most popular and most fashionable instrument among the zhiqing.

They began with a song about their hometown, a piece based on an earlier melody, "The Same Old Autumn Water," from the 1930s, with new, somewhat melancholy lyrics. Holding the pink harmonica in her hands, Apricot cocked her head and lost herself in the music, her gleaming eyes staring into the distance at the apricot grove on the slope. She was wearing a checkered blouse and, with her hair tied into two short braids, her guileless, innocent manner was captivating.

> "The happiness of years gone by
> Turns to loneliness before me.
> Where has the dream gone?
> I look out with teary eyes,
> Dear Mama.
> When will I be able to come home?
> The raging waters of the Jin River,
> The splendid People's South Road
> Are the same as always."

The lilting harmonica strains reminded them of the buildings in Chengdu's Wangjiang Park, the unending traffic on People's South Road, the flowing waters of Huanhua Creek, as well as the enchanting fields of golden rapeseed flowers.

They were seventeen, fresh out of high school, although some of them had actually completed only two years. Responding to the call of the great leader, Chairman Mao, these boys and girls had just arrived in Lanjiang in Yunnan two months earlier. Zhong Tao's sister, Apricot, a fifteen-year-old middle school student, had joined him in the Yunnan border area, several thousand *li* from home, a place where they'd expected to find "bananas above their heads and pineapples under their feet" everywhere; what they encountered was a shock. Their meals consisted of turnips boiled in water and blanched cabbage. They had to clear the hillside and build their own living quarters. In the daytime, they made adobe blocks and cut bamboo until they nearly dropped from exhaustion. So when dusk descended and they could finally rest, naturally they thought of home and of their parents.

Tears brimmed in some eyes. Then, as the harmonica tempo picked up, they switched to a rousing tune:

"Go to the countryside,
Go to the border area,
Go to wherever the motherland needs us most."

Now they were reminded of their departure from Chengdu, seen off with gongs and drums so loud they nearly shattered the sky, red flags flapping in the wind, earsplitting shouts of farewell, and the tear-streaked faces of their mothers.

The setting sun lengthened their shadows and turned the apricot flowers a fiery red. Qiangzi had discovered the grove a few days earlier by accident; flowers in this alien land were a pleasant and comforting surprise.

"Who'd have thought we'd actually see apricot flowers in far-off Yunnan."

"They're so pretty."

Qiangzi, charmed by Apricot's harmonica, fixed his gaze on her, prompting her to stop when she spotted him. "Why are you staring at me with those cow eyes?" she yelled.

He turned and said softly, "I'm not."

"Liar! Your punishment is to sing us a song." She wrinkled her nose and began to play again, sending her braids flying.

"Let's get Qiangzi to sing for us," Xia Yuhong echoed Apricot.

"Yes, sing us a song." The others joined in.

Unable to fight them all, Qiangzi relented and cleared his throat.

"The girl plays the harmonica.
The boy sings.
The boy and girl are having a great time,

Two birds in a nest.
The boy wants a fan box."

Since "fan box" meant having a romantic relationship in the
Sichuan dialect, everyone jeered and cheered, then the girls and boys
broke into song. They were hot-blooded youths who dreamed of
turning the world red and changing the face of the earth. Simple,
naïve, fanatic.

"Dark Boy" began to sing "Song of the Zhiqing," which they'd
just learned; the others quickly joined in, their voices loud and
sonorous one moment, low and sorrowful the next:

"Say good-bye to Mama, say good-bye to my dear hometown,
The golden days of a student are entered into history books, never
*   to return.*
Ah, the road ahead is so arduous, winding and endless,
The footprints of life beached on a remote alien place.
Leave with the rising sun, return with rising moon,
Our sacred mission is to repair the earth with great devotion, it is
*   our destiny.*
Ah, my beloved, I bid you farewell and I will head into the
*   distance,*
Where the flower of love will never bloom, never bloom."

A breeze blew past the apricot grove, a heartbreakingly pretty
sight that transfixed Xia Yuhong. Falling petals flew off into the
sky.

"Ah, an apricot rain," someone cried out.

"Yes, an apricot rain."

The young Zhong Tao gaped at the raining petals; for the first
time in his life he could feel its heart-stopping beauty. It was lovely
and yet sad, something none of them would ever forget. As they frol-
icked amid the apricot rain, someone began to sob.

* * *

The light flickered under the pomegranate lampshade on the table. Zhong Tao was still humming the song as he recalled Xia Yuhong's transfixed face.

Ding Lan, also lost in thought, looked at him with tears running down her cheeks.

Youthful days, ideals and ambition, rosy dreams, along with their boasts of dyeing the world red: it was all just like yesterday.

The harmonica came to an abrupt stop. Zhong's face resembled a bronze statue; Ding Lan returned to the present.

"Do you know why this place is called Milan Café?" she asked.

"Because of its Italian flavor?" Zhong said, referring to Milano, the capital of Lombardy, in Italy.

"No, it's because the owner was a Hong Kong girl called Milan."

"Really?"

"She left, but the coffee shop has stayed."

He asked about some of their college friends; she told him they were all quite busy.

"Qi Xiaohui asked me the other day when we could all get together again."

"We'll see," he said.

"You be careful, OK?" she said in a worrying tone.

"I have one more thing to do, and then it'll be finished."

The blue flame never stopped dancing before his eyes; a heart-rending scream persisted.

"Don't forget, you don't know anything," he said slowly, staring at her eyes.

She nodded. "But—"

She was about to say something, but Zhong cut her off. "Let's talk about something else."

"Have you heard anything from Xia Yuhong?" she asked.

Zhong shook his head.

"A friend who returned from study abroad told me she once saw her at an Art Festival at the University of Pennsylvania. She's still single."

Zhong listened but said nothing.

"Later I heard she came back to Chengdu to see her family and asked about you."

A light of hope seemed to flicker in his eyes, but then he sighed. "We had the good fortune to meet but not to be together."

"How's your aunt?" she asked.

"I should go back to see my family." He clearly had something on his mind.

— 4 —

A black tea café, half a block from the Landmark Building. Close enough.

It was lunch break and Nie Feng had asked Feng Xueying to meet him. Before leaving Shenzhen, he wanted to know as much as possible about Zhong Tao, Hu's executive assistant.

Nie could not explain his interest in Zhong. All he could say was, as a journalist, he thought Zhong was somehow enveloped in mystery and intrigue. From the perspective of the case, he was a peripheral person in the eyes of the police, and Nie wanted to know exactly what role he'd played in the drama.

Ever since his return from Lesser Meisha, he knew that he must see two people: Ah-ying (Zhong's colleague) and Ding Lan (Zhong's friend from college).

Ah-ying was wearing a flax-colored short-sleeved blouse over pants with wide stripes. Her oval face, framed by shoulder-length hair, gave her the look of a well-educated white-collar worker.

After they sat down, Nie ordered a cup of jasmine tea; Ah-ying, lychee black tea.

"I didn't realize you were still here," she said after the pleasantries had been dispensed with.

"I'm heading back in two days."

"Have you found anything useful?"

"I'm running out of time," he said unhappily. "I'm afraid any follow-up report on Hu's death will have to wait until the case is solved."

"I've heard that the investigation is stuck," she said, sounding upset with the progress of the police investigation.

"Who told you that?"

"Everyone in the company is saying so. Somebody even said it could be a woman, you know, *cherchez la femme*."

The rumors were getting out of hand.

"What has Assistant Zhong been up to lately?" Nie asked, to change the subject.

"He's not the assistant any more. Got promoted to VP," she said sharply.

"Right, so I heard. That may be good for Landmark."

"Maybe."

"When did he come to work for Landmark?"

"Last summer." After Ah-ying proceeded to tell him how Landmark had gone about filling the position of executive assistant to the CEO, Nie Feng no longer had to wonder how Zhong had become Hu's right-hand man.

Zhong Tao, who had been working for a Shenzhen brokerage, was a successful stock trader who was well known in the South China market. He surprised everyone by applying for the Landmark job, since he had no real estate experience. The position was for executive assistant and chief of administration, with clearly delineated qualifications and a high annual salary—three hundred thousand yuan. Naturally, there were many applicants and the competition was fierce. Zhong did not stand out at first; he came to the interview in a black polo shirt, and wearing a beard—borderline slovenly. The other candidates came in suits and polished shoes, all neat and tidy. Ah-ying thought he looked familiar, eventually recalling that she had attended one of his talks on the market at a brokerage.

Zhong went straight in to see Hu himself, without first stopping at her office, so she thought they'd made a prior arrangement.

Hu had interviewed several MBAs who had returned from overseas for better opportunities in China, even the marketing chief at a real estate firm. They were all outstanding candidates, but after meeting with Zhong, Hu offered him the position. Many in the company wondered why Hu would hire someone with no experience as his assistant.

It turned out that Hu had been impressed by Zhong's performance in the realm of finance. Ah-ying heard that he helped Landmark acquire more than a billion yuan in equity within the first two months of his employment.

"I see." Nie nodded. He followed with more questions about Zhong.

"Maybe he'll go back to trading stocks," she said. "They say he was an amazing trader. His old company tried hard to keep him."

"Does that mean he may have had a special reason for coming to work at Landmark?" Nie probed.

"Now that I think about it, that's quite likely." She took a sip of her tea.

"Why do you say that?"

"Well, Mr. Hu offered him three hundred thousand yuan plus a two percent share of stock. That's an attractive offer. But if you look closely, a top trader would likely make more than that."

Nie thought her analysis was right on target.

Whatever the "special reason," it was not something Ah-ying would know. She did say that Zhong was a cautious but hard worker, with an outstanding performance record, winning Hu's complete trust and positive comments from everyone in the company. Even Zhou Zhengxing, Hu's deputy, was impressed. Some of the young women found him attractive, but he did not respond to their advances. A man in his forties was like a vat of aged liquor, or a hefty novel, but no one had tasted the liquor or knew anything about the novel. He was single, had no family or girlfriend, and seemingly never dated. That was unusual.

Nie thought that Ah-ying acted differently when she talked about Zhong, as if puzzled by his idiosyncrasies or displaying feminine admiration. Or, perhaps, both.

Then the topic of Hu's funeral came up.

"Who could have sent that eerie wreath?" he asked.

"Very likely a woman." She sounded quite certain.

"Why do you say that?" he asked, surprised.

"I saw a strange woman there."

"Really?" Obviously, he'd underestimated Ah-ying's instincts.

She told him that during the viewing of the body she'd seen a woman in a floral blouse standing by the back door. She'd never seen her before, and no one had paid her any attention, since they were all looking in the direction of Hu's body. Even if someone had spotted her, most likely they'd have assumed she was a funeral home employee. But Ah-ying was curious, because it was nearly 11:00 A.M., and the woman had looked at her watch twice.

"People were stunned when the wreath was delivered, which threw the memorial into chaos. But the woman had a peculiar look on her face, almost as if she admired the wreath, like watching one's own child on the stage."

"What did she look like?"

"I didn't get a good look. She wasn't close enough and only stayed a few minutes."

Nie thought it was logical for the person who ordered the wreath to show up at the memorial. She'd be willing to risk it in order to witness the dramatic effect it created; it would certainly be gratifying.

"Can you guess her age?" he asked.

"Middle-aged."

That matched what he'd learned at the shop.

He said good-bye and walked outside, feeling energized. What

Ah-ying had told him was important, for it proved that it was neither Zhu Mei-feng nor Ah-ying who had ordered the wreath. It had
likely been a third woman.

One thing he had not expected was that Ah-ying had kept from
him the information that the woman actually appeared in one of
the photographs taken at the memorial. Her identity would be revealed by an investigative agency. But that would happen later.

Next, Nie Feng met with Ding Lan at the editorial office of
Woman magazine.

The magazine had a nationwide circulation of several hundred
thousand, but their editorial offices were rather cramped, a common
situation for magazines affiliated with a publishing house. The editorial staff was well paid, despite the low regard in which they were
held by the publisher, since their salaries were tied to the magazine's
circulation.

Ding Lan's tiny office was crammed with a desk, a file cabinet,
and two chairs, leaving little space for anything else. Her desk was
littered with manuscripts, mail, and other items. The covers of every
issue decorated her wall; bundles of the latest issue waiting to be
posted occupied the corners.

There was barely room for him to stand.

"Sorry this is so cramped," Ding apologized, then offered him
one of the chairs and poured some tea. She looked to be in her early
forties. Dressed in a V-neck chiffon sweater, she was an energetic,
animated conversationalist, and was considered to be one of the top
female editors in the business; many of the contributors to *Woman,*
including well-known writers, had sat on that chair and decided on
topics to write about in discussions with her.

"We're in the same line of work," he said.

"I quite like *Western Sunshine;* it reminds me a bit of *National
Geographic,*" Ding said. He was pleased with her positive reaction.

"That's what we're striving for, to be China's *National Geographic.*"

"Zhong Tao tells me you're also a graduate of Sichuan's C University."

"Right. I was a journalism major, class of '88. You and Zhong were ahead of me; you're both so accomplished."

"You flatter me," Ding said with a smile.

They talked for over an hour. She impressed him with her forceful, competent, and straightforward attitude.

"What's your favorite spot in Shenzhen?" Ding asked.

Whenever she posed that question to outsiders who came to Shenzhen, either for pleasure or for business, the usual answer was "the Dingwang Building," or "Window of the World." But Nie's choice was a new one for her.

"Lesser Meisha Beach."

"Really!" That surprised her.

He went on about his impression of Lesser Meisha. He'd been to Sanya in Hainan and Beihai in Guangxi, both famous beaches. Because of the white sand, Beihai was known as a silver beach, while the sand at Lesser Meisha had a light gold tinge, which was rare. "Blue ocean and yellow sand" was Lesser Meisha's claim to fame. Then he mentioned the stone jetty, Lovers' Lane, and the barbecue ground, with its grove of rubber trees and pits shaped like hexagrams.

The conversation turned naturally to the reunion on the night of the twenty-fourth.

"I heard you had a great time at the barbecue reunion."

"Yes, it was an unforgettable night."

"Why'd you choose Lesser Meisha? Isn't Greater Meisha bigger?"

"Greater Meisha is too noisy. Lesser Meisha suited us better."

She could be telling the truth, he thought.

"Five men and two women, drinking and playing finger-guessing games till dawn. It must have been a lot of fun," he said with a laugh. "I hear you finished off three cases of beer, and that everyone was dead drunk."

"How did you know that?" She had to laugh.

"Zhong Tao told me."

"He and Qi Xiaohui got drunk as lords playing finger guessing games."

"I hear he was no match for his drinking pal, that he actually got sick."

"He's not a big drinker, but likes to play one." He could fathom her concern for Zhong in her comment.

"He left the grounds before everyone and went back to his room to rest, didn't he?"

"Not really. He was only gone about twenty minutes. He went back to change clothes. I was with him."

That was exactly what the police had told Nie.

"I admire him," Nie said. "One of his schoolmates said he was a rising star in the South's stock market."

"That's true. He's a financial genius."

"Then why did he leave to come to Landmark?" Nie asked, catching her by surprise.

"Well," she hesitated, "maybe it was just fate."

"Fate?" Nie recalled hearing someone else say that.

"The position at Landmark was really attractive," Ding explained, as if realizing that she'd said something she shouldn't have. "I heard it was very competitive, with many talented people fighting over the position. Executive assistant to the CEO, and all that."

"And Zhong Tao got the job."

"Yes. His strengths outshone everyone else's."

"What I heard was that the CEO, Hu Guohao, was his patron saint."

"Hu Guohao?" Something flickered in her eyes. "A playboy CEO," she added contemptuously.

"Playboy CEO?" Where had he heard that before?

Ding rummaged through the pile of newspapers on her desk and handed one to Nie. It was from *Urban News* two days before; a short piece in the second section reported the incident at the memorial, with a close-up photo of the blue wreath. He was surprised to see that it had already made it into the papers:

SURPRISE OMEN AT MEMORIAL FOR
REAL ESTATE TYCOON HU GUOHAO

"A WELL-DESERVED DEATH" INSCRIBED ON STRANGE
WREATH THAT DESCENDED FROM THE SKY

PLAYBOY CEO'S AMOROUS TRAIL WHEN ALIVE;
A FOG OF MYSTERY AFTER HIS DEATH

"LOFTY ASPIRATIONS, WILD AMBITIONS,
A PLAYER'S FLIRTATIONS." DOES SOMEONE
HAVE SOMETHING TO HIDE?

"From our perspective at *Woman* magazine," Ding Lan said, "'a well-deserved death' is a nice epitaph. A disgusting man who abused women ought to have a worse end, regardless of whether he was a high official, a nobleman, or a wealthy businessman."

Nie was surprised by the vehemence. Was she speaking as a magazine editor or as a woman? He sensed something else in her angry comment, but had yet to figure out what it was.

Based on information Xiaochuan had given him, Nie knew that the participants in the reunion had told pretty much the same story. They'd had a great time at what was a regular reunion. Ding Lan did not look like a calculating person, nor was she secretive, and she was a fan of *Western Sunshine*. What he hadn't expected to find was that she seemed to have feelings for Zhong, and that piqued his curiosity. Nie knew that Zhong was a 1977 graduate in International Trade from Sichuan's C University, and that Ding was the class of '79. They hadn't been in the same department, and yet they had a special relationship, so what else connected them? He couldn't stop mulling over this new discovery.

. . .

After Nie left her office, it dawned on Ding to wonder what lay behind this fellow alum's visit? Was there anything hidden in his questions?

She picked up the phone and dialed Zhong's number.

Back in the guesthouse, Nie turned on his laptop and visited C University's Web site, where he found Zhong's name on the alumni page for the International Trade class of '77, the year the college entrance exam was reintroduced after the ten-year Cultural Revolution, during which schools were closed and just about everything was halted. Many zhiqing finally were given a chance for fair competition and were admitted into college without worrying about their family background. It was a life-changing experience for many. Zhong clearly belonged to this group.

Then he checked out Hu Guohao.

After keying in Hu's name, several people with the same name popped up: the CEO of a pharmaceutical company, a bioengineering professor, and an old revolutionary from some county in Guangdong. He also found news of Hu's death, including a feature piece on him. A brief bio was appended.

Hu Guohao, renowned real estate entrepreneur.

1942, born in Henan.

1960, joined the revolution at the age of eighteen. Notable accomplishments, awards.

1981, initiated real estate development in Guangxi and Hainan, with outstanding performance in a fiercely competitive field. Managed to survive Hainan's real estate bubble.

1992, moved to Guangdong, where he and a partner established Landmark Realty. Within eight years, his talent had produced remarkable yields: the Landmark Building, Yayuan Plaza, Xincheng Garden Estate, and other housing developments.

1998, began to attract domestic and international media attention; interviewed by America's *Fortune* magazine, the BBC, China's CCTV, Phoenix TV, and domestic print media.

2000, January, chosen by *China Managers* magazine as the Best Real Estate Manager.

To Nie's surprise, Hu's life in the 1970s was a blank. Why was that? He was puzzling over the question when his cell phone rang. It was from the maid at home. His grandmother's birthday was coming and his mother wanted to know when he'd return.

"In the next day or two." He realized that his deadline was the next day.

"Has the case been solved?" his maid asked.

"What case are you talking about?"

"Don't try to pull something on me." She raised her voice smugly. "I read your article in the latest issue of *Western Sunshine*."

It turned out that his editor in chief had added a postscript to his article, reporting that four days after being interviewed by this magazine's reporter, Hu Guohao was found dead on Lesser Meisha beach. A special report on the investigation was forthcoming.

"You little imp. I didn't know you could play detective."

"Really?" She sounded flattered.

"Keep it a secret between us, and I'll bring you seashells from Greater Meisha beach."

"Sure, if you keep your word."

SEVEN

The Second Victim

— 1 —

July 6, Thursday, the eighteenth floor of the East Square Building.

Hong Yiming's body was found in his office at 11:55. Cause of death: poison.

After he arrived at his usual time of 9:00 A.M., Miss Lin, his secretary, had made him a cup of Green Snail Spring tea, as always; he'd signed some documents and did not leave his office. No scheduled meetings that morning. At 11:10 he called to have his driver get the car ready at 11:30; he had a lunch engagement at Hotel Oriental Regent. The driver waited till 11:45, and Hong still did not show. As a former soldier, he was known for his punctuality, so the driver assumed he'd been delayed and waited another ten minutes. When Hong still had not shown up, the driver finally called Ms. Lin.

She called Hong's extension. No answer. She then knocked at his door. No response. So she pushed the door open and saw Hong leaning back in his chair, a terrifying look on his rigid green face. Blood oozed from his nostrils; white foam had gathered at the corners of his mouth.

She screamed, so shocked she could barely walk. Staff from other offices rushed over and immediately called 110.

Police from the city's criminal investigative section arrived first, followed by Cui, Xiaochuan, Yao Li, and police technicians. By then the office had been cordoned off with yellow police tape, obviously by the squad from the city, led by a detective heading a special unit. Cui had a brief conversation with the man before beginning his own investigation.

A preliminary examination showed that Hong had died of acute poisoning. The bloody nostrils and foaming mouth were classic symptoms. Based on the state of the body and information provided by the secretary, he had died between 11:10 and 11:35.

The police began their crime scene investigation as a technician took photos. Nothing seemed out of order in the office, except for a bulge on the rug under his feet. Before he died, he'd suffered convulsions and violent spasms, both symptoms of poisoning. The golden yellow wrapping of a piece of liqueur-filled chocolate lay on the rug by his feet. Yao Li bent down and picked it up; one glance at the wrapping made her shudder. She instinctively looked over at Xiaochuan, who knew what that meant and made a terrifying face.

Twenty-five pieces of green mint candy and seventeen pieces of chocolate liqueur candy remained in the lotus-shaped crystal dish. Yao Li bagged them all.

They questioned some of the employees, including his secretary, his driver, and the upper management staff. A common impression was that Hong had been behaving in an unusual manner over the past few days. He seemed uneasy and less carefree, no longer talking and laughing as before. Miss Lin thought he seemed to have something on his mind, for he'd been openly agitated recently. Once he'd blurted out that he dreamed he was being chased by an old man dressed in red, and had woken up in a cold sweat.

Hong enjoyed a contented family life, no problems with his wife. They had a daughter studying in Canada, whom his wife was visiting at the time. She'd been notified of Hong's death by phone. There

was no note, but the police found a piece of paper in one of his drawers with the character "山" and a string of numbers, identitical to
the one they'd found in Hu Guohao's briefcase.

"Another 'red tower mountain!'" Yao Li said, while Cui was
studying the paper.

Was this some sort of death curse? What did the character mean?
Could Hong have killed himself? If so, why? Could he have been
frightened into suicide by the "death curse"? Normally suicides left
notes, but not Hong.

Cui was stumped.

After they finished at the crime scene, Hong's body was delivered to the Public Security Hospital for an autopsy. In his stomach
and vomit the ME found traces of Tetramethylenedisulfotetramine,
commonly known as TETS, or, in simplest terms, rat poison. A le-
thal white powder, odorless and tasteless, its toxicity was more than
a hundred times that of arsenic. A dose of six to twelve miligrams
was enough to kill. It was what had killed Hong.

Of the candy Yao Li brought back, the twenty-five mints were fine,
but they found one of the chocolates had been doctored. The liqueur
had been replaced by rat poison. Which meant that either someone
had altered two pieces of candy in Hong's crystal dish, or had filled
the candy with rat poison beforehand and sneaked it in among
the other pieces in the dish. Made in Shanghai, the candy was
available in any of Shenzhen's supermarkets. Hong Yiming had eaten
one of the poison-filled chocolates that morning, thus eliminating
the possibility of suicide. The police found two incomplete fingerprints on the yellow wrapping paper, but they turned out to belong
to Hong. No prints were found on the remaining pieces of candy.

In retrospect, they realized that when Hong had asked to see the
police three days before, he had already received the sheet of paper
and sensed an imminent danger. What he hadn't known was that
when the killer delivered the paper, he may also have included two
pieces of poisoned candy, as a random weapon that killed when the
victim picked up one and put it in his mouth.

"Why did the killer doctor two pieces of candy?" Yao wondered out loud.

"Two bullets, to increase the probability," Xiaochuan said.

"Not only that," Cui said. "You see, two pieces would shorten the time of his death by half, so the killer's point was to quicken Hong's death."

"How does that work?"

"If one piece is poisonous, the chance of Hong dying each time he ate a piece would be eighteen to one, but if there are two, the chance would eighteen to two, or nine to one."

"I could have been a victim of that nine-to-one chance," Yao Li muttered to herself.

"Thank God we didn't accept it that day when he offered us the candy," Xiaochuan said with visible apprehension and relief.

"Who would have imagined that the CEO's office at Big East was a death trap." Even Cui was stunned.

"Does this have anything to do with the land at Tiandongba?" Xiaochuan wondered aloud.

"You mean a competition for real estate profits?"

"Right."

"But didn't Zhou Zhengxing give up the bid for the land?"

"But he didn't give up on Landmark's dominant position."

Hong's sudden death rocked the security establishment, and sent a shock wave through the city. Before the police had determined the cause of Hu Guohao's death, Hong Yiming was found dead in his office. Barely two weeks separated the two deaths, and both victims were real estate tycoons. And both had been recipients of a mysterious sheet of paper.

A meeting was held that afternoon at the Y District Public Security Office. Chief Wang of the Municipal Investigation Bureau (MIB) was in attendance, with instructions from the city government. A short man with a crew cut, his face reflected the somber mood. The meeting ended with a decision to tie the investigation of the two cases together, with Precinct Chief Wu in charge and Cui Da-jun his deputy. MIB would send over some of its best investigative officers as reinforcements. It was to be an all-out effort; they had a month to solve the cases.

Cui was under the gun, with mounting public attention and the deadline set by his superior. There had been signs before Hong's death, and his death could possibly have been avoided; Cui blamed himself for the oversight. Hong likely had held information back, which led to his death, but that was no excuse for the leader of the crime squad.

At the meeting, Chief Wu focused their discussion on material evidence they'd found at the crime scene.

First, technicians had confirmed that the sheet of paper in Hong's drawer was of the same quality as the one found in Hu's briefcase. The font and size of the string of numbers appeared to be the same. The symbol for "山" was handwritten and also closely resembled the earlier version (the police were already referring to it as "red tower mountain"). It was clear that both had come from the same person or group of killers, and that the reasons for the two men's deaths were closely related. Knowing what the symbol and the numbers meant would be a key to solving the cases.

Secondly, the killer had planned everything meticulously. Using doctored candy was a clever method of "random killing," meaning that the victim could die at an unspecified time, making it easy to have an alibi. And only Hong's fingerprints were found on the paper and the candy wrapping.

But the police knew that killers always make a mistake. They needed to determine how the candy got into Hong's office as another key to solving the case.

Cui, Xiaochuan, and Yao Li reported on the investigation. Preliminary questioning at the crime scene that morning had cleared Ms. Lin and the janitor who cleaned Hong's office, both of whom were beyond suspicion. They had also talked to the night security guard, but had found nothing suspicious. Hence, the likely killer was a visitor Hong had seen in recent days.

Cui and his officers had met with Hong Monday afternoon, and since they believed that Hong had felt he might be in danger, Cui had asked Ms. Lin about Hong's visitors between Monday morning and Wednesday afternoon.

She showed them the visitor's logbook.

On Monday morning Hong had seen three visitors: two of them were friends from Master Trading Company (GM Qian and the marketing director), the third person was Landmark's Zhong Tao, who had arrived at 10:00 and left at 10:45. Ms. Lin recalled that Hong had asked Zhong over to talk about payment of a loan Hong had made to Hu Guohao. During their meeting, Hong had taken a call from his daughter in Canada.

Monday afternoon, Hong met only with Cui and his officers, after which he kept his door shut and saw no one else that day.

Tuesday morning, Hong met with his production manager to discuss the bid for Tiandongba.

Tuesday afternoon, Hong went on a business trip to Zhuhai; he was away the whole day and his door remained locked.

"Did Zhou Zhengxing, Landmark's CEO, come to see Mr. Hong?" Cui asked.

Miss Lin's answer was negative.

"Can you show us what he did from Thursday to Saturday?"

She turned the page and read for them.

July 1, Saturday: Mr. Hong spent all day at the Southern Real Estate Elite Forum at the Mission Hills resort and did not come to the office.

June 30, Friday: Mr. Hong spent the day in Guangzhou at two business meetings. His door was locked the whole time.

June 29, Thursday: in the morning he was too busy to meet with the heads of two interior design firms. Around 10:30 Hu Guohao's widow, Zhu Mei-feng, came to Big East and met with Mr. Hong in his office. Miss Lin had no idea what they had talked about.

"Mrs. Hu was here last Thursday?" Shocked, Cui snatched the log from the secretary to look at it himself. Zhu Mei-feng's name and time of her visit were clearly recorded.

"When she left, Mr. Hong walked her to the elevator. I overheard him say something about his hope that Mr. Hu was looking down on them," Ms. Lin offered.

What a remarkable coincidence. In the short space of three days, Zhu Mei-feng and Zhong Tao had both come to see Hong Yiming. It was entirely possible that one of them could be the killer, since they both had an opportunity to touch the crystal dish. Of course it was also quite reasonable for them to talk about issues remaining in the wake of Hu Guohao's death. Besides, it would have been difficult to plant the doctored candy in front of Hong.

During the meeting at the station, one of the officers had mentioned another possible suspect: Zhou Zhengxing.

"Zhou's alibi for Hu's death is not strong enough. He had plenty of time in Nan'ao to dispose of his enemy, a whole hour, from midnight on the twenty-fourth to one o'clock."

"This is something we can't overlook," Chief Wang said.

"But we haven't found any clues in Nan'ao," Cui said unhappily. "Our investigation of Zhou Zhengxing is going nowhere."

Then Chief Wu posed an interesting question:

"What made Hu Guohao and Hong Yiming targets by the same killer?"

"They worked together in Hainan, each running a housing development and real estate business. Zhou Zhengxing would be the prime suspect if the murders were done for business profits," Chief Wu said. "One of the victims was the man he wanted to replace as head of Landmark, the other one Landmark's major competitors."

"I agree that we should continue looking at Zhou," Cui said.

"Hong Yiming told us that he and Hu came from the same place in Henan," Yao Li offered, "so maybe they had some other connection."

The comment made sense to Chief Wang. "Let's look for that connection and put Nan'ao aside for now. We can always come back to it if there are new developments."

The meeting ended with a resolution to conduct an all-out investigation and surveillance of the prime suspects.

Nie Feng learned of Hong Yiming's death when Xiaochuan called after the meeting at the station. The death came as no surprise and yet was totally unexpected. His apprehensive demeanor in the days shortly before his death indicated that he sensed that his life was in danger, but even the police had not expected it would actually happen and so soon.

Xiaochuan informed him of the weapon—poison-filled chocolate liqueur candy.

"Poisoned candy! Perfect for a random killing, or a distance murder, a clever and secretive means of carrying out a murder, since the killer would have an airtight alibi."

"Hong Yiming actually offered us candy when we saw him Monday afternoon."

"I'll bet none of you took him up on his offer."

"Of course not. If we had, it might not be him who was dead. There were eighteen pieces altogether, two of them were poisonous, which meant that each piece had a one-in-nine chance of killing someone."

"Not if the killer laid those on top," Nie corrected him. "Then the chance would have been one out of three, or even two."

"My God, why didn't I think of that?" Xiaochuan sounded like he was gasping.

"Why don't we meet and talk about it?" Nie wanted to know more.

"Sure. Where would you like to meet?"

"How about the 110 Coffee Club?"

"110 Coffee Club?" Xiaochuan got the joke—the police hotline—and laughed. "OK."

Nie then called his editor at *Western Sunshine* to update him on the latest developments.

"Mr. Wu, something big has come up. Another big shot has died." Nie could hardly hide the excitement in his voice.

"Oh yeah? Who?"

"The CEO of Big East Real Estate, Hong Yiming."

"Another real estate tycoon!"

"I was going to fly back tomorrow, but—"

"No, no way. You can't keep delaying. There are important interviews waiting for you here."

Nie Feng knew the editor was mainly concerned about expenses.

"Just give me a few more days. There'll be a break in the case any day now."

"Are you the lead detective now? Give me a break. You have to come back."

"I think I've found traces of the murderer."

"First you say something about finding clues and now it's traces. All the speculation in the world won't help you solve a case." The editor was unconvinced.

"Then how am I supposed to write a follow-up article?" Nie was trying every angle.

"Three days," Wu relented. "That's all I can give you"

"Only three days?" Nie sounded unhappy.

"That's right. After that, you'll have to pay for things out of your own pocket." Money was the editor's best weapon.

"Yes, sir!"

— 2 —

Nanyuan's Ming Tien Café.

Nie Feng was seated in the same window booth as before. The same ponytailed waitress brought him a glass of water.

"What would you like, sir?" she asked with a big smile.

Nie took a look at the menu. "Japanese rice with braised eel. Make that two."

When Xiaochuan arrived, the waitress was bringing up the eel dish in red lacquered trays filled with fine little plates of side dishes, so typical of Japanese cuisine. There was also a small bowl of miso soup with purple seaweed for each. It smelled wonderful, so they began eating right away, while Xiaochuan filled Nie in on the "death notice."

"Identical to the one Hu Guohao got?"

"Yes. Another red tower mountain, according to Yao Li," Xiaochuan said.

"Yes, I see that. The symbol does look like a red tower mountain. I hadn't noticed that before."

"Yao Li is an admirer of yours. She asked me to give you her best."

"She did?" Nie asked jokingly.

Scratching his head, Xiaochuan smiled and changed the subject.

"Do you think that sheet of paper means something?"

"At the very least, it means that the same person killed Hu Guohao and Hong Yiming, and the pair of murders were meticulously planned and carried out. The killer is very smart."

Xiaochuan was pleased that things were starting to become clear, even though there were still too many puzzles, too many questions.

"Also, the death notice was clearly meant to frighten the victims and make them feel like they were being hunted down. This fits the profile of revenge killings."

"Revenge killings," Xiaochuan repeated.

"Yes, but only if my analysis is correct." Nie paused and, with a look at Xiaochuan, continued, "And if so, the key to cracking the case is to decipher the motive for revenge."

"Decipher?"

"Yes. Not to find actual clues, but to figure out what the red tower mountain symbol and the string of numbers mean. Oh, and that strange wreath. They're all there in front of our eyes, and we have to find out what message they were intended to convey, what secrets lay behind them. I'm pretty sure the victims knew before they died."

"So how do we go about deciphering them?"

"I have to leave in three days, so I won't be much help."

"Will you still follow the case after you return to Sichuan?" Xiaochuan was obviously disappointed Nie had to leave.

"Of course," Nie said. "I'll follow up, so we'll know what happened, and I have to write a story about it. So don't forget to share any new information with me."

"No problem." Xiaochuan knew that Nie wanted an exclusive, a trait shared by every reporter worth his salt.

"Did you drive here?" Nie asked.

"I did."

"Then come with me."

"Where to?"

"You'll see. You want to decipher the symbols, don't you?"

They climbed into Xiaochuan's blue-and-white patrol car and headed for Shennan Road. It wasn't far, Nie told him, and they were there in no time—Shenzhen Book City. It was getting late, but the place was crowded with book buyers and browsers.

Xiaochuan parked behind the building and they rode the elevator to the second floor, where they passed stands for new books and bestsellers, before reaching the Economics section.

"We need to look for books on the study of Chinese characters, so why don't we spread out?" Nie said.

"Under what category?"

"Cultural education or ancient books."

Xiaochuan nodded and disappeared around a corner.

Nie searched through half the section, but all he saw were books on economics and business management, in addition to history and biographies. Finally, he asked a salesclerk, and learned that books about language and Chinese characters were on the fourth floor, while the third floor housed literature, children's books, and educational material.

He went up to the fourth floor, which was packed; cookbooks and books on cosmetics and fashion had been given the choice spots, next to special shelves for books on technology and computer science. Medical books were in the back. Surrounded by people and books, he felt lost, until he spotted "Language and Chinese Characters" in a neglected corner, where he picked up a copy of *On the Origin of Chinese Characters,* a second-century treatise on the Chinese writing system by Xu Shen.

Since it was quiet there, he sat down and patiently flipped through the pages, eventually finding the character he was looking for—"山," for "mountain"—in a style that looked a bit like the symbol on the sheets of paper. The annotation read: "Vent means to vent the qi / myriads of objects and creatures are born / there is a tall rock." Old Mr. Xu should have been annotating the meaning of "山" but Nie was confused; what did venting the qi have to do with the mountains?

The writing style, or font, to use modern lingo, Small Li, was promulgated by the First Emperor of China after uniting the country. Nie recalled a class in classical Chinese in college, in which the teacher had told them about the origin of the Small Li style and its counterpart, Big Li. The two were similar, though Small Li was less ornate and more picturelike; he assumed that an earlier style would have an even greater pictorial look, so what came before the Small Li? It must have been the writings on oracle bones, ancient writing carved on tortoise shells and the shoulder bones of oxen.

So off to look up oracle bones. At the information desk the staff located a book entitled *A History of Chinese Oracle Bone Studies.*

In the chapter "Common Examples of Oracle Bones" was a list of frequently used characters. And that was where Nie Feng found a listing for the character for fire, "火," in three different styles. The first had a rising middle that made it resemble a tower, while the second, Nie was shocked to see, was nearly identical to the symbol on the sheets of paper.

Just to be sure, he took out his copy of the paper from Hu's case file. They were virtually identical. So, that's it! The symbol was not "mountain," but "fire."

After wearing out all that shoe leather, figuratively speaking, to decipher the meaning of the symbol, suddenly there it was, right in front of him.

"I've found it!" he yelled out happily.

He quickly clammed up when he noticed the curious looks from shoppers around him.

Naturally cautious, he was struggling to find corroborative or contradictory examples when his cell rang. It was Xiaochuan.

"Hey, Mr. Nie, which floor are you on?" The young officer sounded excited.

"The fourth. By the shelves on language and Chinese characters."

"I think I've found the book you're looking for. It's called *The Story of Chinese Characters*."

"Is it good?"

"Simple and easy to read."

"Great. Come on up."

Xiaochuan had found an ancient pictographic version of "火" that resembled the one in Nie's book, but with a curved bottom, which on closer examination, looked like a Chinese ingot, a lifelike pictorial illustration of flames.

Nie Feng was visibly excited when he scrutinized the ancient pictograph for "fire."

"You're a bloodhound today!" Nie praised the young officer, who blushed. Xiaochuan could not suppress his excitement as he asked Nie how he'd thought of finding clues in the oracle bone texts.

"I got an inspiration from Officer Yao's comment of 'red tower mountain.'"

"The symbol refers to fire, but I don't believe Hu Guohao or Hong Yiming ever studied oracle bone texts," Xiaochuan said. "So how would they have understood the killer's meaning?"

"Some things are actually quite simple, but we often overthink them," Nie said. "This symbol is a good example. The killer drew a simple picture to indicate fire. If fire had a special meaning to someone, then that person would immediately have seen it as a representation of fire. For anyone else, it could have meant almost anything."

Energized by their success, Nie Feng and Xiaochuan happily walked downstairs.

"What an incredible, wonderful discovery!" Xiaochuan was beaming.

"It's like finding the key to solving the case."

"The key to the case, you think so?"

"Yes. Now that we know what the pictograph means, it will lead us in the right direction."

They walked up to the counter, where Nie paid for the two books.

"So this means that fire is connected to the deaths of the two real estate tycoons." Xiaochuan guessed.

"I think so, and maybe the killer as well."

"The killer?"

"I'm just guessing." Nie said cautiously. "If time allows, I'd like to conduct another experiment."

"Need my help?"

"Not on this one. The police have been fully mobilized, so you're busy enough." He paused and thought before continuing, "Don't share our secret with your Mr. Cui, not just yet."

"Why not?"

"He might not buy it."

"All right, I won't tell him."

— 3 —

The next afternoon.

Zhou Zhengxing exited the Landmark compound in a black Audi. A black VW parked across the street fell in behind him. The VW was driven by Zheng Yong, with another officer in the passenger seat, both in street clothes.

"Chief, this is Squad One," Zheng whispered into his walkie-talkie. "The target is on the move."

"Don't lose him," Cui said on the other end.

"Yes, sir."

Zheng sped up and caught up with the Audi as it headed toward Shennan Road.

Twenty minutes later, a red BMW drove out of the Landmark compound; Zhu Mei-feng was at the wheel.

Across the street, a white van started up to follow the BMW.

"Chief, this is Squad Two. The phoenix has left its cage. I repeat, the phoenix has left its cage."

"Got it. Don't lose her."

"We won't."

Half an hour later, the black Audi drove into the Municipal Government compound and stopped in front of the administrative building. Zhou Zhengxing got out and entered the building, to conduct business apparently. His driver drove over to the parking lot, turned off the engine, and waited.

"Chief, Squad One reporting. Target arrived at the Municipal Government Building."

Zheng Yong parked across the street to stake out the location.

"Keep tabs on him, and don't leave." Team Leader Cui was at the command center in the Y District Public Security Office.

"Yes, sir."

Ten minutes later Squad Two called in.

"Chief, Squad Two reporting. The phoenix has returned to her nest," meaning Zhu Mei-feng was back in her beauty salon.

"I see. Stay with her." Cui sounded disappointed.

"Chief, this is Squad Three. Target is on the move." Xiaochuan.

Cui picked up his walkie-talkie.

"Good. Don't lose him." His voice was higher this time.

Xiaochuan's target was Zhong Tao, in a black Buick, leaving the compound.

Xiaochuan and Yao Li, in a white van, fell in behind the Buick as it traveled down Shennan East Road, passed the Opera House, the News Plaza, and the Municipal Government compound, before turning south on Shangbu Road. Xiaochuan closed to within a distance of thirty meters.

The Buick turned onto Nanyuan Road and stopped in front of an upscale coffee shop. Zhong parked his car and went inside. Xiaochuan pulled up outside a restaurant across the street and observed the coffee shop with Yao Li. The sign above the door read Sicily Café.

"Chief, Squad Three reporting. Target entered a coffee shop on Nanyuan Road; looks like he's meeting someone."

"Got it. I want to know who he's meeting."

"Will do."

Xiaochuan fixed his eyes on the coffee shop.

The car was like a steamer on that hot afternoon, so Xiaochuan cranked the window down a bit. About ten minutes later, a familiar figure appeared in their field of vision. The man was strolling along as if on springs, with a devil-may-care attitude. The green T-shirt, beige baseball cap, and white cloth sack with red straps were unmistakable.

"What's he doing here?" Yao Li muttered. He was about to enter the coffee shop.

"Ah, I see," Xiaochuan said as he dialed Nie's cell.

"Hey, Nie Feng, it's me, Xiaochuan. I'm in a van across the street."

"Oh." Nie stopped, turned to look, and said, "I see you."

"Did you ask Zhong Tao to meet you here? Need any help?"

"Call me in twenty minutes," Nie whispered into his cell. "Say you've got something for me." He hung up and walked into the coffee shop.

Dark red curtains hung in front of tall rectangular windows beneath a domed roof. There were two levels, both tastefully decorated. The bottom level was divided into eight cozy rooms with homey satin-covered sofas, circular rattan tables, and European-style desk lamps. Labels and logos, ads, and maps for coffees from around the world decorated one wall. A variety of coffeemakers adorned a wooden counter, which, set against two large orange chandeliers, gave the place a special feel.

A waitress in a white apron came up as soon as he entered.

"Your friend's waiting for you upstairs, sir."

Nie looked up to see Zhong nodding at him.

A wooden staircase abutted the redbrick wall facing the entrance. Photos of movie stars from around the world covered the wall. Nie held on to the metal railing as he climbed the stairs.

The upstairs section was quiet, with an unobstructed view of the seats downstairs. Nie sat down and commented, "Nice place."

"My college friends sometimes meet here, but I don't come very often," Zhong said.

Nie had called him earlier that morning, telling him that he was due back to Sichuan in two days and would like to see him before he left. Zhong quickly agreed and picked the place to meet. He seemed to be in a good mood.

"What would you like, Mr. Nie?"

"Whatever."

"Their Blue Mountain is the best."

"I don't care for it, too sour for my taste."

"A bit tart, but rich and aromatic with a long finish. That's precisely why people like it." Zhong sounded like a connoisseur.

Nie ordered a mocha, while for Zhong, it was Blue Mountain. The waitress quickly brought their coffee in green frosted cups trailed by enticing fragrance.

"I see you like mocha," Zhong observed. "It has a strong, rich flavor."

"I know nothing about coffee, so I pretty much close my eyes and point," Nie said as he added milk and sugar, stirred the coffee with the tiny spoon, and took a sip. It was indeed rich and strong. "When I'm busy, I drink Maxwell House instant."

"Good to the last drop." Zhong smiled as he recited the famous line.

Nie also smiled. Zhong seemed to be in an unusual mood. Gone was his serious, dour demeanor, and he was more talkative. Nie had no idea why, but he felt a closeness to Zhong; maybe it was because they'd attended the same college.

Zhong picked up his cup, now with a light golden sheen, and took a sip; it was perfect.

"You don't add milk or sugar?" Nie asked.

"The best way to drink the best coffee is unadulterated. Some people even insist upon brewing it when the water temperature is exactly ninety-two degrees Celsius, saying that it brings out the natural coffee flavor and releases the beans' soul. But that's hard to do. I'm OK as long as the water is above ninety degrees." Zhong took another sip before continuing, "I don't use cream or sugar, so I can get the richest flavor possible. It's a little bitter at first, but after savoring its lingering taste, you realize what it means to say 'after the bitter comes the sweet.' Oftentimes, life is like a cup of coffee with no added sugar; you must taste the bitter in order to enjoy the sweet taste later."

Nie Feng found Zhong Tao's ability to connect coffee to life interesting. In his view, this older fellow alum appeared to be outstanding in every respect—talent, personality, taste, and intelligence. In addition to the humor typical of most Sichuanese, he seemed shrouded in intrigue and exuded masculine charm. Could such a likeable, exceptional individual be a killer? Nie wasn't sure, unless there had been some sort of blood feud with his boss.

What secrets were hidden behind the splendid façade of the Landmark Building? Nie was reminded of his last visit to the place.

"I heard harmonica music the last time I was at Landmark."

"Harmonica?" Zhong asked. "Do you remember the tune?"

"I heard it in the lobby. It sounded familiar, but I can't recall its name." Nie began to hum. "I'm a bit off, but it sounded like this." He was embarrassed.

"It sounds like 'Apricot in the Rain,'" Zhong said casually.

"You're right. It did sound like 'Apricot in the Rain.' I heard that at C University's anniversary ceremony."

"Someone said you're also a graduate from C University," Zhong said affably.

"Yes. I was a journalism major, class of '88."

"I wrote the lyrics to the song," Zhong said lightly. "A zhiqing musician from the Sichuan Conservatory wrote the music."

"No wonder it sounds so moving."

"So you're easily moved." Zhong laughed, with a friendly mocking tone.

"You can interpret 'Apricot in the Rain' two ways." Nie felt like showing off. "One comes from *The Thousand Poems,* which goes, 'The apricot rain fell on my clothes, barely wetting them / the willow wind blew past my face, a mild chill.' It depicts early spring, when apricots bloom amid a fine rain."

Zhong listened wordlessly.

"But I like the other interpretation better," Nie continued. "'After a gust of wind, the petals flutter down from the trees—'"

"'And all we have left are the setting sun and the apricot rain blanketing the ground.'" Zhong picked up the line from the song.

"It's a beautiful line," Nie gushed.

"But do you understand the true essence of the scene?" Zhong asked, his casual tone tinged with a hint of sorrow. Nie held his tongue.

Zhong looked over Nie's head, his gaze cast into the distance, which gave Nie a feeling that the man had experienced many trials.

Or maybe there was something almost wild about him. The silence in the room was stifling, despite the easy-listening saxophone music.

"Were you admitted into C University after returning from the countryside?" Nie was hoping to learn about Zhong's background.

"That's right. I was one of the lucky ones to have a shot at college after 1977, when the entrance exams were reinstated."

"I heard that many Chengdu youths were sent to Yunnan as part of the construction corps."

"That was where the students from my high school went."

"Oh, where in Yunnan?"

"Lanjiang."

"Which part of Yunnan is that?"

"Ever been to Yunnan?"

"No."

"So you wouldn't know even if I told you." Zhong seemed reluctant to continue. "It's on the border with Burma."

"I guess the zhiqing have lots of stories to tell."

"The young have no regrets, as they say, but the price was too high." That was all Zhong said.

The waitress came over with hot towels.

"May I take a picture with you?" Nie Feng asked abruptly.

"Sure." Zhong did not hesitate. So Nie took out his Pantex and handed it to the waitress.

"Would you take our picture?"

They posed by the table, Zhong standing with his arms crossed and Nie smiling. The waitress clicked, a light flashed, and Nie's cell phone rang.

"This is Xiaochuan. I went to the Nanyuan Guesthouse, but you weren't there."

"Ah, I'm at the Sicily Café, chatting with Mr. Zhong."

"I've got what you're looking for. Want me to bring it over?"

"If it's not too much trouble."

Nie closed his phone and said to Zhong, "That was Officer Wang; he's bringing me some material."

"About the case, I assume," Zhong said casually, though he seemed to be referring to something else. It piqued Nie's interest, so he decided to go ahead with his hunch.

"I have one more question. Maybe you can help me."

"I hope it's not an IQ test," Zhong joked.

Throughout their conversation, Zhong had treated him like a younger brother, open, friendly, and personable, which made Nie feel guilty about what he had in mind.

"It's a psych quiz." Nie scratched his head to cover up his awkwardness before fishing out a folded piece of paper from his tote. It was a copy of the one he'd found at Book City, with the two ancient pictographs. The left one was covered up.

"Can you tell what this pictograph is?" He pointed at the uncovered one, an ingot, but his eyes were Zhong's face.

Zhong paused, but then he smiled. "An ingot."

Disappointed, Nie prodded, "Try again."

"Oh," Zhong said. "A mountain, then."

Disappointment.

"I'm slow. That was the wrong answer, wasn't it?" Zhong said.

With a goofy smile, Nie spread the paper out to show both symbols.

"Now look again, and tell me what the right one is."

Zhong's eyes swept back and forth between the two until he hit upon it. "Ah, I see. The right one is fire and the left is the mountain."

"This time you got it right."

"You can't tell unless you can compare them." Zhong sounded pleased with himself, as Nie, playing with the paper, was unsure how much he could believe Zhong.

Xiaochuan entered the coffee shop in street clothes, with several magazines and a large manila envelope tucked under his arm. He looked around until he saw Nie and Zhong, and climbed the wooden staircase.

"Have a seat, Officer Wang," Zhong greeted him.

"Thank you." Xiaochuan said. "Sorry to bother you." He sat down and handed him copies of *Investigative Reference*.

"Chief Wu told me to give you these." They had, in fact, been left in the police car in case the officers needed to refer to them.

"Please thank Chief Wu for me," Nie said to Xiaochuan. "I was giving Mr. Zhong a psych test. He got both symbols correctly."

Xiaochuan could see what Nie was getting at, so he took out several 8 x 10 police photos of Hu's body, one of which was a close-up of his chest.

"There's an intriguing symbol here, too." Xiaochuan pointed to the scratch marks under the nipple, and turned to Zhong.

"Mr. Zhong, what do you think this is?"

Nie was watching Zhong.

"I can't say." Zhong was cool as a cucumber.

"They're scratch marks on Hu Guohao's chest," Xiaochuan said.

"So? What does that have to do with me?" Zhong asked, still calm and composed.

"Nothing. I just thought maybe you could tell us what it is."

"Sorry, I can't help you," Zhong said, seeming to lose interest.

Then, Nie, who had been watching closely, took out a book from his tote, *A History of Chinese Oracle Bone Studies*. "I'm pretty sure this mark is the same as the symbol for fire." He pointed to a page in the book.

Zhong's expression seemed to change momentarily while an imperceptible smile creased the corners of his mouth.

"Why would the symbol for fire appear on Hu's chest?" Xiaochuan's eyes bored into Zhong's face.

"How should I know?" Zhong said.

"I imagine that 'fire' must mean something special to the person who planned the murder." Then Nie raised his voice: "Either that or the victim had a fear of fire."

Zhong's eyes suddenly bulged and his face turned an ugly dark red. At that instant, Nie almost thought he saw fires raging in

Zhong's eyes, and he could tell that Zhong was trying hard to control his anger.

He quickly recovered and said to Nie Feng: "You have quite an imagination."

Xiaochuan exchanged a look with Nie and got to his feet.

"Sorry, but I have to go now."

"So do I," Nie Feng said as he stood up. "Good-bye, Mr. Zhong."

"I'm waiting for a couple of friends. So good-bye." Zhong shook hands with Nie. He had a firm grip.

Nie then walked out with the policeman and headed to the van across the street.

"Hard work, Mr. Nie," Yao Li said as she handed him a bottle of iced black tea.

"Thanks." Nie took the tea, but before taking a sip began talking about the visit to the café. Xiaochuan thought that Zhong did look a bit out of sorts, but he might not have known the significance of "fire." Nie, on the other hand, believed that Zhong knew more than he'd let on, or he wouldn't have looked so shaken and angry. Besides, his alibi was simply too perfect.

"He looked the same that day at the Landmark Building," Xiaochuan said casually, but it struck Nie as not necessarily an innocent comment.

"Which day was that?" Nie asked.

"When Officer Yao and I went to Landmark the second time. It must have been Wednesday, June twenty-eighth."

"Can you describe the visit?"

"A Boeing 747 was on its final approach outside the window, coming in quite low. When we checked with Huangtian Airport, we found that it was a China Southern flight, and that no one on the plane had any connection with Zhong Tao. In any case, we came up empty. But then Officer Yao recalled another scene—scraps of paper floating down from a building across the way, in the direction of Zhong's gaze."

"Scraps of paper? Are you sure?"

"I must say, it was weird," Yao Li said.

Nie gave the new information some thought before asking: "Where were the three of you sitting at the time?"

Xiaochuan told him.

"What time was it?"

"Five minutes till six."

"How can you be so precise?"

"I glanced up at the wall clock."

"Hmm." Nie looked at his wristwatch and sat quietly thinking. "About the same time as now," he muttered to himself.

"Let's go," he said. "Let's take another look."

Xiaochuan had to stay to keep an eye on Zhong, so Nie Feng hailed a taxi and went to the Landmark building with Yao Li.

Ah-ying was surprised to see them.

"Officer Yao, is there something I can do for you?"

"Mr. Nie and I would like to see Mr. Zhong," Yao said.

"He went out this afternoon."

"Could we wait for him in his office?"

"Sure," Ah-ying said, and asked someone to open Zhong's door. She went in with them.

"Would you like me to call and ask him to return?"

"No need," Nie said. "Oh, and please don't mention that we were here."

"I see." Ah-ying nodded, and seemed to understand what was going on. "Please make yourselves at home." She turned and left the office.

Nie walked over to stand behind Zhong's desk.

"That's it. That's where he was standing," Yao Li said.

He looked to the southwest and saw a red sunset outside. It was like bright red blood, or a raging fire.

He was speechless from the sight. Before him was a sea of fire. Now he knew—Zhong had seen fiery burning clouds.

"That must have been like fire. Fire," Nie said.

EIGHT

Tip of the Iceberg

— 1 —

That night, Zheng Yong and his Squad One partner kept watch on Zhou Zhengxing.

At ten o'clock, Zhou arrived at the Opera House. He got out and his driver drove off. Zheng assumed that Zhou was there to see a performance, but he didn't even enter the grand structure. Instead he hailed a taxi, climbed in, and headed down Shennan East Road.

Zheng and his partner took off after the taxi. Under the evening sky, flickering neon lights turned the city of Shenzhen into a place of prosperity and splendor.

The taxi turned abruptly onto Jianshe Road, heading south toward the train station. Zheng Yong stayed with Zhou all the way to the end of Jianshe Road, where the Yellow Lo Wu Control Point Building by the train station came into view. To their surprise, instead of driving into the station, the taxi stopped in front of a brightly lit building at the intersection.

Zheng looked up and saw that it was the Shenzhen Emperor Hotel.

Zhou Zhengxing, wearing a brown sport coat, stepped out of the taxi and was greeted by a pair of doormen in red uniforms as he walked into the lobby, his steps light and springy. Zheng snapped off a few quick shots of Zhou entering the hotel, then told his partner to park across the street while he jumped out of the car, raced across the street, and ran into the spacious, splendidly decorated lobby.

"This is official business," he said to a tall woman at the registration desk who appeared to be the manager, showing her his badge.

"May I ask what this is about?" she asked.

"The man in a brown sport coat who just came in. Which room is he staying in?"

"Oh, you mean Mr. Zhou of Landmark. He's not staying here."

"Is he here to meet someone?"

"Landmark has a business suite here."

"What's the room number?"

"It's a luxury suite, 1618."

"Thank you."

Energized by a premonition, Zheng walked outside and got back into the car. "Something may be up tonight," he told his partner, barely able to conceal his glee.

At that moment, a red BMW glided over from the opposite direction and stopped at the hotel entrance. The driver stepped out, a woman in an orange evening dress, holding a handbag. She had a nice figure and a pretty face, even in profile. A valet came up, took her key, and drove her car to the underground parking lot.

Zheng had an unobstructed view of her face as she turned to enter the hotel, and nearly cried out in surprise.

It was Landmark's current chairwoman, Hu Guohao's widow, Zhu Mei-feng. Luckily, his partner snapped off a few shots before Zhu disappeared inside. Zheng picked up his walkie-talkie and, like a hound in a foxhunt, reported the latest development.

"Chief, this is Squad One. Target entered Emperor Hotel room 1618 a few minutes ago. We've had an unexpected sighting—Phoenix has just flown into the hotel."

"Got it. Don't lose them. I don't want any screwups."

"Understood."

Before he finished, Zheng saw a white van drive up and park a few meters away. It was Squad Two. He rolled down the window and signaled to them; both surveillance teams were elated when they realized why they were meeting here.

Now they knew that something was definitely up and they could barely control their excitement. All eyes were on the hotel entrance.

The residents of Shenzhen, a city that never slept, were obsessed with merrymaking and pleasure seeking. Traffic flowed up and down the streets as music lingered in the night sky. The police spent the night cooped up in their vehicles till 5:06 the following morning, when, in the early light, they saw Zhou Zhengxing come out and get in a taxi, which headed in the direction he'd come from the day before. About fifteen minutes later, Zhu Mei-feng's red BMW emerged from the underground garage and quietly drove away.

Eight a.m. The officers, including those who had stayed up all night, gathered in the conference room to discuss this explosive development. Team Leader Cui presided, with Bureau Chief Wu in attendance. The room brimmed with high spirits; it was as if the officers were soldiers who had just taken an enemy fort.

Zheng had obtained a surveillance video from the hotel and was playing it on a big screen. It showed all the activity in the sixteenth-floor corridor from ten o'clock the night before till six o'clock that morning. A dozen pairs of eyes were glued to the screen.

—A man in a brown sport coat opened the door to 1618 with a key card and entered. The timer in the lower right corner showed JULY 7 22:28. Ten minutes later, a woman in an orange evening dress opened the door with a key card and went inside. The police checked the faces carefully; the man was Zhou Zhengxing and the woman Zhu Mei-feng.

—July 8, five o'clock that morning, Zhou walked out of room

1618. Ten minutes later, the door opened again and Zhu emerged. She closed the door behind her and walked to the elevator.

No one had expected an affair between Zhu Mei-feng and Zhou Zhengxing. The news injected a jubilant air into the room.

"This is a breakthrough," Chief Wu said. "Nearly two weeks have passed since the June twenty-fifth murder, and even though we've zeroed in on a few suspects, we haven't been able to find any solid evidence. In other words, we've been spinning our wheels. Then two days ago, Hong Yiming was poisoned, which further complicated our case. I know you've all been under a lot of pressure, but so am I. So this unexpected development from last night could be just what we need to move beyond this impasse. What's your view on this, Dajun?"

Team Leader Cui was clearly energized.

"I agree with Chief Wu. This truly is a breakthrough. First, though, I want to thank everyone for working so hard over the past few days. We've been stumbling in the dark since Hu's death, but this discovery of a secret relationship between Zhou Zheng-xing and Zhu Mei-feng should go a long way toward providing some answers. For instance, in addition to knowing why Hu's body had algae from the water in Nan'ao, we now have an idea why Zhu reacted so coolly to Hu's death, and how Zhou could so easily take over Landmark's Board. All this was carefully planned, and it worked perfectly." Cui lit a cigarette and took a long drag before continuing:

"First, it shows that Zhou had two motives to commit the murder—power and romance. Eliminate Hu Guohao, and he would gain the long coveted position of Landmark CEO, and get Zhu Mei-feng in the bargain."

"So what role has she played?" Zheng Yong asked.

"Given her relationship with Zhou, it's very likely they planned it together. She was the prime beneficiary of Hu's death and was resentful over Hu's infidelity. So it's only natural that she might plot her husband's murder with her lover."

"I want to hear what everyone has to say," Chief Wu said.

Cui's comments were based on unassailable logic, and were persuasive; the officers all spoke their minds, but were generally in agreement with Cui's analysis and assessment.

Yao Li, who was known to have her own ideas and was not too timid to express them, spoke up. "I agree with Team Leader Cui that Zhou and Zhu could have planned the murder together. But I don't think we've solved everything, especially when we consider all the twists and turns the case has taken over the past two weeks."

"So tell us what remains unsolved," Cui said as he handed a cigarette to Zheng Yong.

"I'm still trying to figure out why Hu's briefcase showed up at the Nan'ao Elementary School. The Nan'ao Police Station talked to the school's security guard, who said he did not see Hu come on campus. So, personally, I don't think we know where Hu was murdered. Also, we've yet to identify the woman who ordered the strange wreath."

That got everyone thinking.

"And what was the motivation for killing Hong Yiming?"

"Come on, everyone, share your views. Don't hold back. We'll have better results if we put our heads together," Chief Wu said encouragingly.

"I have something to add," Xiaochuan said. "There's one major question, and that is, why did Hu Guohao and Hong Yiming both receive those paper notes? We haven't given this enough thought. Mr. Nie said two days ago that this could be the key to solving both cases."

"That *Western Sun* fellow again, still shooting off his mouth."

Someone snickered, maybe laughing at Cui's mocking comment, or maybe laughing at his mistake.

"When does Mr. Nie return to Sichuan?" Chief Wu asked.

"Tomorrow," Xiaochuan replied.

"Hmm. A journalist might be able to see more than us professional investigators. Thinking outside the box, as they say. I think we should consider what *Western Sun* has to say."

Now everyone was laughing.

"What? Did I say say something wrong?"

"It's *Western Sunshine*," Xiaochuan said.

"Oh." Wu laughed with the others before turning thoughtful. "Indeed. We now have two directions of investigation before us— one, find out if Zhou and Zhu planned the murder together, and two, find out if Hu and Hong were murdered for the same reason. It's important to determine which one to follow."

The room went quiet; the officers were either considering both possibilities or they simply could not make up their minds. Finally Cui said: "I think we need to follow up on both."

"That'll work, too." Chief Wu nodded.

"With what we discovered last night, Zhou could be the key to it all," Cui said, exuding a bit of confidence.

"Bring him in then," Wu said with a determined slap on the table.

"There's something else," Zheng added. "Last night we thought we saw another car following Zhu Mei-feng."

"What kind of car?" Cui asked.

"A date-red VW Santana. It was tailing Squad Two's car. And when Zhu Mei-feng left the hotel, it followed her."

"Did you get the plate number?"

"We did. It was a Guangdong plate, B—XX118."

"Find out who owns the car."

— 2 —

That same afternoon. The police issued a formal summons for Zhou Zhengxing.

Zhou was "asked" to meet with the police in a small room on the sixth floor of the Y District Public Security Bureau. Cui Dajun, Xiaochuan, and Yao Li, all in uniform and unsmiling, sat in a row behind a brown desk. Zhou, seated three feet away, hardly resembled the carefree, springy image on the surveillance videotape from the night before.

Team Leader Cui asked about his connection to the case. At first Zhou was curt, with short answers, probably unhappy over the police summons; he had not wanted to come, but Cui was insistent and unyielding on the phone:

"Mr. Zhou, this is Cui Dajun, Team Leader of the Y District Public Security Bureau. Right. We have a few questions regarding the deaths of Hu Guohao and Hong Yiming, and would like you to come down to the district office this afternoon."

"I've been awfully busy these past few days. I'm afraid I won't be able to make it."

"These are homicides I'm talking about. I'm sure you understand how serious that is. If you won't cooperate with the police, we'll be forced to take drastic measures."

What Cui meant by drastic measures was the possibility that he would request a bench warrant to force him to report to the police. The Public Security Code for criminal cases stipulates that suspects who are summoned but fail to appear without good reason can be brought in forcefully to be interrogated at specified locations. In other words, the police would be sent to bring the individual in, and if he resisted, he'd be handcuffed.

"Is that so? I didn't say I refuse to cooperate with the police." In the end, Zhou came over soon after hanging up.

"Did you go to Nan'ao Elementary School the day Hu Guohao was killed?"

"I did, in the afternoon. I was there for a computer donation ceremony. I spent the night with my mother at my family home in Shuitou Village. You can check with neighbors."

"But we found his briefcase on the school's athletic field. How can you explain that?"

"I didn't see him that day, and I have no idea how his briefcase ended up there." He sounded as if he might be lying, but he could have been telling the truth.

"And where were you between twelve and one the next morning?"

"Your officers have checked that out. I was sleeping at my mother's house."

"Any witnesses?"

"My mother."

"One's mother doesn't count. That's common legal knowledge; you should know that."

Zhou looked embarrassed, but quickly recovered. "What proof do you have that I wasn't there?"

Touché! Cui changed the subject.

"The medical examiner has proved that Hu was drowned at Nan'ao." He watched Zhou's face very carefully. "And you were in Nan'ao that day. Is that a coincidence?"

"Wasn't his body found at Lesser Meisha?"

"Lesser Meisha was where the body was dumped. We know he was killed in Nan'ao."

"In Nan'ao?" Zhou looked genuinely surprised.

"Yes. And, we also know that you and Hu had not been getting along well lately. You wanted to take over as CEO."

"Office rumor." Zhou cracked a smile. "Things like that happen in every company. How could you believe that?"

"But someone heard you and Hu in a heated argument the day before he died."

"There were things he and I disagreed on, but only about running the business. It was nothing out of the ordinary."

"Mr. Zhou, were the problems between you and Hu limited to business?" Cui dragged out his voice.

"What are you implying?"

"What am I implying? You're the one who should know that."

Zhou's face stiffened, as if sensing a trap.

"Where were you between ten last night and five this morning?"
Cui decided to go on the offensive. Zhou froze and began to stammer, "That—that's my personal business."

"Oh, on personal business?" Cui said. "In luxury suite 1618 at the Emperor Hotel?"

Zhou's face fell; his swarthy complexion began to turn purple.

Cui decided to launch the fatal assault and signaled Xiaochuan to start the video. Xiaochuan turned on a player they'd set up ahead of time, and the hotel corridor appeared on a small screen against the wall. He fast-forwarded to where Zhou was seen walking into suite 1618. He fast-forwarded again, this time to show Zhu Mei-feng, in her orange evening dress, opening the door and entering the same room.

Zhou looked completely defeated; he leaned back in the chair with his eyes closed.

"How do you explain this incredible scene, Mr. Zhou?" Cui asked pointedly.

Zhou was cornered. "I can't deny that." He squirmed in his chair. "You must promise me one thing."

"What's that?"

"You have to promise not to make this public." He'd lost his composure but not his dignity. "My wife mustn't know about this," he pleaded softly, "nor the company employees."

"They won't." Cui nodded and gave his word.

Zhou then told them about his affair with Zhu Mei-feng.

"When did it start?"

"Over two years ago."

"Haven't you heard the saying, 'thou shall not fool around with your friend's wife'?" Cui said, taking the moral high ground. "Hu Guohao might not have been your friend, but you'd worked together for nearly ten years. Don't you feel bad about sleeping with his wife?"

Zhou's response shocked them all.

"You have no idea what kind of person Hu Guohao was. He

had many women, too many to count, actually." His contempt was striking.

Xiaochuan and Yao exchanged looks.

Zhou went on to tell them about Hu Guohao's unsavory sexual escapades. Hu, in a word, was a sexual predator. Whenever and wherever he saw a pretty woman, he had to have her; but once he was tired of her, he'd toss her aside and find another. With his enviable wealth and expansive nature, few women were immune to his charms.

"There's a secret door in Hu's office that leads to an opulent room. Supposedly for him to rest, it was actually his pleasure den. Ah-ying was the only one who knew about it."

"Then how did you know about it?" Xiaochuan asked.

"He let it slip one night when he'd had too much to drink."

"Does Zhu Mei-feng know about this?"

"No. She's suffered enough already."

Zhou then described the delicate relationship among Hu, Zhu, and himself. He'd known Zhu Mei-feng ten years earlier, when she was working at the White Rose Karaoke Dance Bar. Barely in her twenties and a graduate of the conservatory, she was smart and pretty—a dazzling beauty, in fact. As the top singer at White Rose, she had many rich suitors, but managed to keep her innocence even though she'd come from a poor family. Zhou had visited White Rose a few times, but had always admired her from a distance. The romance between them began in Nan'ao. Once, on a day tour to Nan'ao, she'd passed out while diving in Xichong. Zhou, who was fishing on the reef, dove in when he heard people calling for help. Having grown up by the ocean, he was an excellent swimmer who could stay underwater for several minutes. She was one step from being a mermaid when he fished her out of the water.

Though it had the flavor of a rescued "damsel in distress" tale, Zhou recounted the incident emotionally. They soon fell in love, and she became his best friend, since he was attached to his wife and told Zhu they could not marry; she was OK with that.

Two years later, Hu Guohao showed up and stole her away. Hu was generous with his money and a determined hunter. Each time he went to White Rose, he first sent over a large bouquet of white roses. At first she was not won over, having sensed a coarseness barely masked by his expansive demeanor, something typical of the nouveau riche. But then her mother experienced kidney failure and needed a large sum of money for a transplant. Having just suffered a tremendous business loss, Zhou was unable to help. Hu Guohao, the newest tycoon and Zhou's biggest competitor, heard about Zhu's problem and quietly paid for her mother's operation. Then he made arrangements for her brother to study in Canada, following that up with a promise to marry her. Wanting her to be happy, Zhou decided to end the affair, even though Hu would not have been able to marry Zhu Mei-feng if not for his wealth. Ultimately, Zhu was the reason Zhou and Hu became partners in their ventures.

Zhu had been a good wife who'd given in to Hu's every whim when first married. Later, when she discovered the truth about his many women, she stuck with him despite the deep hurt. She'd always considered him her savior and had tried to reason with him, but to no avail. Nothing she said or did could affect Hu's natural inclinations, so she simply gave up and changed into a different person. She never confronted or argued with him, and turned a blind eye to his affairs. Perhaps out of a sense of guilt, Hu maintained a civil façade in public.

No one knew how much she suffered, until one day, a drunken Zhou revealed his undying love for her, and she fled back into his arms.

Zhou's open admission of his relationship with Zhu Mei-feng sounded credible, and when he finished, he smiled and crossed his legs, as if having shed a heavy burden.

But Cui was not finished. "Hu Guohao drowned on the Nan'ao coast and his briefcase turned up there." His gaze bored into Zhou's face. "You were in Nan'ao that day, and you and he had clear and serious conflicts of interest. Now you've come clean regarding your affair with his wife, maybe it's time to do the same in regard to the homicide."

"You can suspect me if you want, but what evidence do you have?" Zhou rebutted calmly.

That was the point. The police had no evidence indicating that he had committed the murder, and Zhou knew it. On the other hand, while the interview did not unravel the mystery at Nan'ao, they had learned of Hu Guohao's secret room, which could help them solve the case.

"We'll stop here today. If you need to leave Shenzhen, either for business or personal reasons, please let us know," Cui said.

"Sure." Zhou stood up and shook Cui's hand. "Good luck with your case."

Yao Li handed Zhou the interview transcript, which he signed, and then turned and walked out.

"Quite a guy, huh," Xiaochuan muttered.

"Hu Guohao first lost his wife, then his life," Yao Li said with a sigh. "Too bad."

Cui's reaction? "The Landmark waters run deeper than we thought."

— 3 —

The Landmark Building. Its glass curtain wall reflected a blinding light.

The police were back in Hu Guohao's office to see if there was indeed a secret room. There were five officers this time, led by Cui Dajun, with Xiaochuan, Yao Li, and two evidence technicians with their tool kits. They were all in uniform; the formality so unsettled Ah-ying that she reacted with nervous caution.

"For the purpose of our investigation, we need to check Hu Guohao's office," Cui said, while Yao showed Ah-ying a search warrant.

"Mr. Hu's old office now belongs to Ms. Zhu, our new Chair-woman of the Board."

"Is she in?" Cui asked.

"Landmark's affairs are being handled by the new CEO, Mr. Zhou. Elder Sister Zhu doesn't come in very often."

"Well, then, open the door for us. We'll notify Ms. Zhu of the results of our search."

Ah-ying took out a ring of keys and opened the door to the office. It looked the same as before, with hardly any trace of the new owner, a clear sign of Zhu Mei-feng's absence. The African crocodile was coated with dust. Cui took a look around. The enlarged photo of the Landmark Building on the center wall was still dominant, as were the trophies and award certificates in the glass display case. The walls were covered with textured material so seamlessly applied there was no hint of a door anywhere. Cui tried but failed to find it, so he turned to Ah-ying.

"Would you please open Mr. Hu's resting room?"

Caught by surprise, Ah-ying froze, looking unnaturally uncomfortable.

"We have credible evidence that there's a secret room behind these walls," Cui said.

Now that he'd forced her hand, she walked wordlessly to the glass case behind the desk and opened it. Then she moved the third trophy to reveal a small black button, which she touched gently; a hidden door in the wall soundlessly glided open.

Xiaochuan and Yao Li exchanged looks, barely able to conceal their surprise. Both were reminded of the secret code, "open sesame," in *The Arabian Nights*. Mr. Hu was quite ingenious.

The police officers entered what seemed like the pleasure dome of an Arabian sultan. It was a windowless suite; the bedroom was nearly thirty square meters in size, with thick metallic red curtains making it seem airtight. On the wall hung deer heads and Burmese swords, which were infused with intrigue in the dim yellow light. The suite was furnished with dark imported furniture and an entertainment cabinet edged with curved lines. The Thai wood bed was two meters wide, and on the wall above it hung an embroidered picture of a lascivious, naked woman, à la Goya's *The Nude Maja*. The room was more lavishly appointed than a five-star hotel suite, but lacked its elegance and style. The bathroom, too, was equipped with fancy imported fixtures and a spa tub. The gold-plated levers and faucets sparkled, giving it the patina of luxurious vulgarity.

What surprised the police were the mirrors that seemed to be everywhere—at the vanity, on the dresser, on the wall across from a desk, even behind the toilet—and all in carved frames. There was even one beside the marble vanity, a round mirror with a metal frame and a swing arm. When his curiosity got the better of him, Xiaochuan walked over to take a look, only to see his own face, now enlarged and puffy, staring back at him with a foolish grin. Every line and every blemish showed. Obviously, Mr. Hu had often studied his face in this mirror.

The room was supplied with a Sony VCR and DVD player. The police looked around the bedroom and the bathroom, but found nothing of interest, except more lavish details. Cui then went to open the closet; it was filled with men's casual clothes and gaudy women's underwear, as well as several pairs of Lacoste swimming trunks. He pushed the hangers aside. There it was—a steel gray wall safe; above the chrome handle was a dial pad.

"Can you open this?" he asked Ah-ying.

"No," Ah-ying said. "Only Mr. Hu knew the code." She turned and walked out.

"Give it a try," Cui said to one of the technicians, a lock specialist.

The technician opened his tool kit and took out a small box with an LCD screen. Then he donned a set of headphones, connected the electro heads, and worked on each number, turning a knob on the box. Soon with a beep, a number appeared on the screen. He repeated the process until he got all six numbers.

"There you are."

Cui punched the six numbers one by one and the steel door swung open.

The top shelf of the safe was filled with cash totaling 600,000 RMB, 150,000 Hong Kong dollars, and 20,000 US dollars. A small drawer lined with blue velveteen held gold necklaces, rings, and other types of women's jewelry. The technician took photos; Yao Li made notes of each item. The bottom shelf held four VCR tapes, a couple dozen DVDs, and dozens of Viagra pills. There was also a small wooden box that contained pictures of Hu and different women making love, each more graphic than the next. There was even a photo of group sex. They turned on the Sony player and put in a videotape. It turned out to be porn.

So Zhou Zhengxing had told the truth about Hu and all his women. Which meant that at least some of what Zhou told them was credible. But there was no clue as to how and why Hu had died.

"Who'd have thought that a high-ranking executive like Hu was actually a sex fiend," Xiaochuan said indignantly.

"A sexual predator," was Yao Li's comment.

As they were about to leave the secret room, Xiaochuan spotted something. He noticed that a framed photograph of Greater Meisha beach appeared to be lopsided, as if someone had touched it but failed to put it back right. He walked over, took down the photo, and turned it over on the desk. Then he carefully removed the cardboard backing

There were two photos. One, fitted against the glass, was a Greater Meisha beach scene; the other was tucked between the beach photo and the cardboard backing. He turned it over to reveal Hu Guohao and Ah-ying in a very intimate pose with what looked like the beach behind them (there were sand and coconut palms). A blanket on the sand indicated that it might have been taken in the fall. Hu was wearing a red swimsuit, with his arm around her waist. In a black-and-white swimsuit, she was smiling at the camera.

"A lovely couple," Yao said.

"We'll take the photo with us," Cui said.

Ah-ying should have gotten rid of the picture, but she hadn't. Why? Maybe it had been there first and the beach photo was put in later to cover it up. But why hadn't she removed or burned it?

Or maybe it was quite simple—she was too fond of being in the photo with Hu to part with it.

— 4 —

The Arrival Hall at Shenzhen's Huangtian Airport. Nie Feng was returning to Chengdu. Xiaochuan was there to say good-bye.

He'd purchased a discounted ticket, a little more expensive than a hard seat on the train.

"Where did you go yesterday?" Xiaochuan asked, holding Nie's bag for him.

"I went to Nan'ao. It's a beautiful fishing village."

"Too short a trip to take in the sights, I take it."

"You're right. I went to do a bit of investigating on my own," Nie said. "Nan'ao remains an important coordinate on the map of the case."

"Find anything interesting?"

"Not sure yet. But I did find something modestly worthwhile."

"We searched Hu Guohao's office yesterday afternoon. He had a secret room, his pleasure den."

Nie was reminded of the evasive look on Ah-ying's face when he asked her about a safe.

"Did Feng Xueying know about the secret room?"

"You mean Ah-ying, Hu's personal assistant?"

"Right."

"She did. In fact she opened the door for us," Xiaochuan said. "We found a picture of her and Hu. He had his arm around her waist; they looked quite intimate."

"I see," Nie said. "She must have been more than just an assistant to him."

"Do you think she was his—secret sweetheart?"

"What do you think?"

"Could be." Xiaochuan nodded. "Otherwise, why would she be the only one who knew about the secret room?"

"You need to check her out," Nie Feng said. "Oh, and besides Zhou Zhengxing, there's another likely suspect."

"Zhong Tao?"

"Yes."

"But he had an alibi," Xiaochuan said. "How do we shoot holes in that?"

"That's the biggest puzzle of all," Nie thought out loud, just as Xiaochuan's cell rang.

"Hello? Who's this?"

"Yao Li. Where are you?"

"We're in the west wing of the Hall, waiting for his boarding pass."

"Oh, I see you."

They had no sooner hung up than she was there with them, breathing hard. Still in uniform, she was carrying a paper box tied with red twine. Her face was flushed from running, but that added a spirited glow.

"Nice to see you, Officer Yao," Nie said.

"She came to see you off," Xiaochuan explained.

"Thank you." Nie was surprised. "But there's no need. You're so caught up with the cases."

"This is from my father to your father." She handed him the package.

"Er—" Nie was puzzled. "Your father—"

"Yao Zhenting. You met him once." It was a very famous name.

"Ah, Superintendent Yao." Now he knew who she was. It was a secret known only to those in the criminal squad. There were few female officers in the criminal division, but she had refused to take a cushy office job at the bureau level after graduation, insisting on working on the front lines.

Before he entered the gate area, Yao Li conveyed a message from Chief Wu.

"Chief Wu would like you to share your views with him if you think of something after your return."

It was a friendly request and a sign of trust, which made him very happy. It also meant that the Shenzhen police had agreed to let him keep track of the case until it was solved.

"Chief Wu has spoken highly of your analysis of the case," Yao added. "He says you'd be an outstanding police officer if you decided to change jobs."

"I'm flattered."

"I agree with his assessment." Yao's straightforward comment was underscored by the glow in her eyes as she gazed at him.

"So do I," Xiaochuan joined in.

Nie scratched his head, a bit tongue-tied from the compliments.

"You have to work on the case, so why don't you go on back?"

"All right. We'll say good-bye here then." They shook hands with him and left.

Zheng Yong was giving Team Leader Cui his report when Xiaochuan and Yao Li returned to the station.

"Sit down and listen to what he has to say," Cui said. They took a seat.

"We checked out the car following Zhu Mei-feng," Zheng said. "It belongs to a commercial investigative firm called Yinsida, a private detective agency that investigates employee loyalty, client credit standing, counterfeit goods, men and their mistresses, extramarital affairs, locating whereabouts, things like that. I hear business is good."

"So who's checking up on Zhu Mei-feng?"

"The agency told me the client registered online and gave no name."

"Bullshit," Cui fumed. "What does online registration have to do with a name? They're just trying to keep their client's identity secret."

"What do I do next?"

"Go back there," Cui said in a steely voice, "and remind them that private investigation is illegal under our country's current laws. They should be prepared for the consequences if they refuse to co-operate with the police."

Cui was right. Zheng Yong went back to Yinsida and told them exactly what Cui had told him to say. He received an answer right away, and they were surprised to learn that the client who'd hired the PI was Hu Guohao's personal assistant, Feng Xueying.

NINE

Fire! Fire! Fire!

— 1 —

Nie Feng arrived at home with his white tote and a travel bag.

The first to welcome him home was the ecstatic Yahoo. Overjoyed, the little poodle ran around the house with his shoe in its mouth, looking silly, almost like a wind-up dog. The maid, Xiao Ju, was also surprised but happy to see him.

"Brother Nie is home," she announced

His grandma came up, smiling so broadly her mouth risked staying forever open.

"*Aiya!* How did you get so dark and skinny?"

"You look just like Louis Koo," Xiao Ju joked.

"What's a Louis Koo?" Grandma was not up on her Hong Kong entertainment.

"A Hong Kong movie star, a hunk. He has an incredible tan from swimming so much," Nie Feng explained, bent down close to the old woman's ear.

"So that makes you a hunk, too."

"Impossible. Grandma, you know I've been ugly since the day I was born."

That made Xiao Ju laugh; her face turned a bright red.

He took out gifts for everyone: for grandma, some little sweetheart cakes—the old lady had a sweet tooth—and for Xiao Ju, a necklace made of seashells.

"It's so pretty. Thank you!" Xiao Ju gushed.

"These are for Dad, from Superintendent Yao." He produced the package from Yao Li; inside were two bags of Jamaican Blue Mountain coffee.

"Your Dad's in Beijing at a meeting," Grandma said.

"What about gifts for Aunty and Elder Sister Nie?" Xiao Ju glared at him as a reminder.

Nie's mother was an obstetrician, his older sister a radio host who came home only on weekends.

"Sorry, but I ran out of time. Next time, I promise."

He washed up and called his editor in chief.

"I'm back, Mr. Wu."

Wu started out with compliments on his good nose for breaking stories, his tenacity, endurance, and so on.

"You wanted me back so badly, you must have plans for some overseas travel," Nie said in jest.

"I knew it would take longer than two weeks to solve your cases, unless you were Sherlock Holmes," the editor said in a mild, even tone.

"Why don't you tell me what you've got for me?" Nie knew how his editor operated.

"I'd like you to go to Mianyang to interview a TV magnate. It'll be our next issue's cover story."

"I see. But I've depleted my expense account."

"Go to the accountant before you leave. I'll sign for it."

"Thanks. I'll leave tomorrow." Nie wanted to get the interview over with as soon as possible.

"No hurry. You just got back. Take a couple of days to rest."

"Will do."

• • •

Xiaochuan phoned Nie the following evening to tell him that Hong Yiming's wife had flown back from Canada to arrange for her husband's funeral. When they asked her about Hong's social network and business associates, the police learned that he and Hu were not only from the same county in Henan, but had been comrade-in-arms in the same unit as part of the Yunnan Construction Corps. She'd heard that from her husband.

"I'm thinking that might be helpful in disentangling Hu and Hong's connections," Xiaochuan said.

"I agree." Nie was elated. "This is important." He pondered this news as he put down the phone. Why wasn't it part of Hu's résumé? Was this how the two deaths were connected? He took out a pen and jotted down his thoughts:

Same hometown—good friends—business partners—rivals—together in ...

He looked at what he'd written and decided to add *"one-time"* before business partners, and after a long meditation, finished the last item: *together in Yunnan Construction Corps.*

But which unit in the Corps? And where exactly in Yunnan?

Zhong Tao had also been in the Yunnan Construction Corps. Had he known Hu Guohao and Hong Yiming there? Now that thirty years had passed, tracking down anything to do with the zhiqing would be extremely difficult.

He placed a call to the C University library the next morning, but was disappointed to learn from the librarian that they had nothing on the Cultural Revolution. His next best bet would be the provincial library. After wolfing down his breakfast, he raced out of the house, jumped on his bike, and took off.

As a reporter who spent much of his time conducting interviews, he was not a frequent visitor to the library, and was surprised to find that it was crowded into a tiny space. A low yellow wall with glazed tiles framed the entrance. The library's name was carved into an ivy-draped marble boulder. A guard sat in the entrance to watch over bicycles left by patrons. After parking his bike, Nie walked inside and was immediately unnerved by the dilapidated state of the place. Crossing the deserted lobby, he walked up the dark terrazzo stairs, as if roaming in the wilderness alone. It had to have been at least thirty years since the building had had its last maintenance.

The third-floor special collections area, with its ancient furnishings, looked to be the best place to read. There were three rows of small, Chinese-style rectangular tables, ten in each row. Seven or eight readers sat at the tables, their heads buried in whatever they were reading.

Nie sat down in a corner to search for information related to the zhiqing, accompanied by the hum of the free-standing air conditioner.

Behind the reference counter two librarians helped locate material for patrons. One was middle-aged, wore glasses, and was dressed in a linen skirt with floral patterns. The other, younger, librarian had on a blue apron and was seated at a computer. Both were highly professional, knowledgeable, and happy to serve. They helped to compensate for the library's shortage of facilities.

It took Nie more than an hour to get his hands on a few magazines from the Cultural Revolution era, along with several volumes of zhiqing essays, some of which had yellowed pages and required careful handling. He studied a photo album entitled *Up to the Mountains and Down to the Countryside,* which contained more than a hundred black-and-white photos that recorded the life of Chengdu's zhiqing in Yunnan—carrying kindling on their backs, building houses, cutting down rubber trees, driving tractors, dancing, taking vows, sending petitions, and so on. A large photo showed the zhiqing from Rongcheng County leaving for the countryside. A team of young girls with braids, carrying their backpacks and washbasins on their backs, red flags over their shoulders, and photos of the great leader in their hands, strode proudly down People's

South Road. In the dim background stood a white statue of Mao and the outline of an exhibit hall; their faces were a blur, but the picture managed to capture their vigor and vitality, further enhanced by the sight of crowds seeing them off.

From 1971 to 1972, tens of thousands of Chengdu zhiqing, including Zhong Tao, had set out from under the statue of a hand-waving Mao, heading to the vast territory of the Yunnan border area.

As he read on, Nie spotted an article "Lan'que Ridge and its Ten Graves" in a small pamphlet with a blue cover entitled "Souls of Zhiqing." He was shaken to his core when he finished, for it chronicled a tragedy in the zhiqing camp at Lanjiang, Yunnan, where twenty-eight years ago, a raging fire had immolated ten zhiqing girls.

It was a clear, moonlit night. A Shanghai zhiqing was secretly reading *Songs of Youth* inside his mosquito netting. At a time when the Red reigned and books were scant, romance novels like *Songs of Youth* were banned because of their feudalistic, bourgeois content, which was why he had to read it at night, in secret. It was getting late, but he couldn't put it down. Then he had to go outside to relieve himself. As he climbed out of his bed, he accidentally knocked over the kerosene lamp inside the net, which then caught fire. Panic-stricken, he batted at the fire with his sheet, but in no time the fire incinerated the net and leaped up to the roof, igniting every flammable item in the hut along its way: bamboo, couch grass, clothing, wooden table, and more.

It took less than a minute for the fire to engulf the bamboo hut. Flames shot into the night sky sending dark smoke roiling. The boy was dazed; all he could do was yell, "Fire! Fire! Fire!" Some were awakened and ran out of the burning structure half naked, screaming for help along the way.

The huts were built in rows, sharing walls, all made of bamboo frames with couch grass roofs. Just about everything inside was flammable. So when the fire destroyed the first hut, the other huts were doomed. Fanned by the wind, the fire spread across the rooftops, accompanied by the crackle of burning bamboo and flying sparks. The youngsters ran out of their burning huts, creating a chaotic scene. A girl in the second hut ran out in bra and shorts, while one of the boys escaped from a hut two doors down. The bolder ones even ran back in to rescue items.

By the time the last survivor, one of the boys, fled to safety, all the rows of thatched huts were engulfed in flames. Then an old staff worker noticed something unusual.

"Look, Commander. Why is the fire blue over there?" He pointed to the third hut, where blue flames rose up amid the thick black smoke. He knew that wood, bamboo, and cotton produced only reddish-yellow flames and that fire turned blue when fat was present. But the commander ignored him, too busy rescuing his own jars of pickled vegetables. Two or three minutes later, the thatched roof on the third hut collapsed, reducing the power of the fire, although blue flames continued to lick through the thick smoke.

"Commander, something's wrong there," the worker called out to the leader again, prompting him to have some of the boys poke through the charred remains inside.

The article continued:

Everyone was stunned by what they saw.

Ten female zhiqing were inside, a huddle of shrunken, embracing arms reduced by the fire to black charcoal. Their bodies were no more than three feet long, head to toe, their faces were unrecognizable. It was a horrific sight. When they were pried apart, patches of intact skin were still visible on chests that had pressed tightly together.

Why hadn't they escaped?

An on-site inspection showed that they could not have escaped in time because the door had been secured with thick wire. In their panic, they were unable to undo the wire, which was fastened to the burned doorframe.

They'd been afraid that someone would get in. Ten girls sleeping in one hut, and they'd been afraid of someone. Who was that person?

They hadn't told anyone of their fears, and now they would never be able to.

A profound sadness welled up inside Nie Feng as he closed the pamphlet. History seemed to solidify at that moment. It was quiet all around him, but for the hum of the air conditioner. To his right an old man in a checkered T-shirt was reading a thread-bound book with the help of a magnifying glass. Ahead of him a brown-haired woman in a light blue short-sleeved shirt was flipping through a thick journal.

Suddenly Zhong Tao's face flashed before his eyes—the unusual look on Zhong's face as he gazed at the sunset. What did the fiery red sunset signify?

He opened the pamphlet again, and on the last page he saw that the tragedy had taken place at Lan'que Ridge in Lanjiang, where the 2nd Company of the 4th Battalion of XX Regiment of the Yunnan Construction Corps had been stationed.

And it had happened on June 24, 1972.

"June 24, 1972." Nie mumbled the dates as something stirred in the back of his mind.

Why did the string of numbers look so familiar? Had he seen it before?

"The library is closing, sir," the woman in the blue apron called out from behind the counter.

"You close at noon?"

"It's our lunch break."

So he gathered his stuff, stood up, and was ready to hand in the library books. By accident one of them was upside down, and

suddenly his heart skipped a beat, followed by sudden enlighten-
ment. The numbers on the death notices were 42602791.

Back to front it was 19720624.

June 24, 1972!

He was in a dark mood on his way home.

When his bike took him past People's South Road, he looked up
to see the white marble statue of Chairman Mao in front of the Exhibit Hall, and a sense of temporal displacement crept into his
mind. The statue of Mao waving his hand was twenty-seven meters
tall, and after many decades of change and the transformation
brought on by economic reforms, it remained at the spot, still pointing to the southern sky. This was probably the only one of its kind
left in the whole country. A miracle. Workers standing on scaffolds
were brushing it with gray powder.

Twenty-eight years earlier, on this street, thousands of Chengdu's middle school students had crowded onto military trucks heading south to the Yunnan border, in the direction the great leader
was pointing. He could see it in his mind's eye, with the ceaseless
beating of drums and clanging of gongs, and the shouts soaring into
the sky.

Nearly three decades had passed. People's South Road was
now taken over by streams of motor vehicles, a common sight in a
modern metropolis. What happened to the dreams of those youngsters? Nothing but this white marble statue, with its hand pointing
to Yunnan, remained. An old-timer at the magazine once told Nie
that a member of the political consultative conference had suggested taking down the statue to spare the old man the blistering
sun and pouring rain. The suggestion had been accepted, with one
condition: it had to be taken down quietly overnight. No explosives,
no crane. Which was why the plan was scrapped and the white
statue remained where it was. Nie had no idea whether the story
was true or not.

— 2 —

Nie Feng was sitting in his living room, waiting for a phone call.

The phone rang. It was a friend at the City Writers' Association.

"You should talk to a Cheng Xiaowen at the City Labor Bureau. She was one of the Chengdu zhiqing who went to Lanjiang. She's been active in social work."

Nie took down Ms. Cheng's cell number and thanked his friend. He had to talk to someone who was there when the ten girls died. He called the number; it rang and rang, but no one answered.

That evening, when he was online, a woman called. He could hear children's voices in the background, so he reasoned that she must be calling from home. It was Cheng Xiaowen, who promptly agreed to Nie's request.

"I'd like to know more about the zhiqing situation in Lanjiang."

"Sure, but call back tomorrow morning when I'll know a good time to meet."

He called again the next morning; the phone rang but still no answer. So he tried calling the City Labor Bureau. When the call went through, Ms. Cheng herself picked up.

"Who told you to contact me?" She sounded friendly.

"A friend of mine, Zhong Ping, with the City's Writers' Association."

"I don't know anyone by that name."

"He was a zhiqing himself, and he told me you are quite well known. He also said you like to help people."

"What do you want to know?"

"I'm a journalist at *Western Sunshine*. I'm working on a piece."

"You weren't a zhiqing, so I doubt you'll be able to do a good job." She was certainly direct.

"I'm not writing about the zhiqing. I just need some background for my story," Nie explained. "Specifically, I want to know more about the ten girls in the 2nd Company of the 4th Battalion."

"The ones who died in the fire. It was a horrible death. I was in the 4th Company."

"Can we meet to talk?" Nie asked, a bit too eagerly.

"Why don't you take a trip to Jiaolin Villa at Mt. Fenghuang first? You can take the ninety-nine bus to the end and spend two yuan on a three-wheeled motorbike to the Zhiqing Activity Center," Ms. Cheng suggested. "Take the tour, and we can do the interview after you have a better sense of the era."

"I'd like to meet with you first, if it's not too much trouble."

"In that case, how about ten thirty tomorrow morning? I'll be in my office."

"Thank you very much."

When Xiao Ju saw Nie's smile, she couldn't help asking, "A date? Who is it?"

"A lady."

"Of course it's a lady." The young maid pouted.

The living room phone rang the following morning at ten o'clock. Xiao Ju picked it up and then yelled into the study: "Brother Nie, it's for you, your lady."

"What are you yelling for?" Nie picked up the phone; it was indeed Ms. Cheng.

"Xiao Nie, a meeting just came up at the office, and I'm afraid I can't meet with you today."

"Well," Nie was disappointed, "we can work something out tomorrow then."

"Sure." She hung up.

Xiao Ju gloated over his disappointment. "Did she stand you up?"

"Buzz off!"

He decided to go ahead and visit Jiaolin Villa first. He found a taxi outside the Zhiyuan Building and told the driver to head for North Gate.

"Where to?"

"Mt. Fenghuang."

They drove through the outskirts, a scene of anarchy, with all kinds of motor vehicles raising columns of dust. Along the highway they passed bicycle repair shops, small furniture stores, and fruit stands. Then they were out in the fields, where rapeseed plants were harvested and chard was covered in dust.

Mt. Fenghuang was not far from his apartment building, Zhiyuan, on the north side of the city. The trip cost seventeen yuan. The driver found the address and stopped outside Jiaolin Villa, where cement posts framed the entrance. A plaque on the left indicated: RONGCHENG ACTIVITY CENTER FOR FORMER YUNNAN ZHIQING. A flagstone path, a small plantain grove, and a pond.

The manager gave him a brief description of the place. She said that activity center members did not live on-site since they had jobs elsewhere, but when they held their regular meetings, the place came to life. The owner of Jiaolin Villa had been a zhiqing, and made one small building available free of charge for the reunions. But the villa itself was run like a revenue-generating resort.

She showed him around the small building. One room roughly fifteen square meters in size was designated as "Zhiqing Archives." Nie stayed behind to browse; the collected items were common and yet precious—black-and-white photos of the zhiqing performing manual labor, yellowed newspaper clippings, little red books with Mao's bust, notices stamped with red seals for transferring back to the city, and so on. Two glass display cases stood in the middle of the room. The one on the left housed publications dealing with the zhiqing life, while the one on the right exhibited pamphlets such as "Commemorative Album for Yunnan Zhiqing," address books, and more. There was even an army-green photographer's vest with IN MEMORY OF LANJIANG ZHIQING RETURNING HOME stenciled on the back.

After the tour of the small building, the manager had a young man in blue worker's clothes take Nie to the teahouse.

After skirting two ponds framed by weeping willows, they reached the teahouse, a long structure made of bamboo, surrounded by plantains. Chinese roses were in bloom along the path. It was obviously not a reunion day, for only one table was occupied, by a group of tourists playing Mah-jongg. The place was quiet enough to hear frogs croaking in the ponds and the intermittent sounds of tractors from beyond the wall.

"This is our bamboo teahouse. You'll find zhiqing souvenirs here, also," the young man told him.

The furniture was all made of bamboo. He sat down and ordered tea.

Pictures were pasted on the walls all around, including photos of Chengdu zhiqing returning to western Yunnan. The teahouse was encircled by a light blue cloth curtain a meter tall and thirty meters long. He got up and paced the area, experiencing a sensation of riding a soundless wave. The curtain was filled with inscriptions, all done hurriedly with writing brushes in brown, blue, purple, red, and a somber black; some big, some small, and in various styles, all jumbled together; the ink on some were blurred from moisture, while others had faded. These were valuable records from a memorial retrospective held nine years before in the Square on People's South Road; it had offered an opportunity to the Chengdu zhiqing, who had experienced so many hardships, and their children to talk about their lives.

Nie took out his notebook and began to jot down what he was reading. The first were from young hands:

> *My mother was a Yunnan zhiqing; her name is Zhang Yan—by Kang Kang, June 9.*

> *I'm the daughter of a zhiqing sent to fortify the border; my father is Liu Weidong—by Liu Wei.*

> *My parents were in the 3rd platoon of the 7th Regiment. I love to hear my mom talk about Yunnan—by Zhou Xiaobing.*

Two lines of a palm-sized inscription flowed on the upper edge of the curtain:

Time seemed so imposing at this moment.

It relates a true story to those of us who came later.

Below that, a couple of lines in dark green by a primary school student displayed raw emotion:

I saw the exhibit; I can't forget the forest of green, green rubber trees and red, red coffee beans.

My parents were zhiqing and I envy them their youthful days.

Next to that, in a heavy brown script:

I curse those days!

I envy you—a Chengdu zhiqing stationed in the border town of Gengma, who never left.

He moved forward and saw some lines in purple in an upper-right corner; they had been scrawled in a hurry by a nameless zhiqing. Both the contents and the writing style were like a shout:

Was it an ideal? Or was it an aspiration?

Was it exile? Or was it deception?

Please ask history to give the answer.

Time, history, stories of China's zhiqing. Who could answer these powerful questions?
Finally he found what he was looking for:

Souls attached to Lanjiang, impossible to forget!—by the 2nd Company of the 4th Battalion of XX Regiment.

The abbreviated line was written in dark blue, heavy and forceful.

Nie stared at the inscription and took out his pen to copy it, when he saw, below it to the left, another inscription, water-damaged and barely readable:

Youth—regret.

Below that a slogan in green:

Long Live the Spirit of the Border Brothers!

It was from the 10th Corps.

He paused momentarily before continuing to search the curtain, as if propelled by a hunch. The crowded inscriptions were like thousands of voices echoing in his ears, voices of the young; a rousing vigor in some, indignation in others, and still others patently naïve. Yet they merged into a single voice as a pointed reminder of China's past.

Row after row of blazing inscriptions flew past his eyes:

Eight years of wind and rain, blood and tears;

I've cursed, but mostly I find the past unforgettable.

And another:

The rubber trees will never forget.

All the inscriptions were signed.

A line at the very bottom, in slanted red characters, was like a raging fire:

Youth has no regrets, but the cost was too high.

Nie Feng was too emotional to know how he felt; Zhong Tao had once recited those lines to him. He walked to another corner, where, beneath lines about missing former zhiqing lovers, he happened upon several lines written in thick, black ink:

I can forget everything,

But not my first love in Yunnan.

My love, my eternal hatred, and a debt of blood.

You, hypocritical tyrant, run all you can,

But I will find you.

The lines, penned by someone called Dark Boy, sounded like a call to arms or a vow. It astounded Nie Feng; reminded of something, he hurried back to the small building and asked the manager to take out the address book. There he found some of the names from the original 2nd Company of the 4th Battalion, XX Regiment. On one of pages was the name Zhong Tao and his address, and underneath his name was that of Ding Lan.

It had never occurred to him that Ding Lan could have been a zhiqing as well. She and Zhong had been in the same company.

He finally met Ms. Cheng the next morning. She was in her midforties, with her hair cut short and a bit on the heavy side. Dressed in a dark short-sleeved blouse with tiny floral patterns, she looked capable and experienced. Her office was not big, but had two desks placed side by side, and along the wall were several silvery-gray file cabinets; it looked like the typical office of a civil servant.

"I went to Jiaolin Villa yesterday," Nie said.

"How was it? Did you learn anything useful?" she asked eagerly.

"Quite a lot. But I still have some questions."

"What about?"

"Did you know Ding Lan?"

"I did. She was in the 2nd Company of the 4th Battalion."

"What about Zhong Tao?"

"I did, but not well. We weren't in the same year in high school."

He brought up the fire and the knotty question of why they'd shut themselves in with wire.

Ms. Cheng then told him what she knew: The first one to spot the fire and try to put it out was someone they called Second Uncle Dong, the village head at the time. The fire had indeed been caused by a Shanghai zhiqing reading secretly at night, but there was no consensus as to what he was reading. Some said it was *Song of Youth*, and some said it was *Miss Jenny*; a later article claimed it was *A Young Girl's Heart*. In any case, one thing was clear: he was reading a banned book.

"I read that the door was secured with thick wire," Nie said.

But the former zhiqing, who had been in charge of propaganda work, said she'd been away from Lan'que Ridge and had only visited the scene the following day with the 4th Battalion propaganda team. She had heard nothing about the door.

"It must have been a rumor," she said.

"Could someone have covered it up?"

"I don't believe so."

"Do you know if I can find anyone who was there when the fire broke out?"

"That would be hard; it's been nearly thirty years."

He'd heard that when the Chengdu zhiqing had returned from Lanjiang, some were lucky enough to get into college, but most went to work in factories, which meant they were scattered all over the place. The eight years spent in the border region had cost them the best years of their youth, along with the many opportunities that would have given them a better life. Instead, most returned to the city and wound up with menial jobs. Now some of those had been "downsized" as a result of changes in the economic system. Only a few of those witnesses were still around.

"I really would like to interview at least one who was there," Nie stressed.

Ms. Cheng thought about it and gave him a name.

"Her name is He Xiaoqiong, a clerk of the 2nd Company of the 4th Battalion. She was there when the fire broke out. After she returned, she worked in the benefits office at the Progressive Shoe Company, but we've been out of touch for a very long time."

In the days that followed, after wrapping up his interview with the TV magnate in Mianyang, Nie spent all his spare time searching for He Xiaoqiong.

After many phone calls and online searches, he learned that the Progressive Shoe Company had folded years before, its site now occupied by a mall of boutique shops. He was about to give up the search when he happened upon a newspaper article. In "Laid-off Couple's Exquisite Paper-cutting," a downsized husband and wife had found a way to support themselves by developing their paper-cutting skills. Their artistry had gained them fans not only in China, but in places like Japan, as well. The husband had once worked at Progressive. Nie phoned the newspaper and spoke to the story's author, who then gave him the couple's phone number.

At last his persistence paid off, for two days later, with an address from the "paper-cutting husband," he found Ms. He Xiaoqiong in the mailroom of a dormitory on Huzhu Road.

"How did you find me?"

"Cheng Xiaowen gave me your name."

Ms. He wore glasses and was dressed in a floral blouse that day. She was articulate and obviously cultured. He learned that she had gone to work at a community organization after being laid off, and was extremely busy.

"Oh, so it was Duckie."

He'd heard that the zhiqing all had nicknames, and that some of those names—like Duckie—had stuck.

In that tiny mailroom, she recounted the past for him. Sadness crept onto her serene face when the topic of the fire came up.

"It was simply horrific. Too terrifying for words."

Her recollection of the cause of the fire was consistent with what he'd heard elsewhere. She said she'd lived in the second hut with six other young women. The ten who had died in the fire had lived in the next, and larger, hut.

"Have you heard that the reason they couldn't get the door open was because it had been secured with wire?" Nie asked.

"I don't believe so."

She told him she'd gone to bed earlier than usual that night, exhausted from the day's work, and had fallen asleep the moment her head hit the pillow. Heat woke her up later that night and she opened her eyes to see fire leaping onto the thatched roof, from which burning couch grass was dropping. It was a scene of sheer chaos, with people screaming. An old staff worker tried to move stuff out and rescue children, while the boys helped get the girls out, ignoring their belongings. In all the confusion, she saw one of her roommates, a Miss Huang, jump over a bamboo fence. A few of her roommates ran back inside because they were wearing only shorts and bras. The men, who were stripped to their waists, shouted for the girls to flee. The fire burned for over half an hour. No one re-called who saved whose life.

She said she'd pushed the bamboo fence over so she could escape, but had fallen to the ground. Her right arm and forehead had suffered burns, so they'd carried her to the township clinic that night. She didn't recall much about what happened next at the scene.

"Why couldn't they open the door of the third hut?"

"Maybe they propped a bench against it, and couldn't open it when they panicked."

"Was the door completely blocked?"

"Yes, safer that way."

"Were they afraid someone might sneak in at night?" Nie stared at her, "Who were they afraid of?"

She hesitated. "It's been so long. Some things are hard to talk about." She seemed reluctant to say more.

Two residents walked in to pay their cable bills, so the conversation came to a brief halt. After the residents left, Nie asked her:

"Do you know Ding Lan?"

"Of course. We were classmates. Her nickname was Silly Girl." She laughed. "She was also in the second hut, and was the last one to escape."

"Did she suffer any burns?"

"No. I guess that's why people say that silly people have all the luck."

"Do you know Zhong Tao?"

"He was also in the 2nd Company of the 4th Battalion. Why do you ask?"

"I heard that Ding Lan was his girlfriend." Nie decided to try a bluff.

"That's not true. His girlfriend was Xia Yuhong, the prettiest girl in the company."

Xia Yuhong, not only the prettiest, but also the most talented girl in the company, and Zhong Tao had been a couple, Ms. He told him. She did not know why they broke up, but everyone felt sorry for Zhong Tao. His father had died of lung cancer when he was young, and he and his sister had been raised by their mother, a primary school teacher. She had died the year he entered middle school and the two orphans managed to get by with help from a distant aunt. He and Xia Yuhong had been middle-school classmates, class of '72; his sister, Zhong Xing, and Ding Lan were two years their junior. The Chengdu zhiqing were mostly sixteen and seventeen years old when they traveled to Yunnan; Zhong Xing, the youngest, was only fifteen. Zhong Tao, famed for his combative nature at school, seemed unafraid of anything, and would go after anyone who dared to pick on his baby sister.

"Anything special about him?" Nie asked.

"Since he was very dark, everyone called him Dark Boy," Ms. He said casually.

"His nickname was Dark Boy?" That was surprising news.

"That's right." She nodded.

So Zhong Tao was the one who'd written *"eternal hatred and a debt of blood."*

"Zhong Xing was the youngest of the ten who died in the fire." Ms. He sighed.

"I see." Nie was saddened by the tragedy.

She added that Ding Lan had been in love with Zhong Tao. Her brother, Ding Qiang, whose nickname was Qiangzi, was a childhood friend of Zhong Tao. They were buddies. Qiangzi vanished the day before the fire.

"What was the name of your company commander?"

"Hu Zihao."

That night Nie Feng sent Xiaochuan an e-mail to inform him of what he'd learned:

Dear Xiaochuan,

How's everything? Any recent developments in the 06/25 and 07/6 cases?

I did some sleuthing after returning to Sichuan and here's what I've found: 28 years ago, a fire broke out in Lanjiang, Yunnan, where the 2nd Company of the 4th Battalion was stationed. Ten zhiqing girls from Chengdu died in the fire, including Zhong Tao's younger sister, Zhong Xing. This might explain why Zhong would look so strange at the sight of fiery sunset clouds. It may even be connected to the "fire" symbol on the two pieces of paper. Also, Ding Lan and Zhong Tao were in the same platoon; her brother, Ding Qiang (nicknamed Qiangzi), was Zhong's buddy, and she was in love with Zhong.

So, the alibi she provided for Zhong could be false, which means that the 25-minute absence is a problem for Zhong and may well be the key to solving the case.

Please share this with Chief Wu and Team Leader Cui.

I've also decoded the string of numbers; it's the date of the fire, June 24, 1972, in reverse.

But I have yet to determine if Hu Guohao was connected to the fire. And what about Hong Yiming?

I may make a trip to Yunnan one of these days if I have a chance.

That's all for now. Please give Officer Yao my best.

Nie Feng, 07/15

— 3 —

Two days before Nie Feng sent his message, a fifth suspect emerged.

It was a beautiful morning at the Mei-feng Beauty Salon. Zhu Mei-feng walked into her office and sat down in her leather chair. The salon remained the center of her daily life even though she had now inherited Hu's wealth and become chairwoman at Landmark. She loved the elegant, quiet place, and the girls working there were her friends, which was why she still came to work every day.

Ah-lan, in a pink uniform, walked in with a steaming cup of coffee the moment she sat down.

"Good morning, Miss Zhu."

"Thank you, Ah-lan." She nodded and picked up the day's newspaper—nothing but current affairs and some gaudy inserts for cosmetic products. Plus a thick manila envelope.

She picked up the envelope; it felt heavy. A white piece of paper the size of a cake of tofu, with her name and the salon address printed on it, had been stuck in the middle of the envelope. There was no return address. She tore open the envelope, which included a stack of 7 × 7 photos. One look took her breath away.

They were photos of her trysts with Zhou Zhengxing. Some had been taken at the beach in Nan'ao, showing them holding hands and hugging; some were of them having dinner at Jiaoye Restaurant, or kissing in the suite at the Emperor Hotel. The most shocking ones were of her with Zhou in bed, stark naked, making passionate love.

A chill ran down her spine. At first she was merely upset, but that feeling was quickly followed by an unknown fear.

Who had taken the pictures? Was there an eye in heaven watching her at all times?

She'd gone swimming at Nan'ao and enjoyed dinner at the Thai restaurant with Zhou Zhengxing after Hu Guohao's death. It would not have been hard for someone to photograph them in public places like that. But who could have taken their pictures in bed in the hotel? She took a quick mental survey of the suite—the door was locked from the inside, the curtains were drawn, and the lights were dimmed. The photo seemed to have been taken from above their heads. Then it hit her—a canopy directly above the bed, the perfect hiding place for a camera. How terrifying! Who would have hidden a camera there?

She shook the envelope, and a folded slip of paper fell out. Only three lines of text:

Need money. Please wire 200,000 RMB (an insignificant amount to you) to China Merchant Bank All-in-One-Card # 00200XXX1238, under the name Ma Yin.

You have three days. Do not delay or call the police, or be prepared for the consequences.

I believe Madam would not want these amorous pictures forwarded to the media.

Who was this blackmailer, Ma Yin? And how did she get these pictures? Zhu knew this was serious, but she sensed something fishy about it. Her initial reaction was to call Zhou Zhengxing. But when the call went through, she hung up before he picked it up.

She couldn't tell him about it, at least not yet; he mustn't be involved.

Though this was blatant blackmail, she could not call the police, and most of all, she could not let anyone else know about the contents. The blackmailer obviously had planned everything carefully, including the amount. She was right; two hundred thousand RMB was nothing to her, after having inherited her late husband's wealth.

After some deliberation, she decided to follow the instructions. As the saying goes, money takes care of all problems. Two days later, she removed two hundred thousand yuan from the cash in the safe, which had been returned by the police. Then she drove to a branch of the China Merchant Bank near the Diwang Building, where she deposited the money into the account specified by the anonymous letter. An idea occurred to her before she completed the transaction.

"Miss, could you check the card number and tell me where Miss Ma Yin lives."

"You're wiring her money, but you don't know her address?" The clerk looked up from her screen and eyed Zhu.

"It's not my money. I'm doing it for a friend."

The clerk tapped a few keys and said, "The card number is from the Guangzhou area. That's all the information I have here."

That was strange.

"The cardholder opened the account in March, when depositors weren't required to use their real names," the clerk explained.

"I see."

So there was no telling whether Ma Yin was a man or a woman, and it was likely an alias. Zhu felt uneasy when she left the bank. Little did she know that two other people received similar envelopes on the same day she received hers. They were Zhou Zhengxing and Zhong Tao.

Zhou's envelope, with his name and address printed on the outside, included copies of the same photos sent to Zhu Mei-feng.

Need money. Please wire 200,000 RMB (an insignificant amount to
you) to China Merchant Bank All-in-One-Card # 00200XXX1238,
under the name Ma Yin.
   You have three days. Do not delay or call the police, or be prepared for the consequences.
   I believe, Mr. Zhou, you would not want these amorous pictures to be seen by your wife in her sickbed.

Zhou's wife, saintly kindergarten teacher, had set up her own
neighborhood day care center for some extra income to help her
husband start a business. She worked hard but never complained;
the day care center was a great success, and she handed all the money
over to her husband, who had made his first fortune in interior fit-
tings. Unfortunately, she was paralyzed from the waist down in a
traffic accident. Zhou treated his wife well and did his best to make
her happy. Knowing about him and Zhu Mei-feng would be a savage, maybe even fatal blow. The blackmailer obviously knew that his
wife's happiness was Zhou's weakness.
   After some hesitation and a calculation of the pros and cons, he
withdrew two hundred thousand yuan from his personal account
and wired it to the China Merchant Bank account specified by the
blackmailer.
   The envelope Zhong Tao received contained only six photos.
Three had been taken at Hu Guohao's memorial: one was a close-
up of the blue wreath, enlarged to the point that the words on the
memorial scrolls were clearly visible. The other two were of Ding
Lan, one a full-body shot, the other a medium shot, both showing
her strange expression. Dressed in a dark blue short-sleeved blouse,
she appeared to be standing near the rear entrance of the auditorium, with wreaths and shadowy figures in the foreground. The

other three photos had been snapped secretly, most likely when
Zhong and Ding had met at the Milan Café. It was a tight space and
the interior light was a dim orange, but the photos had good light
exposure, which meant the photographer was a pro.

The note read:

Need money. Please wire 200,000 RMB (an insignificant amount to
you) to China Merchant Bank All-in-One-Card # 00200XXX1238,
under Ma Yin.

   You have three days. Do not delay or call the police, or be prepared for the consequences.

   I believe, Mr. Zhong, that you would not want your confidant,
Miss Ding Lan, to be entangled in the unsolved murder of Hu
Guohao on June 25.

The blackmailer was in for a surprise—three days went by and
no news from Zhong.

At noon on the fourth day, Zhong Tao received an anonymous
call from a woman.

"Is this Mr. Zhong Tao?"

The voice seemed muffled, as if the caller was covering her mouth
or had a cold.

"Yes. What can I do for you?"

"Your three days are up, but no money, Mr. Zhong."

"Oh, it's you, Ma Yin."

"You're a smart man, Mr. Zhong, and I don't suppose you'd like
those photos to fall into the hands of the police."

"Are you blackmailing me?" Zhong asked calmly.

"I'm short of money and would appreciate some help, Mr. Zhong."

"Sorry, I can't help you," Zhong said impassively.

"Aren't you concerned about the consequences?"

"What consequences? Hu Guohao's memorial was open to the
public. So those photos mean nothing."

"It's not that simple. They show that Miss Ding was intimately interested in Hu Guohao's death."

"That's pure speculation."

"Not quite. I also know that you were somehow involved with Hu Guohao's death."

"Is that so? Who are you, anyway?" A hint of wariness crept into his voice.

"Who I am isn't important. What's important is that the money must be wired right away."

"I'm afraid you're going to be disappointed," Zhong said coldly. "I think you should put a stop to this right now. You know that blackmailers suffer a very unpleasant fate."

The caller hung up.

— 4 —

Y District Public Security Office. The Criminal Division Chief's Office.

Xiaochuan came in with a report for Team Leader Cui.

"Chief," he said, "something's up with Zhu Mei-feng."

"So tell me what it is."

"She just wired two hundred thousand yuan to an All-in-One-Card account holder at the CMB."

"So?"

"We asked the bank to check and, get this, first, it isn't her account, and second, another wire transfer in the same amount went into that account on the same day. And it was from Zhou Zheng-xing."

"Really? That's no coincidence." Now Cui was interested. "Whose account is it?"

"Someone called Ma Yin, no other information."

"An anonymous account."

"That's right," Xiaochuan said. "Should we get the Bureau to freeze the account?"

"We will, when the time comes."

"Something's going on."

"That's for sure. Keep a close watch on the account."

"Yes, sir."

Two days later, a woman phoned Zhu Mei-feng at her salon office.

"Hello?"

"Is this Chairwoman Zhu?"

The caller's voice sounded strange, somehow distorted. Zhu could not tell the caller's age.

"This is she. And you are?"

"Ma Yin. You've heard the name before?"

"Ah—" Zhu's paled.

"I want to thank you, Chairwoman Zhu, for the two hundred thousand yuan," the caller said politely.

"What else do you want?" Zhu was on the verge of hysteria.

"You're a smart woman, Chairwoman Zhu." The caller made a point of emphasizing Zhu's title. "We can call the whole thing off if you'll wire another two hundred thousand."

"What? You want another two hundred thousand?" Zhu could hardly get the words out.

"You heard me." The caller was relentless.

"So how do you call the whole thing off?"

"The day after the money is wired, you'll receive all the negatives."

"Who are you?"

"Who I am isn't important. What's important is your public image and reputation, Chairwoman Zhu."

"How do I know you'll keep your word?"

"I'm a woman, just like you. And I won't go back on my word. But remember, you have three days." With that, the caller hung up.

Zhu put down the phone, feeling as if she were waking from a bad dream. She sat frozen in her chair; the more she thought about the call, the more frightened she became. Finally, she picked up the phone again and called Zhou Zhengxing's cell.

"Lao Zhou, it's me. I need to see you now."

I'm on my way to the city government office. What's so urgent?"

"I can't talk over the phone. I'll meet you at the Tangyi Tea House."

"Let's not meet outside." Zhou looked at his watch. "Come to my office, two thirty."

"At Landmark?"

"Yes."

"All right. I'll see you then."

Zhou turned off his cell and told the driver, "Go back to Landmark."

Ever since the interview with the police, Zhou and Zhu had been especially careful with their meetings. He assumed he was being followed, so Landmark would be the safest place to see her, given their positions at the company. No one would question a meeting between the Board Chairman and the CEO.

He was back at Landmark at two ten. Twenty minutes later, Zhu arrived in her red BMW.

Zhou's personal assistant, Ah-mei, greeted Zhu cordially outside the Chairwoman's twenty-fourth-floor office.

"Ah, it's you, Big Sister Zhu."

"I'd like a cup of coffee."

"Of course. Mr. Zhou said he needed to talk to you about some company business."

"Please tell him I'll see him now."

"Yes."

A few minutes later, Zhou calmly strode across the hallway, entered the Chairwoman's office, and closed the door behind him.

Zhu handed him the anonymous note.

"I received this five days ago."

"I got one just like it," Zhou said, "along with a stack of pictures of the two of us."

"Really?" This was something she'd never expected. They looked at each other.

"Did you wire the money?" he asked her. She nodded.

"I thought the money would take care of the problem," she said. "But she phoned me at the salon today. She wants another two hundred thousand."

"So she isn't happy with four hundred thousand."

Zhou had obviously paid also, which increased Mei-feng's sense of unease.

"A greedy goddamn woman!" Zhou cursed.

"Why don't I wire her the money. She promised to give me the negatives."

"No." Zhou shook his head. "Even if she gives you the negatives, you can't be sure she hasn't made copies. She could ask for another two hundred thousand, then four hundred thousand, even six hundred thousand."

"So what do we do?" Zhu Mei-feng was clearly frightened.

"The best solution is to shut her up forever." He spit out the words in a low voice.

"Don't do anything stupid," Zhu warned him, looking increasingly worried.

"That, of course, would only be a last resort," Zhou said to ease her mind. "She just wants money. Why don't you put her off for a couple of days and see what happens."

"What if we tell the police?"

"Let's not do anything rash before we know who she is."

"She sounded to be in her thirties."

"Try this," Zhou said. "Change your phone at the salon to one with a caller ID."

"Good idea, I'll do it right away."

• • •

The blackmailer's goal was six hundred thousand yuan, which she believed she had coming to her. She had planned to get the money from three separate sources, two hundred thousand each, but had not expected that the money from Zhong Tao would not materialize. That had necessitated a call to Zhu Mei-feng for more.

Had Zhu and Zhou known this, a tragedy could have been avoided.

After installing caller ID on her phone, Zhu followed her normal routine—arriving at the salon in the morning and leaving at five thirty in the evening—for two tension-filled days.

Nothing happened.

Until the third day. The woman called again at noon.

"Is this Chairwoman Zhu?" The same muffled voice.

"Miss Ma Yin?"

"Right. I want to remind you that the money has not arrived."

Zhu glanced at the caller ID and could not believe her eyes.

"I, I know." She tried to mask her shock.

"You don't think you can get out of this, do you?"

"No, not at all. It's just that I have a bit of a cash-flow problem." Zhu strained to sound convincing while stealing another glance at the caller ID. She was sure of the number.

"For a rich woman like you, this tiny amount shouldn't be a problem." Now the blackmailer began to sound brazen.

"It's the truth. Please give me two more days, will you?"

"Are you playing games with me, Madam Chairwoman?"

"Of course not. I gave you my word." She spoke gently in hopes that her sincerity would come through.

"All right." The blackmailer hesitated before giving her ultimatum. "I'll trust you this time. But remember, I must have the money by noon in two days. If not, you'll have only yourself to blame when the scandal hits." She hung up.

The tension had Zhu trembling and breaking out in a cold sweat. When she recovered, she dialed Zhou's office.

"Lao Zhou, it's me. Go see who's in my office."

"Why?" Zhou was puzzled.

"Ma Yin just called from the phone in my office at Landmark."

"No!" Zhou was understandably shocked. He opened his office door; it was lunch hour, so the hallway was quiet. He raced to the Chairman's office, where the door was ajar; the secretary's office was deserted. Sensing that something was amiss, he pushed open the door and walked in. There was no one inside. A ray of bright sunlight slanting in through the window shone on the surface of the desk. He stared at the black record-a-phone, lost in thought. Only two people at Landmark had a key to this room: Zhu Mei-feng and Feng Xueying.

He turned to walk out, but before he shut the door, someone called out to him.

"Are you looking for Big Sister Zhu, Mr. Zhou?" It was his personal assistant, Ah-mei. "She hasn't been in for a couple of days."

"Was someone in there just now?"

"Ah-ying was. She said Big Sister Zhu asked her to put some stuff together."

"I see." Now everything was clear. "Where is she now?"

"She just left—for lunch, I think."

"All right," Zhou said, "Don't tell anyone I was here."

"I won't."

— 5 —

Xiaochuan went in to see Chief Cui.

"Chief," he said excitedly, "Ma Yin just withdrew some money from the account."

"Which bank?"

"CMB's Beiling branch."

"How much?"

"Forty thousand. She wanted two hundred thousand, but the clerk wouldn't let her, saying the bank had to be notified two days in advance when the amount exceeded fifty thousand."

"What did she look like?"

"We ran over to the branch office as soon as we received the call. The clerk said the woman was wearing dark shades and was on the young side. We checked the surveillance tape; it looked very much like someone from Landmark."

"Who?"

"Feng Xueying."

"So it's her. I should've figured that out." Cui slapped his desk. The Landmark Building was like a black hole hiding unfathomable secrets.

"Check her out at once, her background, recent movements, and her social network."

"On it, sir."

Something unimaginable occurred on the day after the police turned their attention to Feng Xueying.

On the night of July twentieth, a traffic accident occurred on a quiet street in a Beiling residential district. A woman, a white-collar worker, was struck by a speeding car and died on the spot. The car, a black VW Santana, sped away, heading northwest.

The first responders opened the victim's purse to see who she was. Her ID identified her as Feng Xueying, secretary to the Chairman of the Board of the Landmark Group.

Chief Cui, Xiaochuan, Yao Li, and a crime scene technician, as well as the city traffic police were soon on the scene. Feng Xueying lay across the sidewalk on the narrow, dimly lit street, her head bathed in blood, her face barely recognizable. The ME noted that her right leg was shattered and that she had at least four broken ribs. The car had to have been speeding to cause such damage. Shards of broken glass were found near the victim, probably from the car's headlights.

An eyewitness told the police that the car sort of crept along the nearly deserted street, until it was ten or fifteen meters away from the victim, when the driver turned on his high beams and sped up, giving her no time to escape. The terrified eyewitness managed only a brief look at the plate: it was a Guangdong plate whose last three digits were 144.

The police immediately set up roadblocks northwest of the site.

A search of Feng's purse produced, among the usual women's items, keys, an All-in-One-Card from CMB and a four-millimeter pocket-recorder mini tape, as well as a used surgical mask.

When they returned to the station, Cui told Yao Li to get a pocket recorder for the tape they'd found in Feng's purse. He inserted the tape and pushed PLAY. As a soft, scratchy noise emerged from the tiny speaker, Cui, Xiaochuan, and Yao strained to listen.

A conversation between a man and a woman came up first, exposing Feng's blackmailing scheme:

"Is this Mr. Zhong Tao?"

"Yes. What can I do for you?"

"Your three days are up, but there's no money."

"Oh, it's you, Ma Yin."

Xiaochuan and Yao Li exchanged looks.

"The woman's voice is muffled. It doesn't sound at all like Feng Xueying," Yao whispered. Cui waved for her to keep listening.

"You're a smart man, Mr. Zhong, and I don't suppose you'd like those photos to fall into the hands of the police."

"Are you blackmailing me?" Zhong asked calmly.

"I'm short of money and would appreciate some help, Mr. Zhong."

"Sorry, I can't help you," Zhong said impassively.

"Aren't you concerned about the consequences?"

"What consequences? Hu Guohao's memorial was open to the public. So those photos mean nothing."

"It's not that simple. They show that Miss Ding was intimately in-terested in Hu Guohao's death."

"That's pure speculation."

"Not quite. I also know that you were somehow involved with Hu Guohao's death."

"Is that so? Who are you, anyway?" A hint of wariness had crept into his voice.

"Who I am isn't important. What's important is that the money must be wired right away."

"I'm afraid you're going to be disappointed," Zhong said coldly. "I think you should put a stop to this right now. You know that black-mailers suffer a very unpleasant fate."

The conversation came to an end, followed by a soft, scratchy noise.

"That didn't sound like Feng Xueying," Cui said.

"She disguised her voice," Xiaochuan said. "I think she used the mask we found in her purse when she withdrew the money, and also during the call. That way no one could tell it was her—"

Cui raised his hand to stop him, as another conversation began, this time between two women.

"This is she. And you are?"

"Ma Yin. You've heard the name before?"

"Ah—"

"I want to thank you, Chairwoman Zhu, for the two hundred thousand yuan."

"What else do you want?"

"You're a smart woman, Chairwoman Zhu. We can call the whole thing off if you'll wire another two hundred thousand."

"What? You want another two hundred thousand?"

"You heard me."

"So how do you call the whole thing off?"

"The day after the money is wired, you'll receive all the nega-tives."

"Who are you?"

"Who I am isn't important. What's important is your public image and reputation, Chairwoman Zhu."

"How do I know you'll keep your word?"

"I'm a woman, just like you. And I won't go back on my word. But remember, you have three days."

The chief pushed the STOP button.

"It's clear now," Cui said excitedly. "Feng Xueying was blackmailing Zhong Tao and Zhu Mei-feng, which led to her death. So it's likely that either Zhong or Zhu killed Feng to shut her up."

"Zhong Tao sounded calm," Xiaochuan said, "and didn't seem like he would take such a drastic measure."

Yao wasn't so sure. "You forget that he warned her that blackmailers usually suffer an unpleasant fate."

"That sounded more like friendly advice to me," Xiaochuan said.

"Warning or advice, it doesn't matter. Zhong is under suspicion," Cui interrupted the two officers. "Feng Xueying must have known some of Zhong's secrets, in particular his involvement in Hu Guohao's death."

"Right," Xiaochuan agreed. "Otherwise, Hu's assistant wouldn't have blackmailed him for two hundred thousand."

"I obviously underestimated this woman." Cui admitted his oversight.

"But Zhu Mei-feng sounded weak and scared on the phone," Yao said uncertainly. "Besides, she doesn't look a like a killer to me."

"Let's see if there's anything else," Cui said as he pushed the PLAY button.

Another conversation between two women sounded after the scratchy noise.

"Is this Chairwoman Zhu?" The same muffled voice.

"Miss Ma Yin?"

"Right. I want to remind you that the money has not arrived."

Cui and his officers exchanged knowing looks; things were clearing up.

"Please give me two more days, will you?"

"Are you playing games with me, Madam Chairwoman?"

"Of course not. I gave you my word."

"All right, I'll trust you this time. But remember, I must have the money by noon in two days. If not, you'll have only yourself to blame when the scandal hits."

When the police went through Ah-ying's office, they found a journal. It gave a clear picture of her thoughts and emotions.

Feng Xueying had been one of Hu Guohao's mistresses. She was also a loyal dog: for four years she'd given him her body and affection, had watched over the Board for him, and had served as his eyes and ears. Like the Sphinx crouched at the foot of the pyramid, she kept her eye on everyone in the company. Hu had promised that when the Tiandongba deal went through he would reward her with six hundred thousand yuan and send her to study in Australia. But before that promise could be honored, Hu died. She had searched every inch of his office and secret room, but nothing had turned up, no will, nothing.

She felt she had been robbed, and could not swallow the disappointment. So she'd proceeded to blackmail people whose secrets she possessed. The secrets varied from person to person, but every phone call had worked to perfection. There was no talk of going to the police. She had been prepared to stop once she had six hundred thousand in hand; she would quit her job and fulfill Hu's promise for her to study in Australia.

There is an apt phrase in the famous novel *Dream of the Red Chamber*: "She was too smart for her own good, and in the end she paid with her life." Feng Xueying's greed and scheming led inevitably to her terrible end.

"Ah-ying was one of Hu Guohao's playthings, but wound up being buried along with him," Xiaochuan said with a sigh.

TEN

Re-creation of the Crime Scene

— 1 —

They were getting close.

The police discovered that the black VW Santana had been stolen. It was found abandoned at a garbage dump in the northern outskirts of the city. The last three digits matched those provided by the eyewitness; blood—Feng Xueying's type—was visible on the dented hood, and one headlight was shattered. The car belonged to the owner of a computer company who had parked it outside the Jingtian Plaza Hotel at noon on July twentieth. He'd come out after lunch to find it missing and had reported the theft to the police. The police found no clues; technicians managed to lift a few blurred fingerprints from the door handle.

Obviously Feng Xueying's death was no accident.

Based on Feng's taped conversations with Zhong Tao and Zhu Mei-feng, the police had found a link to Hong Yiming's murder; both Zhong and Zhu had been to Big East prior to Hong's death, which meant they had both a motive and the opportunity to plant the poisoned candy. The police now believed that, in addition to Zhou

Zhengxing, Zhong Tao and Zhu Mei-feng had to be considered suspects in the string of murders.

The Y District Public Security Bureau put out an APB for Zhu Mei-feng, only to discover that she had vanished.

On the night Feng Xueying was killed, Zhu boarded a train at Lo Wu bound for Hong Kong. The staff at Landmark told police that she'd called the office around five that afternoon to say she had to be away for a few days to care for her ailing mother. After that, no one in the company could reach her; she'd turned off her cell. So they called her mother, who, it turned out, wasn't ill at all, and had no idea that her daughter had returned to Hong Kong. Chief Cui went directly to Landmark with Xiaochuan and Yao Li, but the CEO, Zhou Zhengxing, did not know where she was.

Hu Guohao's widow, Zhou Zhengxing's mistress, and Landmark's Chairwoman of the Board had fallen off the police's radar screen.

That same day, Zhong Tao boarded a plane for Chongqing. Zhou Zhengxing told the police that Zhong was scheduled to attend a Western China realty conference. Zhou had approved the leave, which would last about a week.

In questioning Zhou in his office, Cui's investigation was now able to reference the contents of the blackmail letters.

"So now we know that Feng Xueying targeted more than Zhu Mei-feng and Zhong Tao."

"That's true," Zhou said. "I was the third victim."

"So you wired two hundred thousand into Ma Yin's account."

"Yes."

"Why didn't you call the police?"

"In all candor," Zhou said as he took the letter out of his drawer and handed it to the policeman, "I didn't want my wife to know."

Cui glanced at the letter and could not suppress a grin. The blackmailer had hit Zhou where it hurt. Xiaochuan and Yao exchanged a glance.

"Well, I'll take this with me," Cui said to Zhou before leaving. "And I hope you'll continue to cooperate with us."

Bureau Chief Wu lit a cigarette as he listened impassively to Cui's report. He'd stopped "quitting smoking," thanks to this series of murders, which had them all stumped.

The blackmail letter to Zhou showed that Feng Xueying knew only about his affair with Zhu Mei-feng; it mentioned nothing about Hu's murder. That could have meant one of two things: either Zhou and Zhu had nothing to do with Hu's death, or they were involved but Feng did not know that. There was, of course, a third possibility: the blackmailer thought that threatening the two people to expose their affair was enough to get what she wanted.

"What do you think?" Chief Wu asked Team Leader Cui and his two young officers.

"Feng Xueying had an unusual relationship with Hu Guohao. She'd been his personal assistant for four years and his lover for some of that time, so she must have been privy to something. It didn't sound like she was making it up when she threatened Zhong Tao over the phone with her knowledge of his involvement in Hu's death," Cui said.

Chief Wu nodded in agreement. "Zhong could be our prime suspect in Hu's death."

"Mr. Nie said early on that we shouldn't overlook him," Xiaochuan said.

"Not that *Western Sun* again!" Cui said unhappily, which made Yao Li laugh.

Chief Wu puffed away as he mulled things over. As the lingering smoke slowly dissipated in the air, his suspicions of Zhong increased. But how was Zhong involved in Hu's death? Feng was no longer available for questioning, and the police had found no evidence of his involvement. What else lay behind the fog-enshrouded mystery?

"Let's take another look at Zhong's alibi." He stubbed out his cigarette.

Xiaochuan and Yao Li repeated what they knew, but failed to poke a hole in Zhong's alibi.

"I agree that Zhong has to be considered a suspect in Hu's death, but we can't crack his alibi. We have nothing to dispute his explanation for that twenty-five-minute absence," Yao said, stating the obvious.

There were two entrances to the Lesser Meisha Resort, the main gate and a side door, both of which were guarded 24-7. Yao and Xiaochuan had shown Zhong Tao's and Ding Lan's photos to the four night-shift guards, who could easily recall pretty much any rare tourist who passed through either entrance after eleven o'clock at night. None of them recalled seeing Zhong or Ding on the night of the twenty-fourth. The resort cabins, on the other hand, were not monitored; once the tourists were given a key, they could come and go as they pleased, so there was no one to verify that Ding had helped Zhong back to his cabin to change clothes. She was the only one who knew exactly what had occurred during those twenty-five minutes.

"That's the blind spot in Hu's murder case." Chief Wu banged his knuckles against the desk. Cui nodded in agreement.

"We were surprised to see Ding Lan at Hu's memorial," he said. "And she is Zhong's alibi for the twenty-five minutes he was away. Something is fishy here."

"Mr. Nie sent me an e-mail a few days ago," Xiaochuan said, looking somber. "He said he'd discovered that Ding Lan and Zhong Tao belonged to the same zhiqing regiment of the Yunnan Construction Corps back then, and that she's been in love with him ever since. Mr. Nie stressed that she may have provided a false alibi for Zhong. He asked me to tell you both that Zhong's absence is highly suspicious, and could be the key to unlocking the case, once we determine exactly what occurred during those twenty-five minutes."

"He has a point there." Chief Wu nodded.

"Why didn't you tell us sooner?" Cui glared at Xiaochuan.

"Didn't you say you don't have time to listen to nonsense from *Western Sun*?"

Ignoring him, Cui continued: "Let's assume that Ding provided a false alibi. Then where did they go during those twenty-five minutes? And what could they have possibly done? I did a rough calculation. It takes three minutes to walk from the barbecue grounds to the main entrance and four to five to the cabin, which means ten minutes for a round trip. If they stopped for five or six minutes, that would give them a little more than ten minutes left. They'd have to have grown wings to make it to Nan'ao and back in that amount of time."

No one laughed at the image of wings on their suspects. The air in the room was heavy, suffocating even, as they sat there, pondering the mystery.

— 2 —

Nie Feng's study in the Zhiyuan Apartment Building. It was a sweltering summer night. Nie was wearing a sleeveless top, his fingers flying across the keyboard of his Lenovo laptop. He felt good, having just finished writing up his interview with the TV magnate, when he saw he had new mail. It was a message from Xiaochuan.

His eyes lit up, thinking it must be about new developments in the Shenzhen cases. He hit ENTER and Xiaochuan's e-mail leaped onto his screen.

Dear Nie Feng,

How's everything? It's been several days since I received your latest e-mail. There's been a development in the case: on July 20 Feng

Xueying was fatally struck by a car. Our investigation shows that it was no accident.

We found conversations between her and Zhong Tao and Zhu Mei-feng on a tape she made. Zhong and Zhu could well be involved in Hong Yiming's murder, since both had been to Hong's office and had a motive and the opportunity to plant the poisoned candy. We consider them suspects in all three murders—Hu, Hong, and Feng.

Zhu Mei-feng has fled to Hong Kong and we're looking for her.

Our biggest problem is Zhong's alibi. We've checked and rechecked those twenty-five minutes, but haven't come up with anything. As you know, Lesser Meisha Resort has two ticket entrances, the main gate in the west and a side door to the east. They're both guarded twenty-four hours a day. Few tourists go through the gates after 11:00 at night, so the guards would remember if Zhong and Ding passed through between 11:05 and 11:30. When we showed Zhong's and Ding's pictures to all the guards on duty that night, no one recalled seeing them.

We also checked the resort cabin, but found nothing worth noting.

All this means that our investigation into Zhong's role has reached a dead end. Chief Wu calls those twenty-five minutes our blind spot. Everyone, including Yao Li and me, are frustrated. We don't know if we'll ever solve the cases.

I'll stop my depressing note here.

Please give Academy President Nie my best.

Xiaochuan (22/07)

Nie stared at the screen as he mulled over what he'd just read.

It was stuffy in the room, which was penetrated by loud music from a nearby club, but he focused on cracking Zhong's alibi. Chief Wu was right about the twenty-five minutes being the blind spot in Hu's murder. It was the key to solving the case. So he opened to a page in his interview book and stared at the triangle on the Dapeng Bay map, which he'd drawn while attending the case meeting.

It was a rough sketch of a narrow triangle—the three points being Greater Meisha, Lesser Meisha, and Nan'ao. Greater and Lesser Meisha formed the short bottom line of the triangle, the sharp acute angle reached a point in the lower right, at Nan'ao in southeast.

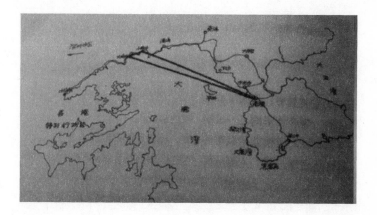

The more he looked at it, the greater his sense that there was something strange or abnormal about the shape, but he couldn't put his finger on it. It just looked unnatural, forced even. The bottom line was too short, while the acute angle was too sharp, presenting the image of a shard of broken glass, or a dagger pointing to the lower right, as if at some arcane truth.

He took out a pen and began to write.

Point 1: Greater Meisha (around 7 on the evening of June 24, Hu Guohao disappears outside Seaview Hotel)

Point 2: Lesser Meisha (around 6 in the morning of June 25, Hu's body found by the pier)

Point 3: Nan'ao (the afternoon of June 30, Hu's briefcase shows up; red tide is found in the water in which Hu drowned)

He turned to the previous page to review his notes from the meeting.

June 30, afternoon, the Criminal Division Office of the Y District Public Security Bureau.

Questions regarding Hu Guohao's death:

One, why did Hu Guohao go to Nan'ao? Was he summoned there by that mysterious phone call or did he suddenly decide to go for a swim there?—the former is more likely.

Second, how did he get there? By bus, taxi, or a car sent to Greater Meisha by Zhou Zhengxing?—need to follow up on this.

Third, how did Hu drown in Nan'ao? Did he suffer a heart attack while swimming? Did Zhou murder him while they were swimming together?

Fourth, how did Hu's body wash up on the beach at Lesser Meisha? If he drowned while swimming in Nan'ao, the body could not have drifted twenty km to Lesser Meisha. Highly unlikely that Hu would suddenly decide to swim across the Dapeng Bay and drown near Lesser Meisha when he overextended himself.

So was his body taken there by car? by boat?

It takes an hour to drive from Lesser Meisha to Nan'ao on the mountain road, making it impossible to get there and back in twenty-five minutes. And it would take a speedboat at least an hour and a half to get there by the shortest route. So Zhou Zhengxing replaces Zhong Tao as the prime suspect.

He looked up from his notes and stared out the window, where the clear summer evening sky sparkled with stars. Then his eyes lit up when a question formed in his head.

What they had talked about (including the four questions) at the meeting was based on the premise that Hu had gone to Nan'ao and drowned there. That was based on two pieces of "ironclad evidence":

Nan'ao's algae-infested water was found in Hu's body, and his brief-case turned up at Nan'ao Elementary School.

But these leads led nowhere, and the police were faced with a riddle: how had Hu's body wound up at Lesser Meisha? No one in Nan'ao had seen Hu on June twenty-fourth from that afternoon till midnight; the police had checked all the places he could have visited, including Nan'ao Elementary School, Nan'ao Port, all the restaurants and teahouses and seaside swimming pools. Nie's own quick visit to Nan'ao before returning to Chengdu had turned up "witnesses" who proved otherwise.

So what exactly was going on here?

A hunch sent him back to the map, where he studied the narrow triangle he'd drawn. Suddenly he sensed that the triangle was pointing at something, some place actually, and that place was Nan'ao. Things were beginning to make sense.

He took out a city map of Shenzhen and stared at the area near Dapeng Bay.

If Nan'ao was indeed the crime scene (because of the algae and the briefcase, both of which pointed "consciously" to the fishing village), Zhong Tao could not have committed the murder and dumped the body on the beach at Lesser Meisha within twenty-five minutes. He had a perfect alibi.

But what if he reversed the process? That is, instead of Nan'ao, the crime scene was a spot reachable in twenty-five minutes. That would be Lesser Meisha, at a secluded spot near the barbecue ground. Then Zhong Tao would have had the opportunity to commit the murder.

But how could he explain the algae in Hu's lungs?

"The type of algae found in the body ascertains the place where the person drowned." That was the ME's analytical principle. Algae that could only have appeared in Nan'ao was found in Hu's lungs, which was why the police determined that he had drowned there. But all that really proved was that Hu had taken in water with red tide somewhere near Nan'ao. In fact, there were two possible reasons for how he had Nan'ao water in his lungs.

One, he drowned there and breathed in the local water.

Two, he was somewhere else, but breathed in Nan'ao seawater and then drowned. Someone would have to have transported Nan'ao water to wherever Hu was killed. If so, this was a methodically planned, meticulously executed murder that required several conditions:

One, the murderer had intimate knowledge of the red tide trend in Nan'ao.

Two, the murderer had the time and opportunity to get water from Nan'ao.

Three, the murderer had a way to lure Hu to the scene of his death.

Nie had checked the local papers, where he'd found reports on red tides, available to anyone who cared to look them up. Zhong Tao was smart enough to hit upon the idea and form his plan. He could easily fulfill the second condition: from June twenty-second, when severe red tides appeared in Nan'ao, to the afternoon of the twenty-fourth, before the reunion at 7:00 P.M., he had at least fourteen hours to make the round trip.

Based upon what the police later learned from Hong Yiming, any person who could meet all three conditions had to be well known to Hu and trusted by him; otherwise, he would not have been so easily called away by a brief phone call. Zhong fit that description well also.

As for Hu's briefcase, it had been intentionally tossed at the elementary school to lead the police to Nan'ao. In fact, it wasn't found until five days after the murder, though no one gave that much thought, since everyone knew that it had been dumped in the weeds and was hard to see. The boy who found the briefcase had relieved himself at that spot three days earlier, and had not seen it. Nie Feng had talked to the boy, a chubby kid called Lai Zhai, on his short trip to Nan'ao.

Nie suddenly felt energized by the thought of a new scenario:

—the primary crime scene was near the barbecue ground at Lesser Meisha beach,

—the secondary crime scene was the stone jetty where Hu's body was dumped, and

—Nan'ao (the school athletic field or the beach) was a fabricated crime scene.

His conclusion: the murderer had cleverly gained time by manipulating locations, thus creating an alibi. He went for his phone and called Xiaochuan's cell.

"Ah, it's you, Nie Feng." Xiaochuan sounded sleepy. "It's three in the morning. What's so urgent it can't wait?"

"I've seen through the blind spot in Hu's murder." Excitement turned his voice shrill.

"Really?" Xiaochuan was jolted awake; he shot out of bed.

Nie gave him a brief account of his deduction and reasons.

"Nan'ao is a fabricated crime scene. Hu was very likely murdered at Lesser Meisha." Nie was clear and direct in his instructions: "Call your boss right away and tell him that the area around Lesser Meisha Resort needs to be searched one more time."

"How about the area outside the villa?"

"That, too. Using the barbecue ground as the radius center, search any place that can be reached in ten minutes on foot."

"Got it."

— 3 —

Team Leader Cui was dubious after listening to what Xiaochuan had to say.

"Could this *Western Sun* fellow be that good?"

"What he's come up with doesn't sound groundless to me," Yao commented.

Bureau Chief Wu, in uniform, walked in at that moment to check on their progress.

"Xiaochuan has something for us," Cui said.

"Tell us." Chief Wu sat down.

Xiaochuan repeated what he'd heard from Nie.

"We've already searched the area near Lesser Meisha. Should we do it again?" Cui asked Chief Wu.

"Better safe than sorry," Chief Wu said decisively. "Get your men together and comb the area by the barbecue grounds. Following Mr. Nie's suggestion, search the area within a radius of ten minutes by foot. Don't miss anything, not even a rabbit hole."

"Yes, sir."

The area singled out by Nie was more like a fan-shaped semi-circle, since the south side abutted the bay of Lesser Meisha. They divided the area into three sections:

First, the crescent-like Lesser Meisha Resort, some four to five hundred meters from east to west, including spots like Chao Kok, Lovers' Lane, the barbecue grounds, the swimming area and beach, the lockers and showers, Haiting resort cabins, Haiyun Pavilion, Bihai Teahouse, and Mei Yuan.

Second, the streets outside the resort's main entrance, including shops, guesthouses, the entertainment district, homes of Lesser Meisha residents, etc.

Third, the Lesser Meisha Hotel and surrounding buildings beyond the east gate.

On the day of the search, roughly a hundred policemen conducted an extensive and intensive search of the three areas, looking as if they would dig into the ground to identity the murder site if they had to. They were very thorough, searching the wooded area behind the barbecue ground and the caves under the wooden bridge at Chao Kok, but no clue of value was found.

Zhong Tao and his schoolmates had spent the night of the twenty-fourth in resort cabins, a row of single-story beige houses separated by low, see-through fences. According to records at the reception desk, they had rented four double rooms, each bed costing 168 yuan, which included passes to the swimming area and a self-serve barbecue dinner. The guests were given keys to their cabins, which allowed them to come and go on their own. That meant the resort staff had no idea whether Zhong and Ding had returned to the cabin, and if they had, what they'd done there. And, since more than a month had passed, and many guests had used the cabins, it would have been impossible to find any trace of them. A search of the cabins yielded nothing.

The Green Bay Teahouse consisted of a line of small bamboo pavilions nestled against a shaded path lined with coconut palms. Each was under twenty square meters in size and came equipped with bamboo chairs, tea tables, and sleeping accommodations. In addition to enjoying a restful cup of tea, tourists could spend the night there if they liked. Young waitresses in blue tie-dyed blouses were on hand to provide services related to tea drinking. Zheng Yong led officers in a search of every pavilion and questioned every waitress. It appeared that neither Zhong nor Ding had been there that night, and they found no trace of Hu Guohao.

Next to the enclosed plum garden behind the Green Bay Teahouse were the luxury guestrooms of Haiyun Pavilion and the shower rooms. By the time the police finished combing through these places, they had completed a thorough search of the Lesser Meisha Resort.

They found nothing.

That did not preclude the possibility that Zhong Tao and Ding Lan had left the resort during those twenty-five minutes. While there was no record of their using the main entrance or the east gate, they could have found another way to exit. In fact, the search team made a discovery after the search spread to the other two sections.

Xiaochuan and Yao Li stumbled upon an unexpected clue when they went to search the Lesser Meisha Hotel. A walk of five minutes took them from the barbecue ground to the east gate, which opened to the hotel's tennis court and its surrounding greenery. They skirted the tennis court, crossed a parking lot, and arrived at the hotel's side entrance; once inside they took the corridor to the left and reached the hotel lobby after passing the day spa.

The sparkle of the lobby's green marble floor was enhanced by the mirrored posts. This was their second visit to the hotel; on the day after Hu's corpse was found on the beach, they'd come to check on his stay at the hotel and look for his clothes. They'd shown their badges and asked around, but none of the staff on duty that night had seen him.

The service manager walked up from behind the counter. It was the same woman as last time.

"Hello, officers."

"We need some more information about June twenty-fourth."

"But it's been over a month." The manager did not seem inclined to cooperate.

"Can you tell us who else was on duty that night?" Yao asked.

"Hmm." The woman turned and called out to a staff member, "Go get Ah-fen."

When Ah-fen, a short, chunky girl with freckles arrived, Xiao-chuan showed her two pictures of Hu Guohao.

"Did you see this man on June twenty-fourth?"

Ah-fen studied the pictures and shook her head.

"How about this one?" He handed her another picture. It was a shot of Zhong Tao.

"He looks like a guest who was here that day."

"Really!" Xiaochuan and Yao Li nearly shouted. Ah-fen pointed to a corner of the verandah teahouse.

"He was sitting at a table over there, with a pot of milk tea."

A post blocked all but a corner of the black granite tabletop. Xiao-chuan saw a rattan chair.

"Why do you still remember him?"

"He looked different, like he was waiting for someone," Ah-feng recalled. "And, it was a woman who picked up the check." She told the officers that she'd asked the woman where the man had gone, and the woman had told her he'd gone to the bathroom.

"Is this the woman?" Xiaochuan showed her Ding Lan's picture.

"Yes, that's her!" Ah-fen recognized her immediately.

Xiaochuan and Yao Lin looked at each other knowingly.

"Do you remember what time it was?"

"Yes, it had to be around seven thirty in the evening." Close to the time when Hu got his call.

"Look at this again. Did you see this man around the same time?" Xiaochuan pointed at Hu's picture. Ah-feng examined the picture carefully and shook her head again.

"No."

For members of the criminal division, the unexpected discovery that Zhong Tao and Ding Lan had been present at the Lesser Meisha Hotel on the evening of the twenty-fourth was like a shot in the arm. After a month of spinning their wheels, the investigation team seemed ready to solve the case.

The focus of the search now moved to the third section: the streets and residential area around the resort. Rows of restaurants, hotels, guesthouses, clubs, pubs, and hair salons lined the slope beyond the resort. A brisk walk from the barbecue ground out to the main entrance to the business district took six to seven minutes.

After checking every retail concern and talking to anyone remotely related, including hotel and guesthouse registration desks, restaurant owners, club managers, waitresses, salon workers, and more, the police found nothing. The last place to check was the residential area, which presented problems, owing partly to the squat, simple rentals that were scattered here and there.

With a young local cop as a guide, Cui began the search with Xiaochuan and Yao Li. Behind the houses a towering banyan tree stood in front of a small temple with pink stone steps and walls, the roof topped with yellow glazed tiles. A narrow alley, no more than a meter in width, spoked off from the temple gate; close to a dozen squat houses with green roof tiles, rusty metal windows, and peeling walls lined both sides of the alley. Above each door hung a small blue For Rent sign.

They checked every one of the nineteen rentals; four of the least livable ones had been vacant for over two months, while migrant workers from Hunan, all employed at a nearby construction site, currently occupied thirteen. The last two, stacked with bricks and sand, were obviously being remodeled.

The local policeman summoned all nineteen landlords, but none of them had seen Zhong Tao or Ding Lan, and could supply no information regarding Hu Guohao. Since any outsider would stand out in a place like this, the search had come up empty. Morale sank among the team, including Xiaochuan and Yao Li. Team Leader Cui was in a foul mood.

"I was right. We should never have listened to that *Western Sun*. See where it got us?" Cui appeared to be upset with himself, but that did not make Xiaochuan or Yao Li feel better. They knew to keep quiet.

— 4 —

That night, when Nie Feng turned on his computer, a message from Xiaochuan caught his eye.

Hi, Nie Feng,

Chief Wu took your advice and sent nearly a hundred policemen to comb the three main sections of Lesser Meisha (the area within a ten-minute walking radius of the barbecue ground). We even searched the streets, the residential district, and other hotels in Lesser Meisha; we pretty much turned the place inside out.

We were exhausted, and we found nothing that would pinpoint

the primary crime scene of Hu's murder. The result was disappointing, to say the least.

Yao Li and I did make an unexpected discovery when we went to the Lesser Meisha Hotel: Zhong Tao and Ding Lan had tea in the lobby on the evening of the twenty-fourth. Other than that, we didn't find anything there either.

That's all. More next time.

Xiaochuan 7/22

What went wrong?

Staring at his computer screen, Nie laughed unhappily. The bouncing red logo, Yahoo, in the upper left corner was getting annoying; it seemed to be mocking him.

Xiao Ju stuck her head in to say, "Brother Nie, a phone call for you."

"Who's it from?"

"Your editor in chief, the old paper fogey."

"Watch your manners. How do you get off calling him that?" Nie glared at her as he got up to take the call in the living room; she made a face as he passed by her.

"Hi, Mr. Wu. What's up?"

"How's your 'follow-up report' coming along?"

"Almost there; they're on the verge of drawing in the net."

"Are you on a fishing expedition? What's this talk about drawing in the net?" Wu joked.

"Sorry, I got carried away. What I meant to say was, the end is in sight." Nie laughed.

"There's an international scholarly conference in Sichuan's Guanghan County on the Sanxingdui ruins. We've been invited to do a special report, and I want you to go."

Now the real reason for the phone call became evident.

"I'm swamped. I'm in the middle of finishing the report." Nie was not keen on accepting the new assignment.

"They asked for you specifically," the "old paper fogey" said before playing his ace card: "Shall I send a car for you?"

"Send a car for me?" That was unusual.

"That settles it." The editor hung up before Nie could object, though he was already thinking about something else. For at that instant, he recalled what Xiaochuan had once told him: Ding Lan owned a car.

That clarified things considerably. He ran back to his study, where he unfolded a Shenzhen map and examined it carefully, his gaze stopping at Lesser Meisha Bay, as he tried to recall the scene when he was there on July fourth.

(Flashback 1) The beach ended at a backwater, where the waves surged, each higher than the one before. He turned back and spotted a botanical garden beyond the embankment. A profusion of flowers in all colors peeked out from under a canopy of subtropical trees. His curiosity piqued, he hoisted himself up onto the embankment and rested his chest against the low wall of what was a seedling garden, like a different world. The garden abutted the lawn of the Lesser Meisha Hotel.

A short jump was all one needed to be at the hotel; just beyond the lawn was a parking lot. Ding Lan's white Citroën could have been parked there, waiting.

(Flashback 2) The following morning at the Haiyi Teahouse, a tourist mentioned that he and some friends had been there the previous weekend and had heard birdcalls in the direction of Lovers' Lane in the middle of the night. Nie had walked down Lovers' Lane toward Chao Kok. On his left was the levee and to his right the hills. Green plastic chairs were placed at irregular intervals for tourists to rest under the shade of trees. A towering old banyan tree not far from the pier created a verdant umbrella with its leafy branches. On the trunk was a plaque carved with the inscription HUNDRED-YEAR-OLD IMMORTAL BANYAN.

He'd stood under the tree and looked up at the many bird nests. White egrets, dozens of them, were perched on the branches. They must have been startled by something when they raised a fuss that night. A winding stone path behind the tree was littered with fallen leaves. Bent at the waist, he'd parted the low-hanging branches and climbed up the damp stone steps to the top of the slope, the outer edge of the resort. Across the chain-link fence, a small brick house rose out of the underbrush, like an abandoned watchtower.

From where he stood on Lovers' Lane he could see the tops of buses passing by the fence, and it dawned on him that the highway connecting Greater and Lesser Meisha was above him.

If, on the early morning of the twenty-fifth, when all was quiet, a car was parked beside the highway, the murderer could have taken Hu's body out of the trunk, carried it over his shoulder, crawled under the fence, and reached the pier by walking down the slope. It was the shortest route. The squawking egrets were proof that something had disturbed them.

Nie called Xiaochuan and asked for Chief Wu's cell number.

"How are you, Chief Wu? This is Nie Feng."

"Oh, Mr. Nie." Chief Wu was slightly hoarse.

"I'm sorry to bother you so late at night, but I have something important to share with you."

"Please go ahead."

"I made a mistake in my analysis of the primary crime scene in Lesser Meisha. I overlooked something."

"What was that?"

"That Ding Lan drives a white Citroën."

"A white Citroën?" Chief Wu repeated.

"Yes," Nie said politely but confidently. "So the crime scene had to be within five to seven minutes by car. I did a quick calculation: It takes roughly five minutes to walk from the barbecue ground to the sapling garden east of the beach and climb over the fence behind the Lesser Meisha Hotel. Ten minutes for a round trip. If it took five minutes to dispose of Hu's body, the remaining ten of the twenty-five minutes could have been used for transportation by car.

But if the killer climbed the slope from Lover's Lane and crawled under the chain-link fence behind the hotel, that would only take three to four minutes, or about six minutes both ways. He'd still need five minutes to dispose of Hu's body, which would have left him with fourteen minutes, a seven-minute trip each way."

"Five to seven minutes by car. That would mean that the primary crime scene could have been farther than we'd thought."

"Right. And that larger area would then cover a place I'd overlooked before—"

"Greater Meisha!" Chief Wu blurted out.

"Yes, it was Greater Meisha."

"Thank you so much, Mr. Nie." Chief Wu slapped his hand on his desk and got up.

Time to focus in on Greater Meisha.

Chief Wu personally took charge of the second, larger-scale search.

A gentle slope, Qitou Ridge, separated Greater and Lesser Meisha, which were six to seven kilometers apart. The whole eastern part of Greater Meisha fell within the search area, which was anywhere inside an arc that could be reached within five to seven minutes by car from Lesser Meisha; that included most of the beach at the Greater Meisha Resort, the Pearl Garden Hotel, the Meisha Hotel, a clinic, and Meisha Market, as well as two residential districts—Shangping Villa and Chengkeng Villa, where only a few dozens families lived.

Cui and his officers began a systematic search, assisted by police dogs. To be safe, they extended their search area beyond the original arc. The local police station also sent all the policemen they could spare to aid in the search.

Two rows of small duplexes with ceramic tile walls and low fences, so typical of Guangdong houses, stood in the shadow of towering white apartment buildings near the Pearl Garden Hotel. The team entered the area and discovered a small family shrine next to a tall banyan tree. A round stone table surrounded by eight stone stools had been set up under the tree. The shrine had yellow tiles and glazed roof tiles; one inside wall of a tiny courtyard was decorated with a colorful drawing depicting "luck/wealth/longevity/happiness," the other with a mosaic painting of "five good fortunes of longevity"

A half dozen dilapidated houses stood behind the shrine, with peaked tiled roofs, old wooden doors, and peeling whitewashed walls. No house numbers, probably because they were too old, but with an occasional number painted in red. The last three buildings on the right were all quite similar. When Cui and his officers reached them, he sensed something: the place looked abandoned and overgrown with weeds, the perfect crime scene.

They searched the first two houses, but found the last one locked. A local cop fetched the owner, a kindly, graying woman in her sixties.

"Is this your house?" Cui asked.

"Yes." She nodded.

He asked her to unlock the door. It was pitch-black inside; even the floor had turned dark and dirty. A small space was created with red bricks covered in lime, possibly a makeshift shower room. Further back a brick stove was topped by an old stove connected to a liquid gas tank. Odds and ends, including some plastic buckets, were piled next to the door.

A water faucet next to the stone steps outside the door was connected to a hose; moss covered the damp ground. A paved open space some three or four meters wide in front of the row of old houses was wide enough to park a car.

"Did someone rent this house last month?" Cui asked the woman.

"Yes, a woman."

"What was her name?"

"Wu Li, looked to be in her forties."

Xiaochuan showed her several photographs.

"That's her, Wu Li, the woman who rented this house." The owner picked out Ding Lan from a stack of college photos.

"Wu Li? Did you check her ID?"

"These are temporary rentals, we never check IDs," the old woman admitted openly.

Cui cast a glance at the local cop, who looked embarrassed. Obviously they weren't enforcing rental regulations. The landlords cared only about the rent, and neither checked renters' IDs, nor notified the precinct station.

"When did she come?"

"Early last month, I think, on a weekend. Let me see. It was the first or the second of June. She said she was renting the place for a couple of workers from her hometown. She paid me three hundred yuan for the month."

"Did anyone else show up after that?"

"I don't know."

"So you collected the rent and said to hell with everything else." The local policeman reprimanded her with a look.

"We try to stay out of our renters' business."

"When did this Wu Li end the lease?"

"End of June."

"Anyone staying here now?"

"No. No one has rented it since."

The police secured the scene and began a search. Several filthy towels were draped over a bamboo pole set up as a rack opposite the door. A wooden staircase with no handrails stood against the left wall; it swayed when they climbed it into a small room with walls formed from waterproofing tiles. It was a dark room with cheap furnishings, but clean enough, with a bed, a table, and two chairs. A common plastic washbasin rested on the floor. Xiaochuan pulled back the bedsheet and found a white plastic bucket with the capacity of about twenty-five liters, half filled with a murky, brackish liquid that had a fishy smell.

Cui summoned a pair of uniformed technicians with a phone call.

"Let's see what we have here," he told them.

One of the gloved technicians took pictures from all angles, while his partner, also gloved, removed a small tube of dusting powder from his metal case and brushed it on the door handle, the edges of the table, and the plastic bucket for fingerprints. In the meantime, the other searchers combed the area around the rental unit. Behind a window they found a balled-up strip of yellow duct tape on which the technician retrieved half a thumbprint. The prints and bucket were taken back to the station as evidence.

The technicians found a match the following morning. The prints from the door handle and table were too smudged to be of any use, but they got two clear prints from the bucket, an index finger and a thumb, which matched a partial print from the yellow tape. They matched Zhong Tao's prints, which they'd earlier retrieved from a drinking glass.

Everyone on the team was too excited for words. After a month of groping in the dark, they were finally zeroing in on their target. The backslapping and high fives ended, however, when they received the test results of the bucket's contents: nothing but concentrated seawater, with no trace of algae, evidence that could have solved the first murder.

Xiaochuan and Yao Li were sent to Guangzhou with the liquid for further testing at the Nanhai Environmental Monitoring Center. Under a high-powered microscope the sample was murky and specked with shreds of something.

They quickly learned the reason from the director, who told them that algae has a very short life span. A new generation is normally produced every few hours, which is why it is termed explosive growth. At best it can survive a day or two, but in an oxygen-deprived bucket with dim lighting, it probably died very quickly. In liquid form, it can be seen under a high-powered microscope a couple of days after it dies, but after that, the cells disintegrate and are impossible to detect under any microscope.

The two officers left disappointed. Cui was naturally unhappy with the result, since they had hoped to use it to make their case. Now they could end up with nothing but wasted effort.

Only by finding Nan'ao algae in the water could they prove that the rental unit was where Hu was murdered. They found a lip print on the yellow tape, most likely from Hu when they sealed his lips, but his body had been cremated, so they would never learn if it was his. In addition, they found no trace of Hu in the rental unit—no cell phone, no clothing, and no fingerprints. Zhong Tao and Ding Lan could easily say they were secretly carrying on in the rental, which amounted to nothing, except perhaps unsavory personal behavior.

Chief Wu decided to put Zhong Tao and Ding Lan under round-the-clock surveillance.

— 5 —

The Sanxingdui Museum in Guanghan. In the luxurious exhibit hall, a group of visitors, looking quite scholarly, were standing in front of a glass case displaying a giant bronze mask, as an exuberant female docent cheerfully explained:

"This is the world-famous bronze mask known as the Zhuyang Mask. At one point thirty-eight millimeters wide and sixty-five millimeters high, it is generally considered to be the largest in the world. Please take a close look at the bulging eyes, which are symbols for ancient Sichuan. As some of you know, the pictograph for Sichuan on the oracle bones has a large eye on top."

The specialists listened with interest and knowing smiles. The mask was the size of a millstone, with a large mouth, bulging eyes, a towering nose, and fully expanded ears like the crescent-shaped tips of ancient spears. With its unusual shape and eerie features, its inherent mystery elicited wondrous sighs from the visitors.

With a conference attendee badge around his neck, Nie Feng trailed the team of scholars, listening absentmindedly and frequently checking his watch. His mind was a thousand miles away in Shenzhen, where the police ought to be tightening the net around the murderers. Finally his cell rang at four fifteen; it was from Xiaochuan. Nie answered while racing out of the exhibit hall.

"Good news, Nie Feng!" Xiaochuan's excitement was palpable. "Based on what you told us, we found the spot where Zhong and Ding stayed; it was a rental unit in Greater Meisha and may very well be the place where Hu Guohao was murdered."

"Really!" Nie could hardly surpress his own jubilation.

"Yes. We're chasing down all leads. You're amazing." Xiaochuan went on to tell him about the crime scene investigation. The discovery of the bucket with seawater did not surprise Nie, but he wondered why Zhong would leave his print on the bucket. The case showed that he was a mastermind who had meticulously planned every step. Was the print a careless mistake, did he not have time to remove all traces, or was there another reason?

"Did you find any of Hu Guohao's prints at the scene?" Nie asked.

"No, but we found a strip of used yellow tape with Zhong's print. There was another print but we have no way of knowing whose it is."

"Any sign of Hu's clothes?"

"No, nothing."

"They did a thorough job of cleaning up," Nie muttered.

He completed his interview that afternoon and, after gathering additional material, returned to Chengdu that night. The trip took half an hour. Sitting in the back of a taxi, Nie closed his eyes, feeling quite elated. Yellow and green fields broke up the dark night as they raced along the highway, while a montage of scenes flashed through his mind. Zhong's carefully planned and executed murder scheme slowly took shape in Nie's mind.

On June twenty-fourth, from 11:05 to 11:30, Zhong Tao and Ding Lan carried out their plan. At 11:10, they climbed over the low fence on the eastern shore, found their way to the parking lot of the Lesser Meisha Hotel, and climbed into her white Citroën. Five minutes later, at 11:15, they arrived at the Greater Meisha rental unit.

Within five minutes, Ding helped Zhong "execute" Hu Guohao, whom they had drugged with sleeping pills.

11:25, they drove back to the parking lot at Lesser Meisha and retraced their steps.

They were back on the barbecue ground at 11:30.

At around three o'clock that morning, Zhong sneaked out of his cabin, climbed over the fence, and drove the Citroën to the rental unit in Greater Meisha, where he loaded Hu's body into the trunk. Then he drove to the highway near Lovers' Lane, parked and turned off the headlights. He took Hu's body out of the trunk and carried it over his shoulder, crawling under the chain-link fence, and startling the egrets perched in the banyan tree. He walked down the stone steps to the beach at Lesser Meisha, where he dumped the body.

He had to have driven to Nan'ao beforehand to get the seawater. But why kill Hu Guohao? What was his motive? This was the key.

Feeling he had to make a trip to Yunnan, Nie Feng called the editor at home.

"Mr. Wu?" Nie said from the taxi. "I've finished the Sanxingdui interview."

"That was fast." Wu sounded pleased.

"I'd like three days off." Nie paused. "For a trip to Yunnan."

"Yunnan? To Shangri-la?"

"I wish."

"Or, maybe you're going to Lugu Lake for a little hanky-panky," the editor joked.

"It has something to do with the Hu Guohao case." Nie ignored the joke.

"New developments?" The editor turned serious.

"Don't know yet. That's what I want to find out." Nie added, "But I have a hunch that the key to solving the case is in Yunnan."

"When do you plan to leave?"

"Tomorrow, if possible."

"Sure." Nie had not expected his editor to be so quick to agree.

"I'll give you four days. But with one condition—give me a report on the Western Flower Show."

So that was what the old fellow had in mind, turning Nie into a reporting machine!

"Then I'll have to charge my expenses to the magazine."

"No problem. You're on!"

ELEVEN

Melodious Harmonica

— 1 —

July twenty-fourth, Monday, Zhong Tao returned from his business trip. Exactly a month had passed since Hu Guohao had been found dead.

The soaring glass curtain wall on the Landmark Building continued to reflect a blue sky with puffy white clouds. Stepping out of the elevator on the twenty-fourth floor, he sensed something different in the air. Dressed in a short-sleeved shirt and a date-red tie, he showed the wear and tear of travel on his darkened skin. As he neared his office, he was surprised to see the secretary's office deserted, while the chairman's office door was sealed with official tape stamped with red seals.

He had spoken with Zhou Zhengxing on the phone when he was off traveling in the southwest, and had learned of Feng Xueying's death. He was quiet for a long time when he heard the news. "Are you still there?" Zhou asked.

"She died for nothing!" was Zhong's response.

All the employees he passed in the hallway gave him strange looks.

"Mr. Zhong, you're back," some greeted him with a nod.

"Hmm." He'd been away only a week but it felt as if it had been a lifetime ago.

He went into the CEO's office, where he briefed Zhou on the Chongqing real estate conference. Zhou looked tired. He asked a few questions about the conference before turning to the subject of Landmark's recent troubles.

"What do they know about Ah-ying's death?" Zhong asked.

"The police think it was deliberate." Zhou intentionally avoided the word "murder."

"Why is Chairwoman Zhu's office sealed?"

"We haven't heard from her for a week, so the police decided to secure the scene, to be safe."

"I see." A pensive look appeared on Zhong's face.

In fact, the police had issued a warrant for her arrest.

After Feng Xueying's death, the police retrieved Zhu's cell phone record and found that half an hour before Feng was killed, Zhu had made several calls to a cell with an unknown number, and that five minutes after the car hit Feng, Zhu received another call from that number, which lasted only four seconds. After that, Zhu shut down her cell. The police requested the subscriber of the unknown number; it belonged to a parolee nicknamed "Big Beard," whom they arrested in a foot massage place three days later. The thumb print on his left hand matched one they found on the car handle of the black VW, forcing him to confess that Zhu had paid him two hundred thousand yuan to kill Feng Xueying. She'd given him a hundred thousand up front and another hundred thousand when he finished the job.

But it was unclear whether Zhou knew all this.

The new boss at Landmark pulled himself together and told Zhong that recent events were damaging the company's image and credibility. The media had stormed the building, and all Shenzhen was enjoying the spectacle. Some of the city's Realtors showed sympathy over their plight, others were licking their chops.

"What's most important now is for us to stand firm and make sure the business runs as usual. We have to minimize damage to the company." Zhou stressed that they were all in it together. "Oh, and the police have been asking about you, too."

"Me? Really?" Zhong said, impassively.

That night, at the Jiujiulong Mongolian Barbecue, the largest self-serve hot-pot restaurant in Shenzhen, Ding Lan and Zhong Tao met for dinner; it was her treat, as a way to welcome him back.

Jiujiulong, with enough seats for hundreds, charged 38 yuan per person, with free soft drinks. The food was cheap and good, so it was full just about every night. A dazzling display of food was placed neatly in the middle of the rectangular room, with clearly divided sections for barbecue pieces, hot-pot ingredients, precooked dishes, and salads and fruit. The variety of food was impressive: all sorts of seafood, crab, fatty beef, mutton, fish heads, and vegetables; there were even dozens of varieties of ice cream and desserts.

They sat across from each other at a small hardwood table, with a bubbling, steaming hot pot between them enveloping them in a rich, mouthwatering aroma.

"The mutton tastes great!" Zhong dipped a string of fatty mutton in his sauce and put it in his mouth.

Ding Lan just looked at him and smiled. "You have no table manners."

"You think so?"

The diners at the next table, young men who looked like migrant workers, were talking and smacking their lips loudly as they ate, oblivious of others and their own table manners. Crab shells and legs were piled high on their plates.

"Did you see your aunt when you were in Sichuan?"

"I did. She's in poor health."

"Who else did you see?"

"Our middle-school class supervisor."

"Oh, Euclid."

The class supervisor, surnamed Ou, was a former soldier who had been transferred to teach plane geometry. The students gave her the nickname "Euclid," partly because her name sort of sounded like that, but also because of her subject.

"You still remember her? Her hair has turned completely gray."

"How time flies. I remember how fashionable she was, wearing a red sweater under a faded yellow army jacket. And she permed her hair."

"Her memory is as sharp as ever. She can still name just about everyone in the class."

"Really?"

"Some members of our class look her up when they go back to Sichuan."

"Did she give you any news of Xia Yuhong?" Ding couldn't hold back.

"I asked about her." Zhong smiled. "She gave me her e-mail address."

He was told that Xia Yuhong was teaching at the University of Pennsylvania in the US, where she had become a well-known sociology professor. She'd returned to Sichuan to see her family last spring. She was still single.

"Did you contact her?"

"I did." Zhong told her that he was surprised to receive her e-mail reply from the States. Xia did not bring up their zhiqing days, but she did say she hoped to see him.

"The two of you are finally back in touch," Ding said, her expression a mixture of happiness for Zhong and envy.

"It'll never be the way it was before," Zhong said calmly.

"When will you leave?"

"I'm waiting for a visa. It's a North American Tour, stopping in Canada first."

"You should leave as soon as possible."

"I know. How about you?"

"Don't worry about me. I'll be fine."

"Still, you have to be careful. And take care of yourself."

"Please give Yuhong my best," Ding said teary-eyed.

— 2 —

Nie Feng walked out of the Kunming Airport with his duffel bag.

He'd taken a morning flight from Shenzhen, arriving in Yunnan at 9:05.

"Long time no see, Springtown!" He stopped to look around; on the tarmac a giant billboard displayed a string of numbers:

07/24/MONDAY, 9:25 A.M.

It's been a month since Hu Guohao's death, he thought to himself.

He'd made an online reservation for a room at the Sunshine Holiday Hotel. To save time, he decided to take a taxi to the hotel, check in, and headed to the flower show. He planned to use three rolls of films and write up a story of about five thousand words, which he estimated would take a day and a night to complete.

The following afternoon, his work on the flower show behind him, he made a series of visits to offices connected to the Yunnan Construction Corps. Zhong Tao and the zhiqing past occupied his mind the whole time.

The one-time farms of the Corps were now under the jurisdiction of the Provincial Land Reclamation Bureau. He checked with the statistics and data department of the Bureau, where a Ms. Pang, a former zhiqing herself, told him that all the files from before 1995 had been transferred to the Yunnan Archives by government order. There a guard checked his ID before letting him enter the building, where he immediately felt the weight of history. A relief mural of national people's customs adorned the wall facing the entrance, while the wall next to the staircase was filled with old photos of Yunnan's minorities taken by foreign visitors in the waning days of the Qing dynasty.

The third-floor restricted-material reading room was a large, quiet room, with thirty or more wooden desks, and five computers on a table against one wall, two of which were being used by an elderly, scholarly-looking man in a striped T-shirt and a young woman with long hair. Three female staff members sat behind the glass window of the circulation desk.

"My name is Nie Feng," he told them. "I'm a reporter from *Western Sunshine* magazine. I'd like to check out some zhiqing files."

"Oh, we're sorry," one of them, a short-haired woman in glasses, said, "but we're in the process of reorganizing the documents. Why don't you come back the day after tomorrow?"

"The day after tomorrow?" Nie hesitated before asking politely, "I made a special trip and am on a tight schedule. Could you possibly make an exception and let me look at them now?"

"I'll have to check with our section chief." The woman turned and walked to the back.

She came back in a moment and said to Nie, "The old files are being moved to a new storage site, so it really can't be done today."

"Well, thanks anyway."

After leaving the Yunnan Archives, Nie decided to make a trip to the border region. At the Yunnan Land Reclamation Bureau, he asked for directions to the site of the Lanjiang Farm, where the 2nd Production Team, formerly the 2nd Regiment, was located. Directions in hand, he took a taxi to the Southgate Railroad Station to buy a ticket from Kunming to a place called Guangtong. He had been given three phone numbers: the farm office, the farm political department, and the farm director; this last number would change everything for Nie in his search for the truth.

The bus terminal was next to the train station, and an abrupt change of heart had him opting for a long-distance bus ride to Lanjiang County. At the ticket window, he asked the uniformed ticket seller how long it would take to get there by bus. "No idea," she replied with an inscrutable look, as if she were selling a space shuttle ticket to the moon. Nie could only shake his head and make the best of things.

— 3 —

At seven o'clock that evening, the yellow bus set out. The bland interior had rows of double bunks furnished with patterned bedding and pads, all thirty-two of the tiny spaces occupied. The driver, a trim, middle-aged man, told him they'd be in Lanjiang the following morning, making it a twelve- to thirteen-hour bus ride. Nie's bunk, number eight, was in the middle, next to the window. As soon as they left the city, the beds began to jolt and swing, so he tightened the soiled, green safety belt around his waist, prepared to die with the bus if it happened to roll over.

Nie decided that the two TV sets—one in the front and another in the back—were there purely for decoration, since they were not turned on even once during the trip.

As they left the city, he rested his head against the pillow and watched the scenery pass outside the window—dark mountains, stands of trees, a starry sky, and lights, all imbued with a romantic aura, particularly the sparkling stars and the Milky Way. He had thought he'd fall asleep and wake up in Lanjiang, but the bus swayed too much for him to sleep soundly. His nightglow watch showed 1:00 A.M. when he awoke the first time, and 3:30 the second time. Amid the constant swaying and the unreal sense of movement, he could not escape a feeling that the bus would just keep going and he'd never reach his destination. It was almost as if they were orbiting a giant oval track, going round and round.

At five in the morning, when the world outside was still shrouded in a dark fog, the bus passed an open market, where old men whose heads were wrapped in kerchiefs had taken positions in front of cloth sacks. There were also a few people who had come to sell young livestock. But it was too dark to see their faces.

The bus continued its jolting journey. When he opened his eyes again, the sky had lightened to a grayish blue. He looked up at a hazy half moon peeking out from behind dark clouds. He fell back to sleep, and the next time he woke up, the sky was a fish-belly gray. Finally, at 6:30, they reached Baoshan, where the bus stopped and the driver turned on the interior lights.

"Baoshan," the driver shouted, "this is Baoshan. Anyone getting off?"

No one made a sound, so he started off again.

Dawn came at 7:00. He looked out the window as the bus wound its way cautiously along a circuitous mountain road. When they passed a craggy ridge, he saw a dam down below with murky yellow water oozing its way along. He assumed they'd be in Lanjiang soon, but the bus driver told him they still had far to go. They rode and rode for a long time until the bus stopped at a little shop with no name, where the driver woke up a passenger who was supposed to have gotten off at Baoshan.

They set off again and passed a turn on a switchback, where he spotted tiny diners with signs advertising local specials such as "Tengchong Snacks" and "Braised Chicken." We must have entered the Tengchong region, he thought as he sank into a slumber. The bus windows were speckled with raindrops when he woke up again; it was drizzling outside.

On and on they went; the bus now seemed to be penetrating low-hanging clouds. The rain was falling in sheets as he checked his watch: 9:30. "We'll be in Lanjiang around noon," the young man in the next bunk said. Nie realized that he shouldn't have believed the driver.

He gazed out the window at the local vegetation: trees whose names he didn't know, banana groves (maybe plantain, hard to tell), corn, sugarcane, and rice paddies on embankments. The houses were mostly rammed-earth, some with redbrick walls and green roof tiles; firewood was stacked in front and in back. Here and there he spotted a dish for satellite TV on a rooftop.

They reached the city of Tengchong at 9:50, where they spent forty minutes idling at the stop, for no obvious reason. He wondered if the bus needed water, but the driver offered no explanation. They set off again, but were kicked off the bus before they even left the city center. The five passengers who had remained on the bus were "sold" like livestock to the driver of another bus (later Nie heard they each netted fifteen yuan for the driver). Finally they resumed their westward journey. The second bus was even shabbier than the first and so crowded he found himself suffocating. The speakers blared revolutionary oldies such as "Nights at the Military Port," "Ode to Coral," and "Red Lilies Blooming in Crimson." Luckily the window could be slid back and forth, so he cracked it open to breathe in cool, pleasant mountain air that carried the rich fragrance of ripening rice.

The young man was right, it would be noon before they reached Lanjiang Farm. So he called ahead on his cell, but no one answered at the office and the political department line was busy. He tried the farm director's office; it went through and a Miss Yang picked it up.

"Hello, this is Nie Feng, a reporter from *Western Sunshine*. I'll be in Lanjiang at noon today and would like to travel to Squad Two. Would I be able to get back to town by five this afternoon?"

"No problem. It's not even twenty kilometers." Miss Yang added that he could catch a minibus in town, a convenient choice.

"Just tell the minibus driver you're going to Squad Two. Everybody knows it. When you get there, go see Squad Leader Xi."

"Thank you very much." Now he felt better.

The day began to clear up about then, the blue sky decorated with puffy white clouds. Groves of bamboo seemed to have overtaken the mountains, painting the hills a lush green. Yunnan bamboo grew as high as a three- or four-story building, much taller than the bamboo in Western Sichuan.

At 11:30 they were in Mangxi, followed by more mountain roads.

It was 1:30 in the afternoon when they finally arrived at Lanjiang Bus Terminal.

The first order of business was to buy a return ticket. But he was told that the 7:00 air-conditioned bus was sold out. His other option was a 4:30 bus, with no air-conditioning. There was only one ticket left, but he had to pass since it would make his schedule too tight.

The streets of Lanjiang were underdeveloped, but alive with taxis, driven mostly by women. Being on a tight schedule, he skipped lunch (breakfast also, actually) and hailed a taxi. The charge was five yuan to go anywhere in the city. They reached an intersection where some minibuses were parked, but none of them knew exactly where the farm site was. Flustered, he hailed a light green Geely taxi and negotiated a fare of seventy yuan for a round-trip; it was a rocky road and tough going.

The driver, a young woman with single-fold eyes, was dressed in a sleeveless tank top. A fuzzy toy bear hung from her rearview mirror. When she heard where Nie was going, she said with a sigh, "That was so horrible. Seven youngsters killed in a fire."

"No, there were ten who burned to death, and seven who suffered serious burns," Nie corrected her. Twenty-eight years later, and people were still talking about the tragedy.

After leaving town through the western gate, passing over a section of paved road, and crossing a bridge (over the Lan River), the taxi was soon bumping along the "rocky highway." Potholes and small rocks had the taxi jolting and rumbling along, raising a column of dust. He learned from the driver that she was originally from the farm area, where both her parents worked; but she had not been back for a long time. She got on her cell phone to ask a friend where to turn. Then she asked where the ten zhiqing women were buried, and Nie thought he heard the other person say "on the side of the road."

The Lan River embankments were planted with rice, bamboo, and sugarcane. In the distance, green mountains were set against a backdrop of white clouds. The driver told him that the farmers who worked the embankments were locals who were relatively well off. According to her parents, the zhiqing had opened up farmlands on the mountains through backbreaking work.

The sun came out, a sweltering ball of fire. He felt the top of the car heat up. After seven or eight kilometers, the taxi turned off the highway onto a road that was barely wide enough to accommodate the car. The sides of the road were overgrown with shrubbery with tiny scarlet flowers in dense clusters and an unusual fragrance.

"They're called lantana; we plant them on the roadside as fences."

"Why aren't there any rubber trees?" Nie asked.

"The rubber trees are off in the remote mountain areas." She pointed into the distance.

When they approached a trio of locals, two old and one young, the driver asked for directions. "You took the wrong turn," the young man told her. "You should have taken the next turn up the road." So she backed up, returned to the rocky highway, and continued on, crossing a small concrete bridge. But that didn't seem right to her, thinking they should have kept going on the earlier route. So she asked some women working in the field, who gave her the right directions. They backed up, turned down the former path, and kept at it for a quarter of an hour, when the road curved to the left. It didn't take long to reach a hill where the road abruptly turned steep. The driver stopped to ask a bare-chested man who was chopping wood by the road if this was the 2nd Company site. He nodded wordlessly.

They continued rumbling along a road that was now red soil dotted with broad leaf shrubs.

Nie fell quiet, as he recalled the inscriptions on the blue curtain and experienced the solemn feelings of a man on a pilgrimage.

This was where it had all happened.

I've cursed, but mostly I find the past unforgettable.

The rubber trees will never forget.

Youth has no regrets, but the cost was too high.

The taxi continued uphill.

"We'll be there soon. The mountain in back is called Lan'que Ridge," the driver said.

"Blue Sparrow Ridge, that's a pretty name."

Soon they spotted houses, five or six brick houses with green tiled roofs and rammed-earth walls. Old timers sitting in their doorways looked at them curiously. "They're farm owners. They enjoy a much better life than the farmworkers."

The taxi was barely crawling when they reached a fork in the road. She stopped to let him out, backed the taxi up, and parked. "I can't turn the car around up there."

So they started walking and, a dozen meters later, were abreast of a towering banyan tree with a trunk so thick it would have taken five adults linking arms to encircle it. The locals called it 'the big green tree.' Nie trailed behind the driver as they followed the winding path past the big green tree. Scattered along the slope were a few old brick houses with wide eaves and clothes on lines drying in the sun. Trash trees grew in front and behind the houses, mixed with bamboo and a few banana trees. He heard a dog barking somewhere.

Outside a house with a bamboo fence they met an old man dressed in dark green clothes with his pant legs rolled up. They walked in to greet him. He was short and almost skeletal, with a blind left eye on a wrinkly face, but he looked friendly and approachable.

When they told him why they were there, he said that Squad Leader Xi was out, but he'd take them to visit the graves of the ten zhiqing.

"They're on Lan'que Ridge," he said.

Nie asked him if he knew any other old staff workers at the farm.

"Old Fu was one of them."

The old man said he'd arrived a year after the fire, but Old Fu had been there since the early days of the farm, so he'd be the one to talk to about the fire.

"Could I see him later?"

"Sure."

The old man led them out of the village, down a small path. The 2nd Company lived and worked on the slope, beyond which were the deep mountains. Rain from the day before had muddied the path, and it didn't take long for Nie's sneakers to be coated in slippery mud. Lantana bloomed all around them, like drops of blood. An old man leading two water buffaloes came up the path and stood aside for them to pass. In addition to the lantana, the path was flanked by bamboo and banana groves, as well as sugarcane that was taller than an adult. After trudging along the winding path for a quarter of an hour, the old man stopped. Shrubbery and a sparse rubber tree grove stood to the left; towering sugarcane to the right.

"That's Lan'que Ridge," their guide said as he pointed to the sugarcane, greatly surprising Nie and the taxi driver, who saw only what appeared to be an impenetrable stand of sugarcane. But before they could say anything, the old man parted the sugarcane and ducked in, climbing ahead of them up the hill. Nie felt the leaves cut his face and arms, but fortunately a dozen meters or so later they were free of assault from the leaves. Before them was a deserted plot overgrown with waist-high weeds.

"Right here," the old man said. Rocks protruded through the undergrowth.

Nie parted the weeds in front of him, revealing a headstone with a still-legible inscription, HERE LIES COMRADE WAN XIAORONG. He continued on and exposed a light rusty-red stone with a newly painted inscription, HERE LIES COMRADE ZHONG XING, to the right of which was a line of text about the girl and the time of her death. A red five-pointed star was carved in the top of the tombstone, and traces of burned paper were still visible on the small stone slab in front of the tomb. Headstones for the other girls were visible nearby.

Nie Feng stood still, besieged by a turbulence of emotions.

On his way over, he'd tried to envision what it would feel like to see the graves. Would he be standing silently under a bloodred setting sun? Or shrouded in a drizzle as rain wet his face? He hadn't expected the ten girls' graves to be overrun by weeds, brambles, couch grass, and other nameless vegetation.

Nie sought out all ten graves and stood before each of them, bowing silently as a sign of respect.

The weed-infested field fronted a grove of apricot trees, whose blooming season was long past. As he gazed at nothing in particular, he thought he heard the melodious harmonica strains of the sorrowful "Apricot in the Rain" coming to him out of the distant past.

Looking up at the relentless ball of fire, he discovered that all ten headstones faced northeast—the direction of their hometown, Chengdu. That might well have been the final wish of the ten girls sleeping under the ground.

After quietly taking a few pictures, he experienced a sudden attack of dizziness. He hadn't eaten all day and the tough climb under a blazing sun, plus the emotional encounter with the past, made him so weak he had to sit down on the grass, ignoring the old man's warning against leeches.

When former zhiqing returned to visit the site, the old man explained, they first contacted the farm, which gave them a chance to clear the grass and tidy up the area. But Nie's unannounced visit had made it impossible for the farmworkers to do anything, so he was seeing the area in its natural state.

Ten youthful souls rested quietly under weeds on a deserted mountain. Nie had the eerie feeling that when he parted the grass it was like parting their hair to reveal their young faces frozen in stone. They'd been so young, no more than sixteen or seventeen. Like delicate March apricot flowers falling to the ground in the rain, their lives had ended before they'd had a chance to bloom. In modern cities, girls that age were pampered in their families and in society. They ate at McDonald's, wore Nike shoes, idolized the cool-looking Jay Chou, went crazy over "Little Swallow" in the TV drama about a Qing princess, chatted away with their online Prince Charming. . . . They would never learn the sad stories of these girls, who had been their age so many years before.

Just listen to the childish voices of the young visitors to the blue curtain:

> *I saw the exhibit; I can't forget the forest of green, green rubber trees and red, red coffee beans.*
>
> *My parents were zhiqing and I envy them their youthful days.*

Nie felt himself tearing up, so he got to his feet. Behind him only a few of the rubber trees planted by the zhiqing many years before were left. Slits on the trunks released a milky, glue-like substance that flowed into a rubber bowl underneath.

"We only get a third of the rubber we used to get," the old man said.

It was almost as if, after bleeding for twenty-eight years, the trees were drying up.

— 4 —

Nie Feng and the taxi driver followed the old man to his house, a structure with thatched rooms in front and brick rooms in the back to rest. They sat at a table in the thatched front, and as Nie talked with the old man about the 2nd Company zhiqing, his wife, a friendly woman with graying hair, prepared some local tea for them. After being sautéed in an iron wok, it tasted like Iron Buddha tea.

Their guide offered to look up Old Fu. "He's not in," he said when he returned.

"I saw him a while ago," his wife said.

As the only staff worker who'd been at the scene of the fire, Fu would prove to be an important witness, so the woman went to find him, but she returned with the same message.

Nie was wondering where Old Fu might be when a heavyset old woman stormed in.

"They've already conducted an investigation, haven't they? So why do it again?" she complained loudly.

She was wearing a sleeveless blouse; a pair of gold earrings dangled from her ears. She was, it turned out, Old Fu's wife, and had also been a worker at the farm. Nie told her about his magazine and his visit, explaining that he just wanted to hear about what happened from Old Fu, and that it was not a renewed investigation. She explained that four of the eight huts had already caught fire when she heard the alarm, but she was busy taking care of her own children. Nie wondered about the rumor that an old staff worker saw blue flames, probably from burning fat. Mrs. Fu neither confirmed nor denied the rumor.

"That was Old Dong," she said, "and he's dead."

Nie then brought up the other key element: after the fire was out, someone noticed that the bamboo door to the third hut had been sealed with wire, which was, they realized, why the girls had not been able to escape. Old Mrs. Fu did not deny that either. "It was like this door," she said as she pointed to the bamboo door in the thatched room. It, too, was secured by a coil of thick wire.

When the driver asked about the bodies, Old Mrs. Fu looked pained and made a tiny gesture. "They were shrunken."

At Nie's request, the old man and Mrs. Fu took him to the fire site, on a slope not far from where they'd been. It was a weedy plot of land slightly over a hundred square meters. A brick house with a tiled roof on the top of the slope was where Fu and his wife lived.

They told him that no one had thought of building on this spot over the past three decades.

Nie had trouble sorting out his feelings as he took some pictures. He was reluctant to say good-bye; so were the old villagers. He was given a packet of tea as a souvenir.

When they neared the big green tree on their way downhill, they spotted an old man squatting beneath it. Wearing a gray shirt, he had a weatherworn face.

"You must be the reporter." He was smoking a cigarette.

"Yes, and you must be Old Fu." Nie could not believe his luck.

"My old lady didn't want me interviewed," Old Fu said with a smile. He'd obviously been waiting for Nie. So Nie sat down next to the old worker from the Construction Corps.

He'd been on site all night, helping to put out the fire and saving anything he could. Nie sought out every detail, no matter how insignificant it appeared.

In the end, Nie was able to confirm what he'd read: After the third hut, where Zhong Xing and the other nine girls were sleeping, burned to the ground, the survivors found a latch made of coiled wire. When Old Fu helped with the bodies, eight of them were huddled together, while the other two lay by the door, where they had obviously tried, but failed, to open it. The height and body types showed that they were Zhong Xing and Wan Xiaorong. One of the surviving girls told them about Wan Xiaorong's facial moles, and that on the train ride to Lanjiang, she'd said to Xia Yuhong, "I got rid of all but this mole between my brows. It points the direction of my future." It had not helped her avoid the tragedy.

Old Fu also told Nie that more than two hours before the fire, he'd heard someone knocking on the door of a hut down below. He was asking Zhong Xing to come out and talk to him, which created a commotion inside the hut; the girls quickly locked their door. Fu even heard the girls' panicky shouts of "It's Grinning Tyrant." Fu had stuck his head out the window and, in the dusky light, seen a stocky figure that resembled their company commander.

"Shit!" The man had cursed hoarsely at the locked door and stormed away.

What an incredible find for Nie Feng. He took a copy of *Western Sunshine* from his tote bag and showed it to Old Fu. A close-up shot of Hu Guohao was on the cover.

"It does look like him, especially the nose and those ratlike beady eyes." Old Fu snubbed out his cigarette.

Nie then showed him another photo, a faded one from a newspaper in Hainan; Hu was wearing a sport coat.

"That's him. The Company Commander, Hu Zihao."

"His name is Hu Zihao?" That came as a shock. So Hu Guohao was in reality Hu Zihao, Commander of the 2nd Company.

Nie asked why some people said they hadn't known about the wire on the door.

"Commander Hu wouldn't let us say so."

"Why?"

"He was the local overlord; the zhiqing kids all called him Grinning Tyrant."

The old man told Nie all about Hu's evil deeds. He was well known for his lust for women and had raped countless girls in the company, sparing only the plain-looking ones. He'd arrange for a girl to stand sentry alone at night, and when it got dark, he'd drive the only jeep in the company to the checkpoint, where he'd rape the girl. He was also fond of barging uninvited into the girls' huts for bed checks; he'd lift their mosquito nets and reach in to grope the girls, who would be too frightened to make a sound. Even in public, he'd touch the girls and shamelessly proclaim: "This is the only way to eliminate barriers for us to be like a family. It's benefical to the revolutionary work."

The 2nd Company had been designated an elite unit, but Hu had used his position to commit criminal acts, putting everyone on edge.

Some of the girls would scream if they heard a mouse in the middle of the night, thinking it might be Hu's footsteps.

"Have you heard the name, Hong Yiming?" Nie brought up Hu's old friend.

"Do you know him?" the old man asked him.

"I've met him."

"He was 2nd Company's political instructor; he and Hu were from the same village."

"So that's it." Everything suddenly became clear to Nie.

Nie asked what happened to Hu afterward. The old man said the zhiqing rapes were eventually exposed and Premier Zhou Enlai personally conducted investigations. Eventually, more than a dozen soldiers in the 16th and 18th Regiments of the 4th Division in Hekou County were punished. The 1st Divison in Jinghong County executed three, and sentenced two to death with a stay of execution; two others were sentenced to life in prison. Hu Zihao's evil deeds were also uncovered, and he was removed from his position while being investigated. When Commander Jia of an independent battalion in the 1st Division and Commander Zhang of the 2nd Regiment were executed, Hu knew his days were numbered, so he slipped across the border into Burma. Based on what the zhiqing told the investigators, at the very least Hu would have been sentenced to death with a stay of execution, and the person who tipped him off was none other than Hong Yiming, the political instructor and an old comrade of Hu's, whom Hu had once saved in combat.

Hong was later punished for alerting Hu, and left the army before retirement age. The zhiqing later learned that the two scoundrels were responsible for the disappearance of Ding Lan's brother, Qiangzi.

Now everything made sense.

The old man told how the wailing that night drowned out all other sounds. Zhong Xing's brother, Zhong Tao, had been on sentry duty at the edge of the village and knew that something was wrong when he saw the blue flames over Lan'que Ridge. He ran all the way back, but by the time he reached the site, the third hut, where his sister and her friends lived, was nothing but charred rubble, with only a few lingering wisps of dark green smoke. The Dark Boy was dazed but tearless, as he desperatedly clawed at the ashes; all he found was a burned harmonica.

Before Nie and the driver left the big green tree, the old man told them that a middle-aged man had come to visit the graves a few days before. He'd also offered sacrifices at Shizi Cliff in the mountains. The old man had never seen the man before, but based on his description, Nie believed it must have been Zhong Tao.

Nie looked up at the sky as a myriad of emotions surged inside. He could almost hear the outcry in the inscription.

I can forget everything,

But not my first love in Yunnan.

My love, my eternal hatred, and a debt of blood.

You, Grinning Tyrant, run all you can,

But I will find you.

TWELVE

Heartache at Lan'que Ridge

— 1 —

(Flashback/A few days earlier)

On the slope at Lan'que Ridge, Zhong Tao parted the weeds to reveal Apricot's grave as he recalled the scene of blooming apricot flowers twenty-eight years earlier. The flowers had weighed down the branches and painted the slope in pink. Under the setting sun, a gust of wind had sent the petals flying and dancing in the air before settling to the ground.

"Ah, Apricot rain," someone had said.

"Apricot rain," they all had echoed. "Apricot rain."

The beautiful apricot rain had been a bright spot in the young boys' and girls' days of hardship in the border region. That and the sorrowful "Song of the Zhiqing." Apricot always played her harmonica as accompaniment each time they sang the song. Zhong Tao could recall how she'd dressed in a checkered blouse, how her small hands had held the pink harmonica, and how she'd cocked her head as she played, losing herself in the melody.

He could almost see the look of innocence on her face, as he squatted by the grave to light incense and burn spirit money that sent orange flames dancing in the wind.

A blue flame appeared before his eyes. The accursed, nightmarish blue flame, lapping at his heart for twenty-eight years.

Zhong kept feeding spirit money into the fire. The flames quickly swallowed the yellow paper and turned his face bright red. Tears welled up in his eyes as he muttered: "Apricot, I've come to see you. I've avenged the evil deed and humiliation for you and Yuhong."

Dark green smoke wafted into the air along with charred pieces of paper.

"You can rest in peace now," he said, staring at the red star on the headstone.

He could not bring himself to dwell on what had happened that evening twenty-eight years before, when an evil specter roamed the grove of rubber trees. It was that devil in a green army coat who had ruined his beloved and destroyed his happiness.

On that day, Apricot was collecting rubber sap at the farthest edge of the grove, behind Lan'que Ridge. Hu Zihao, who'd had his eyes on her for a long time, sneaked into the grove for an opportunity to assault her. Several girls in the company had already fallen victim to his sneak attacks. Apricot was preparing to return to their base when she saw, to her horror, the evil Hu Zihao about to pounce on her. She threw down her bucket and took off running, but Hu came after her. He grabbed her from behind, threw her to the ground, and began to unbutton her pants. Apricot tried to fight him off and yelled for help.

Xia Yuhong, Zhong Tao's girlfriend, heard the scream on her way back from work; she ran over and was shocked when she saw what was happening.

"Mind your own damned business! Get out of there," Hu barked shamelessly.

"Help me, Sister Hong," Apricot called out to Xia, who, without thinking, rushed up and pulled Hu off Apricot. She had no idea where she'd found the strength and courage.

"Leave her alone, she's still a kid," Xia pleaded with Hu, while turning to Apricot. "Run, Apricot. Hurry."

"What about you, Sister Hong?" Apricot was shaking all over.

"Don't worry about me. Run now. Quick."

Apricot, her face a ghostly white from the fright, ran down the slope.

"Very well, then, you can take her place." The enraged Hu leered, an evil light shooting out his beady eyes.

Finally sensing her own peril, Xia Yuhong began to back away.

He pressed forward with a lascivious smirk, reaching out his evil hands to cover her mouth while dragging her off to the side. He jumped on top of her with lewd delight. "Who'd have thought a beauty like you would give herself to me? I'm going to have a good time with you today." She kept fighting him off. When he forced his lips on hers and stuck his tongue in, she bit down hard, sending blood oozing out of the corners of his mouth. Enraged, he took out his pistol and hit her on the head with the butt, knocking her out cold.

Apricot ran back to the base and told her brother what had happened. Dark Boy and Qiangzi picked up clubs and ran up the hill to rescue Xia Yuhong. Hu Zihao was long gone when they got there, and Xia lay unconscious and bathed in blood under a rubber tree, her lower body naked and stained with blood.

Dark Boy burst out crying as he carried Yuhong back to the clinic, where they managed to save her life. But the damage was done; she woke up and couldn't stop sobbing.

"Why didn't you fight? Why?" the young, ignorant Dark Boy questioned.

She was quiet, humiliation and agony written over her ashen face.

"Say something. Why don't you answer me?" Dark Boy demanded again, which was like sprinkling salt on a wound. In despair, she raised her weightless hand and slapped him, as large tears rolled down her cheeks.

Dark Boy realized his mistake too late; nothing could be done now. At that moment an unbridgeable barrier was erected between the two lovers. She began to avoid him and refused to be his girl-friend. An open wound remained with her; she changed into a dif-ferent person, a depressed and glum loner. Two years later she was accepted into a college in Guangdong through an army recommen-dation and stayed behind to teach English after graduation. Then she went to study in the US.

But the tragedy wasn't over yet.

Hu Zihao and Hong Yiming went to a meeting at the regiment office the day after Hu's assault on Xia, and were gone all day. That night, Dark Boy and Qiangzi lay in wait on a path the two men had to take to return to base. They hid in a dense grove of trees, their eyes fixed on the path ahead; behind them was the shadowy Shizi Cliff. It was dark when they heard Grinning Tyrant humming a Henan tune as he walked toward them, followed by a tall figure, Hong Yiming. The political instructor was a calculating, manipu-lative man whom the zhiqing nicknamed Red Fox.

The youngsters felt their blood surge as they spotted their mortal enemies. When Hu was almost upon them, they leaped out of their hiding place. Dark Boy swung his club and hit Hu in the calf. Hu stumbled and grabbed for the club, knocking it out of the hand of the seventeen-year-old. Panicky, Zhong Tao held onto Hu with all his might, keeping him from pulling out his pistol. In the mean-time, Qiangzi kept swinging his club, hitting Hu on the head and on the body. Hu yelled and struggled. It was too dark to see his face and both young men's faces were a blur.

The three of them were in a tangled mess, like a pair of young wolves battling a panther. Red Fox circled them but was unable to help his company commander. But Hu was, however, a seasoned, battle-tested soldier, and with a shout, he struggled out of Zhong's grip and whipped out his pistol. At that critical moment, Qiangzi, with incredible speed, took out a rubber-slitting knife he carried on his leg as protection. The knife was eight millimeters in length with a narrow, razor-sharp blade with a slightly upturned tip.

When Hu released the safety on his pistol, Qiangzi thrust with his knife; Hu turned his face as a reflex, but a warm sensation erupted on his neck. He reached up to touch it and realized that Qiangzi had cut him on the chin, a wound that would leave a permanent scar. The frightened Dark Boy took advantage of Hu's pause to knock the pistol out of his hand.

At that moment, Hong Yiming grabbed Qiangzi by the waist before he could charge Hu again.

"So, it's you, Qiangzi." Hong was surprised. But Qiangzi ignored him and struggled out of his grip.

"Stop that madman, hurry!" Hu shouted.

Hong hesitated, but then shoved Qiangzi from behind.

"Ah—"

Qiangzi stumbled in the dark, lost his footing, and fell over the cliff, trailed by a scream that slowly faded into silence in the abyss. To Dark Boy the scream was swallowed up by Hell.

With his hand on his bleeding chin, Hu staggered out of the grove with Hong's help.

It turned deadly quiet.

"Qiangzi—Qiangzi—" Zhong screamed. His heartrending shout echoed off the cliff.

The fire broke out the following evening.

No one noticed that Qiangzi was missing until after the fire. They did not find his body in the charred remains of the huts. They searched for him for three days but found nothing. Anyone who fell into the black hole beyond the cliff was lost forever, according to the locals.

A rumor made the rounds that Qiangzi had slipped across the border to Burma to become a guerrilla. The zhiqing weren't sure what to believe.

Only three people in the company knew the truth about Qiangzi's death—Zhong Tao, Grinning Tyrant, and the political director, and none of them would tell the truth.

Hu called Dark Boy to his office on the slope the day after the incident.

"Dark Boy, you know why Qiangzi is missing, right?" Hu fixed his beady eyes on Zhong.

"No, I don't," Zhong said expressionlessly.

"Heh-heh." Hu laughed. "He's your buddy, how could you not know?"

Of course Zhong knew, but he also knew that Hu was testing him, to see if Zhong was the second person who had ambushed him.

"You're the company commander, and if you don't know, how do you expect me to know?" Dark Boy turned his head and played along.

Not knowing what else to say, Hu grinned and said: "Anyone who tries to mess with me will be sorry."

Every zhiqing knew what Hu was like: arrogant with an evil smile. Not very tall, he had a broad face and a bulbous nose and was dark-skinned; his voice was hoarse, but that did not stop him from cursing the zhiqing whenever he felt like it, though he always did it with a grin, a dry laugh that sent chills down your spine. Although he was given to squinting when he looked at you, the fierceness of that beady-eyed gaze could scare a person witless. He held the fate of the zhiqing in his hands, having turned the 2nd Company into his own little fiefdom, a primitive tribe where he was the overlord, a lawless individual who did what he wanted with no repercussions. The zhiqing began by calling him Commander Tyrant, changed that to Commander Grinning Tyrant, and then shortened that to Grinning Tyrant.

Hu was the convergence of all desires: a powerful sexual urge and a desire for power, coupled with the need to conquer and to possess. Few of the female zhiqing under his charge escaped his clutches. And Dark Boy knew all too well how much they loathed him, though they could do nothing about it. So he clammed up, fixing his gaze on the bandage covering the knife wound on the man's chin.

If the knife had continued down another two millimeters, it would have taken the evildoer's life. "Qiangzi, you died for nothing," Dark Boy thought silently.

"You can go now." Grinning Tyrant had finally stopped grinning.

Dark Boy turned around, a tear rolling down his dark face. It was all he could do to hold back his loathing and fury as he walked out of the office.

The sunset painted the edge of the sky red as blood. Dark Boy felt his own blood seethe as a chilling voice echoed deep inside: "You mother-fucking, dog-screwing asshole. Just you wait. I am going to lop off your evil head one day." On that day, he vowed to kill Grinning Tyrant, to avenge Apricot, Yuhong, and Qiangzi, and eliminate Hu's evil from society; he would then be willing to die.

Zhong sprinkled a bottle of spirits over Shizi Cliff, his face bathed in tears.

"Qiangzi," he mumbled, "I've finally exacted revenge for you, Yuhong, and Apricot."

After emptying the bottle, he tossed it into the air with a savage force. It arced across the cloudy sky before falling soundlessly into the abyss below. Then he took out his cell phone and dialed Ding Lan's number.

"Xiao Lan, it's me, Zhong Tao. I'm here offering a libation to your brother."

"Really?" Ding's voice had an emotional tremor.

"Do you want to say something to your brother?" Zhong asked, like a big brother, in a tender but sad tone. She remained silent.

"Hello? Are you still there, Ding Lan?" Zhong asked anxiously. Then he heard her sob on the other end.

"Okay," she said, "I'll say something."

Zhong took the phone from his ear and raised it up high in the air.

"Dear Brother, Grinning Tyrant is dead. He died a terrible death." Ding was choking up; her voice seemed to fill the sky of Yunnan. "Red Fox is dead, too. They both deserved to die. Dear Brother, can you hear me? Mom and I are doing well, so don't worry about us. It's been twenty-eight years. Now you can finally rest in peace."

— 2 —

Xiaochuan and Yao Li found another important clue when they checked out buses running through Lesser Meisha.

Buses Nos. 103, 360, 364, and 380 all originated in Shenzhen and stopped at Lesser Meisha before continuing on to other cities, No. 360 going to Nan'ao and No. 364 to Dapeng. The last one usually stopped around ten at night, but on holidays additional runs were scheduled and the buses ran until three or four in the morning.

They located the driver of an air-conditioned bus on the 380 line, a fifty-year-old man named Xie who had many years of experience. He had worked an extra shift on the night of June twenty-fourth, driving till three thirty the following morning. On his last run to Lesser Meisha, he spotted a white car parked on a curve under Qitou Ridge. The windows were closed and the lights off, and there was no sign of the owner. Thinking that the car was having engine trouble, the driver paid little attention and drove on by, not taking note of the license plate. But he was sure it was a Citroën.

The car was gone half an hour later, on his return from Lesser Meisha.

The driver took them to the place and pointed out the spot where the car was parked. They noticed a break in the chain-link fence, big enough for an adult to crawl under; a dozen steps down the leaf-covered stone stairs led to Lovers' Lane. Shielded by tall mug-wort, the opening was not easy to see, but they collected several pieces of red fiber from the fence; a test later showed that they matched one of Hu Guohao's Lacoste swimsuits.

It was finally clear why there had been a tear in Hu's swimsuit; it was likely made when the heavy body was being carried through the opening.

Xiaochuan called Nie Feng to share the news.

"That's it," Nie said, informing Xiaochuan about the cries of the egrets, which took place after three in the morning. Everything fit.

"You should look into Ding Lan's Citroën, and you'll probably need to make another trip to Nan'ao to check out Zhong Tao," Nie said.

"That's exactly what Chief Wu told us to do."

"Great. Oh, be sure to look at the area outside the school wall."

"Why?"

"I went there before leaving Shenzhen, and was told that Hu's briefcase was found by the wall, which separated the school from a street. You might want to ask around to see if anyone had seen a white Citroën parked there."

"Got it."

Without notifying the owner, Xiaochuan and Yao Li conducted an investigation of Ding Lan's Citroën, and found sand on the tires and the undercarriage, but test results produced nothing noteworthy. Then they scraped soil samples from the inside of the fender, a rare red soil with trace elements that proved to be the same as those found in a Xichong sandlot south of Nan'ao. The Citroën had been to Xichong; Zhong Tao could have gotten the seawater there.

They drove to Nan'ao and checked out the school first.

Hu's briefcase had been found in a corner of the athletic field, less than two meters from the enclosure wall, which was nearly two meters high and had a see-through top. Few pedestrians were out on the street beyond the wall. They knocked on the doors of all the houses on the slight rise across the street. When they reached the one on top, they found a young girl with a gimp leg whose parents were out. She told them she was on the balcony one evening over a month ago and saw a white car parked on the street right by the school's wall. A man got out and leaned against the wall as if looking for something, then quickly got back inside and drove away. It was too far to see the license number, though the description she gave of the man resembled Zhong Tao. She couldn't remember the exact date, except that she had gone to the local clinic for physical therapy the day before. They waited till her parents returned and learned that her girl's therapy was on June twenty-ninth. That was four days after Hu's death and the day before the little boy found Hu's briefcase in the grass on the field. This was no coincidence.

Wasting no time, they drove to Xichong, on the southernmost tip of the peninsula. It was a fishing village that faced the ocean to the south, possessing a beach that had turned it into a famous resort. The water there was deeper and bluer than either Lesser or Greater Meisha, and the beach, the thatched huts, and the palm trees more closely resembled natural surroundings. No one at the resort recalled seeing Zhong Tao or Ding Lan.

So what was Ding's car doing here?

"Maybe she had a change of heart before getting this far," Yao Li said as she gazed out at the ocean.

"There has to be a reason," Xiaochuan said.

"A reason, hmm." Yao mulled this over. "Maybe the red tide moved north and the water here was no longer what they wanted. Or it could be a false lead planted by the murderer."

"Say, that's good," Xiaochuan said, making a U-turn and speeding down the road the way they'd come from, raising a column of red dust.

They returned to Nan'ao.

As many as a hundred motorboats were rocking amid the waves at Nan'ao Bay. They were all painted blue or green and looked to be made of wood, but a fisherman told them they were actually fiber-glass. Xiaochuan and Yao Li stood on the shore to look around; discarded plastic bags, paper waste, and twigs floated on the murky surface of the water. This could not have been the water Zhong had taken, and he'd have attracted too much attention to himself if he'd tried.

Xiaochuan asked a fisherwoman in a flowery blouse and a bamboo hat: "Granny, how much to rent one of those?"

"A hundred if you stay close to shore."

"What about going out farther?"

"A hundred fifty."

"What's that over there?" He pointed at a finger of land across the bay.

"Oh, that's Ping Chau, part of Hong Kong. You can't take a motorboat there."

Xiaochuan signaled for Yao Li to take out Zhong's and Dings' photos.

"Granny, did these two rent a boat last month?"

The woman examined the pictures and shook her head.

"How about the others around here?"

The woman handed the pictures to the other fishermen, who passed the photos around, but no one recalled seeing them. Disappointing.

"You can go ask the border police." She pointed to a two-story brown building nearby.

They thanked her and went to talk to a border police officer, a young man in a green uniform with a face rounder even than Xiaochuan's. After checking their IDs, he gave friendly, helpful answers to their questions. Renting a boat required a valid ID and a nod from the police, which meant that the border police checked everyone's ID. This was good news. The young officer went inside and returned with an older colleague, both of them certain that neither Zhong nor Ding had rented a motorboat after viewing their photographs.

The officers thanked their colleagues and returned to their car, disappointed by their fruitless trip to Nan'ao.

"Shall we call in our report to Chief Cui?" Yao Li asked.

"Not just yet," Xiaochuan replied as he dialed Nie Feng's number.

"Hey Nie Feng, it's me, Xiaochuan. We're in Nan'ao."

"Really? Find anything?"

"Someone saw a white car parked outside the school wall on the evening of the twenty-ninth, and saw a man lean up against the wall."

"That's terrific. "Nie sounded excited. "Congratulations!"

"But," Yao snatched the cell out of Xiaochuan's hand, "we still don't know where Zhong Tao got the water."

"Where have you checked so far?"

"Nan'ao Bay, Xichong on the southernmost tip—"

"Have you checked Shuitou Village?"

"Shuitou Village? No. Why?"

Xiaochuan snatched the cell back and held it to his ear.

"It's Zhou Zhengxing's hometown," he heard Nie say. "It's five or six kilometers north of Nan'ao. I think it's worth a look."

"Will do."

Five minutes later they parked in front of the beach near Shuitou Village, about a kilometer distant.

As soon as they stepped foot on the beach, Xiaochuan had the feeling that this place was somehow different. From the embankment, they looked out into the bay, where the color of the water underwent a change—yellow near the shore (likely sandy), then green (glass-bottle green), dark blue farther out, and nearly black at the horizon. Waves lapping on the shore were a display of nature's power.

Motorboats rode the waves with ease.

"Zhou Zhengxing's hometown isn't bad," Yao exclaimed.

"I've never seen such a spectacular view," Xiaochuan echoed her sentiment.

Quite a few tourists were resting under beach umbrellas, while some brave souls were frolicking in the water.

The officers found someone on the beach staff and asked about Zhong and Ding. He, in turn, called over two lifeguards, one of whom recognized Zhong Tao and Ding Lan.

"They've been here."

"Are you sure?" Xiaochuan was so excited his voice changed.

"I'm sure."

"Do you remember which day?"

"Not really. It was over a month ago, but I think it was around noon."

"Did you notice anything unusual about them?" Yao asked.

"Nothing in particular." The lifeguard thought for a moment. "Oh, now I remember. When they left, the man was carrying a plastic bucket."

"Really? A plastic bucket? Do you recall the color?"

"White. You see them everywhere." The lifeguard had no idea that he'd just handed the police a significant clue.

Chief Wu and Captain Cui were elated when they heard the news, and everyone working on the special case could sense that victory was near.

"Looks like we're close to solving the case," Chief Wu said when they were all together. "I'm as excited as you, but we mustn't forget we need proof to nail it. We need evidence; solid, unassailable evidence."

"I agree with the chief," Cui said. "For instance, we're pretty sure that Zhong tossed the briefcase over the wall, but he can and will deny it. Likewise, the girl didn't see the license plate and no one took a picture of a man leaning against the wall. The lifeguard at Shuitou Village is a critical witness and that's good, but we need more substantial evidence."

"The algae traces in the bucket have been sent to the Public Security Bureau forensic lab, but they haven't found anything usable. I was told that China lacks the technology," Chief Wu said.

"And, there's another thing. We still haven't figured out Zhong's motive."

"Mr. Nie's conclusion is that it was a series of revenge murders," Xiaochuan said.

"How can *Western Sun* be so sure?" Cui was doubtful. "We need evidence, not speculation, if we're to solve a case."

"Where's Mr. Nie now?" Chief Wu asked.

"In Yunnan."

— 3 —

On his way back to Kunming, Nie Feng looked up some information about the zhiqing in the archives while waiting for a seat to open up on a flight. The same bespectacled, short-haired woman was there; she gave him a form to fill out, after checking his press credentials and a letter of introduction.

After he handed over the form, the clerk helped him locate the "Table of Contents for the Yunnan Provincial Revolutionary Committee Office of Zhiqing Affairs."

Nie spent four hours poring over dusty files and briefings, encountering shockingly outrageous reports about the Hekou Incident, corroborating what Old Mr. Fu had told him beneath the big green tree.

As he read on, he discovered that what had happened in Hekou County was only the tip of the iceberg. Physical abuse, including rape, was pervasive throughout the Construction Corps. Many of the cadres who committed these crimes were decorated war heroes who became local tyrants once they arrived at the regiments, battalions, and companies that were scattered and isolated among remote mountains and fields. Without legal supervision or restrictions on absolute power, they were left to do what they wanted.

The Grinning Tyrant of Lanjiang, Hu Zihao, was one of them.

During those peculiar, twisted times, female zhiqing who were made giddy by the red slogan of "reeducation" sometimes fell into the clutches of authoritarian abusers, like lambs to the slaughter, having lost the protection of their families and the law.

It was true that only a small number of the military cadres committed such crimes; most were law-abiding, diligent, hardworking members of the Construction Corps. But the cancerous tumors on the body of the corps had to be rooted out and punished. Ultimately many of the abusers of power were put on trial; some were executed immediately, some were sentenced to death with a stay of execution, and others were given life in prison.

While reading references to flight attempts by these criminals, Nie Feng came across: "A Company Commander in Lanjiang slipped across the border to Burma and was not heard of again."

That commander must have been Hu Zihao.

Nie Feng closed the file and sat there lost in thought. Hu Zihao had managed to avoid punishment by a military court but could not escape retribution. He had been a commander in the People's Liberation Army, someone who wore the green uniform and red insignia who had gone into battle and won commendations. Why had he, like some others, turned into an evil tyrant once he was sent to the border region zhiqing camp? How had he become a man who bullied other men and raped women?

His evil deeds at Lan'que Ridge were a manifestation of the bestial side of his personality, but had been abetted by the special historical circumstances of the time, which had given the ugly side of human nature an opportunity to manifest itself in its vilest form. In a way, the abusers and the abused were both victims of the twisted age.

Nie Feng thought of someone else who had been raped by Hu Zihao: Xia Yuhong, after she saved Zhong Xing.

Where was she now?

It was impossible to have an accurate count of the numbers of girls raped, because many of the victims hid the assaults from others. Due to the influence of traditional Chinese morality, any girl who lost her virginity came under tremendous pressure and suffered discrimination in society, no matter what the cause. Someone like Xia Yuhong might have been living in pain and remained single; or she could be constantly reliving the nightmare, the blue flames flickering before her eyes; or she might be at peace on the surface but unable to shake off the dark shadows.

— 4 —

Zhong Tao sent Xia Yuhong an e-mail.

Yuhong,

I just returned from Yunnan. On the way I stopped by Chengdu to visit family and went to see our class director, "Euclid." She gave me your e-mail address. She said that when you came back to Chengdu you asked about some of us from the past. Thank you for thinking of me—Dark Boy, a useless, terrible friend.

It's sad to look back on the past. The fire and the nightmare in the rubber tree grove twenty-eight years ago destroyed our love and happiness. But as the saying goes, evil acts will be punished and good deeds will be rewarded; it was only a matter of time before retribution was accomplished. Grinning Tyrant has finally gotten what he deserved.

Do you remember the political instructor, Red Fox, who had a sweet tooth? When the villain who abetted the evildoer was on the phone with his daughter, I slipped two nice pieces of liqueur-filled chocolate candy into his candy dish, and sent him on the road to be with the scoundrel forever.

It's a long story. I hope we can see each other one day so I can tell you all about it.

Dark Boy

Zhong Tao had searched for Grinning Tyrant for nearly three decades.

After Hu Zihao fled to Burma and disappeared, someone reported seeing him at the border and said that he was doing well.

A decade later, Hu transformed himself into a reputable entrepreneur with a new name, Hu Guohao. No one knew exactly what had happened after he fled across the border, but rumor had it that he began as a Chinese herbal medicine merchant. Later he made a great deal of money by smuggling heroin, likely his "first bucket of gold." Then he sneaked back into China and tried his luck in Beihai and Hainan, mainly in real estate. When Hong Yiming was discharged and relocated to Hainan, the two of them teamed up. Unafraid of taking risks, and welcoming competition, they caught the first wave of the real estate boom and became very rich. When others in Hainan's real estate business folded, the two of them moved on to Shenzhen, where they made even more money; there Hong set up a company on his own. Within a few years, Hu Guohao was the head of a realty conglomerate.

Zhong Tao had learned about Hu Zihao by accident from a friend who had seen him in Hainan. By then he was the CEO of a real estate company. His new name was Hu Guohao, and his company was called "Hainan Guohao Realty." Zhong tracked Hu as far as Haikou, but lost him. The real estate bubble had just burst in Hainan and, according to one estimate, billions of dollars were trapped there, while many real estate companies declared bankruptcy. With considerable effort, Zhong received news that "Hainan Guohao Realty" had shut down and there was no news of where Hu Zihao had gone. But then he heard that Hu might have relocated to Shenzhen, which was why he took a job with a friend in Shenzhen—so he could sniff out Hu's whereabouts like a bloodhound.

The Shenzhen boomtown was full of opportunities for the smart and the ambitious. Zhong spotted Hu when he was being interviewed on TV. The camera swept across the man's enormous desk, showing the lifelike wood carving of a crocodile. Hu Guohao looked just like Hu Zihao: a broad face with a bulbous nose, rough dark skin, and beady eyes. He'd put on weight, but Zhong felt he could recognize Hu, the rapist, even if he were burned to ashes. All he needed to confirm his true identity was the knife scar on his chin, but the medium-range camera shot made it impossible to see.

Then, when the hostess asked Hu about his views on the "ecology of the housing market," the camera moved closer and closer. Zhong trained his eyes on the closeup image of Hu on TV.

"'Ecology of the housing market' as a development trend, is one of Landmark's goals," Hu answered smugly. He was looking straight into the camera, thus obscuring the left side of his chin.

Then the camera moved to a different angle, exposing the small pink scar. Either because of the passage of time or a result of plastic surgery, it was barely noticeable. But no matter, the shape and location were unmistakable.

It's him, Zhong thought. It's Hu Zihao. He shuddered. He quickly picked up the phone. "Ding Lan, it's me, Zhong Tao. Turn on your TV and watch the Economy Channel. Right. Got it? Who does that man look to you?"

"Ah, a little like Hu Zihao."

"Yes. I'm sure it's him, Grinning Tyrant."

From that moment on, Zhong closely followed all news related to Landmark. One day he saw an ad in the paper; Hu was looking for an executive assistant. The timing was perfect.

He placed a call to Landmark and spoke with Hu Guohao himself. Zhong told Hu he was working for a stockbroker, but would like to apply for the job.

"We have many talented applicants already." Hu did not sound interested.

"But I may be better than them all," Zhong said with a laugh.

"Oh, really?" Now he had Hu's attention. "Why don't you stop by tomorrow morning?"

Zhong strode into the Landmark Building at 10:00 A.M. Dressed in a black polo shirt and wearing a short beard, he looked slightly unkempt but carried himself in a composed and confident manner. Outside the CEO's office, he saw four people sitting there, likely waiting to meet with the boss. Zhong walked up to talk to Ah-ying, who asked him to wait as she called Hu's office.

"Mr. Hu will see you now." She flashed him a charming smile.

He knocked and entered to see two men, likely company employees, sitting in front of Hu's desk. Hu sent them off and told Zhong to sit down.

"So you're Zhong Tao?" Hu sized him up through slitted eyes.

"That's right."

Zhong managed a calm appearance on the surface, but his insides were churning. So this real estate tycoon was the mortal enemy he'd spent decades looking for. The evil, venal Grinning Tyrant. He was so close he could have reached out and touched him. Hu was heavier, but Zhong would recognize him anywhere, anytime.

"Tell me what's on your mind." Hu's voice was hoarse, as always.

Beginning with his college degree, Zhong related his work experience and his views on real estate. After the usual questions and conversation, Hu asked the important questions, which, Zhong later learned, were the reasons some of the top-tier applicants from overseas were weeded out.

"In your view, what's most important for Landmark at this moment?"

"The first priority is to make sure the supply of capital doesn't run out."

"Is that so?"

"I've studied Landmark's operation, and what it needs most now is capital," Zhong said confidently.

"Oh, how do you know that?" Hu was surprised.

"From friends in the financial business I've learned that Landmark's current loan amount has reached the danger level."

"So, does Mr. Zhong know how to bring in more capital?"

"Of course," Zhong said without hesitation. "I've been in the stock market for many years, and obtaining a line of credit of a couple of billion is no big deal." That brought a smile to Hu's face.

"What about the second priority?"

"In my opinion, the second-most important priority for Landmark at the moment is to snatch the land at Tiandongba."

"You think it's a good deal?" Hu's beady eyes glinted.

"The land may appear to be a chicken rib to some, but it is in fact a slice of choice meat. The one hundred and sixty acres will be auctioned off at around a million, but the value will rise exponentially once the traffic issue is resolved." That was music to Hu Guohao's ears.

"What's your annual salary at the brokerage, Mr. Zhong?"

"Roughly half a million." Zhong gave a low figure.

"Then, I welcome you to Landmark Corp as my assistant," Hu said decisively. "In addition to an annual salary of 300,000, you'll get two percent of Landmark stock. How does that sound to you?"

"Sounds great. Thank you, Mr. Hu."

"It's a deal then."

And that was how Zhong Tao gained entrance into Landmark's power center and became a time bomb ticking near Hu Guohao. He had two weapons the other applicants lacked: one, an understanding of the phrase "know yourself well, but know your enemy better" (his ability to get loans and Landmark's financial bind); two, "give him what he wants" (Hu had his eyes on the land at Tiandongba).

Hu Guohao was attracted to Zhong Tao's experience and his connections in the stock market and finance field; Zhong did not disappoint. Barely two months after he was hired, he used his connections to negotiate a billion yuan loan for Hu, which earned him Hu's trust and elevated him into a position as Hu's right-hand man.

Zhong Tao next met Hong Yiming, now CEO of Big East, when he attended a business banquet with Hu.

"This is my assistant, Zhong Tao." Hu made the introduction. "And this is an old friend of mine, Hong Yiming, CEO of Big East Realty."

Sizing up Zhong, Hong sensed that they'd met before but could not pinpoint where or when. It had been nearly three decades, and Zhong's facial features, in addition to the beard, had changed a great deal. On his part, Zhong was stunned to see Hong, but quickly recovered.

"Mr. Hong has the demeanor of a former soldier."

"You think so? Was Mr. Zhong also in the service?" Hong probed.

"I always wanted to be China's General Patton, but never got a chance," Zhong joked to avoid answering the question.

"Don't underestimate him. This fellow can do magic with bank loans," Hu said to Hong.

"Oh, now I remember," Hong said with a smile. "I saw you once at a stockbroker's talk. No wonder you look familiar. Please feel free to stop by Big East; I'd like to hear your views."

"Are you trying to poach him?" Hu said in jest.

"I wouldn't do that. I'll poach from anyone, but not my old pal."

Hu laughed heartily.

And that was how Zhong got close to Hong. He became a frequent visitor to Big East, and was elated at the opportunity to seek vengeance from both mortal enemies. What a felicitous find. But he waited patiently, dealing with them confidently and giving nothing away, while at the same time planning his act of revenge for June twenty-fourth, the twenty-eighth anniversary of the fire that had taken so much from him.

He planned every step carefully and meticulously. Over time he gained intimate knowledge of Hu's personality, hobbies, and daily routine, including even details such as the particular sleeping aid he took. As a way of avoiding suspicion, he often hitched a ride with Hu to Lesser Meisha, where he conducted a thorough examination of the areas around it and Greater Meisha, the lobby layout of the Lesser Meisha Hotel, and the water conditions at Nan'ao. As for information about red tides, that he learned from a report in a local paper.

"This has been a godsend!" he remarked to himself.

On June twenty-fourth, he called Hu around seven in the evening from the lobby of the Lesser Meisha Hotel, using an untraceable phone card. Hu was having dinner with Hong Yiming at the Seaview Hotel restaurant.

"Oh, it's you," Hu said when he heard who it was.

"My cell battery died, so I borrowed a friend's phone."

"What's up?"

"I ran into Chief Hao of the City Land Bureau. He's spending the weekend here with his wife, and I wonder if you're free to come over. We're at the Lesser Meisha Hotel." Zhong knew that this was an invitation Hu Guohao could not pass up.

"Sure." Hu shut his phone, said good-bye to Hong, and quickly left. Naturally he would not have told Hong about the phone conversation, and would never have imagined that it was a call that would lead to his death.

Zhong waited for Hu's arrival in the lobby bar. On the table in front of him sat a teapot, two ivory-colored cups, and a creamer of milk. He'd slipped a substantial amount of sleeping pills into the black tea and made sure they were completely dissolved.

He watched the entrance. There were many tourists that day, some in swimsuits, and some with small children. Hu entered through the side door after about five minutes. Zhong got up to meet him and led him to the table, a spot he'd scouted out earlier. It was close to the back door but out of sight of the bar counter.

"Chief Hao asked you to wait for him. He'll be right down," Zhong said to Hu, who sat in one of the rattan chairs.

"Did he mention the land at Tiandongba?" Hu asked.

"He did, and he said he wanted to double check with you."

Zhong poured tea for Hu Guohao and added milk.

"Your favorite milk tea. It's hot."

"Hm." Hu tore open a packet of sugar and stirred it in his tea. "This is good," he said as he took a sip, baring his teeth.

"It was made with fresh milk."

"No wonder." Hu picked up his cup and drained it.

A couple of minutes later, a middle-aged woman wearing a black pearl necklace came over and took one of the empty seats.

"This is Ding Lan, an old friend from college," Zhong said. "This is my CEO, Mr. Hu."

Ding smiled.

Hu wanted to compliment her on her necklace, but his tongue felt stiff and his head heavy. "How come I'm so sleepy—" He was out before he could finish the sentence.

With his arm around Hu, Zhong guided him around the verandah and exited through the back door into Ding Lan's white Citroën. As he'd planned, the posts blocked the view from the bar, making it possible to leave without being seen. Ding stayed behind to settle the bill.

Hu woke up to find himself in a dark room, his arms tied behind his back, his mouth sealed with duct tape. He was weak and his head hurt terribly. Where am I? He tried to make sense of his situation, but felt that he'd fallen into a void. It was pitch-black and deadly quiet. A sensation of nausea assailed him and he passed out again.

He was jolted awake by an acute pain. In the dim light, a terrifying face came into view; it was his assistant, Zhong Tao, who had ripped the tape from his mouth. Next to Zhong was the woman in a black necklace, still smiling.

"Take a good look, Grinning Tyrant. Who am I?" Zhong said in a steady voice.

"You—aren't you my assistant, Zhong Tao?"

"Take another look, you asshole. I'm Dark Boy."

"Dark Boy?" Hu looked up, bewildered, and then terror filled his eyes as recognition set in.

"Who—who's she?"

"She's Qiangzi's sister, Silly Girl."

"Qiangzi?" Hu began to shake violently when he recalled the past.

Zhong took out a piece of black metal with razor-sharp edges, and scratched Hu's chest. Beads of blood stained the edge of the piece, part of a harmonica now twisted out of shape from the fire.

"This is the symbol for 'fire' soaked in blood." Zhong spat out the words. "It's time to pay your debt of blood with your life."

"You're—seeking revenge?" Hu managed to sputter his meaningless question.

"Yes. Twenty-eight years ago, you caused the death of ten girls from the 2nd Company and raped Xia Yuhong. Qiangzi also died at your hands. There are many more zhiqing girls who were defiled by you. Grinning Tyrant, you deserve to die a thousand deaths," Zhong said through clenched teeth.

"Grinning Tyrant, you've committed so many evil deeds you will die a terrible death," Ding said contemptuously.

Hu's face turned purple, a fierce glint oozing from his bleary eyes. In desperation, he wanted to call for help, but no sound emerged from his open mouth. Zhong spat on the floor, then picked up a white plastic bucket and poured its contents—dark green seawater—into a large basin, all before the bulging eyes of the terror-stricken Hu Guohao. When the water reached the top of the basin, Zhong reached out and forced Hu's head down into the water. Hu struggled, but his strength deserted him as his mind began to lose focus.

Hu Guohao swallowed a mouthful of brackish seawater as he felt a wave pull him under. Swimming for an hour or two was normally a breeze, why was it so hard now?

That floating white line ought to be the shark barrier. He knew he'd be all right if he could make it that far.

Hu fought to stay above water, but his head weighed him down and he choked on another mouthful.

He was starting to black out. Damn it! Where am I? Have I died and gone to Hell?

He thought he saw a great white gliding up from behind, eyeing him menacingly as it slowly opened and shut its mouth. He struggled to keep his arms moving, but everything he did was like a slow-motion movie scene, unreal and futile. The more he struggled, the faster he sank. A dozen faces—boys and girls, pale with dazzling smiles—floated up from the recesses of his memory. . . .

Now it was flames, licking in the air before his eyes. Were they real? An illusion?

A wisp of green smoke rose up lazily, spreading across the surface like bleeding ink.

Then the scene began to blur.

He tried to open his eyes, but a white mist clouding his retinas blocked out everything. Haze that would not go away turned into a gloomy, sinister abyss, sending shudders through his body.

He could sense that the Angel of Death was inching toward him. His mind was swirling as he heard a faint voice from somewhere up above say, "He's dead."

His heart erupted in a violent spasm, and he began to sink.

That was the last thing he knew.

— 5 —

Nie Feng called Chief Wu from the Kunming airport to give him an update.

"Hello, Chief Wu, this is Nie Feng."

"Oh, Mr. Nie. How are you?"

"I'm at the Kunming Airport. I returned yesterday from Lanjiang, near the Yunnan border with Burma. It's where Zhong Tao was sent down as a zhiqing. I know his motive."

"That's terrific. What was it?"

"Zhong murdered Hu Guohao for revenge. Yes, a serial revenge murder. Hu Guohao was commander of the zhiqing company back then. His nickname was Grinning Tyrant. Hong Yiming was the political instructor, and Hu's accomplice, which was why he, too, was killed. But one thing is clear—he got what he deserved."

"So that's how it was." The news came as a surprise to Chief Wu.

Nie proceeded to reveal the entangled past of Zhong Tao and Hu Guohao, and of Zhong's deep-seated hatred for Hu.

"Zhong Tao's girlfriend, Xia Yuhong, was raped by the Commander of the 2nd Company, Hu Guohao, whose real name was Hu Zihao. After the rape, she left Zhong out of shame and despair. His baby sister, Zhong Xing—Apricot—burned to death in her hut in a fire that also took the lives of nine other girls. They had latched their door with wire to keep the sex fiend, Hu Zihao, from barging in. Hu had his eyes on Zhong Xing, but Xia Yuhong arrived in time to save her from the rapist. Zhong Xing escaped the rape but not the fire."

"So Hu Zihao destroyed the two persons Zhong loved most in life," Chief Wu commented.

"And that's not all. An old staff worker, a Mr. Fu, mentioned a third victim, Ding Qiang, Ding Lan's older brother and Zhong's buddy. The loss of three lives became a wound that never healed in Zhong's life. It changed him completely. For twenty-eight years, he sought only revenge; it was his sole reason to go on living—to find Hu Guohao and rid society of an evil man who had managed to escape punishment for decades."

"So the case is solved. You really are your father's son. On behalf of the district office of the Public Security Bureau, I thank you, Mr. Nie." Chief Wu was almost too excited to finish.

"No need to thank me. All I did was dig up the truth."

But truth can be cruel. Nie Feng had not expected that the truth he'd uncovered was the kind that he'd rather not have to see. Who would pay for this page of bloody history, which had been buried for so long? From the vantage point of a journalist, Nie felt that the fault lay with the red specter of the Cultural Revolution, in which thousands of female zhiqing were violated. It was the tragedy of a scarred nation.

Nie's sympathies lay with Zhong Tao; after shutting off his cell phone, he was utterly disheartened. He phoned Xiaochuan, who was away on an assignment. Nie told him what he'd found in Yun-nan and mentioned his call to Chief Wu.

"Congratulations! You did an incredible job helping us solve the case."

"I didn't do all that much. The police deserve the credit."

"But why didn't Zhong Tao report Hu and see him punished through legal channels," Xiaochuan asked.

"I thought about that, too." Nie Feng paused to think. "It all happened twenty-eight years ago, beyond the statute of limitations. Zhong Tao was smart enough to realize that. You know the law says twenty years is the limit for serious crimes that warrant a death penalty or life in prison. If a plaintiff wants to pursue a case after twenty years, he must petition the people's highest court. Once Hu Guohao transformed himself into a famous entrepreneur with political connections, it would have been extremely difficult to take him down."

"I see your point."

"There may be another important factor," Nie continued. "That is, Zhong Tao wanted to carry out the punishment himself because he believed he was on a sacred mission to right a wrong, and it was the only way his restless mind could gain peace. That's typical of an avenger, and for him, a lifelong goal. Think about the carefully designed 'notice of death,' the 'fire' symbol, and the eerie funeral wreath. Weren't they the products of a vengeful mind?"

"That certainly makes sense." Xiaochuan was convinced. "Remember Miss Bai?"

"The service manager at the Greater Meisha hotel?"

"She left the Seaview Hotel, fired for being sexually involved with Hu Guohao. No one was sure who told on her. We got the story from Miss Bai's best friend at the hotel, who said that Hu tricked her into the relationship. It turned out that one night she was called into Hu's room, where he forced himself upon her. She had always liked him, and had never expected him to do such a thing. She was afraid to call for help, and he raped her."

Xiaochuan told Nie that hotels all forbid their staff from having inappropriate relationships with their customers, let alone a sexual liaison. Miss Bai became Hu's prey, unable both to escape his clutches or to report him. She nearly killed herself because of the humiliation. Afterward, Hu sweet-talked her around, apologizing and showering her with gifts of money and jewelry. She eventually decided to go along because there was no better option.

"So she was also a victim," Xiaochuan concluded. "And then there's Feng Xueying, who was killed over the botched blackmail scheme. She died because of Hu Guohao."

"Any news of Zhu Mei-feng?" Nie asked.

"We heard she fled to Canada. The police have issued a warrant for her arrest through Interpol." Xiaochuan paused. "She thought she could use the two hundred thousand yuan to eliminate further blackmail from Feng Xueying, but probably never considered the price she'd have to pay."

So Zhu Mei-feng was another of Hu's victims, Nie mused. She was trying to protect Zhou Zhengxing when she locked horns with Feng Xueying and, in the end, was guilty of murder by hire. What an incredible link: Miss Bai, Feng Xueying, and Zhu Mei-feng, every woman associated with Hu came to a terrible end. Despite himself, Nie Feng was glad that Hu was dead and that justice was done. Hu deserved what he got—poetic justice. This must have been what people meant by heavenly retribution.

Nie returned to Chengdu. The moment he stepped inside, his poodle, Yahoo, began to run around the house with his slippers in its mouth.

"Good dog, Yahoo. Bring me my slippers."

The praise had the poodle wagging his tail as it dropped his slippers by his feet. The young maid Xiao Ju was next.

"Brother Nie, you're back. There's a fax for you."

"Who's it from?"

"The Shenzhen Public Security Bureau. Looks like they're inviting you back to celebrate." She was grinning from ear to ear.

"It's not such a big deal, you silly girl."

Nie tore the fax off and read it. Not a word about celebration. Chief Wu was inviting him to join the wrap-up session for the case, all expenses paid.

After dropping his duffle bag in his room, he gave Chief Wu a call.

"This is Nie Feng. I just got home. I saw the fax and thank you for the invitation. I'll ask for a leave of absence and get out there the day after tomorrow."

"No need to ask your editor in chief. He already agreed to give you a few days off."

So Chief Wu had talked to the editor. Of course, he'd agree to let Nie go, so long as he didn't have to pay the expenses. In fact, Nie knew that his editor had probably jumped at the offer, because Nie would soon give him an exclusive follow-up story on the murder cases.

"Mr. Nie, there's one more thing to do before we can close the case. We found Zhong Tao's motive, but we lack the evidence to send him to jail. Too much time has passed, and the contents of the water we found at the Greater Meisha rental has deteriorated. The test results—"

"I may have a solution. I was just going to tell you about it."

"Is that so?" Chief Wu sounded dubious. "Go ahead, I'm listening."

"Well, when I was waiting for a flight out of Kunming, I went online and happened upon a site called Windows to Shenzhen, with a brief mention of red tides, posted by a Dr. Zhou at the Shenzhen Oceanic Environmental Monitoring Station."

Nie had contacted Dr. Zhou and asked about the issue of algae life span. Zhou had told him that the life span was indeed short, two days tops under normal circumstances and even shorter in a plastic bucket devoid of light and oxygen.

"Is there a way to identify the algae after it breaks up?" Nie asked.

"DNA sequence!" Dr. Zhou blurted out. "The cells have broken down, but samples can still be taken for DNA testing. But it's very difficult and you have to know what type of algae you're looking for."

Nie interrupted to tell him the names of the algae.

"You compare the DNA sequence with these algae. It's called molecular biology, a cutting-edge field. Scientists outside of China have been working on it, and theoretically they can determine if the fragments in the water are the algae you're talking about from the molecules. But no one has tried that in China yet. It's extremely difficult because you need to collect enough samples to make sure the DNA sequencing is reliable."

"After I thanked him," Nie said to Chief Wu, "I immediately did an online search of 'identification of algae DNA,' 'biological DNA sequence,' 'samples of biological DNA sequencing,' and 'algae DNA databank.' I found nothing useful."

"So we're stuck then."

"When I was about to turn off my laptop, I recalled Dr. Zhou's mention of molecular biology, so, for the heck of it, I typed 'red tide molecular biology' into the search engine, resulting in nine hundred and ninety-eight hits, two of which were very important. One was 'Molecular Identification and Study of Red Tide Algae in Nanhai,' the other was 'Single Algae Cell Preparation and Its Application in Identifying Red Tide Algae Molecules.' Both were government-funded projects, headed by biologists." Nie Feng gave Wu their names.

"Where are they located?" Chief Wu asked urgently.

"Guangzhou," Nie replied. "In the Biology and Life Science Institute at Z University."

"Thank you so much, Mr. Nie. This is invaluable information." Chief Wu was overjoyed. "I'll send the samples over right away.'

Three days later, when Nie arrived at the Y District Public Security Bureau from the Shenzhen airport, the identification had been completed. DNA sequencing showed that the algae fragments in the plastic bucket were the ones they were looking for.

A warrant for Zhong Tao's arrest was issued the following day.

Epilogue

At Baiyun International Airport. Zhong Tao, red duffel bag in hand, followed members of a tour group. When he neared the security checkpoint, he turned to wave at Ding Lan. "Take care of yourself, Silly Girl," he said silently.

Ding waved back, tears sparkling in her eyes. In twenty minutes, Zhong Tao would board an international flight, heading for North America to pursue his lifelong dream. She wished him good luck.

He walked down the blue security check line and stopped at the checkpoint to show his boarding pass and passport. A woman in a CAAC uniform checked his document and then looked up at him.

"I'm sorry, sir, but there's an irregularity with your passport," she said politely as she took it from him. A pair of brawny men came up to take Zhong Tao to a private room

Ding Lan ran up when she saw what was happening but was stopped by two plainclothes airport policemen.

"Zhong Tao! Zhong Tao!" she shouted agonizingly.

Chief Cui handled the arrest. Xiaochuan and Yao were on hand, both looking grave. They'd solved the case, but, strangely, neither of them felt much happiness over the victory. Nie Feng was standing next to Chief Wu, observing the arrest.

Zhong Tao, escorted by the two policemen, came down the escalator. When he saw Nie Feng standing at the bottom, he rewarded him with a serene smile, presumably telling him that he had no regrets.

Nie felt sorry for him, but that was tempered by respect.

It was midsummer. Zhong turned and spotted a pink sunset through the window. A breeze had sent flower petals falling like raindrops.

"A gust of wind sends petals falling to the ground . . . all that's left under the setting sun is the apricot rain." Zhong recited the lines in a soft voice, almost like a somnolent murmur, drawing curious stares from passengers around him.

Nie Feng looked on, his expression showing the complexity of his feelings.

Ding Lan also looked on through teary eyes.

A song seemed to be playing; it was the "Song of the Zhiqing," which had once sent its listeners into a reverie; a chorus of boys and girls echoed in the vast airport waiting lounge.

The song was coming to an end:

Say good-bye to Mama, say good-bye to my dear hometown,
The golden days of a student are entered into history books, never
*   to return.*
Ah, the road ahead is so arduous, winding and endless,
The footprints of life beached on a remote alien place.
Leave with the rising sun, return with rising moon,
Our sacred mission is to repair the earth with great devotion, it is
*   our destiny.*
Ah, use our hands to turn the earth red, and embroider the
*   universe in red.*
Do not doubt the tomorrow we look forward to will be here.